Cut By The Diamond

WHAT HAPPENS WHEN TWO BROKEN SOULS COLLIDE?

Fighting Edge
Book 1

Natasha Allen

This novel is entirely a work of fiction. The names, characters and incidents portrayed in it are the work of the author's imagination.

Visit my website at www.natashaallenauthor.com

Cover Artwork & Design by Samantha Sanderson-Marshall www.
smashdesigns.co.uk

For anyone that's felt too broken, too flawed or damaged to feel loved, this one's for you. Once you conquer that love within, anything is possible….

Being deeply loved by someone gives you strength, while loving someone deeply gives you courage.

— Lao Tzu

Author's Note

This book is an emotional read with several potentially triggering and difficult topics. When I decided to write this story, I knew it was going to be something people either really enjoyed or really disliked. As an author that is a huge risk to take. However, I knew and still believe that it is just as important to tell a story that isn't all smiles and roses. Not everything in life goes the way we hope and plan. I have spoken to so many people that have gone through similar emotions and experiences that occur in this book. So, if there is one thing I hope to achieve, is letting those of you who have been affected by difficult and troubling relationships, is that you are not alone.

Trigger Warnings

This book contains content that might be troubling to some readers, including, but not limited to, depictions of and references to sexual content, depression, suicidal thoughts, alcoholism, drug use, physical abuse, sexual abuse off page, sexual violence off page, childhood trauma including sexual abuse off page, death of family members, domestic violence and emotional abuse. Please be mindful of these and other possible triggers and feel free to reach out to me on www.natashaallenauthor.com if you would like to discuss further.

Playlist

Chapter 1

Robby

The smell of sweat, blood, and disinfectant wafts up my nose as I run the hose over the mats. Despite having a cleaner that comes in three times a week, I still give the mats a good wipe down at the beginning and end of each day. When I say cleaner, it's one of the trainers' aunts who got let go from her job and was desperately looking for some work. To be honest, I really can't afford her, but I felt for the woman. Most of the guys running classes here do wipe downs themselves after each class, and I know some of them even get the students to help, but there's no way I'm risking any kinda lawsuit from someone having caught an infection from one of the damn mats.

The first few beats of *Smokin' Love by* Stick Figure and Collie Buddz blares through the speakers and I'm instantly transported back to the feeling of the warm, humid air in Pattaya hitting my face. Imagining the distant sound of the waves crashing on the shore is a perfect juxtaposition to the strikes and pounds of the guys hitting the punching bags and those sparring with one another on the other end of the gym. Instead of being on the island that feels more like home to me, I'm here. In this small, shitty town, wondering what the fuck I am doing with my life.

Stuck in the cycle of getting up, opening the gym, doing paperwork, getting some training in myself, then more paperwork before closing up, heading home to my empty house, fueling my body, only to do the exact something the next day. Day in, day out. The gym. My gym. It still feels so wrong calling it that. My gym. It shouldn't be mine. I shut that train of thought down straight away. I'm not going down that road right now. I've got enough other depressing shit to keep my mind busy. Like all that damn paperwork I need to stop avoiding and get on with.

"Fuck's sake," I mutter to myself as I grab the mop and bucket and make my way up the stairs, down the virtually blacked out corridor, and to my office. The moaning creak of the heavy door is only another thing that's on the endless list of repairs I need to do to this place. If I had the damn money.

The chair groans beneath me as I take my seat behind the desk and wait for my laptop to start up. Opening up the account's spreadsheet, I aimlessly see if overnight a miracle has happened, and I suddenly have funds I can do some sort of work with. But no, instead there are debts I still need to pay, bills that I'm paying in installments, and for the fifth month in a row, not even enough for me to pay myself.

"Fuck, fuck, fuck this shit," I shout.

The booming echo of my voice bounces across the icy walls of the office. How did Michael and Joseph, make this seem so easy? I never remember my brothers complaining that this was such a money pit. Slamming my laptop shut, I scroll through my phone, looking for anything to distract me from the mountain of stress I don't want to deal with right now. After scrolling through every social media app, I end up catching up on the posts I've missed in a Discord group I'm in.

It's for tattoo enthusiasts in the area. My tattoo artist, Tan, who owns a shop in town, started it. It's cool seeing the different styles of those in the group. None of us show our faces in our profile pictures, it's just a picture of our favorite pieces on our body. Makes it kinda feel like we're in this secret society or something. I let out a huff at how ridiculous that sounds. Even so, there's just something about connecting with people who are into the same things as you, have no judgment, and never dig deeper than needs be.

There are a couple of people on here that I'm sure are guys who train in the gym. Some tattoos look familiar, and I could have sworn I recognized one of them while sparring with a guy.

I've had some that reached out and sent me private DMs asking me about the big chest piece I've got, where I got that done and all that shit. Speaking of DMs, now who is this? Looking at the inbox, I see that there's a message I hadn't noticed before. Clicking on it, the first thing I notice is the profile picture. All I can see is the partial image of a woman hugging her bent knee. She's got a sick piece on her thigh and a sleeve on her arm. Zooming in, I try to see more of the details: flowers, a ship, a mandala pattern, and I can't quite make out the rest. With the dark lighting of the picture combined with her rich dark brown skin, it's just too hard for me to get a clearer look. Then my eyes focus on her profile name. *BlkMermaid*. Well, that's interesting.

Sounds much better than mine, *emeraldgiant.* I don't know why I went with that, probably because I got called it in school and it just stuck.

BlkMermaid: I've gotta say that piece looks amazing. And the way the colors pop is just insane! How much of you is covered, if you don't mind me asking?

What is it about this mysterious blkmermaid that has my fingers twitching to respond?

emeraldgiant: Thanks. Yeah, the colors have held up well, especially considering I got my sleeve done over ten years ago. Still hasn't dulled. At the moment I've got one sleeve fully done, my chest is all outlined but still needs finishing and colored. Plus, I wanna bring it up to my neck. The plan is to be fully covered. Everything except my face.

I don't realize that I've been staring at her profile picture for god knows how long when suddenly the icon above her picture shows she's now online. Chucking my phone onto the desk, I try to busy myself. Not paying any attention to whether or not she's read my reply. I make myself a coffee and stretch out the tight kinks in my neck. By the time I get back, I can see a notification pop up, showing I've got a new message.

BlkMermaid. Wow! That sounds amazing! I'm jealous of how well and vibrant they still are after all that time. You're so lucky! So will you continue with the same style or change it up for the different areas?

Lucky. Ha. I couldn't feel any further away from being lucky right now if I tried. There is honestly not a single thing I feel lucky about in my life. Everything is shit. I hate the weather here. I miss the warmth of the island. Not just the warmth. Everything. I miss the culture, the food, the people, the way of life. Everything is just so much easier out there.

"H̄î tāy t̄hexa c̄hạn khidt̄hụng prathes̄ʹthịy," I say to myself.

Thank god no one else is here. They'd probably have me committed if they found me talking to myself in Thai in my office. Though I'm not sure if being committed sounds so bad. It's hardly a big difference to how I'm living my life right now. Isolation, simple and monotonous routine, same shit day in, day out.

What on earth am I doing back here?

Don't know why I'm asking myself that question when I know the answer. I didn't choose to come back. I needed to. Getting the call that Mom needed to be taken into hospice wasn't exactly one I could ignore. Didn't matter how much I wanted to stay on the island.

Her dementia was set off by the accident and has gotten worse these last few years.

Like I didn't have enough shit and trauma in my life already.

Fuck, I need a drink. Or a joint. I know I shouldn't. I hate that whenever I'm back here, I just can't say no. I wouldn't say I was an addict, but I have an addictive personality. It was bad when I was a teen, but I could always control it. And I did. Until everything changed.

The only place I feel I can consistently stay in control, be clean, and not give in to temptation is back in Thailand.

Screw this. There's no point in me staying here for the rest of the day. Koa will come in soon and he's run this place enough to not need me around.

Grabbing my keys, I make my way to the car and give my guy a call to see if he can hook me up at least until next week when I can pay him.

It takes six tries to start the ignition before this damn piece of junk finally starts.

Days and weeks merge into one long, dark, blurry tunnel. My sleep has gone to shit. I feel tired all the time yet end up staying up all night. When I do eventually get up, I head to the gym, go straight to the office, lock myself in there, and work out how the fuck to pay shit. Some days I push myself to do one class, just to get my body moving. But I've lost twenty-two pounds in the past year. About half of that since coming back here. Loads of my muscle mass has gone. Doesn't help that I'm hardly eating. The only time I feel like I'm even getting an appetite is after a joint. I feel like I'm stuck in a tomb. The loneliness is stifling, yet I can't bear the thought of being around anyone.

I'm stuck in this loop, this hamster wheel I can't get off. The only thing I find any amusement, any distraction in is the Discord group, and the occasional messages with BlkMermaid. I don't know why. We've not spoken about anything deep, not that I would with a stranger. But there's just something about her. Whenever I see that I've got a new message, it's the closest thing to bringing any kind of energy or spark to my day. Like, I can lock myself into this weird and mysterious world when I'm scrolling through the messages. Escaping the hell that is my life.

Waking up to another day, I drag myself out of bed not knowing or even caring what day it is. Before I even leave my bedroom, I can't wait until the day is over and I can climb back into bed. Taking myself downstairs, I switch on the coffee machine and hope that the milk in the fridge is still okay. Just as I'm about to check it, my phone rings and I see that it's my mom's hospice.

"Hello, am I speaking to Robby Black?"

"Yeah, that's me."

"I'm afraid I've got some bad news."

Chapter 2

Carina

"Zion, Kai, can you both hurry already. We're going to be late for school. Come on," I shout up for the fifth time this morning. I swear these kids are trying to send me into an early grave. Doesn't matter that we have the same routine every single day, both boys act like I'm asking them to give me one of their organs or that the distance between their bedrooms and the front door is the same as hiking Mount Everest.

It's too early for this. The buzz from my coffee has already worn off and I'm seriously not in the mood for any of their bullshit this morning. "Boys, for the last time I said let's go!"

Thankfully, the traffic is in our favor for once and I drown out the boy's grunts with the radio. Gone are the days of big squeezes for mommy in the morning, holding onto my leg, not wanting to leave my side and go to school. Instead, I'm lucky if I get a "yeah" in response when I tell them I love them before the slam of the car doors. Checking my mirrors, I pull out of the drop off lane and head to my first patient of the day.

"Good morning, Mrs. Wilson, how are you feeling today?" I ask as I attach the blood pressure cuff to her arm.

"How many times do I have to tell you to call me Susie? You've been my carer for what, three years now? And I tell you the same thing every single time."

I smile at her ribbing, as yes, even though we have the same conversation every time, she always leaves out the fact that whenever I've greeted her by her first name, she's always corrected me. Reminding me she worked too hard in her marriage to earn that name to not be addressed by it.

"I know. Maybe I'll remember one of these days."

"Anyway, enough about me. How are your boys doing?" she asks.

"They're good. Same as usual."

"And how is Kai handling that new teacher you were telling me about? Last time you said he still wasn't sure about her."

"Still not great. One thing I will say is that he hasn't come back crying. And the school hasn't called me in this past week. So, I guess even though it's not great, that's still a bonus."

My youngest is autistic, and it's been a long journey since getting his diagnosis when he was four. No two days are ever the same. With some feeling unbearable and too hard to manage, others are fun and smooth plain sailing. That's one reason why I got into work as a carer. I was lucky to find an agency that allows you to pick your hours, which allows me to do it around the boys' school, then only doing night shifts when my mom has them. We have a rotation of house calls; people that we see daily. Besides changing dressings, helping with personal care, and dispensing medication, a large part of it is just companionship. And most of the patients are really sweet. I've built up my own little dynamic relationship with all of them.

"Well, let's just give it time. For all we know he could just have great instincts, and this teacher might just be awful. And he's just someone that can sense it."

Nodding along, I pour out a glass of water, ready for her to take her meds.

"Now, have you considered my offer from the other day?"

"Hmm? What offer?" I ask, sounding perplexed, although I know exactly what she's talking about. And it takes everything in me to not to roll my eyes at her silliness.

"Oh, you know about me arranging for you to go on a date with my grandson. And if not him, then I was also thinking you could try going out with the handyman; he's lovely and very practical. Just think, you'd never need help to fix or repair things ever again."

It's really hard to keep a level of professionalism while having conversations like this. I remember the day she'd been prying about my love life, or lack thereof. From the second she found out I was single, she's been hellbent on trying to fix me up with someone.

"Susie, we've already had this conversation many times before. I really appreciate you trying to match me up with someone, but there is no need. Besides, your grandson is too young for me."

"Oh pishhhh, age is nothing but a number," she retorts.

"A number that's nine years if I remember correctly. That wouldn't be so bad if he were nine years older than me. But nine years younger? No, that just wouldn't work. Besides, I'm a single mom with a lot of baggage. He needs to be with someone who's carefree, able to go on fun adventures, travel, and enjoy spontaneous dates with. Not me. Not when I need to refer to my calendar and book things weeks in advance."

"You're selling yourself short. You don't look thirty-four. When you first started coming to see me, I thought you were only just twenty, if that. I didn't even think you were going to be old enough to do the job."

"I know. I remember."

It had taken quite a while for her to warm to me. Which was something I was used to in this job. There are many people who get into this profession and treat it as some sort of conveyor belt, not getting to know or really seeing the people as people. Just patients. But for me, it's always been different. Especially as almost all of them are elderly and rarely have family that come visit them regularly. So many are lonely and desperate for company. So when someone comes in, they either latch on to that sense of familiarity, or they behave almost childlike, apprehensive until they know you'll stick around. And that's what Mrs. Wilson did.

"Well fine, if not my grandson, even though I know you two would really hit it off, how about the handyman? I'm pretty sure he's around the same age as you. So you don't have that excuse."

The cheeky twinkle in her eye makes me smile. And to be honest, the only reason I'm not just putting an end to all of this with her is because I can't help but feel warmed at the excitement and enthusiasm she gets. It's like her own little pet project that keeps her entertained between my visits.

"Yeah, I'm pretty sure he is a similar age, and yes it would be great to be with someone that could help with little odd jobs around the house. However, I know I'm not his type."

"What do you mean you're not his type? You're very beautiful. And I could imagine if you put a bit of makeup on and when you are out of your uniform, you look stunning."

"Aww, that's very sweet of you. But you see, I'm not his type, not in that way. Well… you see, I don't think any female would be his type." Raising my brows, I wait for her to connect the dots. I bite my lip when I see the confusion spread across her face.

"You don't think any female would be his type? But if no female would be his… Oh," she drags the sound out a few seconds, "I see."

Giving her a warm smile, I hope she now doesn't come out with some silly comment to which I will have to remind her to be respectful.

"Okay, well now that isn't something we can do anything about, is it? But you know Mary, a few doors down? I could try to set him up with her son. Now *they* would make a brilliant match."

I can't help but laugh. This really is her newfound hobby.

"Have you tried online? I've watched a few infomercials and apparently, it's all the rage nowadays."

"Yes, I have. And I even went on a couple of dates. But like I said before, it's not just me. I've got two kids. In the beginning many men will say that it isn't an issue, but after a while, not being able to meet up at the drop of a dime, them not being the priority in my day to day, they just can't seem to handle it."

"We will find you someone. There is no doubt about it. I will make it my personal mission."

"That's very sweet of you, but there really is no need."

"Hush now. I won't have any of that kind of talk. We will do it. Mark my words."

I don't know why but a part of me almost feels a little scared at the determination in her voice. I think I may have signed myself up for an impossible task without even meaning to.

By the time I clock off, I'm cutting it close with picking up Kai from the speech and language session he has after school. Luckily for me, they have those sessions in school, as opposed to me taking him somewhere else. Honestly, if they didn't, I'd have to cut down my hours even more since there's no one else to take him.

Only another reminder of how everything is always on my shoulders. As much as I wouldn't change my life, I love my kids to death, doing everything alone, dealing with a teenager who's discovering who he is as a young man, along with all the pressures society now lays upon him, while also navigating the forever changing days of a son who's autistic is all exhausing. All the while working, cooking, cleaning, and just trying to keep everything afloat and staying sane at the same time. See, this is what happens when I have any conversations about dating. It only ever triggers the feeling of being alone. Maybe it's about time I found myself a new hobby. I do wanna start working on my fitness again. *I wonder if there are any good gyms or classes around here that would be worth me checking out?*

Parking the car in front of Kai's school, I cut the engine and grab my phone from my purse. Seeing I have a couple of minutes before he comes out, I look at local gyms.

Fighting Edge.

Hmm, the website is pretty basic with only a handful of pictures. Looks like this is some sort of mixed martial arts gym. Maybe that would be a good challenge for me to set myself. I'm not really drawn by the idea of boxing, or MMA, and some of the other classes are for sports I've never heard of like BJJ and Muay Thai. I've heard of Judo but that's not really drawing me in. Krav Maga I think I read about somewhere but there isn't much info on here about that. They have Kickboxing, both mixed classes and women only ones. I've always been keen to try that. Perhaps instead of always putting it on the future to-do pile like I've always done, I should just give it a go. What's the worst that could happen? I try it out, shift some of this weight and actually learn something new? Doesn't sound like too big of a sacrifice.

Chapter 3

Robby

My skin feels like it's on fire. Doesn't matter what I try, nothing seems to help or ease it. It's not like I've never had to deal with my psoriasis before, but fucking hell, this is the worst flareup I've ever had. And it all started three months back when I was still in Thailand.

I'd caught the first plane I could get on after getting the news my mom had passed. I didn't want to, nor could I deal with any of it. I just needed to get away. Away from all the reminders, away from people, just away from everything. And the only place I knew I wanted to go was my favorite island. The only place that feels like home. I had no plans. Hadn't even booked somewhere for me to stay. Just packed a bag and boarded my flight. Luckily, I've been there so many times in the past several years, that I have friends there and could sort out places to stay.

I'd initially thought I'd be able to work through all the shit and eventually grieve; process all that has happened. But I just couldn't do it. I pushed it all aside and buried it as deep into the recesses of my mind as I could. I just couldn't take it. Couldn't breathe. I felt like I was drowning, and there wasn't a part of me that was strong enough to cope with that. So I distracted myself. I tried to do it in the right way at first by signing up and training at one of the Muay Thai gyms. I focused on that for a couple of weeks. My days comprised of training, eating clean, stretching, and meditation. Then I explored the island. Went to the temples, chilled with some wild monkeys. Finally started feeling a bit more normal again and wanted to let my hair down a bit, so I went on a couple of nights out. Let loose, drank, smoked some weed, just enjoyed myself. Only that didn't last long when I got ill, went to hospital, had pneumonia and an infection which ended up setting off the worst psoriasis flare. My money ran out, so I had no other choice but to fly back home.

That was almost three months ago and it still hasn't eased, despite the tablets I've been taking and the creams I've been applying daily. All of which has only made me even more fucking depressed than I've already been. If it was only in one place, I wouldn't care as much. But it's everywhere. I'm covered from the top of my scalp to the tips of my toes. I hate having to look at it, so I'm pretty much always in baggy sweats and an oversized hoodie. I hardly leave the house. If I do, it's pretty much only to grab some basics from the shop or maybe pick up some weed. I stopped drinking after I was in the hospital, and when I first got back, I did actually start going to AA meetings. Not because I felt like I had a problem, but more so I could hold myself accountable. It was the only way to get any structure back. I know I should stop smoking weed, but it's the only way I'm able to relax enough to get into a dreamless sleep or, to be honest, even eat. My appetite is basically nonexistent. I've tried forcing myself to eat but just can't do it. So I just have a couple of puffs and after a little while get hungry. So besides picking up, grabbing some food, or sitting in a meeting, I don't really do anything anymore.

Koa was running the gym while I was away. I honestly don't know what I'd have done without him. He's been checking in with me daily, keeping me up to speed on how things are going. There have been many times where he's tried to get me to come in and do some floor work, some basic training. Hell, he even suggested I join him for a drink, but I told him I'm being sober at the moment. I don't think he was even that bothered about me actually drinking with him, more just to get me to do something, but I just haven't been interested. Have to give him credit though, he never pushes. He'll just make a simple suggestion, then when I inevitably say no, he moves on, focus's back on the gym, and forwards me any bits that I need to sign off on or gives progress updates on how many new members have signed up that week. And where he's been the one keeping everything in order, I've been paying him most of the money I've received in from the monthly memberships. It's only fair, as he's been the one putting in all the work.

So that's left me with pretty much next to nothing to live on. Just about enough to keep the water and heating on and pay for my internet. I guess some would say I'm lucky as I don't have rent or a mortgage to pay as I moved into my mom's house. I guess it's mine now, though it doesn't feel like it. Even just thinking those words leaves a rancid taste in my mouth.

I've dropped a ton of weight too. It's probably the skinniest I've ever been in my life. Not that I've ever been big, but given my six-foot-three stature and all the muscle I've lost, I try to ignore the fact that when I shower I can feel my bones protruding.

During one of the AA meetings, we'd been discussing really letting yourself be open and vulnerable to someone. That could be a friend, partner, therapist, whatever. And basically, letting them see the side of yourself you fear showing the rest of the world. The side that's locked away. The demon you don't want to let out of the cage. Unlike some of the other guys who said they thought it might help those around them understand them better, I knew the opposite to be true.

There is no way anyone could understand how I feel. Never wrap their heads around what I have been through. How could they? Why would they even want to? And besides the fact that I know no one would be interested in hearing me chat about all that shit, why would I risk making myself vulnerable like that? All that would do would be letting myself be exposed for someone to walk all over me as they see me as some pathetic fuck up who can't catch a break. And if there was someone like that, what kinda freak of a person would they be themselves? How screwed up would their own lives have to be to be wasting time and energy with mine?

Nah, there's no point. Besides, it's not as if I have a bunch of people to choose from. My family is basically all gone. I'm not gonna speak to my best friend William about this. All the guys I was close to growing up are not exactly the type you'd chat about this shit with. They're great to train with. To go out and forget about all the shit in life with. Or stay in and get stoned with. But this shit? Nah, not all this.

My phone goes off for the twentieth time this past hour, and I finally push myself up and grab it off the coffee table. It's another notification from that Discord group. To be honest, this group has been the only thing that has distracted me recently. The guy who set it up was going to an expo show and wanted to put a showcase together, so everyone was putting their ideas forward. I even put in a couple of suggestions. It seems the show went well as he's been posting not only two of the bigger pieces he did as live demos there but also some work from other artists he's friends with. Some designs he's shared have been fucking insane. Not all the tattoos are in styles that I would do or get done myself, but I can still appreciate the amazing artistry that has gone into them. For me and all the ones that cover my body, I'm all about colors. The more vibrant the better.

After mom died and when I landed in Thailand, one of the first things I did was log out of all my socials. Just wanted to shut everyone and everything out. And it felt good.

So, just like with everything else, I logged out of Discord and didn't message BlkMermaid, who I'd been messaging back and forth with, or anyone else in the group again. Not until I got back. There were hundreds of messages sent in the group while I'd been away, and I couldn't be bothered to look at all of them. There were a couple that caught my eye, but other than that, I've just been watching from the sidelines. That's where I enjoy most things nowadays anyway. So why is it that despite that, on any other day, the thought of reaching out to anyone usually sets me off in an annoyed and frustrated mood, am I eager to reach out and message her? See what she's been up to? I don't know what the fuck it is, but there is just something that feels almost familiar about her. Some sort of weird connection, like there's some sort of imaginary string pulling me to her. I don't know what it is but I really wanna know why, so that's why I message her.

Emeraldgiant: How has the BlkMermaid been navigating the high seas lately?

Chapter 4

Carina

Well, I'll be damned. That was the exact reaction I'd had when I got the notification on my phone that Mr. Ghost himself—*emeraldgiant*—sent me a DM. That honestly wasn't on my bingo card. I simply thought he'd joined the pile of all those men that suddenly turn into ghosts and vanish.

There was a part of me that didn't want to message him back at first. I don't know why. Maybe there was a stubbornness deep-rooted within me, but to just vanish, no communication out of the blue, to me just feels like a rude thing to do. Yeah, I get it. We don't know each other super well, but still we were messaging back and forth quite a bit. If he'd have felt it was simply too much, he could have just said that. But nope, he just disappeared.

I noticed that he'd not said anything in the group anymore either. And at the beginning that had taken the initial sting out of me thinking maybe I'd come across as too much. Too annoying. I dunno. But there was something about him that really intrigued me. His answers and responses were always a little held back. Like he'd enjoyed our conversations but wasn't giving all of himself. I also got the sense that there's something lonely about the guy. Which was really unfair for me to say, since I don't even know his name, let alone any information about his life. For all I know, he could be married, have a bunch of kids with an enormous family and group of friends, and just simply dipped into this group on the rare occasions he wasn't preoccupied or bored.

Yet that wasn't the vibe I got. There was an air of a lonewolf about him, like he was on a deserted island. Maybe it was that mysteriousness that drew me in. Well, that and his tattoos are hot. Damn, I really hope it isn't the case that he's married. Or in a relationship. Though I don't know why I'm even thinking about that right now.

After he'd disappeared, and I'd realized I'd done nothing wrong, I actually ended up forgetting about him.

I've been really focused on the things I'd set myself to do. Working on myself. And the biggest surprise is, not only did I try out those kickboxing classes, but I've been going to them ever since. Even though it's only been three months, I no longer feel like the newbie in class. I'm still learning but I've really gotten into it. I know I have a long way to go, but I've slowly felt the difference in my body growing stronger and have already lost some weight. But more so, there's a strength there mentally that hadn't been there before. I never could've imagined, even after just a short time, the impact it has already had on my body and my mental health. Now I wish I'd gotten into it sooner.

Even now, as I change out of my hoodie and sweatpants and stuff them into the gym's locker, I'm already itching for the class to begin.

We'd gotten an email that our usual teacher was out sick, so they offered to either cancel the class or if we were ok to have the male teacher who teaches the mixed class. Apparently, I wasn't the only one who didn't mind the male teacher covering as when I walk into the studio, the mats are almost full of the other regulars, already stretching and warming up.

"Heya Carina, how's it going?" Lucy asks as she ties her hair into a topknot.

"Not too bad. I'm interested to see how different today's session will feel with a guy teaching it."

"Oh, it'll be the same. I do both the mixed and women only. And he's great. I've also done a couple of BJJ classes, and some grappling sessions. I swear the man might be big, but he has agility you'd never imagine. Plus, some women do the mixed class only because of him. Or I guess you could say how he looks." The smirk on her face has me intrigued.

"How do you mean?"

"Let's just say he has no shortage of admirers of both the male and female persuasion. Not that it means anything to me," she says with an air of mock indifference.

"Yeah, but that's because you're happily married, and your wife sounds like the coolest person ever."

"Ah, well, I guess that's because she is," she says with a warm smile.

I've met her wife a handful of times, usually in passing in the car park. And I won't lie, I do feel a sense of envy when I see how adoringly they are to one another. You'd think they've gone off to war and are uniting after months of absence, as opposed to an hour and a half at the gym.

Once the class gets underway, it takes me no time to

understand the comment Lucy made. Our teacher, Koa, looks like some sort of god. I think he's of Pacific Island descent. He also tied his long hair up into a topknot. Yes, he's huge, but he has a kindness in his eyes that instantly puts me at ease. And Lucy was right, it doesn't feel any different. Which I guess only goes to show how good of a teacher he really is. As we strap on our gloves and pads, he talks us through the style of sparring he wants us to work on today. Instead of starting from a straight up stance, we are working from a defensive offset.

I can't pinpoint when during the class it happened, but I couldn't get out of my head. There was something about us working or our defensive technique that seemed to trigger memories of my ex-husband. And once he got into my head, I was really struggling to land my hits. Maybe it's because instead of seeing my sparring partner in front of me, all I could see was him. Both wishing and wondering how different things might have been if all those years ago I could have known how to defend myself. Fight back.

I hate that the more time that passes, the clearer things become for me. How, for years, he would gaslight me. Convince me that there were so many things wrong with me. After I fell pregnant with Zion, things got better, but that only lasted about two or three years. Then impulsively, we got married. I agreed as we'd been in that good phase, and I'd convinced myself that he was finally changing. How stupid had I been? I later found out he'd started having an affair with someone he reconnected with at our wedding. I only found out when I was seven months pregnant with Kai. I'd had a terrible pregnancy and was in the hospital a lot. So I tried to do some online shopping, getting the baby things we still needed. That's when my card got declined, and when I looked back at the purchases that had been made, I could put together the trail of restaurants, spas, hotel stays, the lot. All without me. While I was raising our son.

When I confronted him, he twisted things, tried turning it back onto me. I knew I couldn't deal with it then since I just needed to put all my time and energy into getting through that pregnancy. Once Kai was born, I had terrible postpartum depression, so again I just couldn't deal with his bullshit. Instead, I just put up with it. Put up with all the lies. The mental and physical abuse. The fact he would steal money from me. Then when I got the news that he'd been arrested for fraud and two counts of theft, I honestly could have dropped to my knees in gratitude. He only got a three-year sentence, but I knew it was going to be my way out.

I packed up our stuff, and the boys and I moved out, so I was now closer to my mom. The courts granted me a divorce, and I was finally free.

Even after his release, he hardly visits the kids. That's not even my doing. They don't have a good relationship with him, and he makes no effort. Though, he always blames me, stating that I am poising them against him.

So why is it when I freed myself from him, broke away years ago, he still has the power to haunt me now?

Sweat pours off me by the time class is finished. It may have been one of my most underperforming classes, but I still gave my body a good workout. After catching my breath, I stop and chat to Lucy for a bit before I make my way to the changing room and have a quick shower. I don't like that I'm still in a semi-haze from the haunting memories of my ex, and even once I'm showered, moisturized, and dressed, I still can't shake it.

Sliding my feet into my Chucks, I pack up my bag and put my watch back on. I can see I still have time to go to the shop to grab some food for dinner. Making my way out of the changing room, I pass the large mat room where another class has started before passing the octagon that I've never seen being used before. Just behind it, something catches my eye. Walking over, I see some posters. There's a mixture of promo fight posters, but what's intrigued me is the gigantic mural that's been painted at the top. It's a demon head with this snake-like lizard slithering across. The colors are vibrant and really stand out. What is it about that piece that looks so familiar? I don't think I've ever noticed that before. Maybe I've looked at it before without realizing. Though, I don't see how I could have spotted it and not had the same reaction I'm having now. I squint my eyes to see clearer. The initials R.B. written in cursive underneath, though that jogs nothing. Shaking my head, I make my way to the car and head off. Yet the whole time I'm at the supermarket, and as I prepare dinner, the only thing that keeps running through my head is that I recognize that image, the swirls, vibrant colors and intricate patterns seem so familiar and it's bugging the shit out of me that I can't remember where from.

Chapter 5

Robby

It's weird. Part of me wants to say that everything is the same shitty thing it's always been. Which is correct. To a degree. Nothing major has changed. It's not as if my skin has suddenly cleared up. Nor is it the case that I suddenly have any desire to do anything. I'm still only leaving the house to grab food, go to AA meetings, and pick up weed. I stopped at the gym for the first time three weeks ago and joined in one of the evening classes. I went in to pick up some documents and the Muay Thai class that was on was doing partner work and they had odd numbers. I don't know why, but I just jumped in and offered to fill the spot. It was probably one of the worst sessions I've taken part in. My reactions were diabolically slow. Couldn't block shots I know normally I wouldn't have a problem with. That night when I crawled into bed, my arms and legs were so tired I didn't even have the strength to pull the covers over me.

Not that surprising, considering how much weaker I've

become since returning. But it has given me a bit of a push to build back some strength again.

Besides that, the only slight change to my shitty, boring, depressing life has been the reconnecting messages I've had with *BlkMermaid*.

After I reached out to her, she didn't reply to me for two days. I don't know why, but that really bugged me. Especially as I'd seen her comment on the main group chat. When she finally did, I didn't quite get why she had a bit of a shortness to her answers. She acted as if she were annoyed at something, but said nothing. That eased up when she'd asked what I'd been up to, and I'd told her I'd gone to Thailand after getting some bad news.

I didn't want to go into detail, but things seemed to relax from that point on. Last night, she messaged wanting my opinion on something. I don't know what she is going to come out with, but it's almost midday and my curiosity is getting the better of me.

Emeraldgiant: So what is this thing you want my opinion on?

Picking up some eggs and a frying pan, I head to the stove to make some breakfast. I'm starving since I haven't eaten since yesterday afternoon. Turning the music on the speaker, I check the cupboards to see if there's anything I can add to eat. I find a tin of spam which I dice up and remember there's a packet of microwave rice I've not used yet. Plating up, I grab my food and get comfy on the couch. Switching off the music, I turn the TV on, flicking through the channels to find something that isn't annoying.

The ping from my phone draws my attention.

BlkMermaid: I rarely treat myself to sweet things, but I had a dream the other night about these, and I can't get it out of my mind. Now the hard part. Do I go for the cherry crumble or banana cream? [image omitted]

No fucking way. There in the photo is a display case with some damn delicious looking puddings. But that isn't what gets my attention. It's the sign. I know that bakery. It's a little mom and pop place that opened up in town about two years ago.

EmeraldGiant: That's a hard choice. But I think if I'd be picking, I'd go with the banana. Are you there getting them now?

I knew we were in the same state from the group entry rules, but I didn't realize we were in the same town.

BlkMermaid: I was, but I couldn't wait for your response. So I got both. I'll have one, then will share the other 😁

EmeraldGiant: That's E.P.'s Pastries right?

BlkMermaid: Yeah, have you heard of it?

EmeraldGiant: Well, kinda. I live about ten minutes away from it.

BlkMermaid: No way! I don't know why, but I thought you'd be really far away. So we live in the same town. That's insane. And kinda creepy.

Shit, I don't want her to think I'm like stalking her or something.

EmeraldGiant: Listen, I only mentioned it because I recognized it. Didn't mean to freak you out or anything.

My knees bounce as I await her response.

BlkMermaid: Oh no, I didn't mean creepy about you. I meant just in general. It's kinda insane. For all we know, we could have passed each other on the street or been in line at the same checkout. It's kinda funny when you think about it. We've been talking for a while now. Shared our favorite movies, and least favorite tattoos we've seen on other people, as well as other things. We live in the same town, yet besides our profile pictures, we don't know what the other looks like. Nor do we know each other's names.

I don't wanna tell her how unlikely it is that we've walked past each other, especially given how rare it is that I leave the house. She is right though, that it is crazy.

EmeraldGiant: You're not wrong there. Well, how about this? How about I give you my name and my number? That way you'll have two more pieces of information about me. Plus, you won't have to just think of me as the random emeraldgiant while we talk.

I know she will probably say no. For all she knows, I could be a complete weirdo. But I really hope she doesn't.

Our messages are the only things bringing me any entertainment in my life right now.

BlkMermaid: Okay, that's a deal. You give me your name and number, and if you're lucky, I'll message you giving you mine.

EmeraldGiant: Deal

I send her my name and number and I watch as her icon goes from online to offline. Great. She probably changed her mind. See, this is why I don't bother trying to get to know new people. Not here. There's no point. It's a waste of time.

My phone vibrates and my thumbs feel like they aren't moving quickly enough to type in my passcode.

UNKNOWN: 'Hi, Robby, it's Carina. Nice to meet you.'

Carina. That's her name.

Her picture is dark. Not like it's edited, more like a moment captured in a dark room and it's black and white. Squinting my eyes, I try to make out her face but can't see it clearly as she's looking away from the camera. I can make out her body though. She's in a light dress that hugs every curve. Like luscious curves that go for days. With big coily curls that sit like a crown on her head. I think she's on a balcony and I wish I could see more. See her clearer, as what I can make out is fucking hot already.

I don't wanna sound inappropriate, but wow. You're beautiful.

Thank you. That's very sweet of you to say 😊

The thoughts running through my head couldn't be any further than sweet. For the first time in months, my body tingles with sensations of desire. It's been so long, I don't even remember the last time I felt turned on. Hell, I can't even remember the last time I jerked off. It's like I'd lost all feeling down there. Yet from just one look at her, my mind is already flooded with the hottest thoughts I've had in months.

Once we exchanged numbers, it was like the floodgates opened. We pretty much message all day every day.

If you could only have 1 snack for the rest of your life, what would it be?

Ha, now that's easy.

Chocolate peanuts or chocolate raisins. What about you?

Pistachios, I think

Yeah, I like them too.

Favorite drink?

It used to be Long Island. But I don't drink anymore. No, it doesn't mean I'm boring. I just stopped 😉

Just because you don't drink doesn't make you boring

Glad you think like that

Plus I didn't even mean alcoholic 😊

Hahaha, ok, well either vanilla latte or toffee nut latte. Or Rubicon

Ooh, which flavor though?

Lychee or mango. Well, I like all of them if I'm honest. Both the juice and the fizzy one but I prefer the juice

Coffee or tea?

Both. Coffee in the morning, maybe tea in the afternoon

Do you prefer sweet or savory?

Oh, both. I have a sweet tooth for sure! But I like to at least have savory before having sweet. What about you?

Hmm, well, I used to love sweet, but after I had my kids, I think I prefer savory. Now sweet is more like a treat.

Kids? Oh wow. I don't know why, but I wasn't expecting that.

How many kids do you have?

2

Jeez. Okay.

Aww, nice. I have 0. Never been married, never had kids.

That's not a bad thing. Does it bother you I have kids? Don't worry, I won't take offense if it does.

I think about how I want to respond for a couple of minutes. I wasn't expecting to enjoy chatting with her as much as I have. I kinda feel torn. My head and my life are in such a fucked-up place right now. I know it wouldn't be the best time to start anything. But I also don't wanna shut this down.

No, it doesn't bother me… with everything in my life at the moment, I'm just taking my time to be honest, so I have no expectations. Plus, I'm not looking for like a hook up style one nighters or anything like that.

That's nice and very refreshing to hear

Yeah. And no one would want to get into bed with me at the moment anyway. I had an infection and then got bad psoriasis all over my body, which is horrible.

That's why I've not been on dating apps since I've been back. They bring out the shallowest sides of people. So, I guess overall, I'm not interested to see how many people I meet turn away when they know I'm gonna look like this for a few months at least. Plus, I don't wanna like jump into a relationship quickly for the sake of it just because I'm sad and lonely. 😊 Would rather be kind to myself and take time.

Releasing a huge breath, I feel an enormous weight lifted from my shoulders. I don't know why. I hadn't planned on telling her all that. But I'm kinda glad I did.

If you ever have a woman being rude or commenting about your skin in this town, let me know and I'll put her in her place. Listen, I'm a single mom. I'm curvy/plus size, my body is covered in all kinds of marks and scars and tattoos. I'm not a model, don't have the perfect body, and have had enough men say they'd be more attracted to me if I was slimmer or less curvy or even wishing I was taller. I'm not the most confident person about how I look, so I would never judge or discriminate against anyone.

That's also refreshing to hear x

Does it hurt? The psoriasis?

It doesn't hurt, no. Only hurts to look at, lol

I could say I'm sure it's nothing, but I feel like that would dismiss your thoughts and feelings. Well, if it makes you feel any better, I hate having to look at my big boobs every day. On more than one occasion, I've screamed at them and just wished I could detach them and store them in the cupboard. Only bringing them out for special occasions.

Haha, love it. You've made me smile already. Aww, I'm sure it's not that bad. It's all in our head, right?

Her boobs are literally what I'm picturing in my head right now. My cock thickens so quickly I have to adjust my boxers to relieve some of the tension.

Alright, enough about my boobs. How tall are you?

Damn, I'd prefer to stay on the topic of her boobs. But I guess this is more appropriate.

6'3

Oh wow, I'm a whole foot shorter than you.

That's not a bad thing.

She's seeming more and more like a great little package.

Chapter 6

Carina

"Good morning, Mr. Schriver. How are you feeling today?" I ask as I start to change out his dressings.

He's one of my few patients that always sets me off emotionally. I think it's because he lost most of his family in a terrible accident. His daughter, her husband, his granddaughter, and two family friends had all been on vacation when the boat capsized, and the only survivors were two of the stewards and his granddaughter, Amira. She's currently working as a nanny in England so isn't able to visit him.

"I awake to another sunrise, so I guess that's good."

Sorrow mars his face, as it always does. His wife had died several months after the accident, and I know that medically they said it was a heart attack, but I'm convinced it was from a broken heart.

"When I came in, I saw that there was a note on the sideboard that you'll be having your new food delivery this afternoon."

"Yeah, Amira found this new company and set it up on the line."

I don't know what it is about older generations and their mispronunciations with certain technological terminology, but it always makes me smile.

"Ooh, well, that sounds good. Did you get to pick from a menu or are you just going to do a bit of Russian roulette and leave it as a surprise when it's time to cook?"

"I eat everything, so I won't mind what it is, but I do like your idea of spicing things up a bit. Oh, and I forgot to tell you, I got some good news yesterday."

"Oh yeah, and what was that?"

"Amira called to remind me about the delivery, but she also said that the children she is looking after both got into the boarding school the parents have been trying to get them to attend. So in September, they'll be starting there and she will move back home."

For the first time since I've met him, pure joy radiates from his face. "That's fantastic news. You must be so excited?"

"Yeah, I am. But I am worried for her, as I want to make sure that when she comes back, she won't just be worrying herself by looking after me. I want her to live her own life."

"I'm sure she will. Do you know what she's going to want to do work-wise when she returns?"

"I think the same thing. Childcare is what she's always said brings her the most joy. So if you know anyone that'll be looking for help or anything, tell them she will be available from then onwards."

"I will. And if she also offers babysitting, I might just ask her if she wants to work with me."

"That's for sure. She said she feels like she knows you with how much I've told her about you."

"Same goes for me. I can't wait to meet her."

It's true, I genuinely do. If she's anything like her grandfather, I know she'll be lovely. Finishing up with Mr. Schriver, I pack up for the day, then head home to change out of my uniform and into my workout gear, just in time to get to my class. Afterward, I shower at home as I want to deep condition my hair, plus both boys have after-school clubs today, so I've got a little more time. Making myself a herbal tea, I'm able to relax on the couch with my hair wrapped in the thermal conditioning cap. Grabbing my phone, I remember I haven't yet messaged Robby back.

> Hey, just getting a chance to text you back. Today's been good. For once the morning ran smoothly, there were no hiccups with any patients today, and even squeezed in a class at the gym. Currently, just doing my hair and having a mini break. How about yourself?

It's weird, I hadn't expected us to reconnect this way. We text pretty much all day, every day. The conversation stays light and never steering towards anything too heavy. But I get the sense that he's dealing with some stuff. Not that I want or ever would push for anyone to open up and talk about things they aren't ready or comfortable talking about. I've found it difficult to work out what direction this is going in.

Most of the time we just joke back and forth, but sometimes things steer towards a flirtier tone. He didn't shut things down when I'd told him I have kids, and when he said he was just taking things easy in the dating world, I actually really got that. I think too many people nowadays want instantaneous connections and things to happen, and I just always feel that if things happen quickly, then they always end up ending just as fast.

Meh, it's been so so. Nothing exciting. So which gym do you go to?

I started doing classes at this place called Fighting Edge. I don't know if you've heard of it. I never thought I'd be into or feel comfortable at a place like that, but it's really been great.

I watch as the typing bubble pops up several times, then disappears again. Several minutes go by and I'm a little confused. Still nothing. After a further ten minutes, his message finally comes through.

Oh, wow. So I feel like this just keeps getting more insane. Yeah, I know the place. I guess you could say I know it pretty well. My family, well, me, I guess own it. It's mine.

Shut the fuck up. How is this even possible? That can't be. There is no way.

Are you being serious right now or are you pulling my leg?

I'm being serious.

No way. I can't believe it. So you are telling me, we met by chance, then we find out we live in the same town, and not only that, but the gym I randomly started going to a couple of months ago is owned by you? Yet we still haven't met in person despite speaking every day?

Yup. That pretty much sums it up.

I can't tell if this is funny or weird or damn insane. Where neither one of us has really pushed about actually meeting in person, I don't wanna be the one to make the move to do so. Plus, I still can't quite wrap my head around the whole thing. So, not wanting to steer things into any uncomfortable territory, I just try to lighten things up.

Haha, that's crazy. So there's a high chance you'll either work out or find out what I look like, possibly even be there at the same time and be none the wiser?

Yeah, I guess so

Changing the topic, I get us back to our this or that game.

Alright, how about this? Beach vacation or city escape?

Well, I've lived in Thailand for a while within the last five years and it kinda feels like both over there. But I would say beach just because of the hustle and bustle and traffic of the cities I don't like. Cities for a few days only, but beach for a few months.

Mmmm, yes, that sounds idyllic.

Mexican or Indian food?

Mexican, you?

Don't know why I asked because I like all of them. Mexican, Indian, Thai, Chinese, Japanese, Italian. Yeah, I like all foods.

He seems to be really indecisive. I don't know if that's just his personality or maybe he's trying to sound really worldly. It's funny and a little cute though.

Ha, that's good. I always think it's great to try out as many different cuisines as possible. How about Caribbean?

Yeah it's nice, I just haven't eaten that as much as others.

Now that is a travesty 

Are you Caribbean, by any chance?

Yup. Ok, eating in or eating out?

Oh well, it depends where. Unfortunately, the standard of food in lots of places just isn't great and you can often make it a lot better at home. Hahah but eating out is great – in lots of Asian countries it's more common to eat out than at home lol

Really? I didn't know that. Ok, this one is slightly different. Do you prefer short or tall women?

Doesn't matter, just not taller than me haha

Damn, why do men always struggle giving detailed or more in depth answers?

I don't think I've met many women taller than you. How about you?

I'm not too fussy about how tall women are 😁

I can't help but laugh at my silly response.

I think most men prefer short, if I had to guess

It's weird, as I've noticed that whenever I expect him to go in one direction, he never does. Plus, he does a lot of generalizing. I don't know if that's just the way he is or if he's just like that with me.

My last two exes have been complete opposite heights, hahahaha. Tiny and then almost close to me. I've had no preference about women. I'm really open-minded. Would you date a guy that's shorter than you?

Given that I'm only 5'3 I know I should say yeah, I'd be fine, but I'm only really attracted to taller guys. I think if I wasn't curvy, I'd probably be less concerned and not care if he was my height or possibly even shorter. But given my curves, I'd feel too insecure and would worry about crushing him. Like if I hugged him, I'd be scared I'd suffocate him.

Sorry, I know you said it's an insecurity, but that's funny. I get it, that makes sense. Nobody wants to be suffocated in any relationship.

Horror movies or cartoons?

Horror.

Be a good kisser or great in bed?

Great in bed. Kissing's great sure, but it's not the end of anything.

Hmm, I always find it funny how many guys underestimate the power of a good kiss.

Snakes or spiders?

Spiders probably. I'm much bigger than them. Snakes, I dunno, still too unpredictable and dangerous.

Ha. I hate spiders. Like have a serious phobia.

Have sex in the morning or at night?

I know I'm taking a risk at going down this road, but I just wanna see.

> Both. Come on, it doesn't matter the time of day. 😔 I won't be doing that for a long time anyways, so can't think about it.

> Is that because you can't or don't want to? And please tell me to shut up if you don't wanna answer that.

> Because of my skin at the moment. It's everywhere. Horrible. So I can't.

> If it's just you that's deciding that, then that's one thing, but don't let anyone stop you when you wanna jump back into action.

> I know, but honestly, no one would want to, anyway. I don't think you understand. It's all over my body, from head to toe. I've never seen or had anything like it. I just can't and wouldn't enjoy myself or be comfortable enough.

I drop the subject because one, I don't wanna make him feel uncomfortable and two, there's something about the way he feels about himself that makes me just feel so sad.

Over the next couple of days, he's much quieter than he had been, and I would just kick myself that I may have made him feel uncomfortable. Because, in all honesty, I've really enjoyed just having someone to talk to. Even as simple as our conversations have been, it's just felt nice to get messages on my phone that aren't either work related or from the boys' schools, therapists, or doctors. As sad and pathetic as it may sound, I've liked not feeling lonely.

Then one evening, I'm a little surprised when he steers our little game back to the topic of dating.

What would your ideal date be?

Hmm, I don't think I'd want something like a sit-down meal or just going to a bar or something. I'd want something that's activity-based. Like one of those treasure hunt things. Or going to one of those food festivals, or something random and non-typical, I guess.

What's a non-typical date, lol? Well, I can't even do anything exciting like that. As where I'm not doing most of the running of the gym I've gotta give half my pay to my manager who's doing all the work while I'm like this. So yeah, I feel like a bit of a write-off at the moment. Sorry. I couldn't even take you to one of those activity places. I know I sound like a real catch, I'm sure.

Oh stop it! Don't be so hard on yourself. And you've been the most intriguing person I've chatted to in a long time.

I know everyone says not to be so hard on myself etc, but I'm still not sure how to do that. Just going through a lot at once lately that all... things won't be like this, this time next year.

I know it probably sounds hypocritical as I berate myself and the shitstorm that is my life on a daily basis, but I've found the easiest way to get through each day is just faking it till I make it.

And now I'm back home alone and don't know what to do. This is part of my problem.

I'm sorry. I'm also sorry if anything I've said so far has seemed insensitive.

Not at all. I'm not gonna be offended by anything anyone says. It's alright x

Ok, what are your hobbies?

Muay Thai. I used to compete. It's my favorite escape. I love it but, like with everything at the moment, I just can't even enjoy that. Three years ago, I lost both my brothers. And last year my mom died, so I guess I'm still dealing with that too, you know… it isn't easy, but the sun rises again.

Cold seeps deep into my bones. That's so sad and heartbreaking. I knew he was going through some stuff, but I never could have imagined it being this. Tears fill my eyes as sorrow for this man I've never even met washes over me. My hands tremble slightly as I try to find the right words to respond.

I'm so sorry. That's truly awful. I will say, just the fact that you are getting through each day is something you should be proud of. I know when I've gone through some of my darkest times, just getting through the day needs to be seen as a victory. Whether it's something small like just getting up, brushing your teeth, and having a shower–might not seem like much to others but when you're simply surviving, those things need to be celebrated x

Yeah, I get what you mean x

Well, I think you're interesting and I'd definitely enjoy hearing more about what got you into Muay Thai and some adventures you've been on during the multiple times you've been to Thailand. I know you said you're not looking to date, but I'd still like to get to know you better. So how about for now, if you want me to be your friend/random curly-haired tattooed woman to vent to/whatever category you wanna label me as, that's fine. You can always reach out to me if you want or need to.

Aww well that's made me laugh and smile so thank you oh and by the way I love curly and coily hair x

It took me a couple of days to really wrap my head around everything Robby had shared with me. So much started making sense. The ups and downs in his moods, the seesaw of how he seemed to just want someone to talk to one

minute, then flirt the next. Then I guess just that feeling, that knowledge of having someone there.

I realize that by saying I don't need to be a particular label is putting everything into a gray area. Am I just a friend? A confessional? Someone he is simply getting to know? But in all honesty, right now it doesn't matter. We both clearly just want someone to talk to. The only moments throughout the day when I shut off and am not in mom mode or work mode are during my interactions with Robby, and right now I don't want to lose that. And who knows, when we finally do meet, that might be the moment it all becomes clear. He could become the friend I need, or things might grow and bloom into something more.

Chapter 7

Carina

My day was pleasantly filled with surprises. First, my mom called me this morning on the way to work, letting me know she wanted to have the boys for a sleepover tonight, which was great. It's so rare that I ever have an evening off. Plus, as tomorrow is the weekend, I'm also not working. So not only do I get the evening to myself, but I also get to have a sleep in morning as well. Also, two of my patients had procedures in the hospital, so I only had to do half a shift. Given my extra free time, I did one of the earlier conditioning classes I'm usually unable to attend. It was good, my muscles feel loose, and I guess the only disappointment I had was in the back of my mind I was hoping to run into Robby.

Yesterday, he mentioned he was going to head to the gym at some point to do some admin work. His recent messages haven't seemed as anxious and reserved as before, but I didn't want to let myself get carried away. So instead, I focused on myself. I had a long relaxing bath and treated myself by making my grandmother's oxtail with rice. I did cheat, however, and used the pressure cooker instead of cooking on the stove because I was hungry. I laughed as I cooked, knowing if she could see me now, she'd slap me round the back of my head for not making it the way generations before me have done. But come on, when you're hungry, you're hungry. I'm just about to make myself a glass of rum and ginger ale to accompany my food when I get a message.

> Hope your day has gone better than mine. Couldn't sleep last night so only drifted off at about 5. Slept through my alarm to go to AA. Had forgotten to go to the shop to grab some food and then got a call from the gym that there's a leak in the roof. When I went to jump in the car to come here to sort it out, it took eight tries before the damn thing finally started.

Wow, I feel like he's managed to pack in so much in that message. Bless him, he really hasn't been able to catch a break today. Makes me feel bad that by comparison my day's gone pretty well. But at the same time, I can't help that niggling thought that he's always focused on the negative. I get when times are tough it's hard but still, always dwelling on it isn't good. Also, I wonder why he goes to AA. I know he'd mentioned before he doesn't drink, but I now wonder if that's why? I've never dealt with anything like this before, so I have no idea how to broach something like this. Maybe now isn't the best time to ask either.

Yeah, mine's been fine. My mom has the boys tonight. Sorry to hear that you didn't sleep well, and about your car acting up. Were you able to sort out the roof issue?

Kinda. Well, for now. But I'm still here now since I haven't even begun on the paperwork I need to sort. I've just got a headache. Plus, I'm hungry. I'm just sick of everything.

Looking around the kitchen, I get an idea.

Like I said, I don't have the kids, and from the sounds of it, you haven't eaten. I've just finished cooking some dinner. If you want, I could bring some food to the gym. Maybe eating would help clear the headache?

Nervousness slithers through me even though I know the offer I've put forward isn't exactly a big one. It is, however, the first time either of us has put the suggestion of us meeting face to face out there. I don't want him to think that I'm just trying to take advantage of the situation. I'm genuinely not. I would offer that to anyone I was close to or friendly with. I await anxiously for his response.

Yeah, I guess you can do.

I don't know what I was expecting, but part of me feels a little deflated at his tone. Grabbing a Tupperware box out of the cupboard, I dish out some food for him, tasting it as I go and making sure it's all good. I'd been starving before, but now my appetite has been replaced with anxious trepidation. As much as I haven't wanted to admit it, I know that when we meet face to face, it'll be like the bell has been rung. Things will change. Whichever way they do, I know it won't be the same as before.

Once I've got his food all packed up, I just wanna make sure that he's okay with this.

Okay, I've got it packed and ready. Are you sure you're okay with me coming over?

Well, from the sounds of it, you clearly don't want to come over. Fine, you don't have to.

Woah, where on earth did that come from? He's completely taken that the wrong way. Once again it feels like he's actively looking for something bad. Is this part of him and his character that he always jumps to an extreme conclusion or reacts defensively, or is it just because he's currently going through a tough time? I can't tell if this is a red flag or a defence mechanism from him which makes me feel both bad but also a little concerned.

No, no, that's not what I meant at all. I just wanted to double check that it's ok with you. I'm more than happy to head there now. Just with everything you've got going on, I didn't want you to think I was overstepping or anything like that.

Ok, it's fine, everything is still open as normal and there's a class that's just started. I'll be in the office. There's a door next to the men's locker room. Past that door, there's a set of stairs that'll take you right through.

Okay, is there anything else you'd need?

No, that's fine

My mind is so scattered I don't even think about the fact I'm in leggings, a tank top, and an oversized shirt. My hair is still up from my bath earlier and the only thing on my face is my moisturiser.

As I get in the car and make the quick journey to the gym, I think of his reaction. Was that his way of saying he didn't want to see me? That he felt I was just pushing myself into the frame. I really hadn't expected that from him. It's making me wonder if some of the stupid points my ex used to say about me are true. That I'm just annoying and push myself into people's lives when they don't actually want it. Is that what I do? I don't mean to. If someone needs something and I can help, I just do.

By the time I park out in the gym's parking lot, I'm even more nervous. It feels weird as I make my way through the gym, not to train but holding a bag of food for the guy who's somehow and unexpectedly captured my attention. The man who, unbelievably, was right under my nose but neither of us knew. And now, after weeks of daily conversations, I will now finally meet him in the flesh.

Taking a breath, my hands shake as I go to knock on the door. I hear a chair squeak, then finally the door opens.

I have to crane my neck slightly to see his face. Damn, he really is tall. It's crazy, as in one sense he looks exactly like I'd imagined. But at the same time, nothing like that at all. His tall form is covered in oversized gray joggers and a matching hoodie. His eyes are a shade of blue I've never seen before, with flecks of gold and gray swirling through. A strong and chiseled jawline that's peppered with a dusting of stubble. What I had least expected was the color of his hair. Deep jet black that's so striking, it's like something out of a mythical painting.

"Hi." The sound of his voice breaks me out of the trancelike spell I'm under. Clearing my throat, embarrassment washes over me and I barely get the words out. With trembling hands, I pass him the bag with the food.

"Please come in."

He takes the bag from me and motions for me to enter. My eyes briefly scan around me, and I'm surprised at how bare his office is. There's an old leather couch on one side, with some filing cabinets on the other. What takes up most of the room is the large desk in the middle. It reminds me of one of those antique style double desks when two people would easier have room to work simultaneously. "Would you like something to drink? Up here all I have is water, but I can grab something from the coffee machine downstairs if you prefer?"

"Water's fine."

He carefully places the bag of food on top of the scattered papers on the desk and walks to a water dispenser. The only sound in the room is the churning of water pouring out of the machine and into the plastic cup that he hands to me.

"Thank you for this. I don't remember the last time I had a full, proper meal like this. It smells so good too."

Taking a seat on the couch, I make myself a little more comfortable. "It's really no biggie. The timing was perfect, actually. I'd just plated up."

"Cool, so you've already eaten, or do you wanna share?"

"No, no, I'm good. I just hope you like it."

I look away when he pulls out the large container and the utensils I wrapped in a napkin. "Damn, this is good. You're a great cook," he says after he chews and swallows his first mouthful.

My cheeks warm at the compliment, but I just brush it off.

He chews down another huge spoonful of food and something inside me pangs with sorrow. Seeing the way he's demolishing that food, it's clear that someone of his stature would clearly need to eat a lot to fuel himself and from both the sounds and looks of things, he clearly hasn't been eating anywhere near enough. Wanting him to sit and enjoy his food, I tell him about the book I finished reading last night. I can tell it's piqued his interest, because when I summarise what happens, he asks for more details. By the time I finish telling him basically everything that happens in the book, he's finished the whole container of food. And I'd put a lot in there.

"Thank you, that was delicious."

"Well, I'm gonna leave you in peace." I can tell from his eyes that he's exhausted. "But I'm glad we finally got to meet in person."

"Yeah, so am I. You got anything special planned for tomorrow?"

"Nope, nothing really. The boys won't be back from my mom's until early evening. And I'm not working. So I'll just probably end up pottering about the house for a bit. How about you?"

"Nah, nothing, will probably just stay in and chill. If

you want, you can come over for a coffee or something. I know I can't really do anything fun at the moment, but I do have one of those proper barista-style coffee machines. And I know you said how much you like your coffee."

"Yeah, I'd like that. Any particular time?"

"Um… how about I message you when I'm up? Hopefully tonight I'll get a good night's sleep and wake at a normal time."

"Sounds good to me."

With my keys still in my pocket, I go to reach over and grab the empty food container and cutlery to put back in the bag at the same time Robby does. The tips of our fingers touch for the briefest of moments, and my eyes shoot over at him. Once again hypnotized by the magnetic pull from the glacier hue that shows both so much pain and sorrow. It's like being branded, feeling the points on me where his eyes trace over. My lips, my neck, my chest, then back up to my eyes. Then he closes his eyes, taking a deep breath, and gives me the softest smile. I almost miss it with how fast it goes.

"Thank you again for this."

"Was my pleasure. Alright, I guess I'll see you tomorrow."

"Cool, I'll message you my address in the morning."

Giving him a nod and a smile, I make my way back down the stairs, through the gym, then finally out to my car.

As I get into bed, I can only think of one thing. From this moment on, things are going to change. I don't know why or how, but I have this feeling that I will either be able to thaw that frozen castle he has locked himself in, or that ice will sink me to my deepest depths.

Chapter 8

Carina

Why is it that when I don't have my kids, or I don't have to be up early, I am never able to sleep in? Like my body is adamant I have to get up. I can't deny the little bit of excitement I have to see Robby. I'm interested to see his place, as I am curious if his is a home that's just a house, or whether it'll be an extension of him. Will there be parts of him there that I have not yet learned about?

Getting out of bed, I jump in the shower, then get dressed quickly. Because I don't know exactly when he will get up, I make myself a coffee, quickly put a load of washing on, and throw the previous load into the dryer. I wonder if I should put some makeup on. I'm not someone that usually wears it, only really if I'm going somewhere for a special occasion. Yet there is a part of me that wants to make a little more effort. But then again, I'm torn as last night I wasn't wearing any. And I don't really wanna set myself up and start wearing it, because then I'll feel like I always need to. Otherwise if I suddenly see him without, he'll probably think I look ill or something. Deciding to stay barefaced, I change into my more flattering jeans, and even I have to admit my ass looks pretty good in them.

He finally messages me letting me know he's awake and sends his address. Seriously, he even *lives* close to me. Giving myself one last check in the mirror, I do a quick fluff of my hair, then head out.

Just as I'm about one block from his, I see the cute sign of the little coffee shop on the corner. I suddenly remember him telling me his favorite drinks are vanilla and toffee nut lattes. Pulling over, I pop inside and am happy that not only do they sell coffee, beans, and food, but they also sell syrups too. I'm not sure which one out of the two to pick, so I end up getting both. A few minutes later, I pull up to the address he gave me. It looks like a lovely house. There's a cute little water feature out the front, though it's overgrown and covered in some kind of moss or something. To be honest, the whole front yard could look so much bigger and have more potential with a little bit of a clean-up. Not that I'm any kind of gardening expert.

Knocking on the door, I'm relieved that I don't feel the same nerves I had last night. Yet just like last night, I'm once again awash with momentary shyness as he opens the door. I don't know what it is about him. He's not even doing anything, just makes me feel like a schoolgirl who's somehow found herself near her crush. Okay, I really need to get a grip.

"I didn't know which of the two you'd prefer. I thought it's just best to go with both."

I hand him the two bottles of syrup and he tips his head for me to follow him in. Closing the door behind me, I notice the cream carpet and quickly take my shoes off before following in his wake, my eyes are like black holes, absorbing everything I see. His house is so barren that I'm taken aback. As we pass the front room, the only things in there are storage boxes. No furniture. Nothing. Then we walk through this big open-plan kitchen/dinner/living area. The space is beautiful. The kitchen has all the appliances you could need, with a large island in the middle. On the other side of the island, there is a large brown leather couch with a matching armchair beside it. Both are facing a TV mounted on the wall. In the far corner, there is a large desk, almost matching the one he has at the gym. Beside it is a framed poster from the movie *Pulp Fiction* that's leaning against the wall on the floor.

"This is cool. You didn't need to bring anything, though. But thank you."

"My grandmother always said you should never arrive as a guest somewhere empty handed."

Robby huffs a small laugh. "She sounds like a very generous and smart woman."

"She was," I say with a smile.

"Alright, so which one do you want, vanilla or toffee nut?"

"I don't mind, whichever one you choose to open."

"I know for sure both will be open by tomorrow, so you just pick which I open first."

"Okay, let's go with vanilla."

Even though he looks really at ease as he prepares the coffees, I can't help but feel like there's something cold about this house. There isn't any kind of draft or anything. But this place has an almost tomb-like feel to it and I'm not sure if it's because there is nothing personable anywhere or because it feels like there is some sort of dark cloud that looms over us. I say my thanks as he hands me my coffee and sits on the other side of the couch from me.

"I was thinking, you said you liked the sound of that show I was telling you about. Do you wanna watch it?" Robby asks casually.

"Yeah, sure, why not? But you've already seen the first episode."

"I know. But in my defense, I was already dozing, so I probably missed parts of it" he chuckles as he reaches over and grabs the remote.

He finds the show and puts it on. After the first five minutes, I'm hooked. I'm pretty sure at some point he even asked me a question, but I was so engrossed that I didn't really pay him much attention. He makes us another coffee, and I know I'm probably gonna be up late tonight. But even despite the coldness of the house, I still find myself relaxing and just switching off. By the time the episode finishes, I'm desperate to find out what happens next.

"Can we put the next episode on?" I ask.

"I would love to, but it isn't out yet." He laughs, showing me the episode list.

"What? Why not?"

"There's only one a week, and it's just started. So you gotta wait till next week."

"Damn," I mutter.

"That's fine. I think it's Wednesdays that the episodes come out. So if you're not working or finish early on Wednesday or Thursday, you can come over, and we watch it each week."

I've always struggled not getting carried away with excitement, but I'm really fighting myself right now not to be beaming with his suggestion. Because as much as it might seem like a small thing, it means a lot to me that he wants to spend more time together and arrange something that allows us to enjoy and bond on something.

"Yeah, I'd like that. Are there any other shows that are on your watch list?"

"I've got loads, but there are a couple that I wanna watch again because I loved them."

"Oh, really?"

"Yeah, look."

"How is it that most of the shows you watched I haven't and vice versa?" I observe and see the corner of his mouth turn up in a smirk as he shrugs his shoulder slightly.

"Well as that's the case, how about we make a pact?"

"What kinda pact?" I ask curiously as I shift myself to face him better.

"Both of us will pick a show that the other hasn't watched and watch those episodes alongside the series that's released weekly. Then when we finish, we move onto the next one. How does that sound?"

Biting my lip, I suppress the grin that's desperate to break out at the thought of our plan.

"You've got yourself a deal" I declare.

Flicking through the options I decided on a docuseries about Michael Jordan, mainly because I loved the Chicago Bulls when I was a kid. Robby picked Dexter and when I spot how many series and episodes there are, I can't deny the warm feeling I get. Could it be that he's picked something that would take a long time for us to get through? Is it his way of making sure our recurring dates last as long as possible? It's not as if it's anything over the top or excessive, but it's nice. And with the way that he relaxes more and more, no longer sitting on the other side of the couch and instead next to me, makes me feel not only warm and happy but also hopeful.

For the next two weeks between my kids, my job, and doing classes, that's what we do. I go to his house, and we just chill and watch our shows. On a couple of occasions, I was surprised when he sat by his back door and rolled himself a joint. It's not that I have an issue with it. I grew up with my cousins and friends smoking and remember they used to say that smoking weed is the same, if not better, than cigarettes. If you're an adult and you choose to do so, it's up to you. Obviously, being a mother to two boys, I'm not encouraging it, but it's not like I'm going to tell him what to do. Plus, I've noticed him having one always coincides with the days he seems to be really down and depressed. Like he finds some sort of escapism. One thing I guess I don't understand and to be honest, I never asked, was why he was in AA regarding his relationship with alcohol, when he's also smoking. Again, I'm in no means qualified, but surely there must be some sort of correlation between the two.

We've gotten into this weird yet comfortable dynamic of me coming over, always with either food or a new coffee syrup to try. There were a couple of occasions when he'd fall asleep, somehow ending up with his head in my lap. At some point I started stroking his hair while he slept and I'm not sure if it was more for him or for my own self-soothing. I only realized I was doing it when one time I stopped, and he woke up instantly and asked why I stopped. That was when the light little touches started.

An innocent hand on the knee, which, in essence wasn't a big deal but the warmth of his palm penetrated through the fabric had my skin tingling. Or when it would be time for me to leave, having a hug that lasted just a few seconds longer than would be deemed innocent. Feeling his body pressed against mine unlocked a yearning I've not felt for such a long time. Or when I've been leaning on the kitchen island, his knuckles would graze my ass as he'd walk past and have me biting down on my lip so as not to let out a pleasurable moan. With each and every passing encounter, my body felt like it was set alight with yearning desire. I had to actively suppress the urge to moan when his large, strong hand rested on my thigh and his fingers made aimless circular patterns. All the while, I struggled to concentrate on what's going on in the episode.

Also, he loves touching my hair. When he first asked if he could, I said yeah, but did laugh as I asked why. To which he replied he doesn't know what it is, but he just loves curls. So my hair has become his own personal stress toy. He insists on giving a squeeze every time before I leave.

Today, we watched the last episode in the Michael Jordan series, and because I need to leave in about forty-five minutes, we just chat instead of starting the new show.

"With how much you say you enjoy kick boxing, I think you should give Muay Thai a try," he says optimistically.

"Oh yeah? The other day I was walking past the studio as one class was on and there is no way I could handle that. I still have no core or upper body strength. Well, I'm trying to work on it at least."

"Don't be silly. I bet if I got you in a clinch, you'd be able to get yourself out of it."

"Are you insane? Listen, I know I'm not the smallest

woman, but you've been doing this sport for god knows how many years, and you've done actual fights. Come on. You're the one being silly."

It's so rare that he lets out a real, full smile. I almost swallow my tongue when I watch as one stretches across his face.

"Just sounds like you're scared," Robby teases.

"I'm not scared. I'm just realistic." Even I can hear the apprehension in my voice, and watching as he raises a brow proves he could hear it as well.

"Alright, how about this? Instead of you getting out of a lock, how about I'll be on the floor and have to get free of your grip?"

"You want me to sit on you?" I ask incredulously.

"Hahaha, not quite, but kinda. Look." He pushes the armchair out of the way and lays on his back on the floor, stretching his arms out above his head. My eyes rake over his body and erotic thoughts flood my mind as I picture him in that position but with fewer clothes on.

"Now put your knees on either side of my hips and pin my wrists down."

This time it's me raising a brow at him. I can't be the only one that recognises how much this will resemble a sex position.

"Surely this should be the other way round," I mutter under my breath.

"What was that?"

"Nothing. But this is just silly. I'll probably crush you if I get on top like that."

"Stop making excuses and come on."

The slight command in his tone shoots straight through me, and I don't even realize how much I like it until I notice

I'm squeezing my thighs together. My skin feels tight as it tingles with desire.

Shaking my head, I follow his instructions and get into position. Knowing there are only a couple of articles of clothing separating us and being in this position feels like both the best and worst kind of foreplay.

"Now, I want you to really focus and try every way you can to not let me get free."

I give him a nod and tighten my grip around his wrists. My face is only inches from his and I watch as his Adam's apple dips when he swallows. I can feel every slight twitch and movement he makes between my thighs, and I have to fight the urge to rock and rub myself against him.

At first, he tries to buck me off and I almost lose my balance but lock myself tight. As he wriggles beneath me, I move my shin and press it down onto his. First on one leg, then the other. He smiles at that, and I put my full weight down on him.

I let out a breath as my arms get tired, struggling to keep my grip on his wrists. I gasp as, while he continues to try to get free, something long and hard grazes my pubic bone. It takes me so by surprise I release his hands. In an instant, he flips us over so now I'm on my back with him on top of me, my wrists pinned above my head.

Panting, I look up into his eyes, his pupils blown, and my nipples harden as I watch the desire sweep across his features. A rose blush blossoms over his cheeks as he starts to rock and grind against me.

My eyes widen when I feel the thick, long, hard ridge of him and I'm sure my panties are soaked now. A ball of fire burns in my belly as I feel consumed by my desire for him. Slowly, he dips his head forward and brushes his lips against mine. His kiss is so gentle, so tender, it has me craving for more. The stubble around his mouth grazes against my cheeks and the corner of my mouth. The soft warmth of his mouth is the perfect contrast to the rasp of his stubble. My chest hitches as I struggle to catch my breath, though I can't tell if it's from our little role play or because of my desire for him right now.

As he runs the tip of his tongue along my bottom lip, I moan. My nipples ache, desperate to be freed from my bra. Finally, his mouth closes on mine and this time, both of us moan as our tongues slide and explore. He continues to rock his cock against my pussy. I'm only wearing yoga tights and wouldn't be surprised if he can feel the wet patch forming.

The loud ringing of my phone's alarm sounds out across the room, feeling like a bucket of ice water. It's the alarm that tells me I need to be on my way to the school, otherwise I'll be late. As Robby rests his forehead against mine, we both catch our breath.

"Robby… I… I… I," I pant breathlessly.

"Yeah. I know. I get it." The frustrated and dejected tone is evident in his voice. He knows what that alarm means, and he knows I've got to leave.

Without saying a word, he pulls himself up and helps me to my feet. I don't realize why he's smirking at first, but when I look down, I see my suspicions are right. I have a wet patch and my face burns with embarrassment. Leaning over the couch, he grabs the hoodie he'd been wearing earlier and slides it over my head before I've even said anything in response.

"Thanks," I say, sliding my arms through the sleeves. Luckily, with how tall he is and how short I am, the hoodie reaches down to the tops of my thighs, covering any evidence of what just happened.

My face heats and I bite my lip as I think about how good it felt to have his body pressing down on mine.

"You better stop thinking about whatever is going through your pretty little head because you need to go, or you'll be late."

Turning, I look at him, my eyes narrow in annoyance that he seems completely unaffected right now.

Giving him a nod, I grab my purse off the counter and go to put my shoes on. Just before I grab the door handle, I turn and find him standing just behind me.

"Thanks for the coffee."I say still slightly breathless.

Looking down, I see the outline of his still-hard cock through his sweatpants, which brings a smile to my face.

"See ya soon," I say.

Just as I walk out the door, he calls out, "Hey, you forgot something."

My brows crease in confusion, then I laugh as he appears next to me and gives my hair a squeeze.

"I'll see you soon," he says with a grin, and I rush to my car.

As I make my way to the school, I realize a couple of things. One, he's a lot stronger than he looks. Two, he's definitely packing something that felt like it had length *and* girth to it. Three, I can't deny the confidence boost I'm feeling right now. I don't care what anyone says, it feels great when you know that someone, especially someone you're physically attracted to, is also drawn to you. And forth, where the fuck do things go from here? My body has ideas of where it wants things to go, but is he ready for something more with me?

Chapter 9

Robby

I honestly didn't think I'd be back doing my regular training again this soon. Well, I'm doing three classes a week, plus my typical gym work. But that's a hell of a lot more than I have been doing. What's fucking annoying is that my days just don't stay consistent. Some days, if I have a good night's sleep and get up, showered, dressed, and downstairs before like ten, it feels good. Like I genuinely believe everything is gonna be fine. I'll go to one of my AA meetings, or come into the gym to help, and it'll feel like I can get through the day.

But then some shit will happen. Some sort of bullshit gets thrown my way and I'll be back to square one. I'll just head back home and either lay on the couch till I fall asleep or get into bed and hide away from the world. Like it just can't seem to stay as an easy, good day.

Then there is Carina. Well, that's been a whole unexpected turn of things. When she offered to bring me food to the gym and I'd finally meet her in person, part of me wanted to say no. I didn't want her to see my skin. Wanted to wait until the creams and tablets hopefully started making some sort of difference. But then I just thought fuck it. If she's gonna be one of those women that has an issue, then I might as well find out now, rather than further down the line.

All I knew was she had curly hair, tattoos, and that she was black. That was it. So when I opened the door, I was more than a little impressed. She's fucking *hot.* The warm sepia tone of her skin glowed as if there was some sort of spotlight on her. She had a shy smile and luscious lips that any man would be desperate to feel. Her hair was up on her head, with a few tight, curly strands around her face. But it was her eyes that drew me in. Dark yet warm, they were almost black. Hypnotising. Like she has the power to see into the deepest and darkest parts of your soul. Maybe siren was the best descriptor for her as she is almost ethereal. She hadn't lied about her height, but I hadn't expected the voluptuousness of her body. Curves for days. A large chest that was encased in a top that showed just enough to have me fantasizing about seeing more. And her ass was more than a handful, my hands twitching, eager to give it a squeeze.

Then, once she started coming over to the house regularly, it was harder and harder to not think about how her skin would feel beneath my touch. Or when she'd lean over the kitchen island, how good it would feel to peel her leggings off and slide right into her. Feeling the warm, wet heat of her grip me tightly as I pound into her. But I had to suppress those thoughts because I wasn't ready. So at first, I'd made it my mission not to touch her. Not to give in to my base desires. Instead, just focusing on her company. I still can't get over her. I'd not expected her to come into my life. Even though we were only just messaging, I hadn't imagined she'd be a real life part of my day.

Then yesterday had been like normal. She arrived with a little treat like always—it's become a thing she does and I look forward to seeing what she brings, sometimes playing a game in my head to see if I can guess what she will turn up with.

We chilled and watched another episode of the series she chose. But it was as if a switch had been flipped. I wanted, needed to feel more of her. That's when I thought it would be fun to see if she'd take the bait with my little demo suggestion. Even with the fact that in the past year, I've dropped a ton of muscle, I know there was no way she'd be able to keep holding me down. She'd been a little apprehensive at first, but finally agreed. And fuck was I glad when she did. Due to our height difference, I knew for her to pin my hands down, she'd have to practically lay on top of me. The second her full breasts brushed against my chest, my cock thickened in my pants. *Finally.* Finally, what had felt like forever, the craving that had now been slowly, subtly building, was finally going to amount to something. Only just like with everything else in my life, I couldn't have it. Nothing could go simply. The second the blaring sound of her alarm went off, I knew our time was up before we really even got the chance to begin.

As always, things hadn't exactly panned out for me. That's basically the story of my life.

"Fuck it" I say as I push myself off the couch and dash to the bathroom. Turning the faucet on I make quick work stripping out of my clothes and my dick that's still hard springs free. Pre-cum oozes out and I wrap my fist around the head. The second I grip and start stroking, that pent-up desire ricochets through me and has my head rolling back.

Stepping into the shower I start fucking my fist as the water trickles down my back. Remembering how good her body felt on top of me. The softness of her skin and the heat that was emanating from her pussy and burning through the buttery fabric of her leggings has me reaching down and giving my balls a slight tug. The telltale tingles begin to shoot up my spine as I grip my dick tighter. My chest feels like there are bands of steel around it as breathing feels heavier and tighter. Picturing how good it would have felt burying myself to the hilt in her hot, wet heat is what sends me over the edge and has me coming so hard it's like a dam has erupted as my cum sprays across the shower wall tiles.

"Fuck, fuck, fucking hell," I pant as I have to lean against the wall to help me stay standing. Black spots dot my vision and my heart is still beating so hard it feels like it's going to explode out of my chest.

It takes me several minutes to get my senses back, then I quickly wash off before getting out wrapping a towel around me and just about manage the few steps it takes to get to my bed before I collapse on it and fall asleep almost instantly.

Despite sleeping fifteen hours then heading downstairs for a coffee, I must have fallen back asleep for a couple of hours. Damn Carina must have some sort of super powers. My dick twitches as I sit on the couch, reminiscing about yesterday when I suddenly remember this morning I got a message from one of my old training buddies, someone I used to go to school with, asking if I wanted to hang out. At the moment, I've not seen anyone besides Carina. Only the people at the gym while I'm training, but even then, it's not any real socializing. Can't really call the interactions with people from AA anything more than what it is. The only person I see or speak to is Carina. She's the only person I've let come over since I came back. Not only that, but she's pretty much the only person I speak to. Every day. Throughout the day. She's always encouraging me to eat, so I now send her pictures of every meal I make. Often it'll be with ingredients or containers of food she's brought over. She even found these cotton sleep gloves for me to wear when I find my skin intolerable. I'll send pictures of that as I sit there contemplating how boring and pathetic my life is, looking like Mickey Mouse in these white gloves.

Fuck, my life is a shitstorm.

My phone goes off with a message. Reaching over the couch, I grab it, expecting it to be Carina. To my surprise, it's my buddy who messaged earlier, though I'd never replied. He's sent a picture of a nice-looking bud he's picked up. Well, that's got my attention. Either wallow bored, thinking about how shitty everything is, or let him come over and at least get high. It's not exactly a hard choice now, is it?

Alright, you've persuaded me. Pick up some papers and tobacco on your way over as I'm almost out. Oh, and we need to work out who's going to be the one driving to Adam's wedding. Cause I ain't got the money to be paying for no taxi's or shit.

This past week Carina has only come over the once. She said they were short staffed, and she had to cover, which has been pretty annoying. I've gotten used to her company, the fun little treats, and like the little dynamic we've gotten into. So the fact she's not been around has really thrown me.

One, because when she came round, she only really had the time for us to catch up on one episode, which also meant there was no chance for us to carry on any of that hot and delicious fun we'd started last week. Which is really annoying as every time I think back on it, it's gotten my dick hard and had me jerking myself off almost every single day. And just like the first time, every time I think about her, how much I want to fuck her, I always come so hard, and there's so much of it. That never happens. Was it her? Did she cast some sort of spell or something? Or was it simply because I haven't fucked in so long that my body is just dying for release? Either way, it doesn't matter. I still haven't gotten what I want. Each time it feels like I'm only releasing just the smallest bit of tension.

But with her not coming over as often has meant that I've been bored. I've met up with a couple more buddies, but to be honest, it's only because they were up for getting high. And when you've got no drive or desire to do anything, and no one there to push you, it's just the easiest way to pass the time.

I made the mistake of scrolling through the pictures and videos on my phone, which sent me on a downward spiral. Seeing my brothers and Mom set me off. It hurt, physically hurt, hearing their voices. Hearing their laugh, the stupid jokes, it was like having a wound reopen.

A notification interrupts me.

> Heya, just wanted to see how you're doing. Sorry, today's been manic. I didn't even have the time to do the class today. How about you? Did you train today? Hope you've eaten x

Part of me just wants to ignore her. Just be left alone and sit in the lonely sadness that I'm forever surrounded by. But at the same time, I don't.

> Feeling like shit. Haven't eaten today and have been going through photos of my brothers and Mom. Now I'm just on my couch crying pathetically. Sick of this bullshit.

Chucking my phone back on the couch, I head to the bathroom and jump into the shower, wanting to wash away my tears and misery. Wishing the hurt and the pain could just disappear down the drain along with the water. I'm just so tired. Tired of everything. Feeling the familiar thumping pain of a headache coming on, I rest my forehead against the cold shower tiles and only once the water cools, do I finally get out.

Using the cream I got from the doctors, I slather myself from head to toe. My skin briefly easing from the cooling sensation before I wrap myself up in a pair of joggers and a hoodie. Downstairs, I pour a glass of water and pick up my phone. I see that there are three messages from Carina.

I'm so, so sorry. I'm not sure what I could say to help. I wish I could. I wish I was able to take that pain away for you. Saying that things will be ok feels inadequate and almost insulting. I wish I could come over and give you a hug. Or let you squeeze my hair. Or even just distract you, but sadly, I can't. I know it's not much, but I am here for you if you wanna talk. And you might feel like you're alone, but you're not. I'm here. Let me know if there's anything I can do x

The next message she sent came through several minutes after.

Okay, so I know I can't physically help right now, but one thing I know you need is to eat. So I've ordered you a pizza. I also got you some sides and a drink. Again I know it's not much but at least try to eat something x

They said it'll be there in twenty minutes.

She sent that seventeen minutes ago. Then, just like clockwork, there's a knock on my door. Hauling myself up from the sofa, I open the door and the smell of the food makes my stomach rumble. The delivery boy hands me three boxes and a bottle of Rubicon before running back to his car through the pelting rain.

Food in hand, I sit back down on the couch and turn the TV on. Needing something light, I find one of the specials of my favorite comedian. Opening up the box, I see she's gotten my favorite; cheese, pepperoni, jalapeños, olives, and red onions with a side of chicken wings and garlic bread. There is no way I'm going to finish it all, but I can have the leftovers tomorrow.

To my surprise, I demolish almost three-quarters of the pizza, half the garlic bread, and there are only two wings left. Damn, I feel stuffed. Moving the boxes back onto the counter, I refill one glass with some more Rubicon and another with water.

> Thanks for the food. I ate more than I thought I would. Think I'm about to fall into a food coma now.

Laying myself back down on the couch, I feel my eyes get heavy, and before I know it, I drift off into a dreamless sleep.

Chapter 10

Carina

Today's my day off. I did the school drop off and what's even better is both Zion and Kai have after-school clubs today, so I went to the gym and was pleased Robby messaged, telling me to come over whenever.

The other day when I was at the store, I found these frozen raspberry desserts that were absolutely amazing. So I grabbed another packet to bring as the little treat for today. I park the car, then knock on his door. It's surprisingly warm today, so I'm wearing a dress for the first time this year. But what's even more surprising is when he opens the door and he's in just a t-shirt and shorts. I've only ever seen him in loose joggers, I think, since he still tries to hide his psoriasis. Although I honestly don't think it's as intense as he feels it is. It really doesn't bother me in the slightest.

"Come in."

"So I went for something a little different today," I say, following him inside and handing him the frozen raspberries.

"Mmmm, now these sound good." Like a child, his lack of patience makes me laugh since within seconds he's already opened them and tried one. "Damn they're good. These are addictive."

"I know. But so far I've only found one place that sells them, and I don't think they stock that many. So ease up a little and maybe make them last a little more than five minutes," I tease as I laugh.

He pours a couple into a little bowl, then puts the rest of the pouch in the freezer.

"What flavor are you wanting to go with today?" he asks, opening the cupboard that now has about eight different coffee syrup bottles.

"Surprise me."

I take my now usual seat on the couch and make small talk while he prepares our drinks.

"I was sitting out in the garden for a bit this morning. Sun usually helps a bit with the psoriasis. Oh, and I got a phone call from my doctor this morning too. Apparently, I'm eligible to do this phototherapy treatment. He said it's meant to help." Even though he's trying to sound calm, I can hear slight bits of excitement and optimism in his voice.

"Oh really? Is it like lasers or something?"

"No, I think, from how he described it, it's kinda like a sun bed thing. So it's across a twelve-week period where I've gotta go in twice a week. So thirty sessions in total. And you strip down and have that light therapy on you. It starts small, only thirty or forty-five seconds, then goes up like thirty seconds with every appointment, until in the end I think it's six or seven minutes. I can't remember the exact details."

I almost spit my coffee out as I wasn't expecting him to say he has to strip down for it.

"So you just stand in the middle of a room naked?"

He laughs at my surprised face. "I don't think it's gonna be in like a doctor's office. It's probably like a little cubicle. Like an upright sun bed."

"Aahh, I see. So you would just look like an exhibit with a bunch of medical students around you, watching and tracking your every movement?" I ask playfully raising my brows as I widen my eyes comically.

His loud and carefree laugh echoes across the room and brings the biggest smile to my face. I don't think I've ever heard him laugh. Not like this.

"Nah, I don't think it'll be like that. I'm still not sure whether it's even worth me going to. It'll probably just be a waste of time," he says as his shoulders slump.

He keeps doing this. It's like he's afraid to think positively about things. Like he gives up before anything even happens. I don't like it and don't want him to feel like that. How do I get him to stop looking at things as the glass half empty?

"No, don't be silly. It's still worth trying. Plus, now you'll have to go just to prove me right and let me know if there are medical students watching."

"If there are, I'll make you come with me and cover their eyes."

We settle in and turn on the next episode of our show.

Despite the warmth outside, there is a bit of a draft inside his house that has made me shiver a couple of times. Without saying a word, Robby grabs a throw from the armchair and lays it over both of us. It's not the biggest, causing him to edge closer so we're both covered and my body suddenly feels alive at his proximity.

Ever so gently, the tips of his fingers softly brush against my thigh, just stopping short of the hem of my dress. Though I try not to react, I attempt to shallow my breathing as my pulse begins to race. Although my eyes are on the screen, every thought and fibre of my being is fixated on his touches. I have to fight not to fidget.

After what feels like forever, when my body is practically humming with need, the tips of his fingers graze the front of my panties and I have to hold in a groan. Out of the corner of my eye, I find him focused on the TV and I want to scream, begging him for more. As if I said those words out loud, he slides two fingers along the lace edge and down to my lips. I know without even seeing it that his fingers are wet. Still, with a gentle touch, he circles my clit. My hands fist the throw as a shiver runs down my back from how good his fingers feel, but it only makes me want and crave more. My hips grind down against the couch as my thighs open wider, pleasure pooling in my belly. Leisurely, his fingers travel down further until finally they reach my entrance. The rough callouses of his fingers only add another delicious texture. His two fingers don't even get past the second knuckle before my walls clamp down on him, which has me letting out a deep moan. Gripping, eagerly wanting more, despite the slight burn I feel as he struggles to work his fingers deeper. He groans, "Fuck. Your pussy is dripping. So wet. So tight" Robby taunts, finally turning and looking at me and giving me his full attention.

His words only turn me on more. I whimper when Robby drags his fingers out. I can feel his eyes on me, which has me turning and facing him. He brings his glistening fingers to his mouth and sucks my juices off of them.

"Mmmm, I knew you'd taste good."

"Oh, fuck," I pant.

As if a bomb detonated, he pulls me onto his lap and fuses his mouth onto mine. Gripping my hips tightly, he rocks them back and forth against his hard length. I'm so turned on I know I'm dripping on him through my now soaked panties.

His lips leave mine, kissing his way down along my chin, down my neck, along my collarbone, and down to my chest. With one hand still gripping my hip, the other reaches up and slides the dress and bra strap off my right shoulder. Using just his teeth, he pulls the lace cup of my bra down, freeing my breast. His eyes dart up to mine the second he spots my pierced nipples, and I swear his pupils darken even more with desire. My nipples are so hard they ache. His hot, wet tongue licks around the silver barbell piercing. I feel drowsy with desire. His lips pucker as he blows against my now wet nipple, sending a shiver down my spine. The sound of the metal clank against his teeth just before he bites down makes my head roll back.

Switching hands, he repeats the process on the other side. The TV still playing in the background is drowned out by my moans as they get louder and louder. Just when I feel myself getting close, he flips us so I'm against the couch. He stands and shuffles out of his shorts and boxers. The second his cock springs free, my eyes widen, and my mouth salivates. I'd been right. He's got both length and girth. With a perfect curve to it that I know will hit just the right spots. As I lean forward, I look up at him at the exact moment I wrap my lips around the thick mushroom tip.

"Oh fuck," he growls.

The height and angle are perfect as I work him in and out of my mouth. Holding onto my hair, he pushes his cock deeper into my mouth until he reaches the back of my throat, making me gag at first before I swallow him down. Drops of saliva drip from the corners of my mouth and tears roll down my cheeks as I struggle with his length and girth.

"Fuck. Shit. Oh, fuck yes," Robby shouts.

Tears continue streaming down my cheeks as I continue to swallow down every time I gag. My jaw aches, but I ignore it. I'm so fucking turned on right now with how much he's enjoying this.

"I need to fuck you now, Carina," he growls in desperation.

He doesn't even give me a chance to respond as he pulls back, his cock coming out of my mouth with a wet pop, glistening with my saliva.

"You want this as much as I do don't you Carina?" Robby asks, his voice a deep barrelling purr that sends a delicious shiver down my back.

"Yes… god… yes," I declare eagerly.

"Mmm, good girl," he praises, those words make my already overheated skin feel like it's on fire.

Pushing me back, he drops to his knees and lines himself up, rubbing the thick mushroom head against my clit which has my thighs trembling with incandescent desire. Both of us look down as he slowly enters me. The burning ache as my walls stretch around him has me on the prescipice of pleasure and pain. My eyes roll back in my head as my body takes a second to adjust around him. It's tight, as his thick girth makes me feel like I'm full to the brim. Bringing his thumb to my mouth, he pushes it in, and I suck on it before he brings it down to my clit and starts rubbing as he increases the tempo of his thrusts.

"Oh god, yes, oh yes," I cry.

Picking up his pace, he fucks me harder, making my breasts bounce and my back arch. Opening my legs wider, allowing him to get deeper, has my eyes rolling to the back of my head. His fingers pinch my nipple bars, the sting of him pulling them sends a shot of pleasure to my clit. Sweat beads down my back and as his cock edges my G-spot, my orgasm hits like a bolt of lightning. Iridescent stars cloud my vision as euphoric pleasure washes through my entire body. I don't realize I'm screaming until his hand covers my mouth to muffle the sound while he continues to fuck me through my pleasure. Seconds later he finds his own release. He growls a sexy as sin moan, pulling out and coming all over my thighs and pussy lips.

We're both a panting mess, and I genuinely struggle to move. The loud beating sound of my pulse floods my ears. After a few seconds, he rises and walks out, not saying a word. The only sound I can hear is the loud and heavy breathing from both of us. In the distance, I hear the water in the sink running. When he returns, it's with a damp cloth and he hands it to me before finding his boxers and shorts off the floor.

Cleaning myself up, I fix my bra and dress as my body cools from the overheated euphoria I just experienced, and continue trying to calm my breathing.

I don't know why, but once I've finally put myself back together, shyness suddenly sweeps over me and I struggle to look at him.

"Wow. That was great. Do you want some water?" Robby asks, slightly breathlessly.

"Yes, please," I say with a croak.

Why the fuck am I suddenly feeling shy? What the hell is wrong with me?

As he hands me a glass of water, my hands shake slightly, and I awkwardly pass him the washcloth.

"You might wanna throw that straight in the machine," I say as I attempt the lighten the mood.

He chuckles as he takes it from me.

"Damn, I feel empty now," he says, sitting back down on the couch and once again bringing the blanket over us.

"I don't know about you, but I don't think I watched any of this episode. I think we should start it again."

"Yeah, I don't know what happened," he says with a chuckle.

He restarts it and angles himself so his legs are stretched out on the couch, pulling me to lie down beside him, playing with my hair as the episode begins.

It's not long before I notice his fingers have stopped twirling my curls. Gently lifting my head, I look over and see he has fallen asleep. Glancing at the time on my watch, I know I've still got a few hours before I need to pick the kids up, so I know I'm fine. I try to focus back on the show, but my mind is elsewhere.

Damn, I know it's been a long time since I've slept with someone, but that was hot. Even better than I could have expected. To be honest, I wasn't sure we would even have sex.

I can't help but wonder now if this changes what category he puts me in now. Am I still just the curly friend? Or could this eventually turn into something else?

Chapter 11

Robby

It's like now that I've started, I don't want to stop. After that first time sleeping with Carina, I felt drained for the next two days. It completely took it out of me. I don't remember the last time I came that much. It wasn't the case that every time she came over we'd fuck. Sometimes there wasn't really the time. Others I'd be feeling too shit and depressed about everything to even want to attempt anything. But she was good. Even on those occasions without sex, she still helped make me feel better. And today is one of those days.

Knowing she's coming over before she goes to work, I begrudgingly get out of bed, jump in the shower, and just as I finish getting dressed, there's a knock on the door.

"Morning, sleepy." The bright, enthusiastic tone in her voice is the polar opposite of how I'm feeling right now.

"Yeah, I guess it's still morning, technically." I follow her through to the kitchen, as she carries two bags with her.

"Alright. So one of these bags is for physical consumption, the other is more mental."

My face scrunches in confusion. "Huh?"

She unloads one bag. Bananas, protein yogurts in my favorite flavours, oats, eggs, the only brand of tooth floss I like and have run out of, two steaks, and a couple cans of pulses. Instantly my mood picks up when I eye the steaks.

"These look like they'll be good." I pack the food away, leaving out one of the steaks I'll have later.

"Good, I know it's not much, but hopefully will get you eating something good and nutritious."

"Yeah, no, it's all great."

"Now with this bag," she starts, lifting it with a strain and I can see its heavy as she carries it to the armchair. "So remember last week you were telling me about how you want to bring in more money to the gym?"

"Well, yeah. I wanna see if there's any way I can increase revenue without having to hike up the membership prices, which would risk losing loads of members."

"Well, that's what I was going to talk to you about. Or I guess show you. Obviously, this is your area of expertise, and I am in no way business savvy. But the other night I was looking up some other gyms like yours, and really deep dived to see what things they were doing or offering that you aren't, but could."

She pulls out a three-ring binder that's all color coded and neatly filed and organised. I have to smile as she's mentioned several times how much she enjoys making lists and having things just right and easily set up.

"So I can't remember if I ever told you, but I used to experiment with graphics for friends where I used to live, just for something fun to do. It would just be little things like re-designing their logo with a new color scheme, or helping cut and edit videos they would then use on their social media. Again, I am no pro, I just enjoyed doing it in my spare time. Plus, once you get the hang of the software and make some templates, it's actually pretty simple."

"Okay… and what kinda stuff have you worked out I need to do differently?" I ask curiously. I genuinely am intrigued what she's on about or where she's going with this. I've got the feeling that she's a little nervous as she's not giving me her usual eye contact and her hands are fidgeting as she clenches the corners of the binder.

"Well, all you have is a landing page and your gym has next to no social media presence. Did you know you're the only gym offering some of these classes in like a fifty-mile radius? That's insane. But people don't know about it."

She hands me the folder and flicks through pages of printouts where she's done a bunch of original designs.

"So I've printed off just an example batch of graphics that you could use. It's super easy. Plus, if you do it in batches, you can schedule posts so you don't need to be making, creating, and posting things every day."

Flicking through, I'm amazed at how much she's done.

"Then I've put together a couple of samples of how you could improve your website. Plus another thing I think would be a great bonus would be selling merchandise. And if you wanted to go even further, I found a list of small independent suppliers that you could do collaborations with."

Page after page, there are just so many ideas and suggestions, each one detailed with how much time and effort would need to go into it, and with how much money I could make.

"Wow, this is… really cool." Shock washes over me at

just how much effort she's gone to. I don't remember anyone every doing anything like this for me before.

"Again, this is all just me brainstorming and putting together ideas. You might decide you don't like any of this, but I really do feel there is so much potential and you're basically sitting on all this money that you could be making."

"No, it really does look good."

"Oh cool. I'm glad. Anyway, I need to get going but I just thought I'd put this little thing together and you can just have a look through, see if there are any particular bits you'd want to try then you can just go from there."

"Yeah, I promise I will," I say, still reading through the different points she's outlined. I really like the idea of merchandise. That could really look sick. Especially if I got the guy who did the graffiti art in the gym to come up with some designs.

"I hope the rest of your day is good, and the food is okay. Oh, and I also left you a couple of books I think you should give a read. See ya."

"Wait," I shout back, dashing to the door and giving her hair a squeeze which making her laugh, before she hurries to her car and I watch her leave.

It took me two days to go through that folder, then I picked which things I wanted to try first. Carina came over on her next day off and we spent several hours setting all the social media stuff up. I didn't really get it, so I let her run with it. I wasn't completely useless or unhelpful, though. I made sure she always had coffee in hand, and when she took a break,

I'd fuck her and give her an orgasm, which I'm sure helped her get back focused. I must have dozed off at some point because the next thing I knew there was a clattering of something behind me. Pushing myself up from the couch, I find Carina drying and putting away a pot and a pan. Rubbing the sleep out of my eyes, I spot a plate of food.

"Oh, sorry, did I wake you?" she asks.

"No… I… I didn't mean to fall asleep."

She gives me a small smile, then grabs the lap tray I always use and brings over the plate and a glass of water.

"Mmmm, that smells good. What is it?"

"I didn't wanna use up any of the unopened stuff, so I just threw together a little stir fry from some of your leftovers. I've gotta get going to pick the boys up."

Looking at the clock on the stove, I notice the time. Shit, I must have slept for about three hours. Carina just makes me feel so relaxed whenever she's around that I feel I'm in this safe bubble.

"I put your laptop back on charge since I had to keep making sure it wouldn't go into sleep mode, well mainly because you were asleep, and I wanted to carry on working and didn't wanna have to wake you for the password."

I laugh, as it wouldn't have been a problem if she had.

"I've made the changes we'd discussed to your Instagram and Facebook pages. I've done the layout and fonts and tabs for the website, but I still need to do a couple of tweaks, so I've set it to draft so you can look and see how it is so far. Just make sure you don't press the publish button yet, since it's not ready."

"Okay, I'll look at those while I eat. Thanks."

Just as she reaches over to grab her bag, I give her hair a squeeze, and as always, she laughs at the gesture.

"Talk to you later."

"Bye."

I'm not a superstitious person, and I don't know why I keep doing it, but squeezing her hair has become such a habit, a ritual. Like I'm convinced my bad luck follows on the occasions when I've forgotten to do it.

Digging into my food, I'm impressed she managed to put this together with the things I already had here. It's really damn good. I check the two social media pages she'd been experimenting with, and my eyes widen with how good they look. How did she manage to do that in such a short time? I then click on the tab for the website. How the fuck? This looks sick. It's exactly as I described it but I can hardly believe this. She did all of this, cooked, and cleared up all while I slept. The woman is damn insane.

My best mate William, who I hate to admit I haven't made the effort to see enough, joined the class I did today and ended up coming over after.

"So you gonna watch the fight this weekend?" William asks.

"Of course. When have you known me to miss a card?"

"Yeah. I just sometimes hate having to stay up for it," he moans.

"See, that's where my problem with sleep works in my favor. Most nights I'm still up at 4 am." It's annoying but true.

"Yeah, I get it. Oh, by the way, I saw the new page you did for the gym on socials. It looks sick. Did you hire someone or something?"

Pride fills my chest as I see how genuinely impressed he is.

"Hire someone?" I scoff. "Dude, I'm broke enough as is. Nah, a friend did it for me."

"Well, you're lucky you got it for free. I know some people end up spending a fortune getting all that stuff done."

I give him a nod as I grab us both a drink.

"Yo, I'm hungry. You got anything to eat?" he asks the second I sit my ass down.

"I'm not getting up again. You can look for your damn self," I say, rolling my eyes.

"Nice. Looks like you're getting it together. You've got a couple of meals prepped: steak, chicken, some good veggies. Looks good. So what can I have?"

I swear if it wasn't the case that we've been friends since middle school, I'd have thrown him out already.

"Just heat up one of the containers."

That keeps him quiet and he finally just chills and eats.

"Did you make this or is this one of those prep delivery services? 'Cause this tastes good. Send me the number. I need to get hooked up with this."

I go to answer, but quickly shut my mouth. I don't know why, it's not a big deal that Carina made them. She always says that I need to eat, always asks if there's anything she can do. And she always helps and looks after me however and in which ever way I need it. So why is it I don't wanna tell him it's all her? Hell, why haven't I even told him about her?

Chapter 12

Carina

My birthday has always held such mixed emotions for me. When I was little, I remember I was always more worried and concerned that my friends were having a good time at my party, that I ended up never enjoying it myself. I'd spend days meticulously planning and prepping how I'd hope and wish for the day to go, and was always disappointed. Then, as I got older, it just became another day. People close to me would forget it, or not make a fuss, which would simply put me in the mindset that it wasn't a day worth celebrating. So obviously by the time I then had kids, it was never anything I made a fuss about. There was no point. I wasn't going to go out or have a party or anything like that. But I appreciated my mom taking the boys for the weekend.

Where my actual birthday was on the Monday, I thought it would be nice having the weekend off, not working, not needing to do any chores, not fuss or worry about the kids. Then come Monday, take them to school, chill for the day, then maybe treat us all to some takeout.

I'd told Robby my birthday was coming up and that the boys were going to be away. I can't remember if it was his suggestion or mine, but we'd somehow shake things up a bit and have him stay over at my house Friday and Saturday night. I hadn't really thought much of it until after I dropped the kids to school this morning, kissed them goodbye, and told them I couldn't wait to see them on Sunday. But when I got back home and cleared up the mess they'd made at breakfast, it suddenly dawned on me Robby was going to be the first man I've ever have over. Besides my dad, or my mom's husband, or the odd repair man, I've never had another man round. Not since moving here. I know it's silly, and considering how often I've been over to Robby's, it shouldn't be a big deal, but he'd be seeing another side of me. Another part of my world that he hasn't before.

Suddenly, I look at my house through the eyes of someone who doesn't have kids, and what is clean and organized to me probably still looks chaotic to them. So for the next few hours, I clear away every piece of Lego and the millions of pieces of paper that have one small drawing on it that somehow required a fresh piece of paper. Even though I knew he wasn't going to be going into either of the boys' rooms, I still cleared and tidied away all the trash there too. The house is now cleared and spotless from top to bottom. And there's a part of me that loves the fact that I know it's going to stay that way, at least until they return on Sunday.

When the door finally rings, I take a couple of deep breaths before welcoming him in.

"This feels very different," he says with a smirk, making his way through the door and into the living room.

We decide to watch Pulp Fiction, and I have to laugh when he gets through half of all the snacks before the end credits roll.

"What's so funny, missy?"

"You."

"Me? You're laughing at me?" he asks before shifting from his seat next to me on my large U-shaped couch and cages me in with his arms on either side of my head.

The air around us shifts, and I feel myself melting into the intoxicating sexual tension.

Pressing his hips down against mine makes my dress rise up and I can feel the trailing hot blaze of his eyes as they follow the path of my dress as it rises up my thighs, when suddenly those piercing eyes shoot up to mine.

"You've been a very naughty girl, haven't you? Being sat next to me this whole time with no underwear on?"

My pulse spikes as his hands grip my thighs, pushing them wider.

"Were you just going to sit back there like a little tease the entire night? Just waiting to see if I noticed?"

Just like I was over a month ago when we first slept together, my body goes into sensory overload. No amount of self-pleasure can match the feeling of someone else turning you on. My skin heats, my nipples harden as they strain against the lace fabric of my bra, and my pussy drips with arousal as his hands rub and massage between my thighs.

"Look at you, you're glistening. So eager and desperate for me to fuck you, aren't you?" The deep timbre of his voice vibrates through me and makes my toes curl.

"Yes… god, yes… please," I plead breathlessly.

Reaching behind his head, he pulls his shirt off before

bending and slowly sweeping his tongue across my lips, spreading them apart teasingly, and lightly plays with my clit. The pressure of his tongue is so soft it's almost infuriating. My arms and legs writhe against the fluffy pillows around me and I buck my hips, eagerly chasing more. I'm so turned on that when he slips two fingers in, they meet no resistance. Before I even get the chance to luxuriate in more of the pleasure of his mouth on me, he sits back on his knees, pulls me up, and pushes his sweats and boxers down.

"Get on your knees and make it nice and wet. I want my cock dripping."

His orders only spur me on further, and I do as he commands.

There is no finesse, nothing elegant as I work him in and out of my mouth, all the way to the back of my throat. The sound of his moans and groans echo across the room as he holds on to my hair, bucking up into my mouth until finally he lets go of my hair, hooks his hands under my arms, and lifts me back onto the couch. Bending me over so my ass is in the air, I'm face down between the couch cushions.

He lines himself up at my entrance, my heart hammering off the scale with anticipation, before he buries himself deep inside me in one thrust. This angle gets him deeper than any other, and the pillows muffle my screams as I bury my face further in them. His pace is relentless, pushing me higher, filling my body with pleasure. My whimpers, his loud panting, and the slapping of skin as he works his way in and out of me, the only sounds.

I'm so lost in the moment that I don't notice his movement until his wet finger slowly rubs, then breeches my tight hole.

"Oh fuck. Yes… please… more," I cry out.

The tight ring of muscle squeezes against his finger as I'm filled to the brim and my whole body trembles with the added sensation. As I stretch around him, he pinches my clit with his other hand, setting off my release as my body explodes into a million pieces. Spasms of pure, unadulterated pleasure ricochet through every cell in my body, tampering with my sanity. My arms and legs twitch in the aftershocks, and I feel him swell against my inner walls. His thighs are trembling against mine before he lets out a growl-like moan, claiming his own release.

My brain struggles to focus as my body tingles with aftershock pleasure and my damp thighs quiver while Robby disentangles himself from me. I'm barely able to find the strength to sit up as I once again notice how quiet he is after sex. Not uncomfortable, his energy feels more relaxed, actually. He pulls his boxers and sweats back on before asking where the bathroom is. Words fail me as I recover from the onslaught of the raw physical pleasure I've just experienced, so I only manage to point in the direction of the door.

While he's in the downstairs one, I head upstairs to clean myself up, getting back before he does.

"Your house is really relaxing. I don't know what it is, but it just feels super chilled here," he says, while we climb into bed.

"I'm glad. This weekend is meant to be just super chilled, so it would be pretty shit if you didn't feel at ease here," I tease.

He laughs with a huff before reaching down, grabbing my

hand, and placing it on the back of his head. I roll my eyes with a smile as I know that's my cue to stroke his head, which I do. Within five minutes, he drifts off to sleep. I, however, find it much harder. It's been so long since I've shared a bed with someone, not even my kids when they're sick do. They're too old. So it feels really odd having another person here. After almost an hour of tossing and turning, I finally fall asleep, though I find myself waking every time he moves.

During the night, our bodies entangle, and with no words spoken and without the same primal intensity there was earlier, he works his way inside me. It's softer, gentler, with only our combined breaths disturbing the silence of the night.

"Is that bacon I smell?" he asks walking into the kitchen, hair still disheveled from sleep and his nostrils flare reminding me of a sniffer dog following it's favourite scent.

Warmth fills me with how content I feel seeing how at ease he is here in my home.

"Yup," I answer, rolling my lips between my teeth to hide my smile at seeing him.

"Morning, by the way. I wondered where you'd gotten to when I woke since the bed was empty."

His t-shirt rises as he lifts his arms above his head while stretching, and I have to shake my head because all I can focus on is the deep v of muscle and the intricate tattoos along his waistband.

"I woke early and didn't want to disturb you. So, I came down, read a book, and had a coffee."

"Is there any more? Coffee, I mean?"

"Sure, help yourself. Pancakes are ready and I'm just waiting for the bacon to crisp up a little more. I wasn't sure, do you want eggs?"

"Mmmm, normally I'd say yeah, but bacon and pancakes sound good for now."

He makes himself a coffee as I finish cooking breakfast and we eat on the couch.

As the day goes on, a solemnness surrounds him, a sorrow in his eyes that I can't decipher. Even as I attempt to keep things light and jovial, his struggle to even break out the smallest of smiles is obvious.

"Are you okay?" I ask gently.

Rolling his head, he takes a deep intake of breath. An array of emotions flickers across his face and something in my gut tells me he's really struggling right now. I hate seeing him like this. My chest aches and I'm desperate to take away his pain.

"I… I…" His voice cracks with emotions, and I fight the urge to shuffle over and console him. I don't want to overcrowd or overwhelm him and make things worse.

"Tomorrow, it'll be two years to the day since my brothers died." He says the words in a rush, like he's desperate to get them out.

"Jesus, I'm so sorry." I cringe slightly as the words just feel so unhelpful.

"I… The three of us were in the car. My eldest brother, Michael, was driving. Joseph was passenger, and I was in the back. We'd driven up to go and watch a Muay Thai fight. They both loved watching, not just the big pro fights, but also the lower divisions and belts."

My heart pounds as he obviously struggles to get through this memory, his face pinched like he's in pain.

"I'd had a couple of beers as I'd competed the previous week and didn't have to cut or train. Neither of them were ever really big drinkers, so was always easy for me if I wanted to relax and enjoy myself as they would always be the designated drivers."

He swallows before taking a deep, steadying breath before continuing, "The last thing I remember was stretching out in the back seat, falling asleep to the sounds of my brothers debating whether it would be a good idea to start holding charity fights at the gym. Next thing I knew, I was awoken to the loudest sound I've ever heard, then being flipped and feeling airborne and everything just being a blur. Still, to this day, I don't know how many times the car rolled until we slammed into the central reservation. Michael and Joseph died on impact. Because I'd been lying down, I got away with only a couple of lacerations. Apparently, the paramedics and fire service couldn't believe I managed to not only survive but walk into the ambulance. Later at the hospital, I found out a fourteen-wheeler had lost control, and they guess Michael tried to break and steer around it but clipped the back corner of the trailer. And because of the speed, it flipped us."

Tears stream down his face, and I have to blink back my own at hearing the horrific story. Slowly, so he's aware of what I'm doing, I shuffle closer and wrap my arms around him, rocking him gently as he breaks down, releasing the heartbreak as he mourns the loss of his brothers. After a couple of minutes, he gets control of his breathing and sits himself back upright. I give him his space, as I don't want to stifle him.

"So yeah, that was that. Two weeks after the funeral, I went back to Thailand to just escape, forget about everything. I stayed out there for like three months when I got a call that Mom had had a stroke and was in a care facility and jumped on the first flight back. I'd hoped she would get better, and it looked like she was, but after a couple of months, she had another stroke. This one was much worse. It was actually around that time you first DM'd me in that group. Then, exactly six weeks to the day of her second stroke, she passed. I couldn't take it. I needed to leave. Needed to get away. So I did. Back to the only place that really felt like home."

I quickly wipe away the tears from my cheeks, I don't want him to see them. My heart is absolutely breaking for him. He already experienced the unimaginable loss of his brothers, but then losing his mother? No wonder he's so lost and broken. He's experienced more heartbreak and loss than most do in their lifetime. And this all happened in one year.

"Robby, you have been through so much. You have endured and survived things most people couldn't even fathom. I know this will probably sound stupid, but my god, are you strong. Stronger than you know and tougher than you give yourself credit for. The resilience you've shown by simply pushing and getting through each and every single day is probably the rarest thing I've ever seen. Like a diamond."

He looks up at me with sad, quizzical eyes.

"I mean it, you're like a diamond. Haven't been

destroyed from the pressure life has put you under. You're one of a kind."

His eyes soften and I watch the corner of his mouth lift in a slight smile before shaking his head and sighing.

"I'm less like a diamond, more like a demon," he says with a dry laugh before continuing. "My friends all say I'm heartless, so I think demon is better fitting."

"Well, first, I think you're wrong. But how about you being the Diamond Demon? That can be your nickname. And regarding being heartless, that's a really shitty and mean thing for them to say. I don't think you're heartless at all, and as you've said before, I'm always right."

"Yes, I know, but to be fair, they've known me a long time." The laugh that follows sounds hollow and empty.

"Well, the version of you they know is probably different from the one that I've experienced."

"Yeah, that's true. But that's because you're light and sweet and just make things better. You're not sad and miserable like me. Or feeling pretty pathetic, like I am now for opening up and being a vulnerable ass."

Resting my hand on his knee, I give it a squeeze. "Would it help if I shared something about me? Something that shows that I'm not as light and able to make things better as you believe?"

"Please. Yes, please." The sincerity in his eyes is what I'm holding on to as I know what I'm about to share won't be easy.

"I haven't had a loss the way you have. I can't imagine the pain you've experienced. But I have gone through traumas, though. Ones that for many years I'd been made to believe were my fault." I can already feel my throat tighten as fear, shame, and embarrassment slither through me.

I can't look at him as I speak these words, so I stare blankly ahead. "When I was a child, I had a best friend who I was closer to than my family. She meant the world to me. There were some periods when I would stay at her house more than my own. It was her ninth birthday party, and she was having a sleepover." I take a deep breath so I can say this as quickly as possible.

"That night was the first time her father molested me."

Out of the corner of my eyes, I can see him lean forward, the veins on his hand protruding from how tightly he grips his knees.

Mentally detaching myself, I explain the rest. "He continued to do it for a year. The only reason he stopped was because I started my period a couple of months after my tenth birthday. He would tell me that he picked me because of how I looked. So that set off a deep correlation within me that I still get triggered by to this day. Years later, when I met my now ex-husband, who I opened up and told this to, he had several of his friends over for drinks. I wanted to go to bed, but he had other ideas." Swallowing down the bile that fills my mouth, I take several deep breaths through my nose to try and calm my rapid breathing before I continue. "Long story short, he pinned me down to the bed and got his friends to have sex with me." My hands shake as I wipe my sweaty palms on my legs, but inside I feel ice cold.

"You mean to rape you?" His tone is so sharp, so filled with anger it makes me flinch, but I can tell his reaction is not aimed at me.

"Yeah. That was the start of his physical and mental abuse. His favorite line used to be that it's not rape if you're married. Or it's not theft if you're married. He loved using the line 'It's not abuse, it's just a traditional marriage.' Or how he used to try to hide his cheating even though it was so obvious but when I'd confront him about it he'd get in my head and somehow convince me it was my fault. That I was lacking, how my body wasn't what it used to be after the kids, and how it's not his fault if women throw themselves at him. So yeah. That's me. I'm definitely not always cheery or positive, nor do I always have the belief that I can make things better. But I push. I push to get through each and every single day, as I have no other choice."

A weight feels like it's been lifted from my shoulders. And even though I hate going back and thinking about any of that, I weirdly feel better about opening up and sharing this with him.

Looking up, I find Robby looking at me, observing, absorbing. For several seconds, neither of us speaks.

"I just don't know how you do it," he says eventually, his voice softer now. "Just getting on with everything. All I want to do is run away. Go back to my favorite island. My favorite time out there was about four years ago. Training, eating clean, lots of meditation. It just really re-centred me. I wish I could have that back."

Though I'd initially felt relief at sharing something that's so difficult for me to talk about, there's another part of me that feels pissed off that he's not really acknowledged any of the stuff I've just told him. Is it that he just doesn't know what to say? I thought in some way, me opening up would be a way of letting him know that he doesn't need to feel so alone in his sadness. He isn't the only one baring the scars of trauma. Yet with his lack of reaction, and the way he's brought it back round to himself I'm now wondering was it wrong of me to have shared my past. My trauma.

My pain. Does he think I'm somehow trying to one up him? As that couldn't be any further from what I was trying to do. Guilt seeps through my pores and I make the conscious effort to focus back on him and make sure he doesn't think I'm trying to dimmish or out-do what he's gone through and how to cope.

"Well, have you thought about doing that? Maybe going for like a set time, I dunno, six weeks, eight weeks, twelve weeks? You could go there and do a proper reset, then come back stronger than ever."

He thinks about it for a moment, different expressions passing over his face. "I'd love to, but I doubt it. I'll probably go there for a vacation at some point. But I think it would be better for me to fix myself here. Get the gym to its peak. Really turn it into the legacy that my brothers deserve for it to be. Then maybe in like ten years, once all of that's solid and running well and I've done the things I need to in my life, then I'll move out there for good. I'd love to buy a patch of land. Build a house. Maybe set up a gym or some kind of business out there. That's the plan."

I am so overwhelmed with mixed emotions, both from the things he's shared and opening up about my past.

Today really hasn't gone or felt like how I expected it to. But I wouldn't change a thing. Because despite the vulnerability I felt opening up, deep down I know it's something that will help me get stronger. Only cementing that I'm not a victim, I'm a survivor.

"So, what about you? What are your long-term plans?" he asks.

Letting out a sigh, not really sure how to answer as I've not really let myself go there.

"I don't have a proper plan, really. Not like you. Which

I guess is kinda funny considering I love lists and plans. I guess for the next couple of years, just keep doing what I'm doing. Maybe find a way I can work for myself, or work from home, set something of my own up. Keep doing that until my youngest is eighteen and will hopefully go off to college. Which is in like eight years. And then? Then… well, I guess the world is my oyster."

"Sounds good. Sounds plausible. Plus, it's funny. We'll both be looking or starting new adventures about the same time."

I can't help but wonder if we will still be in each other's lives in these futures we are talking about. Will this build into something? Will things fizzle out? Or will we just be blips in each other's lives that we will have forgotten about in years to come?

"Yeah, I guess you're right. Now, as you're the designated Diamond Demon, please tell me you have some sort of superpowers to control time and fast forward the next couple of years?" I ask hopefully.

"Ah, I'm afraid not. But I guess I should make the most of showing you my superpowers before the weekend is up."

Chapter 13

Carina

From that moment, the weekend took on a new vibe. A new air. Something shifted between us. I woke in the night to find his mouth working one nipple, then the other. There was something different when we had sex. It was raw, not through power and intensity, but from the silence. No words were spoken, yet it felt as if so much was being said. I could feel a shift in the feelings I had for this man. A profound respect and appreciation, that despite all odds, he was showing me the most intimate and vulnerable sides to him.

On Sunday morning, knowing it was the anniversary, I wanted to go at his pace. Do whatever he felt like doing. If that was nothing, then so be it. If he just wanted to get high and forget the world, I could understand that. So I was a little surprised when he suggested we go for a walk.

We drove my car down long and winding roads, finally stopping at the beginning of a trail that led toward this vast canyon. Despite the coverage of clouds the air still feels warm around us as we set off on our walk.

I've never come here before. I've always wanted to, but I guess a part of me has always just been too scared. But I don't mind it with his company. We walk for about half an hour, when eventually the clouds disperse as the sun begins beating down on both of us, and where he's stayed pretty quiet the whole time, the only real sounds have been the loud panting from both of us along with the chirps and songs of the birds around us. When we reach the outlook point, he sits in the tall grass, takes his sunglasses out of his pocket, and puts them on. I take a seat beside him but make sure there's space between us so he doesn't feel crowded.

"My brothers and I used to come here when we were kids. Of the three of us, I struggled the most with growing up without my dad. I guess maybe it was because I was the youngest and in my head, they got to have time with him that I never did. I was angry he left. Angry that he could just walk out the door and never look back. So from when I was around thirteen, I think, we used to cycle up here, and Michael would tell me to just scream. Scream at the top of my lungs. At first, I couldn't do it. I thought it was stupid. He would egg me on, prodding and poking until I'd finally snap. And I could just shout out, shout all the things that were bothering me until my throat felt sore. We did that for a while, then they got me into Muay Thai. Even though there were only four years between us, they were a hell of a lot more mature than me. Always."

I'm engrossed as I learn about these two men I'm sure are looking down on their brother, wishing he wasn't suffering the way he is.

"They sound amazing. Sounds like precious gems run in the family."

He gives me a soft smile before looking back out into the distance.

"I don't really know why I thought of coming here today. I haven't been here for years."

The sun casts off the stray tears that roll down his face and he attempts to wipe them from behind his sunglasses. We sit in silence for several minutes. "Is it alright if we go?" he asks, breaking the silence.

"Yeah, of course."

He helps me up and we make our way back down to the car. He's pretty much silent the rest of the hike and the entire drive back.

When we pull up at my house, I'm not surprised he says he's going to head home. "Thank you for coming and keeping me company this weekend."

"Not a problem. I'm sure the kids will be excited to see you when they get back. What are you up to tomorrow?"

"Nothing planned. Not working. So I'll probably just chill here and have a boring adult birthday," I say with a light laugh.

"Why don't you come over after you've done the school run?"

"Okay, sure, I'd like that."

I walk him to his car and before he gets in, he gives me a hug and the compulsory hair squeeze before driving off.

I end up going to bed at the same time as the boys, feeling emotionally exhausted. But my dreams that night were filled with the heartfelt cries of a boy, then those of a man. Both sound lost, hurt, and not understanding why they have been left behind.

I think Zion and Kai's birthday gift to me this morning was that they got up, got dressed, and were ready for school with no issues. It really must be a birthday miracle. When I dropped them each off, neither one slammed their doors. I even got "love you" and "happy birthday." It really must be my lucky day. Once I'm back home, I remember I need to email Kai's paediatrician for an update on his referral. I end up getting lost doing some online shopping and am startled when my phone beeps with a message.

Hey, I'm up, so come over whenever you're free.

Sometimes I envy his ability to sleep in. Though let's be real, it's not as if I actually do it on the occasions when I can.

Alright. I'll head over in about 15 minutes.

I finish off the work I was doing on my laptop, that's luckily been keeping me distracted all morning, then make my way over to Robby's.

The second he opens the door, I can tell something's off. His shoulders are slumped and he's pulled his hood up despite it being 74 degrees outside.

Following him in, I leave my bag on the side like I always do and head into the kitchen.

"You want a coffee?"

"Yeah, sure. You sleep okay?" I ask, wondering if maybe he just had another bad night.

"Shit, as usual. Fell asleep on the couch watching some trash on the TV, then woke up at like two or three or something with this shooting pain in my back then went to bed."

"That's not good. Is your back still hurting now?"

"A bit, but it's more like a dull pain now."

Leaning against the island, I look around and note how his clothes are just chucked around the place, which is really not like him. He's one of the few men I've met who cleans up after himself. So seeing everything in this kind of disarray, used cups and cutlery just left in the sink and his training gear just hanging out of his bag in the corner, is really not good.

A sad smile spreads across my face when I note the elephant print loose trousers he's wearing and remember when he told me he'd bought a bunch of them during one of his stays in Thailand, noting that he found them so comfortable. It's like where he can't run away from the grief and the pain right now, he's putting himself in a protective cocoon.

We take our usual places, music playing in the background, but then he puts some show on the TV. I don't mind at first. I know my birthday isn't a big thing, and it's not like he doesn't know that. We even mentioned it yesterday. But as the hours pass and he ends up dozing in and out of sleep, I start to think he may have forgotten.

It's probably the least we've ever conversed, and even though I know his somber, subdued mood is because of the significance of yesterday's date, there is another part of me that feels a little sad that he's not even mentioned my birthday. I feel guilty for even feeling sad. It's not his fault that yesterday bears such a heavy toll on his mind and heart.

I think it's more that I miss his company. Until now, I honestly hadn't realized just how lonely I feel. I have my kids, and I'm lucky that I still have my parents. I don't take that for granted. But I don't have any friends. Not really.

The closest thing to that are my patients and colleague, Susan. Outside work, the only messages or phone calls I get are regarding the boys. I remember once I had two days off and I could count the exact number of words I said in that time.

When I was younger, I used to be such a social butterfly. But not anymore. Now I'm pretty much the polar opposite. It's not like I'm craving to be around an abundance of people, but I do feel like there is an enormous difference between choosing to be alone, happy in your own company, and not having anyone. I'm not saying you shouldn't be alone, but it should be your choice. And when it isn't, it feels like you're stuck. Like you're trapped down a well, screaming at the top of your lungs, but all you hear is the echo of your own voice.

So having gone from feeling like that every single day to then having someone message you multiple times a day, asking how you're doing, what you're up to, and if you want to spend time together, it's like suddenly you're not alone. Like you've been thrown this rope and there's someone on the other end to help you out.

That's what it has felt like since Robby came into my life. Yet, as I sit here on my birthday, with him asleep next to me, not even a mention, a *'HBD'* text, or even a high five, I can't help but feel lonelier than ever.

Cold seeps through my bones, and I shiver as I blink back the tears. My shivering must disturb him as he awakes.

"Oh… I guess I missed that episode." His voice has a husky tone to it from sleep. "Do you want another drink?"

Looking at the time, I see that the alarm I've got set on my phone will go off in a couple of minutes.

"No. I'm gonna have to go anyway to do the school pick up." The melancholy is clear in my voice.

"Okay. Sorry, I slept so much. I guess I was more tired than I realized."

It takes everything within me to paste an understanding smile on my face. "It's probably best that you don't fall back asleep now, or you'll be up all night again."

"I know. I won't. I need to clear this place up. So that'll keep me busy."

"Good. Okay. Well, I hope you have a nice evening." I swallow down the ball of emotion in my throat, not only from what he's just said, but also the fact that he hasn't even looked at me or noticed the clear discomfort I don't even have the energy to hide.

"Yeah, you too."

As I sit and wait for Kai to come out, I decide to send Robby a message. Maybe if I make light of the fact he forgot, it'll be an easy way to broach it.

I just realized I didn't even get my customary hair squeeze on my birthday! Ouch that's harsh hahahah 😅

OMG!

I'M SORRY

FOR FUCK'S SAKE

It's fine. My curls were looking a little flat today, so it's understandable 😉 I'll make sure to console them this evening heheh 😆

There's just so much on my mind because of yesterday. Then this morning I got the reminder on my calendar that it would have been Mom's birthday at the end of the week too. Sorry I didn't say happy birthday. I feel stupid.

I just wanted to make a joke of it. I wasn't trying to make a big deal out of it. This would have just been an easy way for him to realize he messed up and maybe make up for it next time I see him. Instead, it feels like he's once again jumped to the negative and my gut reaction is to do damage control.

Oh, please don't apologise. And don't you dare feel stupid. I was just joking. I thought it might make you laugh. Yesterday I was so worried about you and even though I didn't know if I could help, didn't know what you needed, all I want to do is help. To try and cheer you up or distract you or whatever it may be you needed. You said your mom's birthday is on the weekend, right? I had an idea I was going to bring up to you about something you might wanna do but didn't wanna say anything, as it's not my place.

I'm just so fucking annoyed with myself. This is just fucking typical. I hate feeling like this. I'm so sorry.

Never apologise for feeling emotional or distracted or feeling any particular way. I'll always make sure I do anything I can to help. Whether that's sitting in silence, being weird and silly, making sure you eat, or whatever else may be. I didn't want to make you feel worse. Especially with what you're currently going through.

No, I'm annoyed because the other day I thought I'm gonna get you some flowers or a gift or something. But like the idiot I am, I forgot.

Don't be. See it as a blessing because if you'd have gotten me flowers, I'd have probably burst into tears as I've never been given flowers before. And trust me, the last thing you'd want to see is me a crying mess 😭

And besides, you were stuck with me all weekend, which is a challenge in itself.

It's never a challenge. And you already do enough. Way more than anyone else does or has.

🙂

I try to distract myself for the rest of the afternoon and do everything I can to not let the boys see or tell that all I want to do is roll into a ball and cry. I plaster a smile on my face and order us takeout. I keep it all in as I tell them goodnight and prep for bed. However, once I get into bed, pulling to duvet up over my head, I finally let those tears fall. What is wrong with me? I feel sad that I've been overlooked, forgotten in a way, but then at the same time, I feel like a shitty person for even thinking that. Am I just being selfish? Have I just expected too much while not being considerate of everything Robby is going through? I feel so torn. All I want right now is a hug. Just a simple hug. As tears soak my pillow, I wrap my arms around myself, knowing that it's all I'm going to get.

Chapter 14

Robby

Finally, it feels like things are beginning to look up. After getting through the anniversary and Mom's birthday, for the first time, I felt like I could breathe. Well, it lasted for about two weeks, then my car kept acting up which was really annoying since I've gotten back to working at the gym every day. Don't know what the hell is wrong with it. Sometimes it takes about ten attempts to get the ignition to start. Once I've got it running, it's fine. But then there were the days it just wouldn't start at all. I'd called Carina pretty much to vent my frustration since she's the only person who knows and understands. She was sweet and said she can add me to her insurance. That if my car doesn't start, and she's not using hers, then I could borrow it. I pointed out that I couldn't do that to her as she's got two kids and needs it for her job. But she shut that down, saying she wasn't giving me her car, just that I could use it if I really needed. And she and her colleague often carpool, but she usually drives just because she's already on route when doing the school drop off, but says if I need it and she'd then have work that she could just ride with her colleague. Plus, she'd been planning on walking more with the kids anyway.

I've finally started putting some muscle back on and can feel my reactions and connections slowly creep back up to where they used to be. It's like my mind has reconnected with my body and is telling me that something might be shit, that I might just wanna give up, but I can do it and get through it. As if I've found this inner strength. This self-belief that I'd lost has come back.

I've even joined a couple of the guys for a drink after training a couple of times. Plus, business has really picked up. I've started seeing a real uptake in money coming in. We've had loads of people join who lived not too far away but never even knew our gym existed until they saw the ads on social media. It's insane. It's gotten to the point that we have a waitlist for some of our classes.

I asked Carina if she could make a couple more batches of posts. I think she's really gotten into doing them and I've told her it would be a great business for her to do on the side since she's clearly got the talent for it. She also sent me the links for mockup designs on some of the merchandise stuff and I felt like a kid in a candy store, desperately wanting them all. I hadn't known that she'd already contacted one manufacturer and had gotten them to put a sample together so I could see if I like the t-shirt material and the colors of the ink. I don't know why I'd just presumed she'd have gotten the gym's logo on it, but no, she'd done better. I burst out laughing when she'd come by with the shirts, and I'd unrolled it to see a diamond with demon horns sitting on top like a crown with the words DIAMOND DEMON printed underneath. I've pretty much worn the t-shirts nonstop since I've gotten them. Koa joked after class that it should be what I go by now. Though I think he thinks it's like a brand or something. He has no idea it's custom-made for me. But maybe he's on the right track. I've been thinking about maybe putting on a couple of amateur fights. And being called out as the Diamond Demon has a great ring to it.

"Yo, Robby, we're gonna go grab a beer and some wings while we watch the game. Do you wanna join us?" one of my buddies, who's also gotten back into training, shouts across the studio.

I'm tired and would love to just chill on the couch and maybe even have some bud, but a nice cold beer and spicy wings sound pretty good to me right now. "Yeah, sure. Why not? I'll meet you guys there. I gotta lock up first."

Once I'm showered and lock up the gym, I grab my bag and head to the car. Just as I'm putting it in the cradle, I see a message from Carina.

> Spoke to the insurance and they said I can easily add you on, so you're covered to use my car when needed. It'll be an extra $45 a month, will need the details from your license, and they have a couple of questions that need like tick box answers.

Nice. That'll at least feel like I've got a good backup just in case. Grabbing my license, I take a picture of it and send it to her. It's funny, I've never shared a car with someone before. This is a first for me, though I guess it's not really a big deal.

Sweet. Thanks. There's my license. Just let me know when you're doing the questions, and I'll answer them.

Today, it only takes four tries before the ignition starts and I drive over to the bar to meet the guys.

"Nah, I'm telling you, man, Valdev still has a good couple of fights left in him. I don't know why so many people underestimate him. That hook kick he did when he fought Simmons was damn near lethal. Or when he put Keefi out cold in thirty seconds," I say, exasperated once again.

"Dude, no one is going to top Maldeife. So you guys just need to put your big girl pants on and accept that fact," William declares.

"We've got four portions of wings, nachos, fries, and one portion of tenders. Is there anything else I can get you, gentlemen?" the waitress asks.

"No, we're good," the four of us say collectively.

Once she walks off, I'm not surprised when Eric pipes up. "She can get me in her bed if she wants. Have you seen the ass on her?"

Everyone laughs before looking over, not so subtly, mind you, to check out the ass in question.

"She's cute, but I like my women with a bit more meat on them," William says with a grin.

"For me, she's gotta be petite. Little pocket rocket that I can just pick up and toss around," Justin counters.

"If you're just tossing her around, I think you're doing it all wrong. Besides, I swear your girlfriend is the same height as you," Eric teases.

"Shut up, Eric. What about you, Robby? If you've got your pick, what are you going with?" Justin asks.

I finish chewing before wiping my mouth and taking a sip of beer. "I'm not too picky. Tall, short, big, small, it doesn't matter to me."

I squeeze my eyes shut as I picture Carina. Thinking about her and her body has my dick twitching, and this really isn't the place for that.

Eric and Justin laugh.

"Well, considering it's been ages since you've properly been out with us, hell, it feels like we've finally got you back and I think it's time we find you someone. That should keep a smile even on your face," Eric ribs.

Shaking my head, I roll my eyes at his stupid idea. "I'm good, dude. Maybe we should get you to focus on your grappling. That way, it'll be easier for you to pick up a woman," I joke.

Everyone laughs, but I'm a little surprised when William's eyes narrow slightly at my dismissal. Before I can work out what his problem is, my phone vibrates in my pocket.

> Ha, that's funny. Your initials are the first three letters of your name. Robert Oliver Black. I don't know why, but I imagined you having a different middle name.

> Oh yeah? What did you think it was?

"Robby, you're up," William shouts as he sets the balls up on the nearby pool table.

I dunno, but if we're sticking with demon themes, maybe something like Forneus or Aamon or even Loki 🤪

That makes me laugh.

HAHA. Now they are a hell of a lot more impressive than what I've got. What about you? What's your middle name?

"What's so funny?" William asks.

"Oh, nothing. Is it my shot?" I ask.

"Mmmm, sure."

I'm replying to some emails when I'm interrupted by a knock on the office door.

"I just got a message from David that he's running late. If you want, I can cover his class. Well, at least until he gets here?" Koa says, leaning against the doorframe.

"Yeah, sure. Would you just prefer to tell him to leave it today and you do the entire class? It'll probably be easier doing that."

"Yeah, no problem. Oh, and I forgot to mention, some guy came in earlier. Said he works for a charity that helps kids and teens that come from troubled homes and was hoping to speak with you about working together on something. I told him you wouldn't be in till later, but he left me his card. I put it in the locked drawer by the reception."

"Okay cool. I'll come grab that in a bit and call him."

I've been really keen to do something meaningful with the gym. Something like this could be the perfect opportunity to utilise the space and facilities in a way that makes an impact. Like I've truly done and achieved something.

He shuts the door behind him, and as I tuck into the sandwich I picked up earlier, I realize I haven't heard from Carina today.

How's your day going?

After about ten minutes, I get a response.

Fine. Just another Wednesday.

Huh. That's not really like her. She's usually cheerier. Unease pools in my stomach and I instantly lose my appetite.

Everything alright? I'm getting the impression something's up.

Just not having a great day. Haven't been sleeping well. Had to get my mom to come down and watch the kids as work messed up and needed me to help set up a new patient, which ended up running over as she has a lot of meds and we're still working on the adjustments she needed with the new aids in her apartment. And Kai forgot his lunch this morning, and the school called, but I couldn't answer, and he then went into a meltdown. So it's just been a bit shit.

Are you at work now?

No, I've just had to stop at the store to grab some stuff for dinner later.

Instead of messaging back, I call her instead.

"Hello." Her voice sounds just as down and subdued as her messages.

"Hey. Sorry to hear you're not having a great day. Do you know what I think will help?"

"What's that?"

"I think you should do a gratitude list. I used to do it back in Thailand, especially on days I was struggling. Some people do them every single day. First thing, after they wake up, they write the things they're grateful for. You can do like fifteen, twenty, twenty-five. There's no set number. But it's a good practice. It helps shift your mind. So instead of focusing on the negative stuff that's burdening you, you look and think about the things you might not even realize you're taking for granted."

"Ummm… really? I don't know if I can think up fifteen things," she says apprehensively.

"Sure you can. It doesn't always need to be big, elaborate things. It can be simple stuff like, I'm grateful for my body—as I'm able to get up and work and look after my kids and work out and whatever. Or I'm grateful that my kids are healthy. I'm grateful that I've got a car that works and turns on from the first go. Or say how you're grateful that you've got your parents, or how your mom is close enough that if you're stuck, she's able to help you out. Grateful that you have your eyesight. Grateful that you have money to buy groceries, or that you're able to cook and that you're able to help people like me out when we're going through hard times. Grateful that you've even been born. What is that statistic of like one in two million for the sperm to meet the egg? Grateful that you've got such a creative mind and come up with sick ideas like you have with my social media and website stuff. See what was that, like ten things already? I bet you can easily come up with another five to at least get to fifteen."

"Mmmm… yeah I guess." She still doesn't have that usual conviction in her voice.

"Come on now. I know you can do this. Don't be silly."

"Yeah. Alright. I'll think on it and do it."

"Good. I know I should do it more myself but too often forget. Alright, I've gotta go, I've got another call coming in. But try it. I bet if you do, you'll be able to turn your day around. Talk to you later."

"Bye."

Chapter 15

Carina

I feel like I'm being spread so thin, I'm about to break. Problem after problem just keeps popping up. Work feels like it's a nightmare at the moment. If it's not problems with the wrong meds being dispensed, it's the office not being updated or at least not updating us that patients aren't even home, instead at the hospital, making those trips completely unnecessary and a waste of time. Today is my day off and Robby asked me to come over. I think the main reason I'm always so happy to go over is because as soon as I step foot in that house, I'm able to shut off. It's as if I've somehow allowed myself to block off all the other responsibilities and rest, relax, and not stress. Not worry. It's become this safe space for me where I can let my guard down and let the minutes and hours just pass by.

A few seconds after I knock on his door, he opens it with a flourish, and I smile when I see he's wearing one of the Diamond Demon t-shirts I had made for him.

"Heya, there."

"You're in a cheerful mood," I say, taking my shoes off and heading inside.

"Better than me sounding miserable," he quips. "Which flavor coffee are you wanting today?"

"I don't mind. But only do half a measure for me. I'm not in the mood for too sweet today."

"I've never asked, and I feel like shit I haven't before now, but I was wondering, what was it actually that made you move here? I know you said before that it was a fresh start, but was there anything that really triggered it? Or was it just wanting a bigger place and stuff?"

It's not that I don't want to talk about it. Nor is it I don't trust him. I think a part of me still just feels embarrassed. Like there are these thin strings still attached to me from my past. Those deep-rooted insecurities are forever present.

"So remember I told you how my ex-husband used to not only cheat, but also steal from me?"

"Yeah, the guy sounds like the biggest asshole."

I huff out a laugh before continuing, "Well, he for sure was. As well as many other things. Anyway, it wasn't only me he stole from. Turns out he'd been skimming money from his work too, and did god knows what other shady shit. He got arrested, they built a case up, and he ended up doing some time because of it. Which was how I could get the divorce when he wouldn't give it to me before. I didn't understand why, but I later found out he'd taken out credit cards and loans and all that in my name and used my computer to do it. So when I tried to fight it, they said they couldn't prove it wasn't me that had taken them out. So I had to pay them off, since they were in my name only and it was affecting my credit. But while he was in prison, I decided enough was enough. I'd gotten some money from an inheritance, cleared all the debts he'd accumulated in my name, and moved. I wasn't even worried where we'd go, I just wanted to get away. The only criteria I had was that it was still close enough to my mom, and there were decent schools the boys could go to."

"Fuck. Damn, that's so shitty. Well, look on the plus side. You've gotten yourself back on your feet and you're doing great."

It's sweet that he thinks I am. Inside, I never feel like I'm doing enough. Not a good enough mom, not a good enough carer. Not woman enough.

"Well, I wouldn't go as far as that." I laugh.

"Don't sell yourself short. Have you kept up doing those gratitude lists?" Robby asks.

"I've tried. It's hard not to just repeat the same points each day."

"I know, but the more you do it, the easier it is. And when you really break things down, the more you'll find that overall your whole mentality shifts."

"Yeah, I guess. The points that I always find easiest to do are regarding the kids."

"See? That's good. The other night I remembered something my mom used to always do and at the time I wasn't grateful for it, didn't appreciate it. And now… man, now I would give anything to have it back. I'm gonna miss it." He pauses and a blanket of sorrow washes over his face.

"You don't have to share with me if you don't want to, but can I ask what it was?"

He lets out a laugh, but there's no humor behind it. "It's not anything grand. It's pretty silly if I'm honest. But basically, pretty much from around my twenty-fifth birthday, she said buying birthday and Christmas presents for us was an impossible task. So she'd decided from that moment on, she would only get us socks and pants for both birthdays and Christmas. Which was funny because she wouldn't just get one or two. Like, she kitted us out to last the year. So yeah, I know it's stupid, but I guess I'll miss it this year."

My heart squeezes at the thought of this sweet, broken man missing something that most people would take for granted. Also, making a mental note for the future. I have noticed that he doesn't bring up his mother as much though. I don't know if that's a conscious thing, or because her death is more recent. Maybe it's still too heavy for him to truly acknowledge.

"Sounds like she had a good idea and great logic," I say with a smile.

"Yeah. Shall we put another episode on?"

"Sure, why not?"

I'm not surprised that he changed the subject. Just as Robby gets up to make us another coffee, my phone rings.

"Hello?"

"Hi, is this Zion's mom?"

"Yeah, is everything okay?"

"It's Tom, his football coach. So we were doing training drills, and there was an incident with another boy who ran into Zion, not realizing he was going after the wrong player. The other boy fell on top of him after and apparently, a loud snap was heard. Zion's in a lot of pain and we've got the medic looking at him and they think he may have either fractured or broken his ankle."

"Jesus. Oh, my god. Is he okay? Have you called an ambulance?" I ask in a frantic panic as I get up and try to find my bag.

“We have called one, but apparently there was a big wreck on the freeway, so it’s currently looking at an hour until it would be arriving.”

“Okay, okay. If I drive up to the field, would it be possible for you guys to help me get him into the car? I can be there in like under ten minutes and will head straight to the emergency room.”

“Yeah, of course. If you drive to the end of the parking lot, there’s a gate at the end. It’ll be open, and you can drive through. We will meet you at the end of the path.”

“Thank you. I’ll see you shortly.” My hands tremble slightly as I hang up.

“Is everything okay? What’s happened?” Robby asks, his eyes bounce between mine as he walks over to me.

“Umm. No, that was Zion’s coach. They were doing drills, I think, and another kid did an offensive tackle or something, landing on him. There was a snap, and they think he’s broken his ankle.”

“Fuck. Is he okay?”

“I don’t know. The ambulance will take too long, so I need to take him to the emergency room.”

“Man, I really hope he’s okay.”

“Fuck. Fuck, fuck.”

“What?” he asks.

“I need to work out something for Kai. Gotta call his best friend’s mom and see if she can grab him after school. I don’t know how long we’ll be at the hospital for. So I’ll need to get him sorted for now. If it looks like we’ll be there for a while, I’ll have to get my mom to pick him up from there.” My mind is scattered as I try to dig my keys out of my bag, dropping them twice.

“Listen, take a deep breath. You’re gonna have to calm

down so you're safe to drive. Right, call that mom and get that sorted first so then you can just focus on what the doctor says. Alright?"

"Yeah. Yeah. I know," I say absentmindedly, my voice just above a whisper.

Chapter 16

Carina

Tired doesn't even begin to describe how the last couple of weeks have been. After arriving at the ER, they x-rayed Zion's foot, and his ankle was indeed broken. Two days later, he was booked in for surgery as they needed to put plates in. He was on bedrest at first, then they changed out his cast so he could use crutches to get around. His school allowed him to work from home, which was good as it meant that he then wouldn't fall behind, but it was a nightmare for me. I had to take time off work at first. Then, once he felt comfortable using the crutches, I was able to pick up a couple of shifts. Not only was it difficult having a teenage boy who was already five-ten and built like a linebacker who was feeling annoyed, frustrated, and endlessly bored at being stuck at home with a broken ankle, but Kai really struggled too. Because of his autism, his emotions run differently as is, but he's really struggled seeing his brother like this. Especially as his brother is his hero. The figure he always looks up to. Who he so frequently relies on. So it's been really difficult.

Having time to myself feels like a long forgotten thing. I haven't felt comfortable leaving Zion for more than a couple of hours at a time, even if I know he could handle it. It's me and my inner guilt that couldn't.

I've hardly done any classes at the gym, and it's made me realize just how much working out and training helps me because my mental state has plummeted.

I haven't seen Robby as often. There have been a couple of flyby visits when I'd been grocery shopping and he asked if I could grab a couple of things for him. It's probably the first time since we met that I picked up on how much I do for him, in comparison to the few and rare things he does for me. Then, when I dropped them off, he'd make me a quick coffee. He has helped by being a distraction though, and I've appreciated that. Like when he sent me some photos of prints that he thinks would look good on merchandise and asked if I'd like to put together some ideas, hoping it would keep my mind off all the other stuff stressing me. Or when I'm having a terrible day and he will send silly memes or suggest digging deep with those gratitude lists or sends photos of his meals when he's out with his friends, proving that he's still eating even if I have been forgetting to remind him.

Last week, my mom came over on my day off so I could really just chill. I hadn't really known what I should do with myself, so I went and did a class at the gym. After that, Robby messaged and said I should join him in his office, he'd been stressed as two guys that had been sparring took things to another level and it ended up in a mini brawl with a bunch of guys trying to break them apart. And he didn't know if he should cancel their membership or not since both guys have brought in a lot of other members with them. So, a way to take off the heat and stress was by a visit from me, which escalated from me on my knees, working him in my mouth, to him bending me over his desk and taking me hard and fast. I was already a sweaty mess, when he asked what my plans were for the rest of the day. I'd told him I'd had nothing planned and he offered me the keys to his place and said I could chill there before he came back, but I turned down the offer because had to get back to the kids.

Getting into bed, I aimlessly scroll through social media. The smallest sparks of pride burst through me when I look at the gym's page and see not only how many followers he's now accumulated, but seeing all the comments and likes on the posts I've created. Scrolling through the posts, a name pops out at me. *Emeraldgiant.* Clicking on it, I see the profile is set to private, but I recognize the tattoos on that back from anywhere. It's Robby's. Hmm. It's weird. He's mentioned before he's not a big fan of social media, so it might just be something he has to interact with those closest to him. There's no point in going into a back-and-forth mental debate, so decide I've had enough social media for one day and instead start clearing through the thousands of photos I have on my phone. I save way too many things and I've noticed it started to lag, so hopefully clearing up some space will help. After clearing a couple hundred, I find a video I'd forgotten I'd saved. It's talking about the importance of journaling.

Before I had the boys, I used to always have a diary.

Ever since I was a little girl. I wouldn't necessarily write in it every single day, but I did it whenever I wanted to just let something out. Then, with the kids and the hell of my marriage, I just never found the time. Plus, there was a part of me that was worried my ex would find it and somehow use the things I'd write about, against me. So I just stopped. Maybe I should start again, though. I did pick up some beautiful leather-bound notebooks a couple of months ago. Remembering I'd stashed them in one of my bedside tables, I pull one out, snag a pen, and let the words flow.

This feels weird. Will probably take some getting used to. I think I'm too old to start this off with dear diary. Gosh, where do I even start? I feel like I should keep this journal as the place where I write the things I feel I can't share with anyone. I can talk to Mom about the kids or work, money or just general life struggles. I can even talk to Robby about certain things. But I guess I don't really have anyone to talk about him. Not right now, at least. So I guess this is what you'll start off as.

Mr. Robby Black. You were not what I had expected to stumble across this year. I think that's something I still struggle with. Like, I wasn't looking for you, but somehow you just appeared. Right there. For all I know, we've passed each other multiple times in the last couple of years, with no idea. Unintentionally, you've wriggled yourself through the little cracks in the thick cemented walls I'd built up around myself. I'm not someone who asks for much, yet you've given me those small, simple things without me even asking. You talk to me when you could talk to absolutely anyone, you choose to give me the time of day. You let me see your most vulnerable side and it feels like an honour and privilege that I can. That level of trust is something some people don't even have with their closest friends and partners even after years together, so I really appreciate that you trust me.

When I'm at your house or even just in your company, you provide freedom, the escape to just switch off. I didn't think I would ever get a chance to do that. Not like this. Not as often. I have a safe space where I can just be me. Carina. There are no bells and whistles. Nothing fancy or unrealistic. Just me. And I guess the thing that's shocked me the most is that we've been sleeping together. I know I'm probably as far from perfect as can be. My skin is covered in stretch marks. My body bears the evidence of having birthed two children. On top of that, I wasn't one of those moms that bounced back. I'm fat. I don't know why that word always feels so hard to say, but it's the truth. And the thing is, I don't even really believe it's a bad word. But I guess society has turned it into one. So because of all those things, I guess too often I just think and question, why would you pick me? Why do you have even a shred of desire for me? You could have anyone. I can imagine if you go out with your friends for a couple of drinks, there must be loads of women throwing themselves at you. So why me? There is a part of me that wonders if maybe you have some sort of weird fetish. I know there are some men out there like that. But at the same time, I guess that would be a little silly. Plus, too much work. I guess in the end it all just boils down to me not understanding why you want to give a single mom with no friends, who isn't hot or pretty, and is pretty much a loser, the time of day. Obviously, this is all so easy for me to say here, as I know you will never see this. So it doesn't really matter. Plus, there is no way in hell I would ever let you even suspect that these thoughts and feelings are going through my head. No way. That would be way too embarrassing. Well, I guess this *will do for now. Maybe by my next entry, I'll have some of these fears and insecurities answered. Or I will have more questions...*

Chapter 17

Carina

"How about we have a movie night tonight? I'll order us some pizza, we grab some snacks from the pantry, and the three of us just lounge out and watch a movie together? Do you think the two of you can go a couple of hours without gaming and spend some time with me?" I ask them as we pull up after Zion finally got his cast taken off at the hospital.

"Yeah, sure," Zion says as he navigates the large boot he's now been given.

"Okay, I guess," Kai says unenthusiastically.

"Wow, you boys sure sound excited," I tease.

"Mom, we said yeah. You're doing it again," Zion says with a raised brow.

"Doing what?"

"I don't know when it began, but you've started acting really weird. Like you keep asking if we can do stuff together. Or you'll dig out old photo albums from when you were younger and I hear you crying, even when you think I can't. It's like you're not wanting to be alone, and the weirdest things seem to set you off."

Damn, it feels weird being read by your own kid like that. But as much as I wish I could deny it, I know he's right. I've found myself feeling really lost with who I am. I can't pinpoint the things that make me happy. I wouldn't know where to begin if I had to explain how my life was going. I feel like I'm in this never-ending paradox. For example, I don't socialize but am desperate to have friends. I don't go out for drinks or anything but on the occasions when say the boys are with my mom or the even rarer ones when they visit their dad Andrew; I convince myself it's just pointless getting dressed up to sit in a bar and feel sad if I drink by myself. So I'll just stay in. I enjoy working out and doing my classes, but then find myself comparing my technique and body to the other women and then doubt myself. I want to create and have amazing memories with the kids, but I also feel like all I want is a break. It's like I can't win.

"I know. I'm sorry. I guess it's just been a crazy few months recently and my head's all over the place. Listen, if the two of you really don't wanna watch a movie with me, that's fine. I'll still order a pizza."

"No. It's fine, Mom. I'm just saying it's okay for you to say you just wanna spend time together. You don't always need to add stuff on."

My heart fills and I appreciate his words more than he could ever know. "Aww, that's very sweet of you. So, does that mean I should leave the pizza tonight?"

"No!" they both shout, making me laugh.

"Alright. You two wash up, then you can go up and play. I'll call you down when the pizza arrives, and we'll pick which movie to watch."

"Thanks, Mom."
"Thank you, Mommy."

Unloading the dryer, I put the next load in, then put another load of washing on. I swear I don't think my washing basket has been empty in years. Doesn't matter how many loads I do, it's just never-ending. Zion and Kai stick to their promise and we do have a lovely movie night. We even end up playing a couple of games of Uno, which can get very heated and competitive in this house. Tomorrow's Saturday, but Mom is taking them out for the day because Susan and I got asked if we could cover a shift.

I remember to set my alarm and try to get a decent night's sleep. Just as I'm about to fall asleep, my phone goes off with a message.

Heya, you up?

Just getting to bed. Everything ok?

I turn the bedside lamp on as I shuffle myself up against the headboard, watching as the typing bubbles keep popping up from Robby.

Not really. I'm at the gym. Was washing down the mats and had my phone playing music on the speaker. I must have put it on shuffle as then Mom's favorite song came on. The same song that was played at her funeral. Now I'm sitting on the floor. Crying. By myself. Fuck.

Oh, bless him. I can only imagine how triggering that must be.

I'm so sorry. Is there anything I can do? Anything you want me to do?

Can you talk?

Yeah, sure.

Seconds later, his name pops up as an incoming call.

"Hi." I keep my tone soft and gentle. Not just for him, but also so I don't wake the kids.

"Hi." If he hadn't already told me he'd been crying, I'd have known from the second I heard his voice. "Can you just distract me? Talk about something different. Something unrelated. I just need to get out of my head."

"Umm, yeah sure. Umm… is there any particular topic?"

"I dunno. Whatever you want."

"Okay, how about some random animal facts?"

"Sure."

"Did you know every dog has a unique nose print? Like, no two are alike." I adjust my pillows behind my back so I'm sitting up more comfortably.

"Really? Yeah, I never knew that."

"Or how about that cats have something like thirty-two muscles in each ear?"

"Is that why their ears twitch so much?" he asks curiously.

"I guess. It would make sense for that to be the reason and not that they just do it out of silliness or boredom."

That gets the smallest huff-like laugh out of him.

"How about this? Did you know hummingbirds are the

only birds that can fly backward?" My fingers circle the duvet as I try and think up more facts I can share.

"That seems like a cool skill to have. A weird one, but still cool. How do you know all these things? Have you got your laptop open and are looking them up?" he asks.

I laugh. "No. Last Christmas, Kai got a book that listed like five hundred cool facts about animals, and he made me read it to him almost every night."

"Ah, I see."

Sometimes when I bring up my kids I get the impression that he doesn't really know how to react or what to say. Like he's still not used to dealing with a single mom or something.

"Do you want some more facts or something else?"

"Hmm, let's go with something else. How about you tell me ten things you would like to do? Sexually, I mean, that you haven't done before but want to try."

I was not expecting things to turn down this road and I'm glad that we aren't Face-timing, as I'd hate for him to see the embarrassing shyness on my face.

"Oh, wow. Umm, let me think."

"And I don't want you to hold back. Be as detailed as you can."

My cheeks warm as I try to scramble and think of what to say. "How realistic are we talking? Are you wanting ten scenarios and role play-type things? Or ten intense fantasies where anything goes?"

"Why not for now we do ten scenarios and role plays. We can do the other one next time. You've definitely got more experience and have tried a bunch of stuff I haven't yet. For sure."

I don't think he means it in a bad way, but his words leave a sour taste in my mouth. Once I got out of my marriage and first started dipping my toe back into the dating pool again, I wasn't looking for anything serious. I was, however, intrigued to try some things I'd never done before.

"Alright, well I guess one fantasy of mine would be to go out for the day with the guy I'm seeing, everything is innocent and maybe we go for some coffee or something, then do a bit a shopping. While at the shop, I'd find a dress I like and go to try it on. After I've taken my clothes off and just as I'm about to step into the dress, he'd quietly push past the curtain and join me. He'd bend me over the bench facing the mirror and it would be hot, fast, and hard, but making sure not to get caught. That thrill and risk would be hot. Then when we'd finish he'd quietly step back out, I'd still try on the dress, then we'd carry on as if nothing happened."

"Mmmm, that's hot. What else?" His voice is like a deep purr and the sound of it has me squeezing my thighs together.

"Go on a treasure hunt. But it's all sexually themed tasks. Say, for example, each person is set a number of tasks, like seven or eight of them the other person has picked and thought up. So it could be going to a particular location and taking a sexy photo. Or going to the store and buying a bunch of items that could be used during some fun play and so on. But all the tasks need to be done and completed together. And if not together, then at least with the other person present. If you complete the task, you get a point. If you can't or won't do it, then you don't. At the end, the winner gets to pick their prize, and the loser has to agree no matter what."

"That definitely sounds like something that's up your alley. And I could imagine that you'd get very creative with your ideas."

"Well, what would be fun about it, is neither person would know how extreme or intense the other tasks are. And then in the end it would simply come down to who's more competitive and who has the greatest desire to win."

As I list off the rest of the list, I notice that a lot of them are challenge-based stuff, like giving oral while the other person is on the phone and that person can't give away what's going on. That the person who's doing the oral has to make the other find their release before the end of the call. If they don't, they will be punished or have to do a forfeit. Or when picking some role play scenes, they all have a bit of a theme that one person plays more of a dominant role, whereas the other a more submissive one. Going through them and explaining them in the detailed way he's asked, I didn't even realize I'd been dragging my hand over my chest until my fingers started toying with my nipple bars. My skin feels overheated and my voice keeps hitching as my breathing increases with the desire running through me.

"I don't think there's a single one of them that I wouldn't enjoy doing. All of them were really fucking hot. And just hearing them and picturing doing them has made me realize something," he says with a purr.

"Oh yeah, and what's that?" By now my voice has a breathless tone to it.

"I think meeting you may be some kind of blessing for me. Bringing me out of my shell more. And perhaps bringing me back to myself in some way. I can't explain it very well at the moment, but I'm sure soon I'll be able to open up even more to your desires. Maybe we could work our way through that list. Because hearing those things, it feels like there's a part of me that has always been suppressed and has been wanting to come alive. And there's just something about you that's making me want to let loose and explore. Give in to it all."

That puts the biggest smile on my face. "I'm glad. I think it's always good to be able to feel safe to explore and try out new things."

"Yup, I absolutely agree. Alright, it's getting late, and I need to lock up here and try to get a decent night's sleep. Thank you. For always knowing how to cheer me up and making me feel better. Night."

"Good night." Hanging up the phone, I realize the time. *Oh shit.* Now I'm going to be tired and likely still turned on when I have to get up in a couple of hours. Great. That's just lovely.

Chapter 18

Carina

"Sometimes I wonder why I even got into this career," Susan says in a huff as we drive to our last patient of the day.

"Oh, don't say that. First, what on earth would you do if you didn't have me to annoy and bug you each and every single day? And second, yeah, some parts of the job aren't so great, but the real core, the essence behind it is great."

"You know, I've never understood how you're so positive and chirpy. Doesn't matter if we are dealing with blood, fecal matter, vomit, dressing wounds. You just always look on the bright side of things. Girl, I really don't know how you do it."

"That's a bit of an exaggeration. I will say that I think what's always been easy for me is that I've never felt like I need to get my head in the zone or like go into work mode, if that makes sense?"

"Umm, I'm not exactly sure what you mean."

"Well, I've always loved looking after people. It's always felt natural for me to be a giver. When I was younger, I always loved playing mom. Whether with my dolls, the dogs, even with my friends. And as I got older, I'd always be the one keeping an eye on everyone. Obviously, when I had the boys, that then became my role full-time. So I guess for me it's just a natural fit. It's like caring for people is embedded in my DNA. And to be honest, I don't know how else to be. I can't switch it off."

"Okay, well, that makes everything click. Like, I get it now. But have you ever wondered if you just enjoy caring and looking after people, or could there also be an element of you that maybe craves being needed?"

"Damn, when did *Dr. Phil* get in the car?" I say teasingly.

For the rest of my shift, her words echo in my head. Do I crave being needed? Is that something that's in my subconscious? The need to feel needed. Is that another factor that's intertwined with Robby? That a part of me over the past couple of months has enjoyed that he has needed me?

Getting into bed, I grab my journal and even before I put the first words down on the paper, a ball of emotion builds in my throat.

Today Susan made a point that has really got me thinking about things. Thinking about what I do. Why do I do them? Which then has triggered something that I've been pushing down for a couple of weeks now, but I know I can't keep ignoring. My feelings for Robby. See?

There. I've acknowledged it. For the first time in years, I don't feel alone. He's allowed me to let my guard down and just be me. But as much as I want to keep denying it, I can't ignore the potent feelings I've developed for him. It's gotten to where my entire mood can be lifted from simply getting a text from him. Or how I have to actively stop myself from filling him in on every little silly thing, or how I have to force myself to not think about how he's doing because he's taking up too much space in my head. Besides my kids, he has taken the next step of who's important to me in my life. And if this was anyone else, and we weren't in this weird dynamic we've found ourselves in, I think it would be easier.

I just... feel scared. When things first started with Robby, with everything that he was going through—that dark cloud that he was under—the last thing I wanted to do was get him to put me, put us into any particular category. I didn't want him to feel the pressure of deciding what label would fit us best. And I really didn't mind at first. But now? Now I just can't deny it anymore. We talk every day. We see each other pretty much every free moment I can. He knows my situation. Knows I've got kids, and it's not like I said I wanted to be alone and single for the rest of my life.

One part of me thinks I should just bury my feelings as deep down as possible and throw away the key. The other side, the other part of me, however, feels that I should tell him. Because in his defense, how would he even know if I don't tell him? Maybe there's a way I can let him know while not making him feel pressured to say how he feels. By doing that, then I can live knowing that I did what I could. I shared my side. Shared my thoughts and whatever will be, will be. The ball will be in his court.

Now the only question is when? When do I tell him? I know what I'm like. Now that I'm fully aware and have acknowledged it, it's going to eat away at me. Maybe I should just do it tomorrow. Tomorrow is the last day of the month and if I did it, say, late at night, then perhaps there could be something poetic about that. Cosmic even. That I just put it out there and if things go badly wrong, then I just start afresh in the new month.

Yeah. I like that idea.

Alright, I guess that's the plan.

Until next time x

I'm so distracted this evening I can't even be bothered to cook dinner, so I ordered the boys takeout instead. Just making myself a snack to stop my nerves from getting the better of me took more mental strength that I care to admit. Even after a long soak in the bath, I'm still nervous. Climbing into bed, I try to think about how I'm gonna word it when a message from him pops up on my phone.

Still at the gym, waiting for them to finish fixing the roof. Damn exhausted. But they did say they think they should be done within the hour.

Considering it's eleven-thirty, I can't help but awkwardly laugh that by around midnight he'll be getting the good news that the gym roof is fixed, but then also getting the message from me.

Damn, well, it's good they're almost finished.

Yeah. And Koa grabbed me some food from the Pete's Deli so I at least have eaten. What did you have for dinner?

A slice of toast and four strawberries

What? Hahaha, that sounds more like breakfast. You ok? You seem a bit off

Technically, it was breakfast, lunch, and dinner all rolled into one

Listen, I can tell you're in a bad mood or feeling down or angry or something. And it's not good that you've not eaten properly. Come on now, talk to yourself the way you spoke to me when we first started talking and I was in an awful place. Like for real, you're the one that pushed for me to really get my head in gear with the gym, and look, I'm here now. So tell me, what's up?

Just as I begin typing a response, he sends another message.

So let's start with this. What did you do after leaving my place? Or if you want, I can leave you alone and in peace if you prefer? X

No. Don't leave me alone, then I'd just be even more of a loser than I already am lol

You're really not a loser. Not at all. Actually, you're the opposite. So that's just silly talk. I think you're cool. Cooler than the other side of the pillow 😁

Ok for one, how did you know that something was up with me? Have you suddenly morphed into a mind reader? And I'm not in a bad mood or angry. I just feel like I'm in this limbo. But in reality, it's not an actual limbo. I know what the issue is but don't wanna face it because when I do, I'll just feel even worse. Sorry if that doesn't make any sense.

It makes sense but also doesn't because you're beating around the bush and not facing whatever you are procrastinating over for too long probably.

Hahah, you're spot on there

Well then, you just need to rip off the band-aid and go for it. Put your feelings aside and attack it. Be in a completely neutral state of mind.

The reason I'm beating around the bush AND not facing it is because there is genuinely nothing I can do to influence it into a direction I'd like. And the second I rip the band-aid off, I know it will go downhill. So if in a situation like this, isn't it better to just not complain, and simply suffer in silence?

There's a part of me that's convinced that he knows what this is all about. Or at least has suspicions. I know men can be oblivious at times, but surely even he can see what direction this conversation is hinting at.

What would silence benefit? Sometimes doing the uncomfortable thing is what needs to be done.

What if the uncomfortable thing makes things worse?

Then you or things will actually work out better in the long run. That's why they call it growing pains.

I've had enough of those to last a lifetime already 🙀

Every one has, doll xxx

☹️

We're all in this together, dealing with our own problems, trying to figure out ways to deal with or hide from them. It's all our own choice. No one can do it for us, right?

I get what you're saying, and I know it's all logical. It's just I can't seem to make that logic click and apply to my own brain. Not because I think it's a bad idea. It's more I don't think I'm strong enough in the short term to handle the fallout I know would happen from me facing the uncomfortable truth.

Yeah, I get that but still.

When I see people who are struggling, I always do everything I can to help because I know those people deserve better.

Yup, I'm aware of that. Now I think you just need to do it. Rip that band-aid off. You're strong enough. I know you are. You can do this.

Yeah, he has to know. Fuck it, I just need to get this over and done with.

Ok. I'm gonna to rip the band-aid off and then I'm going straight to sleep. Let's hope my brain allows me a semi-decent night's sleep instead of overthinking the bad news and awkwardness I'm going to feel in the morning

What do you do when you're a woman, full of scars both physically and mentally? You try putting yourself out there, and after endless nightmares, you meet someone completely random and by chance. Someone who's going through their own difficult storm, but there's something about that person that has you wanting to reach out your hand and be there for them.

And you watch as they slowly start seeing themselves even just a fraction of how you see them. And as the weeks turn to months, you're drawn more and more in. Not just physically (because the guy is hot as fuck, even if he can't see it in himself) but also mentally. This person is the first one who makes you feel safe. Makes you feel like you're not alone. Even just getting a message or phone call from them can cheer you up, even on the shittiest of days. And as much as you've tried to deny it, your feelings for them have gotten stronger. Way beyond simple friends.

But here is the problem. That same person, whenever they are going through a tough time, says how much they wish they could just get away. Are desperate to move back to the place they love. The island that brings them such joy and happiness. And all you want is for that person to be happy and support them with their happiness.

So now you're faced with three choices:

1- you accept that the person doesn't have the same feelings for you and never will.

2- you put on a mask every time they talk about moving back to the island and pretend you're happy for them and support them, although every time they bring up leaving, it's like a punch to the gut. You feel like you're on a countdown until they eventually go and never tell them your true feelings.

3- you tell them how you feel.

What would you say?

My heart pound as I press send. There. It's done. I've said it. As the minutes go by, panic slowly seeps in until eventually he replies.

Wow. Ok. I can't properly respond now because I need to take it all in, and they've just told me they've finished the roof. Plus, I'm knackered. And this deserves a clear and proper response.

Dissapointment washes through me as strongly as the

tide rolling onto the beach in a storm. To say I feel deflated is an understatement.

I understand.

I mean it, though, I will respond. I just wanna do it properly. And I know how your mind's probably going off a million miles an hour right now, thinking things will be weird and awkward. But I promise you they won't. I'll speak to you tomorrow. Sleep well x

I can't even bring myself to say goodnight.

As the first tears roll down my cheeks, I already hate myself for telling him. *Why? Why didn't I just keep my mouth shut? God, I'm such an idiot. Why on earth would anyone in their right mind want someone like me? I'm so damn stupid. So stupid.*

Those words repeat like a mantra in my head as I cry myself to sleep.

Chapter 19

Robby

Get up, make a coffee, monitor the crypto market I've been dabbling in again, eat, either train or do some gym admin, chill, eat, and sleep. That's what I've been trying to do. That's the structure, the plan I've been attempting to follow every day. Some days I'm smashing it. Some days I've felt really good.

Even those phototherapy sessions I was initially apprehensive about going to are slowly feeling like they are helping. My skin has started to clear up. The intense itchiness has gone. I'm glad that I've stuck to it.

I managed to get through the day without some sort of shitstorm being blown my way. But as always, I just can't seem to make that straightforward fluidity work every single day.

On top of that, on the days when shit does happen, I've struggled to know how to handle it. Before, I'd have just gotten Carina to come over and either distract me or make things better. But after she told me how she feels, fuck, I just don't know what to do. We haven't sat down and spoken about it. I just don't really know what to say. And every time I've even thought about it, thought about her in that way, it's as if this tidal wave of stress just knocks into me. Which led to a two-day hangover from hell that made me feel so shitty since I'd been doing so well, not drinking. But life, stress, *fuck*, just all of it has me reaching back for the bottle more often in the last few weeks than I have in the past few months. That's when I realized I need it to stop. I can't carry on like this. So, I ended up looking up flights and short-term rentals in Thailand.

I've found a couple that are actually great packages with training gyms out there. So I could lock in some real training too. Even just going through those ads, reading up on the listings in various towns already made me feel more relaxed, more at ease than anything.

I know I'm not going to hold out here much longer. Maybe I'll last another couple of months. But I honestly don't think I'll be able to make it to the end of the year. I thought I was going to manage longer this time. I really did. But I feel like it's the universe's way of telling me to get the hell out of here.

Right now though, I can't be thinking about getting away. Instead I need to work out where the hell my suit is.

Tomorrow is Adam's wedding. I don't know why, but I thought it was the weekend after next. But when my phone started blowing up earlier and I saw all the boys' messages in the group chat, talking about it being Adam's last day of freedom, that's when I realized it's fucking tomorrow. So that's why I'm tearing through my wardrobe, trying to find my damn suit.

I spend the next hour looking through every closet in the house. Nothing. There's no sign of it. Just when I think

I'm gonna have to take my ass to the mall and buy a new one, I remember I put all my formal shit in a box up in the attic. I only have two full suits. One blue and one black. The black one I'd last worn to Mom's funeral and there's no way I wanted to be looking at that reminder every day when getting dressed, so I stashed it up there.

Finding the box, I bring it down and, to my surprise, the blue suit isn't even badly creased. Once I give it a quick iron, it'll be good. Laying it all out, I'm looking at it and can't work out what is missing. I've got the shirt, the pants, the jacket, the waistcoat. What in god's name is missing? A tie. Where on earth is the tie?

Once again, I haul my ass back up in the attic, searching through every box only to come up empty. Heading back down, pulling open all the drawers, still nothing. *Fuck.* I need a tie. Looking at the time, I see the stores are still open. Grabbing my keys, I run out the door and jump into my car.

"Don't you fucking do this to me," I shout, slamming my fist on the dashboard as I try starting it for the twelfth time. "You've got to be fucking kidding me!" I yell.

Slamming my car door, I storm back into the house, looking for my phone. Grabbing it off the counter, I call Carina.

"Hey, you alright?" she asks.

It's like she's got this sixth sense and before I've even said anything already knows there's something the matter. Which there fucking is.

"No. Not really."

"Oh no, what's wrong? What's happened?"

"My car won't start. Like not at all. First, I couldn't find my suit, spent ages looking for it. Finally found it. Then realized I don't have a tie. Went to go to drive to the store, but the piece of shit won't start. Like at all."

"Man, sounds like you've had a nightmare. You can use mine. I can get Zion to watch Kai, and I drive down to you, then you just drop me back home. The wedding's tomorrow, right?"

"Yeah. I only remembered today. How'd you remember?"

I can hear her light huff of a laugh. "You told me the date, silly. Plus, where you said you were staying the night down there, and with how your car's been acting up, I arranged it so that my mom has the boys for the weekend, in case you ended up needing my car. And look, isn't it good that I did?"

I let out a loud and relieved sigh. "You're a lifesaver. Thanks. Yeah, that'd be great."

"Not a problem. Alright, let me quickly tell the boys I need to pop out and I'll be right over."

"Thanks. See you in a minute."

Resting my elbows on the counter I roll my neck as I'm filled with relief that not only will I now be able to grab a tie quickly, but I also won't need to worry about my piece of shit car not starting when I leave tomorrow morning. Plus, since I'm picking up William and Eric along the way, it'll be even more comfortable driving her SUV than my old one anyway.

Waiting out on the porch, I'm ready as Carina pulls up, gets out and walks over to the passenger side.

"Thanks for this," I say, giving her hair a squeeze and climbing in behind the wheel.

"It's no biggie. There's about three-quarters of a tank of gas, so I think that should cover you."

Looking over at her, I see a soft smile on her face as she fastens her seatbelt.

"I honestly can't believe I got the dates wrong. Can you imagine if tomorrow morning I'd have suddenly realized?"

Her laugh fills the car as I take the turn onto her street. "I don't think it would have gotten to that. Especially as I was going to message you this evening anyway, asking if you're all set for tomorrow."

Well, I'm glad that if I hadn't remembered, she'd have at least reminded me.

"So, have you got anything planned for your weekend off?"

"Nope. Just gonna take it easy. Probably get a bit of housework done. But other than that, I'm just gonna chill."

Pulling up in front of her house, I cut the engine. "Thanks again for this. I honestly don't know what I'd have done otherwise."

"It's really not a problem. Like I've said before, I'm glad I can be of help. Well, good luck with the tie, and drive carefully tomorrow. I'm sure you'll have a great time."

"Thanks. I'll send you a picture of which one I eventually get. And enjoy your time off. I'll talk to you tomorrow."

She gets out and gives me a wave before heading inside. Turning the car around, I quickly make my way to the store.

So I couldn't find a tie. Well, not exactly.

How was there no tie anywhere??

Haha, no, not that. It's just all the ones they had were all weird patterns or designs. I did, however, find a bowtie that's in the same shade as my suit. So I'm gonna rock that.

You'll have to send me a picture of the full look tomorrow before you leave.

Will do 😊

I missed the first three alarms I'd set for this morning, so I'm in a mad rush trying to get myself ready and out the door on time. Just as I'm chucking some clothes for tomorrow in my duffle bag, my phone pings.

William: Yo, what time will you be picking me up?

I'm leaving my house in ten. Will be outside yours in about twenty. Be ready since we're picking Eric up on the way.

Once I'm ready, I make sure I've got everything. Shuffling my phone and wallet in my pocket, I grab my sunglasses off the shelf and chuck my duffle over my shoulder as I lock up. The second I step outside, I'm hit with a wall of heat. Fuck, it's a hot one today. I'm gonna be sweating in this suit. Putting my duffle in the trunk, I take the suit jacket off and gently lay it on top of the bag so it doesn't crease on the drive. Getting in, I connect my phone to the speaker and set off for William's house.

He's waiting outside as I pull up, though I have to laugh when he doesn't realize it's me in the car. Lowering the window, I let the sweet beats of my favorite drum and bass tune flood out.

"Yo, get in."

"When did you get a new car?" he asks, putting his seat-belt on.

"I didn't. Mine's acting up. Wouldn't start. So a friend let me borrow theirs."

I drive the two blocks, and to my surprise, Eric is also ready and waiting outside.

"I messaged him just before you pulled up," William explains.

I beep the horn, getting Eric's attention, and he makes his way over before getting in the back seat.

"Bro, nice wheels."

"It's not his. It's his friend's," William says, though there's a weird tone in his voice.

"Not bad. Does this friend have kids?" Eric asks, chucking his bag on the floor of the seat beside him.

Looking back, that's when I see there's still a booster seat in the back.

"Yeah, they do."

I can feel William's intense, curious gaze on me. Considering he knows all my friends and everyone's vehicles, I know he's trying to work out who this belongs to. Especially as I'm not mentioning them by name. I wouldn't even know where to begin or how to describe the dynamic with Carina. Who she is and the role she has in my life. There's no way I'm having this conversation now. So I change the tune and turn up the music, ready to drown out any questions he's even thinking about asking.

Chapter 20

Carina

"Zion and Kai, are you guys ready? Grandma's waiting outside," I shout up.

No surprise I ended waking up early this morning instead of laying in, despite it being the weekend and it's not as if I have anything I needed to do. Well, not besides packing the boys' overnight bags, which I had to wait to do until they woke up. And unlike me, they both slept in. It sounds like the thunderous hooves of a wildebeest stampede coming down the stairs when in reality it's just a ten and fourteen-year-old.

"You both got your chargers?"

"Yeah."

"Yup."

"Good. Alright, get your shoes on and I'll take your rucksacks out to Grandma's car."

Mmmm, maybe I might relax in the garden for a bit as the sun feels gorgeous today, I think to myself. They've definitely got perfect weather for a wedding.

"Hey, Mom. Thanks again for doing this," I say, kissing her on the cheek before putting the bags in the trunk.

"Not a problem. Besides, you know I love having the boys over." The genuine happiness to spend time with them shows on her face.

Getting my squeezes from both boys, I give them a kiss and wave them off.

It's funny, the house always feels so quiet and empty when the boys aren't here. Deciding to leave the housework for now, I, change into my bathing suit, grab a book, make myself an iced coffee, and relax in the garden.

I get through a couple of chapters before I can't focus anymore, my mind inevitably wandering back to Robby.

It's weird. There's a part of me that can't picture him at a wedding. Can't imagine him in a light, positive, love-filled environment. Maybe it's because whenever I've had any interactions with him, they've always been in the cocoon of either his house or mine. Or the darkness of his office. And even though his emotional levels can be quite high, I wouldn't exactly class them as positive. So imagining him in a room full of laughing and smiling people feels like a giraffe just chilling in a public library. No, that's mean of me. Maybe there's a nice and softer side to him. Perhaps when he's around his friends, he's able to relax in a way that he can't around me.

Besides basic check-in text messages, we haven't really talked since I told him how I feel. Not properly. He never ended up responding to my message. That following morning, I'd been so nervous. In a weird way, I was even more nervous than I'd been when I was getting myself ready to tell him how I felt. I think it was because I genuinely didn't know how he was going to respond. Well, it didn't matter that I'd thought of a million different responses that he may have given me, because he *never addressed it.*

It felt like a punch to the gut. For him not to address it in any shape or form hurts so much worse than telling me he doesn't feel the same way. I'm not delusional. I understand no answer is just as much of an answer. But I just can't, or I guess don't want to face it. Not properly. Because if I do, then it would really confirm what I know deep down, that I am just not in a great place.

I've still not worked through all the trauma from my ex-husband nor have I worked on myself enough to recognize and place the right kind of protective boundaries I both need and deserve. I'm just so used to having spent years not listening to my gut, not advocating for myself, not putting my foot down, and demanding better, that it's like I'm stuck in this toxic default mode where I know things aren't right, but just can't help myself and keep going back for more.

The first time I'd gone to his place after, I didn't really know what to expect. I guess it was good though, since he just acted as normal. No one would ever think that I'd opened myself up to him. Like we'd simply leapfrogged over the whole thing. I guess the only thing I wish for would be for him to fully go back to how he was before. There has been a shift. It's also gone hand in hand with the fact that he's reconnected more with his friends, which I know is a good thing. Maybe there's just a part of me that selfishly misses being needed in a way that he used to need me.

Waking from my little snooze in the garden, I head inside and put on my favorite playlist, letting the music blare out as I have the house to myself. I give myself a facial, buff and moisturize from head to toe, order some takeout, and even pour myself a glass of wine.

I'm making tonight about me.

I stretch out on the couch in my silk sleep shorts and tank, sinking into the luxury of an actual night off when my phone pings multiple times.

Opening it up, I see multiple messages and a video from Robby.

I think I'm a little tipsy

oops

great day seeing friends

(video omitted)

Opening it up, I watch as with slightly shaky hands he turns the camera on himself, giving a goofy smile. A pair of white plastic-looking sunglasses sit awkwardly on the top of his head. He then pans the camera back to himself and speaks to the phone, but I can't hear a word that he's saying over the loud music in the background.

Looks like you're having fun. Though, I can't hear a word that you're saying 😆

It's interesting, I've never seen him under the influence of alcohol before. Ever. I don't think I've ever even seen him drink anything other than water, coffee, tea, or a Rubicon. Surely, the whole point of AA is that you don't drink at all? This really can't be a good thing. Unease slowly creeps its way through me. I guess this is a side of him that others in his life have witnessed, but I haven't.

After about twenty minutes, another message comes through. This time it's a photo of him and two of, I'm guessing, his friends on either side. He looks tipsy, but it's cute as his expression is relaxed, with a big smile on his face.

(Image omitted)

😊 glad you're having a good time

Focusing back on the movie, I only watch a couple of minutes before more messages come through.

you're nice

did you know you have really straight and really white teeth? Great. And a good dentist

I burst out laughing at the bizarre, random compliment and before I even get the chance to respond, more messages come through.

pretty. That too.

hot.

great in bed

Damn, I think he's moved on from tipsy and now is in drunk territory. I'm just about to message him back when my phone goes off again.

you're really great. I know I don't say it, but you are curly. That's what I call you in my head. Curly. Sweet. My curly. You always make me

feel good

better. You do

Despite the jumbled and discombobulated mess of his messages, I can't help the warm and fuzzy feeling I get at reading them.

Aww thank you. That's very sweet of you to say. I'm sure you're having fun and hopefully also getting your dancing shoes on and just enjoying your night 😌 x

I finish the movie with no more interruptions. Clearing away the leftovers from the takeout, I treat myself to the tub of Ben and Jerrys from the freezer and stick the next movie on.

heeey, are you awake?

I laugh at his silly question as it's just past nine o'clock.

Yes. Everything ok?

I wonder what silly thing he's going to come out with now. However, instead of getting another drunken text, my phone rings and it's him.

"Heeeya, babe, there's my curly girl," he says with a slight slur in his voice and there's music playing in the background.

"Well, hello to you too. You having a good time?"

The music suddenly gets quieter, so it sounds as if he's gone somewhere else.

"I am. Well, I was."

"Oh no, what's happened?"

"So I may be just a little bit tipsy. And when I was paying for my round, I kept putting pin number wrong in. Now they've blocked my card."

I cover my mouth to muffle the sound of my laugh. Gosh, it's been so many years since I've had that happen to me.

"I feel bad for asking. But too embarrassed to ask the guys. Could I borrow some money until morning? When I'm home, I've got cash I can give you. You're the only one I trust."

See, even in his drunken state and the silly tipsy antics, it still means a lot that he has a level of trust in me. Allows me to bear witness to a side that others don't.

"Yeah, of course. That's fine. I'll transfer you some money to your other account so you can use your Apple Pay," I say reassuringly.

"Thanks, curly. I call you curly in my head, you know?"

"I know. You said that earlier."

"It used to be black mermaid. Now it's curly. That's what I saved you under on my phone now. Do you know that? Can you see?"

"No, I can't see. But I'm not surprised either. I changed your name to Diamond Demon in my contacts, so I guess it's only fair I got my nickname."

"Yup. You're there. My curly. Thank you, babe."

I try my hardest not to react like a goofy schoolgirl at the term.

I send him over the money, then head to the bathroom. When I return, I see another message from Robby. It's probably just a thank you text for lending him the money. I'm a little surprised when I open it and see it's actually another video.

From the background, it looks like he's gone into a bathroom or something. It looks nice though. He's for sure drunk now, as I can see how difficult it is for him to focus on the screen. "I hope you can come over tomorrow. We chill. Spend time together… I like it when we do that. I enjoy our time together. Our coffee and Netflix sessions are my favorite… they make me feel special. You make me feel special. Feel good. Can't wait to spend more time together."

Then it cuts out. I've got the biggest smile on my face and for the first time in weeks, I feel a level of happiness I haven't had in so long. It shames me to admit but I rewatch that video two more times. My eyes widen in surprise when again another video comes through. This time I watch as he heads into I think a toilet cubicle. He sets the phone up, maybe on a ledge or something, and rubs his hand over his face before facing the camera.

This time I can see on his face he's trying to appear more sober, or maybe he's concentrating more on his words.

"I want you to really understand how much I enjoy time, our time, me and you, together. You're like my comfort blanket… plus you've got a great rack. And fuck your mouth does wonders."

That makes me cringe and laugh at the same time, but I continue watching.

"I didn't expect you. I don't know how, but you just

landed in my life… came at a point where… where I wouldn't have put myself out there."

I don't think he realizes that the angle of his phone means that I can see as he goes to pee. Using the palm of my hand, I cover the bottom of the screen, as that's a sight I could have gone my whole life without seeing.

"I know… I know there's something I haven't said. Something I should have already said. I just don't know how to."

"Yo, Robby, who you talking to?" someone shouts in the background and suddenly the video stops.

"No, no no no," I shout out staring at my phone.

My pulse spikes and I sit myself up, alert and wide eyed as I'm desperate to know if he would have said more and what it would have been. I go to message him, asking why it cut off, but stop myself. Something in my gut is telling me I will regret asking. I'm better off staying silent. Right now, I just need to hold on to the good and nice points he mentioned. I'm too scared to ruin that. I know that's sad and desperate and clingy and insecure of me. If I had a friend telling me about being in a dynamic like this, I'd shake her until she saw sense. I know this isn't healthy. I know it's toxic as fuck. But right now, mentally I just don't have the strength to stand my ground. I don't feel like I'm strong enough to put myself first. So I've just got to keep all these thoughts and feeling locked and hidden away.

Chapter 21

Carina

I'm absolutely exhausted when I wake up, which is unbelievably frustrating since not only is there no reason for me to wake up with Zion and Kai not here, nor do I have work, but also because I've actually slept longer than I usually do. It's almost midday and I must have finally fallen asleep just before two, yet I feel like I could still do with another six hours.

The dream I had was wild. I was in this jungle-like place, lost and alone. Then, out of nowhere, Robby appeared and helped guide me out. We were then suddenly in this tiny village. No one there could speak. So communicating was impossible. They shared their food and gave us a place to sleep, then one day Robby just left. The villagers were unhappy and made me a human sacrifice. They tied me to this altar and just as they went to cut me open, I was falling. Until I landed in the gym.

Only the gym was deserted. I tried escaping out the doors, but they were all locked. I climbed up onto one of the higher ledges to look out the window. There I saw

Robby again, this time outside with his friends. I was banging on the window, trying to get their attention, when the whole place started to flood. But still, no one noticed. Just as the water reached my neck, Robby looked over and saw me. Yet instead of coming and helping, all he did was nod, and turned his back. Once the water engulfed me, I was then suddenly in another location.

This went on and on. In total, there were five times I was left to die, get attacked, or abandoned. I bet a therapist would have a field day on the meaning of it all. I break out in full-body goosebumps at the memory and shudder from head to toe.

Finally, I haul myself out of bed and head downstairs. It's almost lunchtime and I haven't even had a coffee yet. As I busy myself making one, I give the boys a quick call, checking and seeing how they're doing. Mom lets me know instead of dropping them off this afternoon, it'll be this evening instead because they're going to have a barbeque for dinner. After getting some housework done, I grab my phone and, despite telling myself not to, I watch the videos from last night again. Just like I had when I'd watched the second clip through, I feel equally frustrated that he was interrupted and stopped short. I still don't know why he did a second video, but also why that one just felt different from the first. My mind feels like a pinball machine, constantly going back and forth, trying to dissect and analyze every point. Just as I finally give up and accept I'm going to drive myself insane with this, a message comes through from him.

Omg, I'm dying right now 😩

Now, considering he already seemed pretty drunk at about nine last night, and I can imagine they all carried on partying till the early hours, I'm not at all surprised that he's feeling hungover today.

Oh dear. I can imagine you've probably got quite a sore head. Did you get much sleep?

Yeah, I got to sleep around one o'clock. But woke up at six to throw up.

Ew, see, that's just another reason I don't enjoy drinking to that excess. To me, there is nothing worse.

That can't have been fun. But hey, it's better that you get it out of your system.

Yeah, I know

Make sure you keep your fluids up today to flush it all out.

That's the plan

Oh, and your videos last night were definitely something

Videos?

Oh shit, I can't help but laugh that he doesn't remember. Does he even remember asking to borrow money? Maybe I should slip in a little reminder.

Yup. You sent two after I sent that money over. One of which I don't think you realized captured you as you peed 😬

Oh fuck. Yeah, there is no way in hell I am going to watch those back.

So, are you planning on just chilling there today? Or will you head home?

No, we're leaving shortly. Gonna grab some food on the way back, then have a nap. Or see how I'm feeling. I'm stuck between going back and having a nap or to just try to hang on till the early evening and then get to sleep early.

Yeah it might be better to stick it out then get a nice long sleep tonight

What are your plans for today? Your kids back already?

Nothing really planned. Just gonna chill. The boys aren't back yet. My mom won't be dropping them off until tonight. They're doing a barbeque for dinner.

Nice. Well, it's good you get some time to relax. I'll let you know when I'm back and how I'm feeling and maybe you could pop over?

Sure. Just keep me posted 😊

Venturing into the kitchen, I finally make myself something to eat, then end up putting on the final movie I wanted to watch last night.

I must have fallen asleep, because I'm suddenly woken up by the loud ringing of my cell.

"Hello?" I answer without checking to see who it is, my head still making its way through the fog of sleep.

"I'm back. Just had a nice cold shower. As I was in there, do you know what I was thinking?" The purr in his voice wakes me up instantly.

"No, what were you thinking?"

"I was thinking how good it would feel to have my hands run over your luscious curves. That I need the feeling of your mouth on me, licking, sucking, and swallowing me down before I bury myself deep inside you."

Holy cow. Well, I sure as hell wasn't expecting that. How do you go from severely hungover to incredibly horny in only a matter of hours? Not only that, but he's never been one to do a lot of dirty talk, so this is really surprising. My skin tingles with excitement.

"Now that's put a big and unexpected smile on my face," I say breathlessly.

"If you get yourself over here, there'll be more than that on your face before you leave here tonight."

"Fuck," I pant.

The sound of his deep, sexy chuckle only turns me on more.

"I'll make my way over now."

"Sweet. I'll leave the door unlocked, so just head right on in."

"Okay, see you soon."

Hanging up, I dash upstairs, throw on a cute little summer dress, and am out the door in fifteen minutes.

I completely forget that he still has my car. Luckily, it's not too far of a walk and it gives me time to pull myself together and not be completely and utterly controlled by my hormones.

When I approach his door, a thrill runs through me. It's not as if we live in some kind of nefarious part of town, or like he doesn't know that it's me that's about to walk through the door. Yet there's something so trusting and really sexy picturing him being as turned on as he sounded on the phone. Knowing that when he's in these moods, when he gets to that animalistic level of arousal, it's always some of the hottest sex between us. I don't know if it's because in some ways it taps into that feeling of being wanted, being desired so much. I've always felt that there's a big difference between someone being turned on, and a person being turned on by you. To me, they aren't the same. And with how long I have felt that I'm someone who's always lacking, not sexy enough, not desired or wanted, I don't know, it just hits so much deeper.

Stepping through the door, I try to stay as silent as I can. Maybe I even have a chance of sneaking up on him. Slowly I pad through the open-plan kitchen and just as I turn the corner, that's when I spot him. He's sitting in the large leather armchair, only wearing a pair of loose basketball shorts which do nothing to hide his large bulge. I'm guessing he heard me, since he doesn't look surprised.

"You look too angelic in that dress for what I'm going to do to you." The dominating tone in his voice makes me whimper slightly. He raises a brow as a smile breaks out the corner of his mouth.

"I want you to lift your dress up, take your panties and bra off, but keep the dress on. Just push one of the straps off your shoulder. Then I want you to come here and get down on your knees."

My nipples harden and I can feel arousal soak my underwear. This is a complete first. Yeah, he has been dominant and authoritative during sex before, but that's usually in the middle of it. When he's all caught up in the moment. Never like this from the outset, giving me orders in this way. And it's so hot.

Not wasting another second, I follow his instructions. Sliding my underwear down my thighs, I look up and find him with his hand outstretched. I can feel my cheeks heat and know he can see my apprehension, but I don't think he knows why.

"Don't make me tell you again," he says, looking down at his hand.

Filled with embarrassment, I step out of them before walking the few steps over to him and placing them in his open palm. His eyes shoot down as he tests how damp they are.

"Oh, you bad, bad girl. Did you soak these because I'd said I was going to decorate your face? Or are you just so desperate for me to fuck you?"

I'm just about to answer when he shakes his head.

"Actually, it doesn't matter. I think it's time for less talking."

He pushes down his shorts and his hard length springs free. The mushroom tip is a dark red and already leaking with pre-cum, making my mouth water.

Pulling me onto his lap so my knees are on either side of his hips, he lines himself up and spears me with his cock. This angle has him so deep I can feel the tip of his crown just by my cervix. Reckless savageness fills me as the potent lust that's exuding from him makes me feel like I'm loosing my mind and senses.

The grip he has on my hips is so tight I wouldn't be surprised if it left bruises. Rolling my hips, I get into a rhythm as I ride him. A bead of sweat drips down my back from exertion. My fevered skin feels like a burning inferno. I don't know how, but despite the tight fit of us both in this armchair, he manoeuvres my legs so his arms are beneath them with the backs of my knees resting against his inner elbows. Then, he flips us so my back is now against the seat of the chair, and he is on his knees in front of me. This position allows him to take back control and the tempo, his thrusts increasing. The veins on the side of his neck and head bulge and my eyes are transfixed as I follow the droplets of sweat rolling down them. Leaning his head down, he kisses along the slopes of my breasts that have worked their way out of my dress before biting down hard on my nipple. The indentations of his teeth feel like primal markings that set off spasms of pleasure that course through my veins like a blazing fire.

"Please, please give me more," I plead.

I'm desperate for more. I can feel myself building towards my orgasm, but before I can fall over the edge, he pulls out, letting out a groaning roar as he comes, covering my face and chest, his hand wrapped around his shaft as he milks every drop.

He's a panting mess and his whole body shakes as he struggles to catch his breath.

"Jesus woman. I've never cum so much in my life," he exclaims.

My skin cools, and both frustration and deflation slithers through me as all the desire I felt from my impending release washes away. Once he finally catches his breath, he stands and I watch as he collapses against the couch, flinging his arm over his head. Awkwardly, I get to my feet and secure myself back into my dress before walking over to the kitchen sink and washing him off my face and chest. By the time I'm finished, I turn around and find him still in the same position. I make myself a glass of water, then grab my bra off the floor and quickly put it back on. There's no way I can put my underwear back on.

"Damn, that was insane," he says, looking up with the biggest, goofiest smile on his face.

That look, that blissed out and satisfied expression on his face extinguishes the frustration that has built within me when he'd denied me the chance of finding my own pleasure.

"Want a glass of water?" I ask.

"Yes, please. I don't think I can move. My legs feel like Jell-o."

I refill the same glass and bring it over to him, passing him his shorts too.

"Thanks." He taps the seat next to him for me to sit down.

Pushing all my thoughts and feelings aside, I get comfortable and pull the thin blanket over my legs as we settle in, watching the next episode of Dexter.

I'm still reeling a bit from my lack of release, so I don't know why he feels the need to tell me that during the reception, he and his friends had a group of women vying for their attention, clearly eager to have some fun. Nor do I understand why he brought up the fact that, even though he could have, he did nothing with anyone. What on earth was I meant to say in response to that? Did he want some sort of medal or a pat on the back that he didn't dive into the arms of these women? It was so weird and he almost sounded proud of himself. It just made me feel awkward. I didn't like it. And to be honest, I wish he'd never mentioned it but I don't know how to tell him that without sounding jealous, so I don't say anything at all.

He lays his head on my lap and wraps his arms around my waist. Not long after that, his breathing turns heavy as he drifts off to sleep. Looking over at the time, I see I've still got about two hours until I need to head back.

It's not my fault that he fell asleep, so I continue watching the show. He'll just have to catch up on his own time.

When I see it's time that I need to leave, I stroke his hair before gently shaking his shoulders to wake him.

"Robby? Robby, I need to make a move," I say, just above a whisper.

"Hmm, mmm, mmm," he murmurs.

I continue shaking him until he finally awakes. "I need to get going. I'm gonna take my car. Are you taking yours to the garage tomorrow?"

"Mmmm, yeah. Hopefully, it starts. I'll let you know what they say."

I pick up the cushion that's beside me and shuffle out from under his head, putting the pillow in my place. I place the blanket over him, grab my bag, and even before I'm by his front door, I can already hear him snoring again. Getting in the car, I'm pissed about the mess. He's left some clothes, shoes, his aftershave, and sunglasses scattered around. Seriously, is it too much of an ask to at least keep my car tidy? Especially as I'm the one being helpful and letting him use it. I put it all in the backseat, then make my way home in time to hopefully take a quick shower before Mom drops the boys off. On the short drive back, I can't deny that niggling feeling that the more I get to know Robby—the more snippets of him I witness—the more I realize he's not quite as great as I've allowed myself to believe. No matter how much I try and make excuses for his behavior and attitude towards both life and me, I can't keep burying my head in the sand.

Chapter 22

Robby

I honestly thought I'd still be feeling rough this morning. Even when waking yesterday, I could still feel the alcohol in my blood. I'm pretty sure if I'd have been stopped while driving back, I'd still have been way over the legal limit. Why oh why did I think it was a good idea to get everyone onto shots? I guess I just got carried away after the first one, which I took so easily and with the guys calling me 'The Shot King' like they used to back in the day, it all just went to my head.

I remember the wedding. It was nice. Then once the reception got underway, and the vibe changed from formal to chilled and fun, well, the booze was flowing, and everyone was having a good time. I don't even remember half of what happened that night. Just snippets here and there. At some point I remember my card not working, but I must have been able to fix it because I remembered buying another bottle for us. Then Eric was talking to a group of girls who were friends, I'm guessing, of the bride. They joined our table and were giving clear signals to us that they were interested. I think a couple of my mates disappeared with some of them, though I'm not a hundred percent sure. I remember William ribbing me, questioning why I wasn't taking two of the girls up on their offer to get some air. I don't know what I said to him. I think I just brushed it off. I know at some point I was messaging Carina. I don't even want to look at the messages I sent. They can stay in the drunk haze I was in. No need to remind myself of that. And speaking of Carina, I guess that's why I'm not feeling as rough today.

I'm glad she came over. It was hot. I don't think I've ever come so much in my entire life. It was actually pretty insane. But just like she always does, she took it like a champ.

Finally dragging myself out of bed, I remember I need to try and get my car to the shop. After five attempts, it finally starts and I head over, driving carefully to make sure not to stall. I will lose my shit if it cuts out on the way.

After dropping it off, I let them know I'll be at the diner across the street so they can call as soon as they get an idea of what could be going on with it. I destroy a breakfast of pancakes and coffee in no time, so I end up ordering another portion and finishing that off by the time they call me. From the sound of the guy's voice on the phone, I'm not feeling too optimistic that it's just going to be a simple job.

I pay the check then cross over the road.

"I won't lie to you man, there is a lot of work that needs to be done."

I listen as he lists what's wrong and it feels never ending.

"To be honest, a lot of these issues are common with a

car this old, but in order for it to run reliably and with no issues, those are bits you'd need to get fixed."

"And to do that, how much are we looking at it costing?" I ask, though I know I'm gonna hate the answer.

"If we do all that, it's looking like it'll be around twenty-three hundred. That includes labor and parts."

"Fuck," I mutter as I rub my hand over my face. "I didn't even spend that much when I brought it a couple of months ago."

"Also, because of some faults we found during the diagnostic, I legally can't let you drive it off the lot. You could get it towed, if you'd want to take it to another shop, but dude, they'll just tell you the same thing."

My phone vibrates in my pocket, but I ignore it.

"Well, the other thing I could do is offer you cash, and we scrap it."

Damn, what the hell am I gonna do without a car? "How much would you give me for that?"

"The interior is still in good shape, and I'd be able to take it apart and sort some of that out, so how about four hundred and fifty dollars? Like I said, I can do that and give you the cash now."

Hanging my head in my hands, I know I have no other choice. "Sure, fuck it. Just do that."

He walks me over to his office and I sign all the paperwork. Luckily, the only thing I still had in the car was a sweatshirt in the backseat. I'm not in the mood to walk, so I grab my phone to call a cab. Not even wanting to look at the piece of trash, I wait outside the shop. As I wait, I see that Carina messaged me earlier.

Heya, hope it goes alright and you're able to get your car fixed. Oh, by the way, did you by any chance accidentally knock into like a pole or bollard when going to or coming from the wedding? There's a little dent on the front passenger side lol

Shit. When did that happen?

Omg, are you joking? For fuck's sake, I thought that was already there. Listen, just take the keys back, take me off the insurance. I can't believe I've fucking done this.

Looking up into the sky, I just want to scream. Fuck. This is such bullshit. Why does this shit happen to me all the damn time?

Whoa. Calm down. No Robby. Don't be silly. You're probably right. I bet it was here already, and I just never noticed it. It only stuck out to me because when I walked past the way the sun caught it, it stuck out. I had no right presuming and asking if it had occurred while you had it. I'm sorry. That really was unfair of me.

I don't even know what else to think anymore. I'm so tired of just constant annoying awful shit.

Again, I'm sorry. Let me know how your car's going and if there's anything I can do.

Alright. Will do.

I don't bother mentioning what happened. Not right now. I've got too much going on in my head.

When the cab pulls up, it takes the driver about two seconds to tell from the look on my face that I'm not in the mood to talk, and luckily, he stays quiet for the short ride.

Once I'm back home, it feels like the walls are closing in on me. Like I can't breathe. Can't catch a break. How has this become the staple of my life, the constant cycle of never ending bad and shitty things happening to me? Haven't I gone through enough?

Grabbing the empty glass off the counter, I launch it across the room, smashing it against the wall. Pieces of broken glass scattering everywhere. Why do good things never happen to me? Surely I deserve something for once to just work in my fucking favor?

Now, I don't know what the fuck I'm gonna do. Just when I thought I had a chance of things slowly turning around, *bam*, I'm hit with another shit storm. Maybe this is the universe's way of telling me something. Perhaps me now not having a car, not being able to get around and do stuff is a sign. A sign that I should leave. That I should no longer be here. That it would never be possible to build things up so that a few years from now I'd be in the ideal position where I could really properly move over there, have the house I built, have a business, as well as having the gym here thriving. Instead, I should just pack up, sell everything, and go. Because really what do I have going for me here besides constant drama? Constant trouble? Nothing. No one. The more I think about it, the more I realize I'm right. I need to go. I need to just be done.

Just after Mom passed, I contacted a realtor and had gotten everything ready to sell. I'd emptied the place and just kept back the few basics so I could stay. The house had been prepped, photos taken, it was all ready to go. But in the end, I just couldn't go ahead with it and pulled out. Then when I got the money from her savings, I just used that to get on the first flight out. When I returned, I couldn't be bothered to get more things for the house. It was liveable for me. And I was so consumed with the trouble with my skin and working out a way to honour Michael and Joseph's memory by trying to get the gym to take off, I didn't think about selling again. But now, this thing with the car feels like it's the final straw.

Grabbing my phone, I scroll through my emails until finally finding the one from the realtor. At the bottom, I see his number and hit the call button.

"Hello?"

"Hi, is this Ryan Hassock?"

"Yes, speaking."

"Hi, it's Robby Black. I'm not sure if you remember, but last year I was going to put my place up for sale, but then changed my mind."

"Ah, yes, it was a three-bed family home on Glyneman Drive, if I remember correctly?"

"Yeah, that's the one. Well, I was calling to say some things have happened and I will be moving back abroad and I want to sell. Like right now. I don't care if we put it up for under market value. I just need this to finally be sorted and done as soon as possible."

"I'm sorry to hear that something has happened, but I'll be able to help you. I have several buyers that are looking for something like yours. There's a couple that I know that's eager to have something sorted within the next month, since they'd like to be settled before the school summer break is over. Would you have some free time tomorrow for me to come over and see if we can still use the shots we took last year and discuss more?" he asks.

"Yeah, that's fine. I'll be in all day tomorrow so you can come by whenever."

"Perfect. How does eleven o'clock sound?"

"That's fine."

Hanging up, I finally feel a sense of relief. Like, for once, things will fall into place, and before I know it, I'll be back in paradise. The countdown can now truly begin.

Chapter 23

Carina

I'm just heading back from the store. Are you still getting your car sorted or are you home?

I'm home. Come over. I can fill you in.

Alright, see you shortly

I put my phone back in my purse, then drive over to Robby's. I wonder what the issue with the car ended up being. It can't have been that bad if it's already sorted and he's back. At least that'll be one less thing for him to worry about now. As I pull up outside his house, I'm a little confused as his car isn't parked out front. Pulling into the space, I walk over to his door and knock. After several moments, he opens the door. His expression is one of annoyance and frustration and in his hands he's got a dustpan and brush with broken shards of glass in it.

"What's happened?" I ask anxiously as I step inside.

"Where do you want me to begin?"

Following him in, I take a seat on the couch and face him. He pours the broken glass into the trash, then rests his elbows on the counter and hunches over.

"What happened to your car? Are they fixing it now?"

He lets out a dry, sad laugh that sends goosebumps down my spine. "No. They aren't fixing it now. They won't be fixing it at all. They ran some tests and it would have cost more to repair than what it's worth. And on top of that, I couldn't drive it back because something that popped up when they were running the diagnostics made it illegal to be on the road."

I don't mean to, but I gasp.

"So because there was no way I was going to be paying to get it repaired, he offered to buy it from me for scrap. Cash. Which I did. It's done now. Gone."

"Oh, Robby, I'm sorry. That's really shitty."

"Yeah. I know. Well, after that happened, it just made me realize it was a sign. Not that I needed anymore, but this was the final one."

My stomach dips as my pulse races. I have a terrible feeling I know where he's going with this.

"That's why I decided enough is enough. I'm going back to Thailand. I called the realtor who's coming over tomorrow. I need to get out of here. I'm too done, too tired of all this shit."

Every word feels like a punch to the gut. Hit after hit after hit. Not only is he leaving, but he's doing it so fast. And this isn't just like he's wanting to go away for a long vacation. He's clearly done here, choosing to close off everything and move there permanently. He won't be coming back. Not by the sounds of it. Not if he's selling the house. I honestly don't know what to say. I have no words, so I sit there silently. My entire body feels numb.

"To be honest, I think I should have made this decision earlier because as soon as I got off the phone with him, I already felt like a massive weight had been lifted off my shoulders. Like I was finally getting the chance to be free again. Put everything behind me. Plus, besides the gym, there's nothing else for me here. Just pain and memories and a shitty life that just makes me miserable most days. So what's the point? Why put off the inevitable?"

The careless and detached way that he's speaking right now chills me to the bone. My mouth feels dry, and I have to swallow to speak.

"What are you going to do with the gym?" I ask. I can hear the crack in my voice, but I don't think he does.

"I'm still not sure. There's a part of me that thinks I should just sell that as well. But at the same time, I'm worried that would be like dismissing my brother's memories. So I think what I'm going to do for now or like the next couple of months is just keep it all going as it is. The last time I was gone, Koa was running it all, anyway. I'll see if he's okay doing that again until I decide what to do. I'll be fine for money for a while since I'll have the cash from the house. And that'll give me the time to really think about what I want to do."

I honestly don't know what hurts more. The casual way that he's telling me all this or the look on his face where he's clearly expecting me to be happy for him. I'm trying to gather my thoughts, trying to not let him see the effect this is having on me, as I know that's not what he's thinking or concerned with right now.

"So, when do you think you'll be leaving?"

He rolls his neck, and I swear there's the smallest smile creeping at the corners of his mouth.

"Because I'm willing to take a hit on the price, and the realtor said there are some people interested in a place like this and willing to do it all quickly, I'm hoping for max a month. Can't see it being over six weeks before I'm already out there."

"Wow. That soon." My voice is just above a whisper, and I have to blink away the emotion prickling at the backs of my eyes.

"The biggest problem I have right now is that I don't know what I'm going to do about not having a car. There's going to be so many bits and pieces that I need to sort out in the next month. It honestly couldn't be a worse timing. If it was a shorter time, like a week or something, then I'd just rent a car. But there's no way I'm paying for that for four weeks. Not a chance. And I don't want to buy one either since that would be insane just for that short time, plus I would then still need to sell it before I go, leaving me with one more hassle."

"Well, why don't you just continue using mine?" The words leave my mouth before I've even thought about what I'm saying.

"What do you mean? You can't give me your car for a month."

"No, I don't mean give it to you like I'll never use it. We'd just go about it like we have on the days yours wasn't working."

He's giving me his full attention, so I am scrambling to make sense of this illogical plan I've just concocted in my head.

"Well, on the days I'm working alone and with no

breaks and super busy, I will for sure need it. But to be honest, besides those, I could carpool with Susan. So that would be fine on those days."

"Okay, but what about the kids?"

"Well… we can just walk. Zion's been really working hard on building his strength back up after his ankle injury, so that'll help. And Kai enjoys walking."

I wish I felt as strong and assured on the inside as I'm making myself seem on the outside.

"Carina, that would be so great. Seriously, that would be perfect." He walks over and gives me a big hug and kisses my forehead. I can see the joy in his expression that hasn't been there in a while, so I tell myself I'm doing the right thing.

I don't know if it's from the conversation or the sweet hug and gesture or the reminder that despite us sleeping together, I haven't had him kiss me in months, but I can feel myself struggling to hold back my emotions any longer. I don't want him to see me bothered or upset so I move towards the door.

"Alright, well, that's sorted then. I need to get back home. I'm sure you'll fill me in on what gets discussed tomorrow. I need to double-check my schedule, but I'll message you later, letting you know if I'll be able to drop my car to you tomorrow or not."

"Sweet. Hey, don't forget," he says as he follows me to the door, then reaches over and squeezes my hair before waving me goodbye as I get into my car.

I knew in my gut that this day would come. Even on the occasions when you'd said that you would not be going back, not properly, not forever for another couple of years, I still just knew.

You'd bring that island up too often in conversation. Like it became your default reference point. As if it was the only thing you could think about that made you happy. There were some occasions where you've mentioned it so often, I wanted to scream. If I had a dollar every time you brought it up since we met, I could buy your damn airfare over. Even when I'm not with or around you, I swear to god; it feels like that island gets mentioned all the time. I'll be watching a movie or TV show and there it is. Or an infomercial trying to entice you to go on vacation. Ads for discount flights will pop up on social media.

There are times when I wish I never would have to hear about that place ever again. The rational side of me gets where you're coming from. Even the part of me that's a mom can understand that all you want to do is to be happy. If I was dealing with this regarding one of my kids, I'd tell them to live their life. Not to waste a precious moment. But selfishly, I don't want to say that to you.

I don't even think it's just that you want to go. No. That I can understand. Obviously, I've never been there, but even I can admit from how you've described it to me, it sounds like paradise.

What hurts, the thing that feels like such a blow, is the way you are finding it so easy to dismiss your life here. Your presence here. And most selfishly, me. When you say words like there's no reason for you to stay, it's hard not to take that personally. I get and understand that we never discussed, or I guess you never said that you have or had any feelings for me. Not even after I told you how I felt.

Despite that, even if you don't feel any romantic feelings towards me, let's say you only see me as a friend. One that you fuck whenever you want. Shouldn't that at least account for something? Shouldn't that at least hold even the smallest of values? I know it's not as if I have friends myself at the moment, but even back when I used to, I still cared and respected them. Even just joking that you're going to miss this or that, laughing at how in the future you'll make up for lost times or whatever.

I know in the future I will need to really sit down and acknowledge my role, my responsibilities, and my own actions. But right now, I just want to blame you.

I'd never be mean or cruel. But here in this diary I can. I can say how unfair you are being. It feels mean and completely undeserving of being a diamond.

Maybe you were telling the truth that you're more of a demon?

Anyway, my head is hurting, and my eyes are stinging from crying. I know I will need to vent and let out how I'm feeling a lot, so I don't think it'll be long until my next entry.

Until next time.

Chapter 24

Carina

For the next couple of days, I work on autopilot. From the second I wake up, I put on the mask that I share with the world around me, just going through the motions. It's been a lot harder not always having my car than I had expected. It's been next to impossible to go to my classes at the gym. I still speak to Robby daily, but my visits have become less frequent. Mainly because, yet again, it's just too tight of a window. And along with that, on the occasions we have been together, it's as if I have detached my mind from my body. I guess it's been my way of attempting to shield myself. If I give him my body, if I continue supporting him when he needs it, then he doesn't seem to suspect what's going on beneath the surface.

I am becoming good at it. The mask, the shell I put on, is my new uniform.

I'd even tried to busy myself more. On all the days where previously I would have gone over and hung out with Robby, I now have been putting more time, work, and effort into building up my portfolio for the graphic design packages I was doing on the side. I know myself. I know how my mind works. If I allowed myself to have the time and chance to think about him, think about us or what I guess used to be us or could have been us, the weaker I feel. So I have to keep myself busy. Have to preoccupy my mind to stop it from falling apart. And the only times I allow myself to crumble, be weak and vulnerable are late at night in my bed. But the more I hurt, the more my mind feels like it is withering, then the more effort I have to put into my mask.

This evening, as go to put pen to paper, I don't feel like just writing whatever random thoughts pop into my head. No. Instead, I write a poem. A poem that if I were brave, I would give to him. A poem that exposes the very depth of my soul.

Would you even notice if I was gone?
The Earth would continue to turn, flowers would bloom, and your lungs continue to take in every breath.
Yet mine has gone.
My body was only the vessel guiding me through, yet that has now also sunken down into the dark abyss.
Would you miss the care, or could that simply be replaced?
I have tried so hard to be there, to give you all

you need. I would have continued to do so, but
I was never enough.
Not for you.
You never chose me.
Being your rock, your cheerleader, your shoulder, your reminder, your sadness hurt me to see, yet in the end, it was you that hurt me.
Was I only ever a bridge for you?
To help you get by safe and secure, allowing you to go off to where you want to truly be.
Leaving me worn, withered, left behind, just expected to be fine.
How easily will you forget I ever existed?
As time goes on, could it be a simple mention of my name, or someone else's cascading curls that wrap around your mind and spark a fleeting, distant memory of the woman who was once there?
Yet I am now gone.
I ignored the signs for too long, being blind to what I was to you, until finally my place was crystal clear. I was never a real option until you knew you were done.
Now you have what you want.
You are the diamond demon, finally allowing the light to shine through the dark. I helped polish your edges and make you see your worth. I am

now the broken mermaid, wishing just once to be chosen. But I wasn't enough. The darkness that once surrounded you has swallowed me whole into the depths.

Now I can see it was never real.

You never wanted me.

Chapter 25

Robby

I'd initially thought that I could get everything sorted in a month. But tomorrow it'll be almost two months to the day that I contacted the relator and told him to put the place up for sale, yet it still isn't done. There had been no doubt in my mind that I'd already be on the beach in paradise. Surprise surprise, as it always seems to be in my life, things just never work out how I want them to. Instead, I'm sitting in the gym's office, replying to boring emails, filling out annoying paperwork, and just wishing I could be out of here.

I guess the only good thing that's been happening, is that my body is finally back to a really decent level. I've been training harder here than I think I ever have. Usually, I only do this level of intense bodywork over on the island. Yet there has been this drive, this determination running through me that previously was never there. It's also been a lot more fun as where I'm back at the gym more, my buddies have also upped theirs. Then afterward we all grab a bite to eat or go for a drink, or just sometimes come back to my place to chill. Especially since I told them I'd put the house up on the market.

I've been on the phone to the bank for almost an hour, because where the sale still hasn't gone through, I'm seriously strapped for cash. It's been damn annoying. Especially as I know as soon as it's gone through, I'll be comfortable. Knowing I have a lot of money coming my way, but right now, having basically none to do shit with has been driving me fucking insane.

Needing a break from numbers and paperwork, I grab my phone and catch up on the multiple messages that are in the Discord group that I haven't checked out in ages. That's when I see that this morning my guy, my tattoo artist, put up a post.

> I'VE HAD A CANCELLATION FOR A FULL-DAY SESSION ON WEDNESDAY. WOULD ANYONE LIKE THE SLOT? WILL DO IT AT A DISCOUNT. LET ME KNOW AS I'D PREFER TO OFFER HERE FIRST. IF IT'S NOT TAKEN BY LUNCHTIME, I'LL THEN I'LL BE POSTING ON SOCIALS. SO LET ME KNOW.

I've had nothing done in what feels like forever. He's usually booked up months in advance and since he's the only person I'll have tattoo me, I'm desperate to snatch this spot up. Before I even think any more about it, my thumbs slide across the screen, and I send him a private message.

> Dude, please tell me that cancellation spot on Wednesday is still available.

My knee bounces as I wait for his response. That would be so good if I could get him to do some work.

Deni: My man, yes, it's still available. You want me to book you in?

Praise the lord. For once, things finally work in my favor. It's as if the stars have aligned and I'm not being handed a shit hand to play with.

Sweet, yeah, book me in. I'm going to be going away soon and don't know when the next time I'll be able to get in to see you. So if we could just spend the session maybe going over some colors to make them more vibrant, as well as filling in some of the empty spaces and the bits we didn't get to finish last time, that would be great! You can just have free rein to put in whatever you want. I always trust your work and eye.

Deni: Sure. Sounds good to me. Since it's you, and I've already got a couple ideas floating around that would look sick, I'll give you an even bigger discount. So usually for the full day it's $1500, was gonna offer it for $800, but for you I'll do it for $650. I'll see you then bro.

Excitement bursts through me. I don't know what it is about having the needle on me, but I've always found it just chills me out. I spend the next hour flying through all the admin work I've gotta get done as I'm on a high about my appointment. Once that initial buzz finally wears off, I suddenly realize, shit, how the fuck am I gonna pay for it? In my main account I have what I need at the moment to get by. Because he only takes cash, there's no way I can take that off my credit card. Checking my trading accounts, all my money I've got in there is tied up in trades that there is no way I am cashing out on at the moment as they are just too good. Looking through all my options and avenues, annoyance bashes its wiry head right at me as I realize there's no way I can get that all together on such short notice. Especially where I need to be careful until the sale goes through. Just when I think I've got no options left and I'm going to have to cancel the damn thing, an idea pops into my head. Scrolling through my phone, I find Carina's contact and press the call button. It's been a while since I've chilled with her, even if we still message daily.

"Hello?" she answers.

"Hey, babe, how are you doing?"

"Not too bad. Same old, same old. How about yourself?"

"Eh, you know me. When you think things are good and going well, you're suddenly reminded not to get your hopes up."

"Oh no. What's happened?"

"I don't wanna bog you down. I feel like that's all I ever do."

"Don't be silly. How many times have I told you before, I'm always here to listen? Or to help in any way that I can."

Phew, that's what I was hoping she'd say.

"Well, I'm just in this annoying predicament. As you know, the sale still hasn't come through and everything just keeps getting pushed back. Which has been so frustrating. You know how I've told you for ages that I've been wanting to get some more pieces tatted, especially things that are important and both reminders and dedications to my mom, Michael and Joseph?"

"Yeah, I remember you telling me about that."

"I don't know if you saw in the Discord chat, but Deni

put up a post that he has a cancellation in a couple of days and I reached out and he said I could have the spot, one at an even bigger discount than usual."

"Oh, that's great. And the timing couldn't be any more perfect, especially with you leaving and how you won't have anyone else work on you."

"Yeah. I know it would be great. And I thought it would be. I got so happy and excited. Felt as though finally a blessing had fallen my way. But then when I checked shit over, I realized I can't move any cash around at the moment. Everything is tied up until I sell the house. So once again, it just feels as though I'm just destined for shit to happen to me. Like it's just so unfair that I get this chance with this random and unexpected opening, just to have to cancel because I can't work things around. Plus, I'm just gonna feel terrible that not only did he already have someone cancel on him, but now I'm going to have to do the same. It's just such poor practice, and will for sure piss him off. God knows if he'll even want to offer me another spot again in the future."

She doesn't say a word for a couple of moments. When the silence continues to stretch, I look down on my phone to see if we've accidentally been cut off.

"Babe, you still there?" I ask.

"Yeah, sorry, I was just checking something. So how much will it cost you? Because for the past couple of months I've been putting a little money aside each payday so I can save up for a big piece I wanna get done."

"He said he'd do it for six-fifty."

"Oh wow, that's a great deal for him. Well, how about this, I can give you the money I've put aside, so you don't need to cancel and lose this slot. Then when everything's gone through with the house, you can just send it back to me. Means you can get your tattoo done, get those pieces and details for your mom and brothers sorted before you leave. It'll give you something to look forward to and because I've still got a couple of months till I have enough for my piece, you'll be able to repay me way before I would even use it."

"Are you sure? That would really be amazing, babe. You'd be helping me out so much. I really don't know what I'd do without you. You're the best."

"It's okay. I can send it over later today, so it's all done."

"Thank you, babe. You really are amazing."

"I'm really not." I can hear a slight laugh. "Anyway, I've gotta get going, but I'll message you once I've sent that money over."

"Alright, brilliant. Have a good day and I'll talk to you later."

I let out a loud and relieved breath. To say I'm glad that I've got this sorted is an understatement. Knowing that I now once again have something to look forward to, I open up the notes app and start putting together a list of all the things I want to do and get done and sorted before I leave. Trying to get all my ducks in a row so when it's time to leave, I can do so with no worries or feeling like I've missed out on anything.

Chapter 26

Carina

I don't know why I keep doing this to myself. Why do I keep hoping, keep expecting there to be any sort of change? Any sudden shift in Robby's behavior? Not only is it the case that he's *not* getting nicer, kinder, or even just behaving and treating me like he used to in the beginning, he's actually getting colder. More distant.

At first I thought maybe I'm just imagining it. My own insecurities morphing into some sort of paranoia. But time and time again he'd do things, or I guess *not* do things that were just unfair.

For example, when I'd helped him to go to his tattoo appointment the night before, we'd been messaging, and I'd asked him to let me know how it's going. Come the following day and it's evening with still no word from him. I messaged, asking if it all went fine and all he could muster up was to send a thumbs up emoji. Then there was the time I'd told him I would need the car on a particular day. It wasn't for work, but where I'd been feeling so down and just shitty within myself, I wanted to give myself a little pamper day. Get a manicure and pedicure, take myself out for lunch, nothing big and fancy, just something to help boost and lift my spirits. I'd told him I'd walk over to his after school drop off and grab the car. Yet when I walked there that morning, it wasn't there. I'd messaged him to ask and see what was going on and if everything was alright.

> Shit, sorry. Completely forgot. I'd told my uncle I'd help move some stuff for him from his storage unit. We already left early this morning.

Then there was the time he'd asked me to come over because he was clearing some things in his attic and didn't know what to do with his mom's stuff. Like an idiot I went. Helped. Comforted him as he cried. Sat and endured listening to the rinse and repeat cycle of him lamenting about Thailand, which bugged me and I really struggled not to show it on my face. I then felt instantly bad when he starts telling me about it taking so long to sort this sale out, that he now thinks he won't be gone in time for his birthday. A day that on numerous times before, he has expressed how much he is dreading. Not just because of the gift issue he said he knows will trigger him, but also just feeling alone. Feeling abandoned.

I've reassured him he's not and also said if it is the case that he is still here, I can arrange for the boys to stay with my mom. Which would give him the option to stay at mine if he wishes and we can either celebrate if he wants or I can distract him, and we could do all kinds of non-birthday related things. He gave me a nod, half smile, and a thanks in response.

I feel like I've tried everything. When he's given the

impression he's needed space, that's what I've done. When he's complained about being hungry and not having eaten, I've made him food and dropped it off. I've tried everything I can think of, everything he has asked for to help. To be there. To do what is required. But as always, it never seems to be enough. And the frostiness and detached way he's been treating me has only grown more intense.

There have been moments when I have wondered, if it wasn't for the fact that he had my car, was using it every single day, would he have already cut me off? Would I already be in the trash pile, ready to be disposed of, just like the items he had boxed up and left on the curb for anyone to take?

It's reignited that deep-rooted feeling of just being completely and utterly worthless. Something my ex-husband used to relish in reminding me of daily. And I honestly never thought Robby could ever make me feel that way.

I've replayed all the interactions, messages, videos, and voice notes from the last few weeks. Thinking and going over them, I try to see if I can spot something that would tell me why he's acting like this, there are two things that keep popping up. One is that he is spending time with another woman. One he's more attracted to, one who's sexier, skinnier, who has flawless skin and isn't damaged like me. Or that something has happened. Something he isn't telling me.

Over the past six months, there have been countless times that he's shown me his vulnerable side. Broken down in tears, been so fragile that I've had to soothe him like a small child. I've seen him when he's been stressed, over-whelmed, tired and in desperate need. Yet now it's like dealing with a hard, cold brick wall. Long gone are the days of any reciprocation. Even just small and simple things like asking if I'm okay, just don't happen anymore.

I feel like I've become a burden to him. Like this annoying anchor that he can't cut away because he still needs to use my car. Something that I'd only originally offered under the presumption that he was leaving at the end of the month. That was over two months ago. And what's even more ironic is that he's never asked to extend holding on to it. I guess he just simply presumed it would be okay for him to carry on having it. Not caring about how hard it has been for me. And no, I haven't told him how hard it's been. But it wouldn't take anything for him to just ask, double check that it's still okay for him to use it.

I was surprised when I got a call from him this morning asking if I'm free to come over for a coffee. It's been some time since I've had the chance to go over there. Plus, with the frosty tension that's become the new norm from him, I guess a part of me just thought our get togethers were a thing of the past.

My fist trembles slightly as I go to knock on the door. The last time I was this nervous standing on the other side of a door was that first day I met him in person. It's crazy how much has changed since then. Yet there's a part of me that feels like I'm back at square one.

Opening the door, he greets me with a half-smile. "Come in."

My eyes note how even more barren the place feels, which is insane considering the fact that it already felt empty enough as it was beforehand.

We go into our usual pattern of small talk as he prepares our coffees, and I'm fighting to come across as normal as I can.

"So I can see you've been clearing the place even more," I point out.

Robby shuffles slightly in his seat on the couch, adjusts his sweatpants and avoiding eye contact.

"Yeah. I have," he says, taking a sip of drink before continuing, "So, I finally booked my flight. We finally got everything sorted with the buyers and the contracts have now all been signed. It's all done. I hand the keys over on the twenty-second and my flight leaves on the twenty-third."

Numbness wracks through me and I struggle to get my head around it all. Really and truly, not wanting to process and believe the words he's just said.

"I… wow. Um, okay. Do you mean the twenty-third as in five days?" I ask, the bewilderment evident in my voice.

He chuckles. "No. Next month. So in five weeks. Which really makes everything work out perfectly. It allows me to get all my affairs in order and settled. Like you said, I've already been clearing out the stuff here, so I'll get that finished in no time. Plus, I'll be able to prepare the gym for when I'm gone and see and spend time with all the people I'm gonna miss."

Looking down at the cup in my hand, I quickly blink back the tears I can feel stinging my eyes. I take a couple of deep breaths before clearing my throat.

"Well then, I'm sure you're super excited. You now have an official countdown. Maybe you should download one of those apps where it tells you how many days, minutes, and seconds. That way, if you're having a bad moment or a bad day, you can just look and see how much longer you have left, then it'll be easier to not be as bothered since you'll know to the second how long it is until your back in paradise." I waffle on as I try to preoccupy my mind.

I bet he hasn't even picked up on the peculiar vibe of my behavior. He never really has.

"Yeah, I guess. Though it's not that big of a deal. Besides, I'll still be staying in contact with everyone."

He says that with such nonchalance. And I almost have to laugh that he even believes such a thing. Yes, I'm sure he will still be speaking to members of his family, his close friends, guys from the gym and such. But given everything, the shift in his demeanour, the way he has been distancing himself and pushed me away already, he can't honestly expect me to believe that he's still going to stay in contact with me. No. Maybe if things were how they used to be, like back when he would share every little thing he did in a day, what he ate, how he was feeling, what things were going on in his life, if we were having this conversation back then, perhaps I'd believe it.

Even just looking at how the sale went through and he'd booked his flight, I doubt all this happened this morning. I wouldn't be surprised if this all went down in the last few weeks. It would kinda explain things. He's clearly been sitting on this, and because he doesn't see me as relevant, because I'm not someone close to him or hold any form of importance, that's why I'm only finding it all out now.

I'm pretty subdued and quiet for the rest of my visit. Really struggling not to show just how sad I feel that the official countdown is on. That, as much as I knew this was going to be happening eventually, I still can't believe it's real.

For the first time, when it's time for me to leave and I see the heavy downpour outside, I ask him to drive me home. If this were a movie, I would just walk back in the rain and let the raindrops join my tears. But this is reality. I just want to get out of here, wrap up, and hide myself away.

At least until I need to get the boys. On the drive back I think he tries to lift my spirits, letting me know that when he is gone, he'll send postcards from the different islands, pictures of sunsets and sunrises, as well as pictures of cups of coffee. So even though we'll be thousands of miles apart, if he sends me one and I send him one, it'll be as if we are having one together. And honestly, I don't think I've heard anything that sounds sadder in my life.

The day has come. I should have prepared myself better. It was careless of me not to. All I can think of is if I'm struggling so much right now when it's just the case that you told me, you gave me the date, how the fuck am I going to be on the day you fly?

I keep wondering to myself, what exactly is it I'm going to miss? Because logically, the way things have been recently, you've not been nice. Not shown kindness or warmth or anything endearing. You've been the polar opposite. So surely I shouldn't be feeling sad that soon I won't have someone treating me this way any longer?

However, I know it's more than that. I know the sorrow isn't for what's been going on recently. It's for the past.

For how you stumbled into my life at a time I thought no one would. The sorrow that I will no longer have someone. Someone close by that I can turn to. That can be a sounding board for my thoughts, even if they are just meaningless points I wish to share.

It's the loss of the comfort I felt. The way I could shut off the physical comfort of simple human touch. Whether or not that be intimate. Because when you've gone without for such a long period, you crave it more than ever.

For the first time in so long, I didn't feel alone. No longer felt like I was trapped in a deserted wasteland with no one by my side. That emptiness, that lonely wall that had barricaded me for years, had finally been breached. You'd bulldozed it down, and I stupidly thought I was free.

I guess the thing that's the hardest is that what I will miss the most is, while you were still here, I could be naive enough to believe that somehow, someday things could be different. If you were still around, still nearby, then there was still hope.

Hope that I could sway you. As if there would still be the time and opportunity to shift this situationship we were in into something more. The logical side of my brain knows just how stupid that is. Because if you'd have ever wanted more, then you'd have done so.

But that's the thing with emotions. They rarely make sense. Usually staying in the irrational and delusional part of your brain. If this were happening to anyone else, god I would be screaming at them to get a grip, get rid, and just move on. However, it's always so much easier being on the outside looking in.

I know things are going to get harder and more difficult for me before they eventually get better. Logically I know that. I also know that at some point I will be fine. I will get through it. But right now? Right now, I just don't want to. I want to bury my head in the sand and not face any of it.

Because my eyes are already stinging from crying. I don't need them burning anymore.

Until next time.

Chapter 27

Robby

These last few weeks have been pretty wild as I've been sorting out all the shit I need to do and going on a little farewell tour, spending as much time as I can with those that have really been there for me and know deep down I'll miss. It's also probably the most that I've drunk in a long time. I guess I just can't help it when the guys just enjoy my wild antics when I drink. Although I always hate how shitty and depressed I feel the day after. But that's where good old reliable Carina comes in. She and her body are always the perfect hangover cure. Plus the treats and food she always brings sure as hell help too.

I can't believe today is my birthday and I'm still actually here. Not too long ago, I honestly would have thought I'd be celebrating my birthday thousands of miles away, under the warm tropical sun with the beautiful beach just a stone's throw away. As opposed to here in the cold, dreary weather.

The sale of the house finally went through and knowing it will be the last time I'll be hosting anything in this place,

I've decided to do a birthday/leaving drinks mashup. I don't know who was more surprised, me or my buddies since everyone knows how much I usually dislike acknowledging, let alone celebrating my birthday. But I guess this is my way of turning a new leaf. Or as Carina has been harping on for months, celebrating myself and who I am. Not feeling sad and depressed about all the things I don't have or the memories I won't be making with my mom and brothers.

I'd stopped at her place yesterday to pick up the present she'd gotten me as she said it was too big and difficult for her to walk over and carry. When she came to the door with this huge parcel, I had to remind her I've already packed my suitcases, and I've hardly got much room left in my carry on, to which she laughed and said it won't be a problem. That only heightened my curiosity more. And even though I knew I should have waited until today to open them, I couldn't help myself. So when I got back from hers, I opened it.

Boy, could I not stop laughing. She'd put together a present like pass the parcel. The first layer had a pouch of my favorite M&M's. The next a bag of chocolate raisins. Then there was my favorite tooth-floss, a custom T-shirt, a Muay Thai t-shirt, a Muay Thai hoodie, these really cool training shorts and I can't believe how much the dragon print on it looks like the tattoo on my chest. There was a pack of socks and boxers with a note on it.

I know this doesn't replace or account for who you should have been getting these from, but I didn't want you to have a year without them

And right at the center, the last and final present was this cute little stuffed monkey about the size of my hand. There was also a note attached to it, as well as another thick envelope.

When I read the note on the monkey, I could feel my cheeks warm slightly.

I know you'll probably think this is silly, but if there are moments when you're really down or you feel you're all alone, just grab a hold of this cute guy. Talk to him, share what's bothering you. He'll listen, I promise lol. And he can remind you that there's always someone who cares.

What really got my attention was the thick envelope. On the front, written in black sharpie were the words

DO NOT OPEN UNTIL ON THE PLANE.

Turning it over on the back, there was another message.

If you've ever had a shred of care for me, promise me you won't open this until you're sitting on the plane. C x

My initial reaction was to open the damn thing as I really wanted to see what's inside. But where I couldn't control myself with waiting to open my birthday present, I feel like the least I can do is respect her wishes. Just before everyone gets here, I finally look at my phone, which has been going off nonstop all morning with people sending birthday messages and asking about tonight. That's when I see a message from Carina.

> Happy birthday to you, happy birthday to you, happy birthday to Robbbbbyyy, happy birthday to you. Wishing the Diamond Demon a very happy birthday. I hope you're having an amazing day. I know you're spending it with the ones you love and hopefully eating all your favorite foods, opening lots of presents and I have a feeling you'll also be having several drinks to toast. We may have only been in each other's lives for 7 months, but I know for a fact that there is no one more deserving of having a blessed and special day as much as you. Celebrate being the man that you are. Sending you best wishes, happy birthday babe xx

Aww, she's sweet.

> Thank you so much. I opened your presents. They're great. Love the Muay Thai t-shirts and hoodie. The shorts are amazing – I love them, yes, a little small but still ok. And they have a dragon with an orb on it! So cool!! Thank you so much 😊

The loud pounding on the front door, along with William's voice blaring me to open up, has me rolling my eyes and laughing at his impatience. Stuffing my phone in my pocket, I make my way to the front door.

"Now you boys ready to get this party started?"

Chapter 28

Carina

"Mom, Dad said we have to see him tomorrow and stay the night, but Kai and I don't want to. Can you tell him we've got plans or something? I just don't want him to shout at me," Zion says sombrely.

Putting the last plate in the dishwasher before turning it on, I turn to face him. My baby has grown so much. Not only as he nears six feet, but equally emotionally. He may be fourteen, but to me he will always be my baby. My first born. And seeing the anguish on his face about the fact that neither he nor his brother want to see their dad absolutely breaks me. I know how hard this all is for him. Especially as he gets older. Zion, by nature, has the biggest heart and is the most caring and loving boy. Always wanting to see the best in people and protecting those that can't protect themselves.

So I can only imagine how difficult it must be for him. Like there is a war within himself. One side telling him he should and has to see his dad, love him, care for him. But then the other side, the side that grows and matures every single day, has grown to recognize just how toxic my ex-husband Andrew is. The way he flits in and out of their lives. Often, going weeks and months between having contact and even less frequently are the times he sees them.

"Of course, I'll tell him. I'll come up with something. Don't worry. Is there anything you would like to do instead?"

"Well… Henry asked if I wanted to stay the night at his place. His mom and dad brought a huge new TV, and they said I could come over because they're doing a movie marathon."

I smile as I watch the excitement shine brightly in his eyes. Now I understand even more why he doesn't want to stay at his dad's.

"Sure. That's fine."

"Aww, thanks, Mom. You're the best." He engulfs me in the biggest hug, and I have to fight back the tears.

Damn, why am I just so emotional at the moment? Every little thing is setting me off. Not just at home, also at work. It's like my eyes have just turned into faucets that I just can't shut off. Well, I guess one way to stop feeling sad and emotional right now is giving my ex-husband a call. That's always a quick-fire way to guarantee to be filled with annoyance and frustration instead of sad and depressed tears.

A shudder runs through me, just like it always does any time I have to speak to him.

"What do you want?" he mutters as he picks up.

Even just the sound of his voice grates me. "Well, hello to you too, Andrew. Don't worry, I'll keep this short. I was just calling to let you know the boys won't be able to come and see you tomorrow. Kai has an assessment straight after school and after that, both boys have dentist appointments. Because I hadn't known you'd be wanting to have them, that's why I'd booked things all in one go as its easier for me, plus you had mentioned nothing to me about having them, anyway. So yeah, we will have to reschedule."

"Oh, please, you're so full of shit. Just get them to go to the dentist another time. It's not like it's a big deal. Plus, can't you just go to Kai's assessment without him?"

Taking a deep breath through my nose, I roll my eyes at his idiotic request.

"No. I can't rearrange it. Of course it's important. Just because you don't like to go to the dentist regularly, doesn't mean the boys have to follow suit. And obviously I can't go to his assessment without him. He is the one getting assessed. So it wouldn't exactly work without him there."

It takes everything within me not to shout and tell him to piss off. God, he's so oblivious to how everything works.

"Fuck off. You can get off your pathetic high horse. Surely by now you know you never have and never will be better than me. Well, this is all your fault. Thanks for fucking up my quality time I should have been having with my boys, you worthless piece of shit," he screams down the phone before hanging up.

Holding onto the kitchen counter, I hang my head between my arms and breathe deeply. You'd think after all these years he would at least come up with some new insults instead of spewing the same garbage he has for over a decade. But the old words still hurt.

I'd told Robby I was needing to use the car this morning since I had just one call out that I needed to go to. He'd said it was fine and that if I'm free, I should knock when I'm done and we could chill for a bit. That surprised me a little, as I've hardly seen him. We've not even been messaging every day like we used to. So I for sure wasn't expecting an invitation over. I throw a sweatshirt on over my uniform and get out of the car. It's funny as the second I knock on the door is the moment I realize this is the first time I'm arriving with nothing for him. Before, I'd have felt guilty, but right now I can't even bring myself to be annoyed about it. He opens the door and has the biggest smile on his face.

"Hey, come on in," he says before wrapping me in a warm and affectionate hug, which takes me by surprise.

We do the usual coffee, catch up, and putting something on the TV. It doesn't go unnoticed, the way he constantly has some sort of physical contact with me. Whether that's him holding my hand or stroking my knee. It's such a conflicting feeling as the warmth and weight of his hand on me feels so good, so right. At the same time, it stands out so glaringly given how many weeks I've been craving it. And the whole time his mood stays happy and positive. As I shift in my seat, he reaches his hand behind me and pulls me into his embrace as we continue watching. It's weird. The more he does it, the more I relax and just enjoy the company. It feels like how it used to be. Just simple, nice, and just comforting enough for me to really just unwind and let my hair down. At one point, he gets a phone call from his friend. Usually he takes it in the other room and chats there. But today he stays sitting beside me, rubbing my leg and I try to just listen to the show and not eavesdrop on his conversation. I go to cover my mouth when a hilarious bit happens, and he pulls it away.

"What happened? I missed that."

Looking over, I see he still has the phone to his ear, but he's directing the question at me. Why? I try to mouth to him what the joke was, but he just shakes his head and smiles.

"I can't make out what you're saying. Just speak up," he says with a laugh.

What the hell is going on? If I speak up, then his friend for sure will hear me. This is so bizarre. He's kept me so separate from his friends, from the other part of his life, so why now suddenly the change?

"It won't be funny if I just tell it back. You'll have to rewatch it," I say in a hushed tone as I shake my head.

Seemingly thinking I'm in a playful mood, instead of reaching for the remote to rewind it, he tickles me instead. Making me scream out with laughter and he knows just how unbelievably ticklish I am. I vaguely hear him say he needs to go, then hangs up. He continues his relentless tickles until he has me pleading.

"Please… please… I'm begging you. Stop. Please stop," I splutter.

"Alright fine. I guess I'll be nice and stop."

And he does. For the rest of the time that I'm there, he just carries on being nice and sweet. Just as I'm saying my goodbyes, I spot something in the corner of my eye. I recognize it instantly. I keep a straight face and give nothing away as I head out.

As I walk back home, all I can think about is how everything suddenly now makes sense. He's opened his leaving present. That's got to be it. There is no other explanation for it. It's the only thing that makes sense.

He opened the envelope.

Fuck. Fuck. Fuck.

It's funny, because I'd intentionally stayed quiet. Felt I was doing the right thing, giving you space. Also hoping and wondering if you would reach out. And to my surprise, you did.

Today was such a great day. No stress, no fuss or frustration. I got a stitch from how much I was laughing. The whole thing, the entire experience of when I was at yours today made me think of how you know when someone is about to die because of an illness or something? They often have a day or an hour or a small period where they're just like their old self. I think it's called their sunshine day. That's what today felt like.

I don't know if I fully believe all the little puzzle pieces I was waiting for and hoping to be answered were answered. My heart wants to say yes, my brain says maybe, my gut says possibly. I know I won't get the things I'm hoping for. No payback, no gifts, no kisses, no thanks, no I'm sorry, and no letter in response. It's going to be hard accepting I won't get any of them, but I know one day it will be ok. I will get through it.

It won't be today, or tomorrow, or likely for some time. But one day. I have to believe that. Because if I don't, then that's just too terrifying.

Everything right now is telling me you opened your gift. That you are now completely aware of what's inside. Why else would today have been the way it was? There's such a big part of me that is still being stupid enough to hold on to the hope that you didn't. That you actually respected my wishes, that you did that because even if it's in the deepest recesses of your soul, you care. Even just a little.

If you opened it, then obviously there is nothing I can do. It's out there now. It is what it is. And I guess we will see how you are this week as you navigate your last few days here.

For my sake, for me, I really hope you didn't.

Until next time.

Chapter 29

Carina

I've been keeping myself as busy as I can in these last days before Robby leaves. One thing that was kinda funny is that as he was clearing and getting rid of everything in his house, he's given me a bunch of stuff. Now of course I appreciate them, especially when it's items that can replace things I have that are broken or on their way out. But the way in which he seems so happy and proud about it, like he's done some helpful and thoughtful deed. Making a point of it, almost as if he's expecting me to be grateful. Like seriously, I appreciate it and all, but he hasn't gone out to the shops and purchased these for me.

Whatever I didn't take, he ended up taking to the dump. He'd also stupidly not thought about the fact that he has to hand over the keys on Friday morning, and his flight wasn't until Saturday early afternoon. Leaving him with no place to say. I was lucky enough to arrange it so my mom collects the boys from school and will then take them back to hers for a sleepover. So Robby can stay at mine on his last night, then on Saturday morning I'll drive him to the train station, since that'll be the quickest way for him to get to the airport.

There is no denying it, this week my emotions have been absolutely all over the place. I get that he's busy doing all the final prep and all, but it was really hard to hear when he explained that he's doing his individual and proper goodbyes to everyone in his life. That he wants to spend this last quality time with those that he is closest to and who mean the most to him. So obviously after hearing that and then basically not seeing him at all, that's been really hard for me to take.

It hurts.

There honestly is no clearer way for him to point out what he truly thinks and feels about me.

I've got to the point that there's a part of me that's relieved that he's leaving. Not because I wish him gone or anything like that. I think it's more the case that for me, within myself, I don't think I could carry on like this for much longer.

As someone who will always find fault within myself, someone who has spent countless years nitpicking every little thing about me and always believing I deserve the worst and that a happy ever after is just not for me, I've gotten to the point now that I know I deserve better. I don't deserve to be treated like this. I might not be brave enough to stand up for myself and make it clear that I do, but within, that little voice in my head has finally waved the white flag and said it is now time.

This thing, this dynamic, this situationship between Robby and me has to stop. Because if I had to continue on like this, just being so disregarded, so disrespected, and used for his pleasure, his convenience, for him to pick up and toss when it suits him, it would break me to a point of no return. If it went on any longer, I don't think I'd ever, even years down the line, feel safe or comfortable to open myself up or trust a man ever again.

After getting the boys ready and taking them to school, I head back home and give the house a blitz from top to bottom. Since Robby's using the car for the last load before handing the keys over and I can't be bothered to walk to the store, I order a few groceries to get delivered. It isn't much, a bunch of snacks and things to pick on.

He hasn't given me an exact timeline of how the day's going. All I know is that he'll drop off his suitcases sometime soon. Then he mentioned he was going to grab some lunch with his uncle and maybe have a drink to toast him farewell. Then apparently, that's when I'd get a couple of hours with him before we settle in for the night.

I guess a part of me should feel happy that he's at least giving me some time at all. Even if it's last minute. But again, there's no point in dwelling on all that right now.

He drops his cases and rucksack off as he does a flyby visit, not even staying long enough for a coffee or glass of water. When I see the emotion on his face, my heart softens a little as it feels like for the first time, reality is finally sinking in for him. The redness around his eyes shows that he's already cried today, so I just stay quiet, giving him a hug and letting him know to just keep me posted. Leaving the cases in the hallway, I move his rucksack and leave it on the couch, as there's no way I'm risking anything happening to his passport or important documents.

A couple of hours go by, and I decide to have a nice long soak in the bath. Once my hands and feet prune, I finally get out and slip into something comfy.

My stomach rumbles as I haven't eaten yet today, but I don't wanna make anything since I still don't know if he's maybe wanting us to have takeout or me warm something I already have in the fridge. So I guess an apple will just have to do for now. Lazing on the couch, I put a new series on. I get through a couple of episodes, noting that it's gone from afternoon to early evening and there is still no word from Robby. Eventually, my phone goes off with a message.

> Heya, so after my uncle left, I got a message from one of my buddies. So having a beer with him. Started feeling anxious now, like I've forgotten something, or that I'll miss my train or my flight. It's probably just a mixture of leaving and the house being done and just everything that's gone on today.

I'm not super surprised that he's still out. I get it. I feel like it's his own little way of putting off facing reality. And one thing I know about Robby Black is that as much as he claims he's a realist and doesn't dwell on things, that's not the case whatsoever. His next messages come through before I've replied to the first.

> Well, that's life I guess. Things happen we have no control over.

I should double check the train times for tomorrow.

I just wanted to text you because you've been so fucking amazing to me these last 7 months. And I'm just a bit overwhelmed with gratitude to be honest. Cried a couple of times today. Only a little to myself.

Though right now that could be the booze

Oh, this man. I swear he makes me want to hug him and choke him at the same time. How does he finally say something nice, something sweet and vulnerable to me after so long of coldness and disassociation, then *bam*, he just has to add in that he's clearly under the influence?

What time do you need to be at the airport? I'll check train times, etc. I PROMISE you, I will make sure you don't miss your flight. Okay?

Okay

I would say maybe it would be best not to have too late of one tonight because you don't want to be feeling rough on your long-haul flight tomorrow. Also, where you've had a drink, or a couple at a guess, I think it would be best for me to get a taxi and pick up the car. Then, a little later, you can message me where you are, and I'll come and pick you up. Again, I'm not trying to be annoying, but I said I'd make sure I'd get you to the airport on time.

Okay. Need to leave tomorrow morning at around 10ish I think to get to the airport on time.

He then drops me a pin of where I'm guessing he parked the car.

By the time I drive back home, it's just past eight o'clock. I push aside the realization that he isn't likely going to be spending any time with me, not properly at least, before he leaves. I blink back the tears that are desperate to fall, wrap myself in the blanket on the couch, and carry on watching my show. As one episode rolls into the next and there still is no word from Robby, my sadness turns to frustration, then annoyance, then anger. This is really pissing me off; it's eleven-thirty.

You having a good time?

I literally just got back to my buddy's house. I've told him I will be getting picked up soon. He lives on Berwick street.

Alright, I'll look that up. What time are you wanting me to leave?

I honestly want to throw my phone across the room as half an hour passes and there's still no response from him.

Alright, Mr. Demon. I'm sticking to my end of the bargain and making sure tomorrow goes smoothly and I'm also going to make sure you get some sleep. So I will leave to pick you up in ten minutes. I know you probably think I'm being mean and a party-pooper, but it's for the best. You can kick up a fuss and complain all you want once you're in the car and inside my house.

This time I don't wait for a response. I put my shoes on, grab my keys, and make my way to the road he told me his friend lives on.

Following the navigation, I can see I'm about two minutes away when he calls.

"I'm at my buddies," he slurs.

"Cool, what's his door number?"

"52, but you don't need to leave yet. I'll… I'll book a taxi in about twenty minutes."

"Listen, I'm already in the car and about one minute away. It's cold and I really don't want to be sitting in the car outside for ages. So I'll see you shortly."

"Wait… but…"

In the background, I hear a deep voice.

"Listen to her, Robby. It's late."

A minute later, I'm parked out front of the apartment complex.

I'm outside.

He takes another fifteen minutes before he stumbles out the door.

Great.

I get him in the car and head back home.

Soon after we get back, he runs to the toilet and pukes his guts up. Oh, how lucky am I? This wasn't exactly the evening I envisioned. Stripping him down, I get him into the shower before making him brush his teeth and down three pints of water.

Suddenly he seems to have an appetite because he demolishes three bags of snacks. We settle in and I put on his favorite stand-up comedian to lighten the mood.

"Carina, I wanna ask something."

"Um, okay."

"This is our last night. And I was wondering, would you pee on me?"

I choke on my tongue as those are honestly the last words I'd have imagined coming out of his mouth.

"I beg your pardon? Did you just…? Did you just ask me to *pee* on you?"

He looks over at me with his slightly bleary eyes and has the audacity to look perplexed at my question.

"Yes. That's what I asked. I don't see how that's a big deal. I want you to pee on me."

I am completely and utterly speechless. My mouth opens and closes like a fish as I try to form words, but nothing comes out.

"I don't know if this is just you being emotional, or drunk, or god knows what. But for the fact that this is the first time you've ever asked anything like this of me, I'm going to give you a pass and just put it down to everything that's happened today."

"So is that a no then?" he asks, a deep frown creasing his mouth.

It's almost comical, the way he's looking at me with puppy dog eyes. "It's a no, Robby."

"Can I at least fuck you properly, then?"

For the first time today, he suddenly seems more awake.

"Yes. But not down here. It's already one in the morning, so let's head upstairs."

He follows me up like an obedient pup and it takes everything within me not to burst out laughing.

We do end up having sex. And ironically, it's probably the hottest it has ever been. Once both our bodies are spent, I quickly shower, then join him in bed. As I switch off the lights, I'm taken aback when tears silently roll down my cheeks. It's as if my body has suddenly realized that this is it.

"Are you crying?" he asks, lying beside me in the pitch black.

"No."

He wraps his arms around me, pulling me to his chest. "Are you pregnant?"

"What?" I exclaim.

"I was wondering, could there be any chance you're pregnant?"

"What on earth makes you say that? And I swear to god if you say anything about my body I will kick you out and set your passport on fire."

"No. I was thinking about it the other day. And I thought *imagine if she was pregnant.* And I kept thinking about it. Over and over. What it would mean and all that."

I cannot believe he just said that. Or that he even thought about it. Seriously? Does he really think if I would be pregnant, that I wouldn't tell him? Surely he can't be stupid enough to think I'd keep something like that secret and stay quiet as I drop him off, as he goes and lives his ideal life, while I'm left to raise his baby, right? The man is certifiably insane. Just as I go to give him a piece of my mind about his stupid comment, I hear his light snoring.

Emotionally, I'm exhausted. Physically, just as much, yet I take forever to fall asleep. Twice that night, he wakes me up and we have sex again. However, both of those times are slow, soft, tender, and intimate. Which only makes me cry myself to sleep.

The loud blaring ring of the alarm I set, wakes me. I struggle to get myself out of bed. Not just because I think I only slept about two hours, but because I know the time has finally come.

It's all over now.

Chapter 30

Carina

Neither Robby or I have the energy to muster any kind of positive atmosphere. For me, I know it's because I feel like I'm currently holding on by a thread. I'm struggling more and more not to just completely fall apart. He steps out of the shower and gives me the saddest of smiles. I bet he's regretting drinking as much as he did last night. This feels so weird. A mix of a dream and some weird trip after taking mushrooms. There is so much emotion that fills the air.

Wanting to bring the mood up even in the slightest way, I help him as he struggles to repack his toiletry bag.

"You must be starving. How about I make you something?"

"Yeah, that would be great. Thank you."

I busy myself with cooking his breakfast and making us each a cup of coffee.

"Would it be okay if I went out and smoked the last of this in your garden?" he asks, popping his head into the kitchen.

"Yeah, that's fine. When you're finished, just leave the blunt on the brick wall at the end."

I watch him through the kitchen window as I cook. On several occasions, he looks up at the sky, then quickly wipes his cheeks. This is so hard to watch. Everything inside of me is screaming to go out to him, hug him, comfort him. But I know I can't. It's not what he needs. Likely not what he wants, either. All of this is his choice. His decisions. His need and desire to move back.

Just like how I can't give him what he wants or needs regarding any kind of future, I can't comfort and solace him right now. He needs to do it alone.

My tummy is a knotted mess, so I only plate up one portion of breakfast and knock on the window, showing him it's ready. Turning the stereo on to play some chilled music in the background, he eats and tells me about his flight and transfer. We both keep the conversation light and easy, never wanting to get into anything too deep. When my next alarm goes off, I know that it's time to leave.

After checking that he's got everything, we load up the car. He'd mentioned this morning that he wanted to drive by his old house, as he hadn't had time to say thanks and goodbye to his neighbour yesterday before he handed the keys over, so I drive him there.

Damn, I don't know how much longer I can keep these tears at bay. He also asks if he can dash into the store to grab something. As he runs in, I pant out a few breaths, doing everything in my power to just hold on. Just a little longer. Getting back in the car, I see him grab a couple of bottles of water. Putting the car into gear, I merge into the traffic and head to the train station.

Pulling up, I look at the dashboard and see he has ten

minutes until his train leaves. Sitting in silence, I watch the drops of rain as they hit the windscreen. My throat tightens and I don't dare move a muscle.

"Carina. Look at me."

I shake my head because I know the second I do, I will fall apart.

"Please. Please look at me," he says before stroking my coils.

Turning my head, I keep my eyes focused on his neck. With the tips of his fingers, he gently nudges my head up. The second my eyes connect with his, the first tears begin to fall.

"Don't cry. There's no need for you to cry." Using his thumbs to wipe away my tears, he tries to keep them at bay but there's no use. They just won't stop. "Shhh, you don't need to cry. We will still talk. And it's not as if I won't ever see you again."

"We both know that isn't true, Robby. As much as I wish that wasn't the case. We both know the truth."

For a fleeting second, I see a spark of hesitation on his face. As if he genuinely thought we would still, in some shape or form, be in each other's lives.

Leaning forward, he rests his forehead against mine before pulling back and kissing the top of my head. I hear the deep intake of his breath. Looking over at the dashboard, I see it's time for him to go.

"Your train will be here in a minute." I disentangle myself from him and my seatbelt, then step out of the car to lift his cases from the trunk.

"Promise me you'll take care of yourself. Live your life, enjoy the moments, but when you have those hard times, please just remember to look after yourself." My voice is just above a whisper, but I know he can hear every word.

"I will. I promise. I'll call you once I'm all checked in."

Wrapping his arms around me, he gives me a big hug as I cry against his chest.

I wait until he disappears into the station before getting back into the car. Closing the door, I finally let it all out. My body shakes as the sounds of my sobs fill the car. Needing to get home and climb under the duvet, I wipe my eyes and somehow manage to drive back.

Not long after I walk through the front door, Robby calls.

"Oh, please don't say you forgot something important?"

"No... no... I," he sobs.

"Robby, what's happened?"

"Remember, I was telling you about my friend out there, the guy that was letting me keep clothes and other belongings at his house while I came back?"

"Yeah."

"I just messaged him, letting him know I'm on the way to the airport and his wife called to tell me he passed away three days ago," he sobs.

"Oh, Robby. I'm so sorry."

We stay on the phone for several minutes and I get him to do some breathing exercises until finally he's able to pull himself together.

"I'm so tired. I'm scared I'm gonna fall asleep on the train."

"When I checked the times, it said you should arrive at the airport at eleven forty-five. Make sure your phone is on loud, and I'll keep calling it so you're awake and get off at your stop."

"Thank you."

I go to the bathroom and wash my face. My eyes are swollen and red and I look awful.

Monitoring the time, I make sure to call him back. He's awake. He lets me know he's going to call me once he's through security and on his way to the gate.

I don't realize for how long I sit on my bedroom floor staring at the wall until my phone rings.

"My suitcases were over, but luckily they didn't charge me. I'm guessing the flight isn't full. Was also lucky that there were no issues with my derma cream when I went through security. Decided to treat myself to a new pair of sunglasses at duty free and now I'm waiting for them to call my gate number, drinking the weirdest tasting coffee. But you did it. You promised to make sure I got here. And look, here I am."

The smallest smile briefly appears on my face. We then spend the next twenty minutes talking on the phone in what has to be one of the nicest calls we've ever had. It's silly, it's sweet, we both laugh. This feels like the perfect goodbye. Neither of us have weapons drawn, our guards are down, and it just feels like I always wished it had.

"Alright. They're calling my flight. And surprise surprise, it looks like my gate is the damn furthest one away."

"Check you've got your bag and passport and let me know if you're stuck with good or bad seats."

"Will do."

I hope you're able to get some sleep and can be semi comfortable on your flight. You're allowed to open the envelope. That might help keep you distracted during takeoff. Anyway, I really wish you all the best. You deserve it. You deserve the world. Never forget that as much as you might say I don't know you and I'm irrelevant and jabber on and don't know shit lol, I DO know that to your core, you're a great guy. Never EVER forget that. You were the first person who made me feel like I wasn't alone, and I will forever be grateful and appreciate you for even just giving me the time of day, as I know I'm nothing special and have nothing to offer, so it meant even more that you did. And if you ever have moments or days when you're struggling, you know you can always reach out. You might hate me and never want to speak to me again after you open the letter but just remember there is always someone that cares for you, respects you, and wants the best for you. You'll always be the Diamond Demon 💎😈🩶 xx

A few minutes later, he sends a video of himself and a half empty aircraft.

Perfect for your flight!

Thanks for your message. And you're not 'nothing special.' Gonna wait till after take-off and will read the letter! And I won't hate you hahahaha

You don't know that yet. You still might. I guess I'll know if you do, if you still reach out after you land 😉

I let out a deep groaning breath. Part of me still thinks he already opened it prior to now. But there's still a part that hopes he respected my wishes. Which means any moment now he'll be doing it.

Inside the main envelope, there is a bookmark with his initials engraved on it, as well as some Thai Baht. I also got him a small handmade Buddhist string bracelet. He'd shown me pictures ages ago where he'd had one similar to that but lost it. So I found one online and got him a new one. Then there is the main thing. Another envelope.

Inside that is a handwritten letter. A letter I wrote months ago and what's funny is if things had changed, I'd never have even given it to him. I'm sure every woman would have screamed at me not to give it to him. Probably saying it's sad and pathetic and desperate if I do. But even though I'd written it for him to read, I actually did it for myself.

My phone pings and I expect it to be my mom, but it's Robby.

Wow. Finished it. Thank you. I will keep it.

And that was it.

It's over.

The Letter

Now I hope you have followed my instructions and are only reading this either on the plane or once you're there. If you're reading this before, then you really are a naughty boy that you couldn't grant me my last wish.

I'm going to pre-emptively warn you that this isn't going to be a quick little note, so be warned, and you might want to put your glasses on to handle my awful writing.

It's funny because this isn't the first time I've written something to you. It was after I told you about my feelings and knew you didn't feel the same when I wanted to get something out and ended up writing a poem. I needed to get my feelings out in a way that was safest for me to feel the least rejected.

I know the thing I should say is I hope you have a wonderful and amazing time in your new life out in Thailand. And yes, I wish that for you. But for the first time since we met, I'm going to be selfish in our little dynamic. I'm going to say things I know I shouldn't but have wanted to. I guess you could say this letter is more something for me than it is for you. Alas, on this occasion, you'll have to let me have this.

When we first connected, we were messaging frequently, but then you disappeared, and I thought I would never hear from you again. So, I was a little surprised when you messaged again months later. I'll be honest, at first I only replied because I was curious about why you disappeared like a ghost.

I had my guard up as my own insecurities slithered through me. But once we started talking again and you explained the things you were going through, I remember all I wanted to do was give you the biggest hug. I really appreciated the raw honesty and vulnerability you showed. To me, it showed what a true and real man you are.

I remember how nervous I was when I said I'd bring you some food and that'd essentially be the first time we met in person. I'd asked you if you are sure you want to meet me, and you took that the wrong way and said, "Fine, you clearly don't want to come over." I was taken aback as it came out of nowhere and again there was a part of me wondering if this was your way of saying you didn't want to see me. Then when I turned up at your office, I was shaking like a leaf, worried you'd take the bag then shut the door in my face.

Luckily for me, you didn't do that. And so began my regular visits.

The more time we spent together, the more I realized how alone I had previously felt. I'd get excited when I'd get a message asking if I wanted to come over. I suddenly didn't feel alone. But in the same breath, I felt myself struggling with feelings I tried to suppress that continued to grow.

What's ironic, and I actually had to look back on our earliest conversations was when we first started talking, you never actually said you were planning on moving back to Thailand. At least not in the near future. If you did, I don't think I'd have started coming around. You actually said in a couple of years.

Now I'm not holding this against you, and

I get that your circumstances played a part in wanting to leave, but you have to understand it felt like a punch to the gut. And in essence, it was the beginning of the seesaw and conflicting points you would often make.

I get that because of things happening in your life, you wouldn't want to jump into anything. You stated as much, and I respected that. I said you don't need to put me in a category, and I meant it. But that wasn't indefinitely. And that's where things started fucking up for me.

As time went on, I did my best to take things how you wanted and needed. I tried to help by making sure you had food, had weed if you needed it, lent you money, insured you on my car so you didn't have to deal with the stress of yours. I tried my best to make things good for you. I wanted to treat you, make you feel cared for, cherished, and appreciated as you deserve it. Then it became something I felt I needed to do to keep you around.

There was a time I was having a bad day, and you told me to write a gratitude list and when I struggled with things to come up with, you said I should put down that I was in a position to help you out. What's ironic is sometimes I have gone without something because I felt you needed it more.

I think the point when I accepted that you didn't think highly of me was once I realized you'd only talk sweetly when asking for something. You'd add words like babe and kisses to messages on no other occasion than when you'd ask for something.

And please don't take this as me criticizing you. That 100% falls on me. I knew what you were doing, but I was just so desperate to get even the smallest crumbs I would take anything you would give me.

Now here's the bit that gets hard, but if you ever had even a sliver of care or respect for me, I'm begging you to please read this.

I understood and accepted you'd never want a relationship with me. But it still doesn't mean it hasn't been a hard pill for me to swallow. I felt like I was giving you all the things a partner should, way more than just friends would give one another. I'd try to boost you when you were down, be there to support you either with company, financially, emotionally, or any way you'd want.

You got everything out of me.

And I gladly gave it. Doesn't mean it

wasn't difficult that you wouldn't even want to kiss me. Or when I'd say I was down and ask to see you, to just get a hug.

You know earlier I mentioned I wrote that poem? One of the key themes in it was how I've loved watching you slowly come out of your shell. Seeing you grow, noticing the change from how you'd be reluctant to leave your house or your car to you flourishing at the gym and seeing a new confidence blossom out of you. I loved watching that. I felt proud seeing how much stronger you've become.

But what's a little ironic is I think I've diminished.

I questioned if I was only ever a stepping stone for you. A way for you to pass the time until you could spread your wings and find better. And as much as I have had times where I have cried because I felt so unimportant to you, I can also understand that I have to take responsibility too. I allowed you to do those things.

I can imagine right now you're probably hating me, which is the last thing I want. I think that's the main crux of it all. I just wanted you to feel something for me. But all too often, I felt like I was an afterthought. If you felt anything, it would only be indifference.

When you said that your oldest friends said you're heartless, I still agree with what I said. I don't think you're heartless. I do think you are lost. That you don't know 100% what you want, and even if you have a dream, an idea you'd like, I think you don't know how to plan it. How to get to that step. And the thing is there's nothing wrong with that. But while you float like a feather in the breeze, not fully sure where you will land, I think at times your actions can be heartless.

Obviously, like we said, I only know the version of you that you've shown me. You've never been cruel, never been mean, never been violent or aggressive. But there have been times I think your behavior has been 'heartless.' I think you're fully aware of your actions - with me - and know the power you have. And on certain occasions, you manipulated that. But like I said, the fault doesn't simply lie with you. I continuously allowed you to treat me that way. So, for this we share responsibility.

Alright, I'm going to try to wrap this up and I know that there's a chance, through me *writing this letter, I've tarnished any potential positive thought you previously had about me.*

When we met, you made me feel safe enough to be myself. I don't think you ever even saw me done up, dressed well with makeup on. You're tall, you're hot, you've got tattoos, got a big dick, and a pretty face. Though it's not as if there has ever been any question about my physical attraction towards you.

Now, as I say my goodbyes, if you have days when you're down, find some way to think of the positives. I know I should say I hope you find all the happiness in the world, and I hope you find someone who treats you with all the love, care, and respect that you absolutely deserve.

Yeah, I don't want to picture that.

But obviously I hope you find whatever it is you are looking for.

I know there will never be anyway for me to know if you ever finished reading this, but I really hope you do. I guess it's the one way that, despite me not seeing it, it's you showing just an ounce of care for me.

Despite everything, thank you for being in my life for the last couple of months. I'm glad I met you.

As cheesy as it sounds, I will cherish the time we had. And maybe one day you'll remember me, or I might pop up in a dream or even a memory might cross your mind, and it makes you smile.

Goodbye Diamond Demon,

Yours,

Carina

(The Damaged Mermaid)

Chapter 31

Carina

18 months later

"Would you like anything else with that?" The barista's smile is warm and welcoming.

"No, thank you. That's all fine."

I tentatively blow on the coffee, despite knowing it's still going to be too hot for me to drink. Going to take a sip, I squeeze my eyes shut as I burn the roof of my mouth. I guess that's what I get for being so impatient. Deciding it's safer to start on my salmon and cream cheese bagel instead, I take a bite before opening up my Chromebook.

I still can't believe that I finally took the plunge. Last month I handed in my notice because I'd secured enough bookings over the next few months, with more in the pipeline, sorted out my website, and knew I needed to give up my care work so I could devote more time to my graphic design.

Not only have I made the effort work-wise and bettering my home life, but I've also continued working out. To be honest, I'm probably the strongest and fittest I've been since before I had the boys. I tried giving dating another go, which turned out to be an absolute nightmare. First, I kept matching with guys I'd recognize from the gym. And in my paranoid state, I'd convinced myself that they'd had some sort of connection to Robby, perhaps were even friends of his—not that I would know as I met none of his friends. Nevertheless, I freaked out and made sure not to match anyone from this town. There were a couple of guys I met.

One turned out to be an absolute psycho. He was looking for someone pure because, apparently, he used to be a sex addict and now was celibate and didn't want to engage with a woman who'd derail his goals. Like seriously, the guy was insane. I definitely dodged a bullet with that one.

Then there was another guy, Jesse. We'd been chatting for weeks, met up a couple of times for nice and relaxed day dates. It was all going well. Then we'd planned for me to stay the night at his, have dinner, and enjoy his hot tub. All was fine until it came down to us doing the deed. It wasn't his fault he wasn't well endowed, but I tried to work with it as best as I could. Then *bam*, he ghosted. There was no word, nothing. Obviously, I put him in the trash pile, along with all the others that ended up wasting my time or not getting my name right or saw me as nothing more than a fetish.

After that, I didn't want to waste my effort anymore. It was as if the pool was reduced to a puddle and those left in the murky water were weirdos or walking red flags. So I stopped with the dating apps, stopped trying to meet someone. There was just no point.

I have to smile at myself when the light bird chime of my phone's alarm goes off. I need a structured routine. I couldn't simply sit at my desk at home and just have free rein. I'd done that at the beginning, and it seriously messed me up. The hours would just fall away. Now I plan out exactly which things I work on and do each day. Set alarms for when I need to allow myself either stretch breaks or to eat. Like the one going off now, reminding me to drive to the store.

The shopping bags in my hand are heavy as I weave my way through the car park. As I open the driver's side door, my eyes land on a familiar person and the bags falls, slipping to the ground.

My whole body freezes, not believing my eyes. My chest tightens as I struggle to breathe.

"What on earth are you doing here, Robby?"

Chapter 32

Robby

This wasn't the way I wanted to do this. I had the whole thing figured out. But then I'd been driving past and saw her car. I recognized it instantly since I'd driven it often enough. So I'd pulled in and parked right beside her.

At first, I planned to just get a glimpse of her. See her in the flesh for the first time in almost two years. I wasn't even going to get out. I just wanted to see her. The last thing I wanted was to give her a shock and send her shopping spilling all over the dirty ground.

"I'm sorry," I say, bending down and catching the items that have escaped the bags.

"I-I… What are you doing?" Carina stutters.

First looking down at the groceries, I wonder briefly if she means regarding that. Looking up at her confused face, I'm just about to answer when she shakes her head.

"What are you doing here? As in this car park. This town. In this state. This country." Her voice hitches slightly with each word she speaks.

Swallowing, I give myself a second to pull myself together. I can only imagine that she's probably mad as well as shocked. Who wouldn't be in her position, especially after everything?

"I-I…" Clearing my throat, I struggle to get the words out. "I know I don't deserve even just a moment of your time. There is so much I've wanted to say. So much you deserve to hear. I don't even know where to begin. Would it be okay if we grab a coffee or something? Just to talk. Give me like ten minutes. Please?"

Her eyes bounce between mine. There is so much emotion pouring out of them, but it's like a pinball that's scattering across the place and I can't decipher what any of it means. After what feels like an eternity, she finally speaks.

"I… um… just can't believe that you're here. This feels like some sort of weird messed up dream. You should be knees deep in your idyllic life over in Thailand. Not picking up groceries off of ground here."

There's a coldness in her voice that I've never heard before. Her eyes are still wide, and I can see the shock hasn't worn off. Even with the confusion, the shock and unexpected expression that washes over her face, she's still stunning. I swear it feels like she's even more beautiful than I remember, if that's even possible. There's a hesitation that shines through her eyes, and it makes my spine tingle with unease. I'm starting to think that she's going to say no. That she isn't interested in hearing me out. To talk. But I really want her to. Need her to. Even if it's just for ten minutes. I just need to ease my approach. Try to somehow convey my earnest sincerity.

"Carina, I appreciate that this is weird. That you probably didn't expect to bump into me today, but also that you might not want to see me. I understand that. There is so much I've wanted and needed to say, but haven't. Would you give me like ten minutes of your time? We can sit somewhere and grab a coffee, or just go for a walk, anything. Just so I can explain it all to you. I fully understand if you don't want to. And if you say no, I'll respect that and never bother you. But I'd really like to explain. You deserve the truth and to hear the honesty I've been too immature and ashamed to say until now."

My heart pounds like a fast-beating drum. I feel like I'm standing on a cliff's edge, not knowing whether I'm going to fall over or stay on safe ground. I honestly don't remember the last time I was this nervous. I don't know if she's noticed that I suggested going to public places. I really hope she realizes I want to take her out somewhere public. Not hiding her away like she said in the letter. That letter. It has haunted me like a shadow I can't escape but at the same time never wanted to get rid of. She glances down at her watch, and I think I may have blown it. Time feels like it's standing still as I await her response.

"I need to get the food in the fridge and freezer. But I guess you could briefly stop by for a quick coffee," she tells me, but the tone of her voice somehow doesn't sound like her. Her eyes usually give her away but I just can't catch them for a long enough look to see what she's really feeling. But right now I can't focus on that. I need to focus on the positive that she's inviting me over.

Relief washes over me, and I let out a deep breath. Feeling the slightest pang of shame, I can't help but feel that there's also the possibility that maybe she doesn't want to be seen in public with me. Perhaps she's too embarrassed to. Or she might be in a relationship and doesn't want it getting out that she's gone for coffee with me. The second that thought enters my mind, my stomach flips. How had I not thought of that before? How stupid has it been of me not to presume that she's happy and in a loving relationship with someone? For all I know, she could be engaged. Married? My eyes glance at her hand and see there is no ring on her finger, filling me with just the slightest sense of ease.

"Yes, that would be great. As long as you're sure you're okay with that? And like I said, even if you just give me ten minutes. You can set a timer if you want and the second it goes off, you can kick me out." Part of me expects her to laugh, or at least smile at that, but there is a stoicism to her face that remains.

"Yeah, it's fine. Do you remember the way? Otherwise, you can just follow behind me."

I'm nodding before she even finishes talking. "I remember. Let me help you with those bags."

"No, it's fine. I've got it. I guess I'll see you at my place."

From the moment I landed back here two weeks ago, all I've thought of is this moment. As we come to a stop at the traffic lights, I watch as she glances back at me through her rearview mirror. My knee bounces as I'm both curious and terrified to know what must be running through her mind right now.

The drive back to hers isn't a long one, but it feels as if it's taking forever. I continue taking deep and steadying breaths to calm myself. I stop myself from reaching into my inner jacket pocket and pulling out the envelope that has her letter in it. The letter I have reread probably hundreds of times since I last saw her. The pages are crinkled and the white of the paper has faded from not only how often it was exposed to the different elements, but also with just how many times I have run my hands over it. I'm pretty sure I almost know it all by heart now. On so many occasions, it's felt as if those words have left the pages and slithered into the deepest parts of my soul, haunting my dreams, crashing me back down to reality, and above all, holding me accountable. It's been like the biggest form of torture and cure at the same time. I've felt like both a sadist and masochist when I read it knowing the words hurt, feeling the shame in the truth to them, but also understanding and acknowledging that I need to see them. Need to be aware of just how true they are. That has been my penance. One I've put upon myself repeatedly.

That's how I'm going to do it. When I talk to her, when I try to explain it, I'm going to do it like the order of the letter. At least attempting to address and answer every point. For the first time in a long time, I send a prayer that she at least gives me the time to get through that.

Chapter 33

Carina

If anyone had told me this morning that I'd be in the car, driving home with Robby behind me, I'd have laughed in their face. I've been through a lot in my life and have had many shocking, unexpected and insane moments happen. But honestly, I don't think I've ever felt as surprised as I am right now. I can't quite compute that it's him. My forearm hurts with how often I've pinched it to see that this isn't some messed up dream.

In one sense, he looks just like before, but completely different at the same time. He's filled out since that day when I dropped him off at the train station. Looks like he's put on more muscle, but he isn't bulky. Which has made his face less gaunt. His eyes don't look as hollow as they used to be. The shell and the outside of him look better. I can see and appreciate that. I just honestly don't see how he could have had an entire personality transplant and morphed into a different person.

When he asked if we could go for coffee so he could explain, my initial reaction had been to tell him to fuck off.

I wasn't interested. It didn't matter what he had to say. But I guess I was still in such shock that the initial venom that had rolled through me ended up numbing me and I'd reverted to my simple manners of just being patient and open to hearing him out. Also, I don't know why, but I didn't want to go out somewhere with him. For one, he never had been willing or wanting to do that before, so why should I just accept it when he offers it now? But more than that, I honestly don't know what he's going to say, and because of that, I can't gauge what my reactions are going to be. If he tells me something stupid like he's back to sell the gym because he's married and has kids in Thailand and is closing off the final bits that are still connected to him here, then I will get right up in his face and tell him to go to hell.

As I wait to turn at the intersection, I once again glance back in the mirror and see he's still right behind me. I spend the rest of the drive back thinking of every scenario or thing that he might say, yet not one sits right with me or feels like it makes sense.

Parking the car, I get out, grab the bags from the trunk, and walk to the door, not even bothering to look back to see if he's parked yet. Unlocking the front door, I head inside and leave it open, walking straight through to the kitchen and start putting away the groceries. I hear the door close and his footsteps approach just as I'm closing the fridge. Turning, I watch as his eyes scan around. I don't know if he's noticed that I changed things up since he last was here.

"Would you like a tea or coffee?" I ask.

"Coffee, if that's okay, but I'd be happy with either."

I nod and jut my chin towards the dinner table for him to take a seat. Silence falls over us as I make us each a cup, then carry them both over and take a seat on the opposite side, facing him.

"Thank you."

Lifting my cup, I blow on it gently, watching the swirls of steam rise. Then looking over at him, I see him take a deep breath, closing his eyes before opening them and looking straight at me.

"I'd said I would understand if you only gave me ten minutes of your time, and I mean it. So I'm going to just try to get it all out as quick as possible."

"Okay,"

"The biggest thing I want to say is I'm sorry. I am sorry for so much, Carina. I know that sounds like a blanket statement and maybe at one time I'd have simply just said that and left that there. But I recognize that saying that isn't enough."

Wow. Okay, I wasn't expecting that. Saying nothing in response, I just nod.

"On the drive here, I tried to work out exactly what I would say and how I would say it. There are just too many things I know I need to answer for, and I guess it might just be easier to do it in chronological order."

I take a sip of drink and warm my hands around the cup. This feels so weird, so surreal, that I feel a chill work its way through me.

"I'd told you before about how, when we connected in that Discord group, what had been going on in my life and the messed-up place my head was in. And when you came along, the more we talked, the more I got to know you, I think at first it was like the best distraction."

I wince slightly.

"No, I don't mean it like that. Not in a bad way." He's

flustered, but I motion for him to continue. "Sorry, I didn't mean it to sound like that. It's just everything was so fucked up. I'd gotten myself into such a rut that it was like I'd convinced myself everything in my life was bad. Negative. Just really depressing. Yet whenever I'd interact with you, I suddenly didn't think about all those dark and depressing thoughts. You brought this light, this sunshine into what felt like always gray and miserable days. It kinda became a thing I depended on. Then when we met in person, I guess a part of me couldn't really see you carrying on like that. I wasn't able to wrap my head around the possibility that there was someone who was just genuinely nice, caring, sweet, beautiful, sexy, and just such an understanding person."

I think the old me would have had a beaming smile on her face, hearing him say those words about me. And yeah, I guess I appreciate it, but I've gotten to that stage where I've realized I don't need to hear those words from a man to make me feel justified or valued or special. The only real and true way I could ever feel them, ever believe them, is for me to think and feel them about myself. And that's what I've been doing. I now know I'm all those things. I might not be feeling them all day, every day. But as a whole, I know I am each and every one of those.

"I also realized that not only was I depending on you to give me that light, that boost, but it became this messed up thing because as much as I depended on it, I also felt like it was a reminder of how unlike you I was. You'd bring this beam of positivity, stability, and encouragement that I'd thrive on in those moments. I became addicted to it, but after you'd leave, it was as if I'd have the worst come down. I'd crash back into this dark realization. Because for me, you had everything I didn't. You had your life together. Even if shitty things were thrown your way, you wouldn't let it bring you down. You just always got through it."

I shake my head and clear my throat. "That's not true Robby. I didn't always get through it. I've had so many things knock me down. But unlike you, I didn't have the privilege to sit and wallow in them. I have two children that I need to raise. If I have a bad day, I can't just sit in bed and shut the rest of the world out. I could be feeling so depressed, so hurt, so upset and it wouldn't matter. I still need to get up, get them ready for school, do chores, go to work, feed them. There's never the option for me to fall apart."

I half expect him to snap or say something defensively, but he surprises me by just listening and nodding. "You're right. And I'm sorry that in the duration of time we spent together, I now know that I was likely a big factor in bringing you down, hurting you, and making you upset. I need you to know I never did it intentionally. As bad as this sounds, I was in too much of a selfish place to even think about trying to hurt you. Looking back now, I can see how instead of thanking you, instead of being grateful and appreciating everything you were doing for me, I'd just convinced myself that was the norm. Because if I didn't acknowledge just how much you were really doing, all the small little things that no one else would have ever done or ever even thought of doing, then I didn't need to face the reality of just how unworthy I was of you."

A weird sense of redeeming satisfaction washes over me. It may have personally taken me a really long time to recognize that myself, but I did. I have. He really didn't deserve anything I did for him.

"As time went on, and the more I saw you, I found it harder to balance that need, that fix that I'd felt only you could give me, with the reality that as much as you were helping me, boosting me, bringing me back to some sort of better version of myself, it wasn't solid. Wasn't something that I knew could last because in order for it to, I needed to do those things, make those changes and adjustments within myself. So what I should have done is tell you that. Been open and honest with you. But I was too much of a coward. That was also why I kept you separate from my friends and family. It wasn't because I was ashamed or anything. I need you to know that. When I'd read that part in the letter, it made me feel like the biggest piece of shit. I was never, ever ashamed or embarrassed about you. It was me. If I kept you separate, if I didn't let everyone else see just how much I depended on you, how much I relied on all the things you were doing and giving me, then I could stay in that ignorant comfortability."

Keeping my face neutral, I let out a deep breath through my nose. I hadn't realized just how much I'd needed to hear those words. Because despite all the hard work I've done, how much I have put into bettering myself, there was still this little voice in my head that on the days I was down or just not feeling great, would worm its way in and try to convince me that there was something wrong with me.

"As the months went on, I knew I had to either face reality or run away. So I did the easiest thing and ran. Do you remember the day before I left?"

Of course I do. It was a day and night that haunted me for a long time.

"Yeah, I remember." I say in a rush and focus my gaze

on my clasped hands, as instantly my mind is transported back to that night and my throat feels like it's swelling with emotion I'd thought I'd long buried which really takes me by surprise. Especially after all this time.

"In the buildup to that day, to my leaving, I know I'd been distancing myself. I'd been avoiding you not because I didn't want to see you, but because there was such a big part of me that was convinced if I spent those last few weeks, the last few days, even just that last night with you, I'd never have gotten on that plane. You were the one constant I had. The only solid, positive, caring thing left in my life. And as much as I still didn't want to truly acknowledge it, I knew the man I was, the person I was then, was never worthy of you. I couldn't give you the things you deserved. I still had so much I needed to work on within myself. But I was so scared that if I told you, you would just drop me. I guess once again I just reverted to the selfish and easy way out. If I kept you at a distance, then you wouldn't be able to hurt me instead."

I've spent such a long time going back and forth in my head, trying to dissect him, his behavior, all that had happened in those last few weeks. Where I'd been in such an insecure place within myself, I guess I never even considered that his distance could be because of all the good and positive things *I* was. That *I* gave. It was just easier for me to revert to the self-loathing, self-criticizing ways I'd been doing to myself for most of my life.

"When you gave me the envelope with my leaving gift, I'd been so desperate to open it. There'd been so many times I'd play with it in my hands and been just so tempted to rip the seal open and see what was inside. But there was also a part of me that was scared shitless. I knew from how you'd behaved, even just the look on your face when you handed it over or spoken about me needing to only open it once I was on the plane, I just knew there was something big in it. That's what had stopped me. That fear, that worry that you were going to tell me something or show me something where I'd no longer be able to bury my head in the sand, was the thing that stopped me."

He takes a sip of his coffee before reaching over to his jacket that's hanging on the back of his chair. As he does, the sleeve of his hoodie rides up and I spot the frayed bracelet I'd given him. He pulls something out, placing it on the table and I know instantly what it is.

"I'm sure I've already taken more than ten minutes, but please, please let me just answer some points you said in here."

It's my letter. I can't believe he's held on to it this whole time. I honestly don't know what else he has left to say, but I guess curiosity has its way of controlling you. I never thought I'd ever get any response or answer to that letter. But I guess that now I will.

"Okay, sure."

Chapter 34

Robby

Taking out the letter, I unfold it, brushing out the creases of the paper as I've done probably a hundred times before. Raw, palpable nerves slither through me, making me realize just how vulnerable and exposing this feels. Having her bear witness to me like this feels more baring than the times before when she'd see me upset and crying. Clearing my throat, I let out a breath before starting from the top.

"Your handwriting wasn't awful, by the way. And it was the first and only letter I've ever gotten from someone that wasn't like a birthday card. I dunno, it just made it feel super personal."

My eyes skim the first page as I brace myself. I know I just need to get on with it, as she still might decide to kick me out.

"From the beginning, you gave me this sense of safety. Like even before we met in person, you'd somehow wove this security blanket over me. I'd never experienced anything like that before. But I instantly felt so at ease, so comfortable just being raw with you. I didn't have the need or desire to portray myself as anything impressive or something I wasn't. Maybe it's because there was actually a part of me that thought at the beginning that we wouldn't likely ever meet in person. Especially as I'd felt so horrible, uncomfortable, and just completely insecure about my skin."

Looking up, I see her take another sip of her coffee with that stoic expression still on her face.

"I still can't believe you thought I would shut the door in your face after you brought me food that first time at the gym. I'd never do that."

Taking a quick sip myself, I continue, "I think, like you, as our visits and time together became more frequent, I also realized just how much I craved and needed company. But it wasn't just any company. I knew I could have hung out with my friends, with guys that I train with. There was just something about you I'd never experienced with anyone before. You were also right when you said I'd changed my plans. I had. It wasn't intentional, or something I'd really expected. Though looking back, I'm also not surprised."

"Really, why?" she asks, and I can see the genuine curiosity in her eyes.

"Do you mean why did I change my mind or why am I not surprised I did?"

"Both."

I rub my hand over my face and cringe slightly. "Okay, don't take this the wrong way, as it's not a negative reflection on you. This is all on me. But now, after everything that's happened in the past year and a half, I know I left because of you."

Her eyes widen and I can see she's taken aback, so I quickly carry on.

"Like I said, please don't think I mean that in a bad way. It was more the case that without you realizing, you were kinda holding up a mirror to me. The way you are, the way you just keep getting up and going every single day, I couldn't see that without then comparing myself to it. Or I guess comparing how I wasn't doing that. You embodied everything I wasn't. I felt like you had all the things I didn't. You were selfless. I was selfish. You always saw the best in things, and I always saw the worst. You would stick it out and fight through the hard times and I just run away.

"That's why I changed my mind. I knew I'd need to really face up to who I was, how I was living my life, and I was too much of a coward to do that. So instead of behaving like an adult, thinking and being rational, I just left. Ran away from my troubles, my worries. Just like I always have. That's why I left. That's why I'm also not surprised I did."

My heart is pounding against my chest, and I squeeze my hands into a fist at how embarrassing that was to admit.

"It was like the more you gave me, the more I took for granted. I became numb to all the little things you'd do, and that was awful of me. I can't tell you how many times it made me feel physically sick when I thought back on everything, and I was too stupid, too self-absorbed to even say thank you. Before I get to the bit where you'd told me how you felt, told me about your feelings for me, there's something I want to give you."

Reaching into my back pocket, I pull out my wallet and hand her the check I've written. It doesn't go unnoticed that she takes it, being careful to make sure our fingers don't touch.

Her eyes widen, then a frown creases her face. When she looks up at me, I can see both confusion and something else. Anger? Annoyance? I'm not sure.

"Why have you written me a check for four thousand dollars?"

"I understand and can now truly appreciate the small gifts you gave me. But when I thought back about how I never paid you back for the tattoo, or the money at the wedding or the other times I'd borrowed from you, or even the car, I just can't believe you never kicked me in the face. That was truly deplorable of me."

"Okay, but those things together don't come to that sum you've written. I'm sorry I can't take this." She goes to slide it back to me, but I stop her.

"No, please. Please let me pay you back. It never should have been the case that I didn't already do it. And if you don't want to accept it as me paying you back, or for using it for yourself, then please just take it and use it for something that you can do with the boys. I dunno, like maybe putting it towards a vacation for you all, or if you're saving up for their college fund, add it to that. But please just take it. It's the least I can do. Please," I beg.

I can see the war within herself on her face. Feeling engulfed with self-loathing, I hate that through my actions, my behavior, how I had treated her, she's not even comfortable letting me pay her back.

"Okay, fine. Thank you. I'll put it towards something for the kids," she says, giving me a small but sad smile.

I want to address it more, but I'm worried if I do she

will end up changing her mind. So I look back down at the letter and know this is probably going to be the most uncomfortable thing for me to discuss.

"Carina, when you told me about your feelings, when you opened up that you were falling for me, I know I never responded. Again, I was being selfish and didn't want to face up to the truth. And once again, you were left in the wind. I think there was a part of me that wasn't really surprised. I'd got the sense just from how you used to look at me. With the kindest and warmest of eyes. So when you told me, I was obviously flattered but also went into a panic. I knew I'd need to address it, which would have meant for me to open up about my feelings for you, but I just couldn't."

Her eyes close and I'm sure this can't be easy for her to hear.

"I want you to know it wasn't the case that I didn't respond because I didn't have feelings. It actually was the opposite. But I knew I couldn't give you what you wanted. What you deserved. It felt safer keeping you, keeping us in the gray zone we were in, as that meant there was no pressure on me. I didn't have to act or behave in an expected way. It kept me from having to take any responsibility. Especially as I knew that your life was different from any other woman I'd been with.

You're a single mom. An amazing single mom who would always put others first. I'd seen the things you cherish, and I knew I wasn't deserving of you. Of a relationship with you. I couldn't be the man, the person that you wanted. You'd told me how when you did get into a relationship with someone, it would not be something casual, and I understood that. But the more I thought about your feelings for me, and what would happen if I said I'd felt the same and we'd make a real go of things, the more I panicked. I'd convinced myself that instead of seeing a real and true relationship with you as a solid and secure life that could be built on, I saw it as me being held back. That I'd never be able to go on vacation the way I could before. I couldn't just up and leave for a few months when things got hard. I'd have to face up to issues and deal with responsibilities."

Pain and anguish mar her face, and it makes me feel sick to my stomach that my words are bringing that to her. But I just want to be open and honest.

"Not that I felt you were stifling or holding me back. It was that I knew I'd have to grow up. Take responsibility. And I was just too chickenshit to do that. So instead I kept you at a distance. Undeservingly taking from you what I wanted and needed and not giving anything back. It's the worst thing I've ever done in my life.

And I think what was even worse was because of your nature, because of the amazing and kind woman that you are, you just took it. Accepted it. At some point, I think it was just before I'd booked my flight, I was at home thinking about all the things you had done for me, and it made me feel like complete shit. But instead of changing my ways or behavior, I relented. It was like I couldn't face just how kind you were still being to me, so I thought if I behave shittier, make even less of an effort, then you'll just end everything. And in my stupid and messed up head that would have allowed me to keep believing everyone leaves and just gives up on me. But you didn't."

My hands shake and I have to look away when I see tears fill her eyes. I want nothing more than to reach out to hold her and just try to hope that she understands how sorry I am. But I know I don't deserve that.

"You were right when you said that I got everything out of you that a partner would give. I did. And I didn't deserve it. I also didn't deserve you. You mentioned several times that I deserve happiness and good things, but you don't see that out of everyone I've ever met in my life, whether here or on the other side of the world, there is honestly no one, and I mean no one, that deserves happiness, love, and pure affection more than you." I can feel my throat tighten as emotion chokes me. I swallow it down as I need to get through this.

"You are and always have been the rarest diamond. I've never met anyone who cares and gives to others as much as you do. It's one of the best traits about you. It's also something I didn't mean to exploit. But I did. And I need you to know that from the bottom of my heart, the deepest recess of my soul, just how truly sorry I am."

She quickly wipes away the tears that roll down her cheeks and it kills me not to hold her. Take her hand. To kiss her. Something I held back from doing because I knew if I had, if I'd always given in to the temptation and affection of her kiss, then I'd have never been able to leave.

"When it came to my actual departure, I'd done everything to ignore how much I was going to miss you. How reliant I'd become on you helping me, fixing me, boosting me up. Even after I left, in those first few months I was out there, I tried to forget it all. I was stupid. I'd told you I was going so I could live this good, clean, and healthy life without worries or stress or anything draining. But in the beginning, I just numbed myself. Nonstop partying, drinking, just going out and being reckless. The more I could distract myself, the less of a chance I had of having to face reality. I needed to forget you. Forget my life here. All of it. So I tried everything I could."

I see her wince and I know she knows what I'm also talking about. It was so mean and callous of me when I posted pictures with the women that were giving me all the attention. I'd have absolutely lost my shit if it had been the other way around. And I know how much of a double standard that is.

"I'd made friends with these guys, and we were just living up life. Or so I thought. Long story short, they ended up doing the same thing to me I had done to you. Using me, not caring, then leaving me in the lurch without a second thought about how it would affect me or make me feel. It took for that to happen for me to really realize, really and truly understand just how deplorable I was to you. That was such a wake-up call. One I'd seriously needed for a long time. So after that happened, I knew I needed to change. I stopped drinking, smoking, partying. I focused on my training. Upped my conditioning and meditation. I journal every single day. I'd hit rock bottom and was slowly building myself up. That's what I've been doing for the past year. Not just in Thailand, but all over. Every time I had to leave because of my visa, I'd go somewhere else for a couple of weeks before returning. And each place I went to, I stuck to my practices."

"That's good. I'm glad you did."

I give her a sad smile and it hurts how little she is saying, but I still appreciate that she's still sitting here letting me speak.

"Once I felt like I was physically at my best and mentally solid enough, I went to this small little island where there's no electricity, nothing. It's just pure basics. And I was there for seven days. I wanted to take that time to really work out what I wanted to do with my life while having no distractions, no internet, nothing. And I did. I wrote so much in my journal that my hands would cramp up. It was there that I'd decided I want to go with my original plan I'd told you. I wanted to come back here, work on the gym, have it thriving but also I wanted more. When I got back from that island, I reached out to Koa and asked him if he would like to buy fifty percent of the gym. He's been doing such an amazing job running it anyway. He's agreed. And with the money I'm getting from his buy in, I'm going to use it to open another business."

"Oh really? And what's that?"

Before I know for a fact me saying something like that would have lit up her entire face. Her eyes would have shone with intrigue and curiosity. Yet now, it feels like she's just asking to be polite. This detachment, I just feel like I'm not breaking through to her. We might be sat across from one another but right here, right now I feel a bigger distance from her than when I was over in Thailand.

"You remember how much I told you about the food out there and how eating out is so much more a way of life?"

"Mmmm, yeah."

"I want to open up a little restaurant. I want it to be something for me. That represents me. Something I come up with, plan, design, just do everything that's my choice. Not someone else's dream that I just inherited. Something of my own. I want to make it a fusion restaurant. Having a mix of foods and dishes that represent me."

"That's great, Robby. I'm genuinely happy for you."

"So what about you? Have you got any new adventures or plans going on at the moment?" I ask curiously.

"Oh you know, just life as usual. Nothing major. Anyway your idea of opening up a restaurant sounds great. I'm sure it'll do really well."

I know she means it, but I can't help but feel like I'm breaking. As even though she continues to listen, as I spend the next twenty minutes telling her about all my plans and things I want to do and achieve here, there are two things I can't ignore. Every time I try to ask about her and her life, she doesn't get into it. She shuts me out. Never giving me more than the bare minimum. But the biggest kick in the teeth, the most undeniable truth is that she no longer looks at me the same way. That look, that spark that used to shine so brightly in her eyes when we were around each other isn't there anymore. The diamond light that I'd taken for granted for too long has dimmed and I'm more scared than ever that I will never get the chance to see it again.

The alarm on her phone goes off and she rises from her seat and collects our cups from the table and takes them over to the sink. I think it's my cue to go.

"Thank you for giving me the chance to speak. I know you had no reason to but it means so much to me that you did."

She gives me a slight nod and I quickly pack her letter back into my pocket before following her towards her front door. My fingers twitch with the urge to reach out and touch her. Feel those soft curls of hers between my fingers. Fuck just to wrap her in my arms and hug her. But I know I cant. It's never going to happen. I just need to be grateful for the time she's given me today.

"Thank you again Carina."

I don't know what else to say as she holds the door open for me.

"It's okay. See you around Robby," she says softly and the look in her eyes is so haunting, filled with so many emotions, I know those eyes are going to haunt me for a long time.

Chapter 35

Carina

To say that my head was like a minefield in the days following that completely unexpected interaction, or whatever you want to call it with Robby, is an understatement.

The rest of the afternoon and evening after he left, was like I was walking and doing everything in slow motion. First, it was from just the pure shock of seeing him, which would have been a big enough thing in itself. Because I honest to god didn't think he'd ever come back. I was so convinced, so resolute in my mind, that he'd just stay out there forever.

It's been two months since I've known of Robby's return and even though I haven't allowed him to take over my thoughts the way he has in the past, I also couldn't completely ignore him. We don't exactly live in a big city, so it's been inevitable that we've crossed paths. Not only simple things like driving past one another and passing each other down the aisles of the grocery store. And obviously, there have been several times I've spotted him when I've gone to do my classes at the gym.

It's always been these small little pleasantries, asking how we are, what we're up to. One time after a class, we both walked to the coffee shop down the block, each grabbing one to go, but still just acting and conversing as adults.

I've grown past the point of holding any resentment towards him. If I did, it would only be me who suffers from hanging on to that negative energy, and I'm just not here for that. Plus, whatever or however he has been working on himself, I think is doing the trick because he really is putting himself out there into the world much more.

Tonight there's been a little fundraiser at the gym. All members were invited, and they'd set up different tasks and challenges and the winner of each would win either a free month of their membership, or they could choose to donate that money to one of the three charities they were raising for. It was the first time I've really seen him in his element at the gym in person. Watching as he takes charge of the various sections, joking and laughing with everyone.

Looking down at my phone as I'm walking out, I'm putting in a takeout order for collection when I bump into someone, sending my phone flying to the floor.

"Oh shit, sorry," I say before looking up.

"No, my bad," Robby says before squatting and picking up my phone.

"Looks nice."

I momentarily scrunch my brows in confusion.

"I'm guessing that's gonna be your dinner?" he asks.

Looking at the phone, I see he must have noticed the order details I was putting in.

"Oh, yeah. I'm grabbing something for me and my babysitter. Easier than cooking something."

He nods and gives me a warm smile. "Yeah, that's made me super hungry, but I've gotta wait until all this is finished."

"It's been a fantastic turnout tonight. Congratulations. And from what I've heard so far, I don't think anyone has taken up the offer of the free month's membership, everyone just picking to go with the charity donation. So I think you guys will have raised a fair amount in the end. Well done."

"Thanks. I've actually got a whole list of things I wanna do. While I was away I'd really thought about how I could incorporate the community more, and charity events seem to be great for getting people together. I'd love to actually run a couple of my ideas past you and get your opinion on them, if you're open to hearing them."

"Yeah, sure, I guess. I obviously can't right now. But we can work out some other time."

"Well, now that you've got me thinking of food, why don't we grab a bite to eat sometime this week? I've seen there are a couple of new places that popped up since I left that I'd like to try out, and I can tell you about some events I'm hoping to pull off, especially some for kids."

I open my mouth in slight shock as I wasn't expecting this. Momentarily speechless, I look at his relaxed face and try to gauge if this is some kind of joke or something. But there's nothing in his expression that shows it.

"Okay… yeah. Alright."

. . .

"Alright, so run it by me again. Why do you feel confused about grabbing some food with him?" Amira asks, finishing the last of her burrito bowl. Amira might have just started off as my nanny, helping me babysit every once in a while, but now she's honestly the best friend I could have ever asked for.

"Well… I… I'm not exactly sure. I think that's the issue. I don't quite know what's going on or where I stand. I'm not a friend, or a stranger. We have a past. I don't like him in that way, but I also don't dislike him. I just don't know what I am thinking or feeling about this whole interacting with him."

"Well, that's all perfectly understandable. I honestly still can't believe how much you've grown and dealt with things regarding him in the time we've been friends. I honestly hated him, hated everything about him when you first told me all about it. To be honest, if this would all be happening like a year and a half ago, I'd actually advise you against it. Tell you not to bother. It would only do more harm than good."

I nod along with her statement, as I know she's right. There's no way I'd have been able to even consider being cordial with him back then. I was too hurt. Still hadn't believed or loved myself enough.

"Also, I think it might be a good thing. Like you said, you guys do often bump into each other. From the sounds of it, it doesn't seem like he's going to be moving away again soon. So even indirectly, you're going to be in each other's orbit in some shape or form. Especially with the fact that not only do you go to his gym, but Zion's training and classes have increased as he's begun competing and working his way up for belts too. Therefore, you can both either dance around this awkward limbo, like you've been doing, or the two of you recognize that you'll see each other and even if you both don't become chummy friends, at least getting to a place of friendly acquaintances will allow you not to feel uncomfortable."

"I know. I know you're right."

"Plus, once you've grabbed a bite to eat, chatted about whatever you two want to talk about, I think you'll not feel in this weird haze-like brain fog every single time you have an interaction with him."

"Yeah. I think that's it. I just wanna get over whatever weird hurdle we're at so we can just continue to co-exist without there being any kind of awkwardness between us."

I think the only thing I don't want to mention is the going somewhere public piece of this meeting. And I know that it's probably ridiculous, but we'd never done that before and I think that will actually feel the weirdest. I can't deny that I'm intrigued and want to see if there is anything actually different about him. Has he truly changed or is he now just wearing a different and slightly softer disguise, where the man at the core is still the same? It took me a really long time to realize, but when someone shows you their true colors, believe them. I spent so many years with a variety of people, always making excuses, convincing myself that things will change, or that person will get better. Always seeing the best. I'd constantly go through an entire list of excuses for that person's behavior. Perhaps it was a way to protect myself. Because the longer I convinced myself that person wasn't intentionally hurting me, wasn't truly wanting me to suffer and go through immense pain, whether that be physically or mentally, then there would still be a chance they cared.

That was my mentality back then. I no longer think like that. And especially after everything I have gone through with Robby, I know it's imperative for me not to fall back into old traits and habits. I've come too far. Worked too hard. I'm so much stronger now and won't be making any excuses for him. I will listen, choose what I want, and if I'm unhappy or he tries to manipulate or steer things in a direction I don't want or am uncomfortable with, I won't hesitate about putting him in his place and finally closing that chapter with him for good.

Chapter 36

Carina

"Zion, I got an email from your teacher saying all parents need to sign off in your ledger once we've checked your homework," I shout from the bottom of the stairs.

I hear a faint grunt of an answer in the distance and head back into the kitchen to finish their dinner.

Amira should be here in about forty-five minutes to watch them and because my two consultation Zoom meetings both overran, I haven't had a chance to shower and I still need to change. "Zion and Kai, dinner's ready," I shout.

It doesn't take long for them to come herding downstairs.

"Thanks," Kai says and gives me an awkward side cuddle.

"Yup, thanks, Mom," Zion replies as he walks past and takes a seat opposite his brother.

"Mommy, where's your plate?" Kai asks.

"I'm going out to have my dinner, remember? I told you that Amira is coming over to watch you."

Zion rolls his eyes and I know it's not because he dislikes her. On the contrary. I think he's convinced he doesn't need a babysitter. And he's right. He doesn't. But Kai does.

"Oh, yeah. Last time she was here she said she was going to play Roblox with me."

Giving him a smile, my fingers play with his curls before I bend down and give him a kiss on the head.

"Who are you having dinner with?" Zion asks, digging into his food.

Now I'm not an idiot. I'm fully aware that with Zion being older and just having an overall better understanding of life, I can tell that there's more to his question. This isn't the first time in the past year that he's hinted about me going on a date or meeting someone. Ironically, it all stemmed from the time after Robby's departure. There was a day when I'd been so down, I'd gone into my bedroom and called my mom, crying to her on the phone and telling her how much I was struggling. Turns out Zion heard me and later confronted me, asking about what had happened. I never want to lie to my children, so I gave him a PG version of what had happened, omitting Robby's name and the fact that he owned the gym Zion has become obsessed with. It was as if up until that point he'd never thought about me having someone in my life.

"Just a friend. We're going to discuss some ideas about his business and some events he's planning on putting on. And he wants my opinion and input on them."

He observes me, then nods. "So it's like a business meeting?"

"Kinda. Can you two eat with no drama so I can quickly shower and get changed?"

"Yeah."

I get showered and dressed in about twenty minutes, which was perfect timing as the doorbell rings as I leave my room. Running down the stairs, I see the boys are just finishing their dessert as I open the door and let Amira in.

"Thanks again for this."

"Oh, don't be silly, it's not a problem," she says, giving my outfit a once over.

Her expression gives nothing away, but I would bet anything she's wondering why I'm in straight-fit high waisted jeans, a fitted long-sleeved t-shirt, and my favorite Adidas gazelles.

I leave her to settle in as I grab my bag and remember to pack my notebook and pen.

"Alright, I'm gonna head off now."

"Okay. Will you be driving?" Amira asks, waiting next to Kai as he sets up the Xbox on the TV.

"No, I'm actually gonna walk there. It isn't too far and I was sitting at the desk all day. Feeling really sluggish, so I could do with a bit of exercise. But I will get a cab back. It's still warm now, but I'm sure it'll drop by the time I leave."

I must have gotten so into the music I was listening to in my headphones that the beat morphed my casual stroll into some sort of power walk because I arrived five minutes early. Not wanting to just stand around, I circle the block, and just as I get back around to the front of the restaurant, I see Robby pulling up. It doesn't take long for him to spot me.

"Hey."

"Hiya. Did you park round the back or something?" he asks, a little perplexed.

"Huh? No, why?"

"It's just I saw you walk round from that direction."

"Oh no, I walked here but ended up walking faster than I meant to, so I went round the block to kill some time."

We make our way to the restaurant, and he holds open the door for me.

"Have you been here before?" he asks.

"I have, but only when it first opened. We brought my stepdad here for his birthday. The food's good."

A waiter walks us to a table that overlooks the cool fountain in the middle.

"So is the food the reason you picked this place? Are you doing some research for the restaurant you're planning on opening?" I ask, my eyes scanning over the menu.

It takes me a moment to realize that he hasn't responded. When I look over at him, I find him staring back at me again with a confused expression on his face.

"I… I… no, I hadn't picked here for research."

"Oh? Um, okay, what made you pick it?" I ask with genuine curiosity.

"Well, damn, this is awkward," he says, scratching the back of his head.

My brows scrunch in confusion as a blush creeps across his cheeks.

"I'd picked here because I hated when I realized that I'd never taken you on a date before. It was another thing on the list of stuff I regret doing. So when I suggested we grab a bite to eat, well… I thought you got what I meant. But hearing that back now, especially in the context of how we'd been talking about food, and how I'd told you about the restaurant, I really understand just how unclear that was of me."

My mouth is as dry as the Sahara with no sound coming out, complete and utter surprise washing over me. Never in a million years had I thought this was a date. Not only is that clear from the clothes I'm wearing, the lack of effort I've put into my hair and not wearing a stitch of makeup. Also, I wouldn't have brought my notebook and pen if I had had any inkling.

To be honest, I also don't think I'd have agreed to go on a date. Why would I? It's not as if there is still something there between us. Or as if he still or ever had any feelings for me. So I just don't get it.

"Carina, I'm sorry. That was stupid for me to presume. If you want to leave, I fully understand. I've already made an evening I was nervous about even more awkward, and you probably think I'm the biggest tool right now, anyway. We haven't ordered anything, so if you want to just get yourself something to go, I'm more than happy to pay and I promise I won't make this any more awkward than I already have."

The initial shock is slowly beginning to wear off and I finally find my voice. "Why?" I ask.

"Why what? Why am I an idiot? Why did I presume something that's so clear to me now, you could have never presumed? Or why am I nervous?"

"Well, my initial why was why did you want to go on a date? But now I also want to know why you were nervous," I ask with a curious laugh.

He blows out a breath before looking me dead in the eyes.

"When you let me come over and talk it all out when I first got back, I thought it would... I don't actually know what I thought it would do. But I haven't stopped thinking about you. Not only since I've been back. Long before that, too. I guess where you haven't just completely ignored me or tossed me to the side since I got back, I apparently just started letting these hopeful ideas into my head. I just wanted to take you on a date. Or maybe date is too big of a word. I just wanted to take you somewhere nice. Somewhere you deserve."

"Umm, okay. Well, yeah, you really didn't make that clear when you asked. Now, why are you nervous?"

"Isn't it obvious?"

"No. That's why I'm asking you."

"I'm nervous because part of me thought you might not show up. Or that you'd cancel. Then I was questioning what if you turned up but did it more because you're just the nicest person and always wanting to help and be there for people? Even the ones like me that don't deserve it."

"Robby, I've changed a lot since you left. If I didn't want to come here, I'd have said no when you asked. Listen, how about this? This isn't a date, but we will stay and enjoy dinner. You can tell me about the restaurant and some of the stuff you got up to in Thailand. We have a nice evening, and tomorrow is just another day. That sound okay?"

"Yes, I'd like that very much. As long as you're genuinely okay with that?"

"Yeah, I really am."

Although I'm still reeling from his revelation of this being a date, I still want to just enjoy a meal. Mainly to prove to myself that I can.

Chapter 37

Robby

I can't believe how stupid it was of me to presume that she caught on that I was asking her out on a date, but also that she'd have even wanted to come on one. I guess, despite how far I've come in changing my ways, I still have work to do on not just how I communicate, but especially making sure I don't make any expected notions about the way Carina is going to perceive things. It's taken me a while to settle myself enough to I feel relaxed after we gave the waiter our orders.

Watching her across the table, I am drawn to her every move. The way her finger traces along the edges of the napkin or follows the path of condensation along her glass. My eyes are transfixed by the full, pillowy arches of her lips. Despite my best attempts at listening to what she is saying, like a magnet, I'm drawn to her insatiable smile. How had I been so idiotic for so long and neglected to appreciate just how amazing, how captivating her mouth is? Not only does it evoke thoughts of unyielding lust but also a tenderness that I wish I could bask in.

She's literally glowing. Everything about her is shining like the brightest sun. And I know that's all from her own doing. She's brought herself to this peace. This level of contentment. And I am so desperately wanting, hoping, and wishing to lie in the warmth of her glow.

"So, enough about me. Before we get into all the stuff about the restaurant, I want to hear more about your time out in Thailand. Don't hold back," she says, pulling me out of my thoughts with a sweet yet cheeky grin.

I've noticed that she's done this a couple of times now and I can't help but wonder if it's her way of just keeping me at a safe distance.

"Okay, anything in particular?"

"How about you tell me three of your favorite memories you created out there, three of your worst, and three times you'd wished you'd done or acted differently?"

I blow out a silent breath as I'm torn. Torn between wanting to be completely and truly open and honest with her, but also feeling embarrassed. Not just embarrassed, but also slightly ashamed because some of those memories that seemed silly but enjoyable now just seem so stupid. So juvenile. Taking a sip of my ginger ale, I glance back over at her and see her waiting, watching, and for the first time since I've been back, there's a genuine lightness in her eyes as she looks at me. That's all the courage I need.

"Alright. I'll save my favorite for last. It'll be a better way to bring up the mood." My cheeks warm and for the first time in god knows how long I feel a little shy.

"Three of the worst? Hmm… well, I guess the first one would be when I got into the moped accident."

Her eyes widen and even though I vaguely recall telling

her about getting injured, I don't know if I ever fully explained how or why.

"I'd been out with some friends. I think we'd gone out every night for like four or five nights in a row. Running on next to no sleep, nonstop drinking and drugs. Anyway, we were stupid, and usually you can get a lift by riding on the back of a driver, it's like an easier and quicker Uber. But because of our stupidity, we were convinced we were fine and could drive ourselves. Anyway, long story short, because of being under the influence, our reactions and judgments were impaired, and we got into a four bike pile up. I was lucky, as I only cut my foot up and got a couple of cuts and scrapes. But looking back, I can see not only how stupid it was putting myself at risk, but that I could have hurt or even killed someone else. That is something I will never forgive myself for."

My heart pounds in my chest as I recall snippets of that night. To be honest, I don't know how we could even get on them in the first place. Usually, there are enough people that would have stopped that. Not that I can put blame on anyone else besides myself.

"Wow. I guess you really were lucky, as that could have ended so much worse." Her tone isn't belittling, but I can't help but feel shame at just how immature and irresponsible I was back then. Carina must sense my unease.

"What are the other two?"

"One is just that I went for the wrong reasons and approached it all wrong."

Her brows rise with curiosity.

"I've already told you about my regrets and why I felt the need to run. And I remember telling you before I left that I was just going to be training as hard and as much as I could out there. Living this good, clean, healthy life."

She nods along. I'm sure remembering the little speech I used to spout, as a way of deflecting from the truth that I'd been really running away from. My eyes are transfixed, following her fork as she brings it to her mouth. Shaking my head, I focus back on what I'd been talking about.

"I'm torn because a part of me now thinks everything happens for a reason, so as much as I hated how I left, the self-destructive path I was on for that first six or so months, I also don't know if I would be where I am now if that hadn't had happened. But yeah, although I couldn't see it at the time, I regret letting myself get lost. I acted careless, and just overall kept putting myself in situations that I shouldn't."

I eat a couple of mouthfuls of my enchilada, then wipe my mouth with my napkin.

"You might be right. I believe things happen for a reason. That there is some unseen, and I guess unknown fate or path that is set out for every single person. Certain things, certain goals can be achieved by action. Or by working hard towards them. But yeah, I think others are just these designated destinations which we never know or can even predict but somehow the journey we go on takes us there." Carina has always had this way with words. It's not like she says things poetically or anything like that. It's so much more; she always makes me think of this wise woman. Being able to take things and hold a mirror up to them so you're forced into looking at things differently.

"I agree."

Our eyes lock for a moment, and I don't want to look

away. Instead, she's the one to cut the eye contact and cuts up another piece of her food.

"Okay, so what's the last one?"

"Last what?"

"Last worst memory."

"Oh." For a moment, I'd forgotten what we were talking about. Again, I feel torn between being brutally honest and wanting to hide away from the truth. "It kind of involves you."

Her eyes widen and her hand holding her fork stops in midair.

"How so?" she asks, quieter than she's spoken so far this evening.

"I don't know how to say this."

"If you really don't want to tell me, that's okay."

"No. I do. It's just hard."

"Would it be easier if you closed your eyes and just said it as quickly as possible? Think of it like ripping a band aid off."

I think about it for a second and realize that will probably be the only way that I can say it being in front of her. I'm sure I must look like a complete idiot, sitting at a table, closing my eyes and squeezing my hands in my lap. Breathing in and out deeply through my nose, I just go for it.

"I hate that when I was first out there, I wanted to affect you. I wanted you to see all the fun and crazy things I was doing. The shit I used to put on my social media too often was because of you. Or for you. And I know that's so fucked up and so bad. But it's like I knew I couldn't have you, but I still wanted to have this connection with you. I'd post pictures of me with women, being stupid, behaving in ways I know you'd never. A part of me was waiting, almost hoping that you'd block me as it would have meant that I mean so much to you, you couldn't bear to see it."

A bitter taste coats my tongue, and I can't believe I just admitted that out loud. I'm too scared to open my eyes and see her face, but I know I owe it to her.

As my eyelids open, I expect her to be looking at me with hate and vitriol, but there's a beautiful smile on her face. Now it's my brows that scrunch in confusion.

"Okay, I'm sorry. I know I shouldn't find this funny, but it's hilarious. Back then, there were so many times I came close to blocking you. Everyone I spoke to said I should. But I couldn't. And the main reason I couldn't was because I didn't want you to suspect I was affected by the things you were putting up. So it's all kind of ironic."

Wow, that surprises me. If I'd have been in her shoes, I'd have blocked and deleted my ass a long time ago. To be honest, I still don't know how or why she put up with all my shit for as long as she did.

"Okay, let's move on. Tell me the three things you wished you'd have done differently?"

"I wished I'd have cut alcohol out from the moment I landed. That would have made a difference instantly. I also wish I'd have done something out there. Maybe some sort or charity work or helping out or just… something. Using my time, my skills, anything to just do good."

As has become my comfort, my fingers trace along the bracelet she gave me before continuing, "And lastly, I wish I'd have been more sensible with my money. I blew through so much so quickly when I first arrived. Because, despite things being cheaper out there, I still wasted a ton."

"In your defense, a lot of your regrets and things you

wish you'd have done differently are all kind of connected. So it's like a domino effect. And because for a while you didn't block or stop the next one from going down, it's not really surprising that it all went on for as long as it did."

"I know. Add hindsight on to that and it all feels even more annoying looking back on."

"I get that. But it's in the past. You can't undo it. The bell has already been rung, so you just gotta move on and try to do better and be better in the future. And from the sounds of it, you did. Eventually."

Her grin sets off my own and I finally feel myself relax more. As expected, when I tell her my best and favorite memories, it really brings up and lightens the mood.

We both order a dessert, and it amazes me the way she expresses her genuine interest at the things I did to turn my life around.

"Would you say it was one particular moment that set that off? I know you've already explained that incident that happened with those guys."

"That was a big part of it, but there was one day I was at the beach and a storm came in and I just utterly broke. I was crying more than I'd ever before. It was as if this huge tidal wave hit me. I let myself properly grieve the loss of Michael and Joseph. Then also losing my mom. I cried about the things I was doing in my life, the hurt I had caused you, the toxic and self-destructive path I was down. Just all of it. It broke me more than anything. But I think that was what I needed. I had to really hit that worst kind of rock bottom, just so I would have a chance of building myself back up again."

"I can't imagine how intense that must have been for

you. Physically and mentally, but also spiritually. It must have been really hard."

"It was. Earlier, you spoke about fate and things destined to be and happen. Do you really believe that?"

"Yeah, I do. Sometimes I might not like it. Or wish it would be or happen differently, but yeah I believe in it. Why?"

"The day I had the breakdown, or maybe putting it in better words, it was a breakthrough, do you know what the date was?"

She tilts her head and is silent for a moment, probably trying to guess where I'm going with this.

"I'm not sure. But I'm going to take a guess that it's a really important one, or just a random Monday or something that until then had held no significance but now does."

Looking deep into her eyes, I smile. "It was an important date. It happened on your birthday. So what's your guess about the significance of that?" Her mouth opens and closes twice, and she blinks rapidly. This is probably only the second time I've ever seen her speechless. The first being when I went up to her in the carpark at the grocery store.

"I… I…" She takes a gulp of her drink then clears her throat. "I don't know what to say to that."

The old me would either not have mentioned it or would have taken this opportunity to tease her. But that's the last thing I want to do. I just want her to know that I took that date for granted in the past. Not appreciating how important it was since it was the day this world was blessed with her. So it now held double significance for me.

I steer the conversation onto something lighter because she still seems a little lost for words.

By the time our desserts arrive, I've filled her in on all my ideas for the restaurant. I'm not surprised when she puts forward some brilliant suggestions. The woman has always been a genius and has the best eye for seeing potential in something.

I struggle to concentrate on her words, though. She'd ordered churros and I have to fight with every ounce of strength I have not to allow the wayward thoughts in my head to take over. But it's so hard. Watching the way the dusting of sugar glisten on her lips or the way her tongue peaks out to lick it off, has my pants tightening while memories of her hot mouth come flooding back. What really almost makes me lose it and send me to the bathroom like some pubescent teen is when she dips a churro into the warm melted chocolate. I honestly don't know what she's said in the last few minutes because I feel like I'm being hypnotized. Captivated in the smallest movement. Thank god the tables are high and wide. Because otherwise she'd see the bulge that's now getting painful in my pants. It's also meant I've had to eat my dessert unbelievably slowly. Not only because I want to get control over my raging hormones, but I also don't want this evening to end.

What had started out as such an embarrassing misunderstanding—which could have resulted in the dinner ending before it even began, and I'll add that it would have been utterly my fault—has now turned into one of the best nights I've ever had with her. And I would give anything to stop time and just stay like this for hours.

Chapter 38

Carina

It's going to take me a while to really process what's happened tonight. Initially, I'd presumed it was just going to be two people getting some food, discussing plans and ideas about the next business venture Robby is planning. Establishing a new normal.

Throughout the meal, there have been moments where I've forgotten myself. Not in a bad way, but I just let go and allowed myself to enjoy the moment. There have also been a couple of moments where I've found him just staring at me. He'd never looked at me that way before, and I don't know what to make of it. I'm intrigued and confused, which pretty much sums up how I've felt about the whole evening.

"So I was wondering, how did Koa feel when you offered him to buy out half of the gym? Was he surprised? I will say, I obviously don't know how things have gone behind the scenes or with any of the admin stuff, but as a whole, he's kept a really tight ship and stayed on top of all the classes and things going on at the gym."

He scoops a small amount of his ice cream up and eats it. If he eats it any slower, it'll melt into a soup that he can drink.

"I think he was surprised that I offered. I've always known how competent he is, and to be honest, I should have offered it to him a long time ago."

"He's so nice. And such a brilliant teacher."

Robby's eye twitches slightly and there's this little voice in my head that says it's out of jealousy.

"I've seen it even more since Zion started BJJ classes. It can't be easy managing a group of teens. Yet when I've sat and watched the classes, he's had them listening to his every word."

His momentary stoic face then softens as he nods along. "Yeah, you should see all the emails we get about how much he's helped some of the kids' confidence. How long has Zion now been training?"

"I think it's coming up to a year and a half now. Honestly, I'd thought it was just going to be something he tried, a bit of a fad, before giving up and moving on to the next thing. But he's loved it. I honestly can't believe how much it's transformed him."

"I love hearing stuff like that. Especially regarding kids at that age. I remember when I was in my late teens and convinced that I knew it all. Instead of watching and learning from the mistakes my brothers made, I was adamant about making them myself. I really wish they offered more martial arts to kids in schools. I'll have to come and watch some of the junior classes and see how he's getting on."

I freeze as that's something I never did. In all those months we were in that weird dynamic, I never let those two worlds cross. I don't know if Robby senses my hesitation because he says, "I'd never go up to him or anything, not without your permission. And I don't have to have a look at the class if you'd prefer it. I'd never want you to feel uncomfortable or think that I'm crossing a line."

My shoulders relax and I'm surprised at just how tense that thought had made me feel. So, for now, I just give a light nod.

"And how's Kai doing? Everything going okay with him?"

"Yeah, he's actually doing amazingly. I don't know if it's because he's settled into a bit more of a predictable routine or as he's gotten older, he's managed to self sooth and self-regulate some of his emotions, but things have definitely gotten easier with him. Plus, where I often will have Amira over and she also looks after him occasionally, I think it's also helped me as there's someone else around that he can go to, play with, and just open up about how he's feeling."

"That's so good. Sounds like he's made amazing progress. How did you and Amira meet?"

I give him a sad smile before answering. "One of my patients was actually her grandfather. He was such a sweet man, and they've both experienced so much tragedy. He'd tell me about her and how she worked as a nanny in Europe. London, I think it was. I knew how much he missed her, but also wanted her to live her life as much as possible. When she finally moved back home, he'd been over the moon. Even before her return, he suggested she could help me with childcare. Which she did. Sadly, she'd only been back about six months before he came down with pneumonia and passed. I'd already started getting close to her before he died, but I think after he did, we kinda gravitated towards one another even more. And we've pretty much been best friends ever since."

The corners of his mouth lift as he gives me the warmest smile I've seen from him. Even without saying anything, that look, that care and understanding warms me to my core.

"I'm really glad you've found someone that means a lot to you. I'm sure you mean a lot to her too."

Robby tells me all about his plans for the restaurant. I can't believe just how much he already has organized. This version of him couldn't be any more different from the Robby I knew two years ago. That version would give up at the slightest hurdle, have next to no drive, to where he'd struggle even getting out of bed on some days.

"Wow, Robby. I'm really impressed."

"Thank you, that means so much coming from you."

His hand reaches out for mine that's resting next to my plate, but changes his mind at the last second. What I would give to know what is going through his mind right now.

"Is there anything else I can get you both? Or would you like the bill?" the waiter asks, surprising me as I didn't even notice him approach the table.

We both look into each other's eyes, and as much as I've enjoyed this evening, I think now is the best time to call it a night. He must see the decision on my face.

"The bill would be great, thank you," he says, and the waiter nods and walks off.

"I'll book an Uber now actually as knowing my luck, there won't be a car available for a while."

"No. Don't. Let me drive you home. Please. It's the least I can do, and it'd make me feel a lot better if I knew you got home safely." The pleading in his voice is crystal clear, and I appreciate his concern, even if it is unwarranted.

"Okay. Thank you."

His shoulders relax and I'm a little surprised at how much it seems he was expecting me to say no.

He pays the bill, and we make our way out to his truck.

"So, is this yours, or are you just renting it?" I ask as I use the step to climb into the Chevrolet Silverado.

"I brought it. I didn't want to go for something new as that would just be a waste of money, so I found a guy that was selling his truck because he wanted a smaller car. Which has worked out even better, since I'm sure there will often be times I'll need to use the flatbed to deliver and move stuff to and from the restaurant."

Putting the car into drive, he merges into the traffic, and I have to bite down on my lip. Déjà vu washes over me as I remember the first time he drove my car and gave me a lift. It was the first time anyone besides me had driven it. And where I'd never been able to be a passenger princess in my own car, now I was loving every second. Plus, he has this way in which he sits behind the driver's seat that I used to find so sexy. I don't know if it's the angle, or the way his hand rests on the steering wheel, or maybe it's just that I've always had a thing for drivers, that's why I used to love watching the *Fast and Furious* movies.

Pressing my palm against my cheek, I can feel its warm and am glad that he can't see my blush under the cover of darkness. It doesn't take long before he pulls up outside my house.

"Thank you for dinner and the lift home. I know it didn't start smoothly, but I've really enjoyed tonight."

"I have too. Thank you for agreeing to stay. I really

wouldn't have held it against you if you'd have gotten up and left."

Unbuckling my seat belt, I feel a sense of shy awkwardness permeate around us. And it's not just coming from me. There's no way to deny how different this evening has been from any previous interactions the two of us have had. So it's like neither of us knows what to do. Or how to act.

"Well, thank you again. And I'm sure I'll see you around at the gym or something,"

"Yeah. Maybe we could grab a coffee or something? And this time you tell me more about your work and all your design stuff you're doing?" he asks hopefully.

"Yeah, I'm sure we can arrange something."

Reaching out, he pushes one of my curls behind my ear and I swallow a small gasp. It's the first time his fingers have touched me and despite it being only the smallest and simplest of touches, my whole body feels ignited. Ever so slowly, he leans forward and kisses my cheek. How something so small, so innocent, can feel so much bigger, more profound, simply because it's coming from him.

"Good night, Carina," he whispers in my ear.

"Good night, Robby," I reply, climbing out of the truck.

Walking up to my door, I pull my keys out of my bag and open it up. As I turn, I see he's still stopped there, waiting for me to step inside. I give him a small wave, which he returns, then close the door behind me.

Chapter 39

Carina

I never knew furniture shopping could be so complex

I grin, reading the text from Robby, then clicking on the photo he's also sent. It looks like he's inside a warehouse with rows and rows of different furniture.

Yeah, that's a whole other league to what I'm used to. My expertise is with Swedish flat pack items. I'm a pro with those 😁

In the weeks following our dinner, we've had several message exchanges. Not every day, but a couple of times a week. Nothing too heavy or intense, always keeping things light and simple. Could be just checking in or sending silly memes. He once sent a video where it was a compilation of the worst tattoos. That had me crying with laughter at how bad some of them were.

We've also met up for coffee three times. The first one,

he spent most of the time asking all about me. About how my work was going, asking if I could show him the website and he spent ages scrolling through, giving me endless compliments as he looked at all the various designs in my portfolio. I remember feeling like the whole thing was a little like we were in the twilight zone. Not only was it the longest we've talked where I was the focus and center of attention and conversation, but I could tell that he was genuinely interested in what I had to say. He wasn't just simply nodding along, saying the occasional yes. Robby really engaged, followed the points I was talking about, would delve deeper, peppering me with follow-up questions, especially when it was topics he didn't know or understand.

After that meet up, he'd occasionally send me screenshots of when he'd see my work out in the world. And with how specific and niche some of them were, I knew he hadn't just stumbled upon them, and I couldn't help but bask in the warm fuzzy feeling that gave me.

The next time we went for coffee, we were in this little coffee shop that I'd actually never been to. We were sitting in these huge wingback armchairs by the window. He'd shown me photos of the location he and the chef had finally decided on. It's a brilliant spot. Probably the smallest out of all three, but it looks like it has so much potential. I'd also asked what he was doing living wise. As I realized I'd never followed up from when I first asked when he came over to explain when and why he was back. He'd told me then that he was staying in an apartment temporarily, but at the time I hadn't pushed for more. I was probably still in too much shock that he was simply back. I guess I was both surprised and not when he said he'd taken a two-year lease on the apartment, as he didn't want to just buy somewhere rashly, plus he's opening the restaurant, so it would be super intense to both buy somewhere and start up something all at the same time. Robby explained that he's put about ninety percent of the money he had left aside that he will use for when he is ready to buy somewhere, and that extra ten percent he wanted to have as a buffer for the restaurant. So again, I was impressed that he's been really rational and logical with it all.

What had surprised me the most at that coffee meet up was while we were sitting there, two of his friends walked by, spotting us in the window. They both came in, grabbed a coffee to go, but approached us to say hi. It's funny because I've actually seen them both at the gym several times. But the big shocker was when he introduced me, gave me credit for the work I'd previously helped him out with regarding the gym and how I'd been the one that was a lifesaver last time as I'd let him use my car. I don't know if that was some sort of code word as the eyes on both men widened, like they suddenly put two and two together. They were both pleasant enough, and I found it funny when one of them, I think his name was Eric, got a little flirty, and Robby got visibly jealous. I don't care what anyone says, there is no better ego boost than seeing a man who has taken you through every emotion on the spectrum, get jealous when another guy flirts with you.

As much as I've enjoyed our messages and coffee meet ups, I'm still trying to work out where I stand with him. I can't deny that this version of Robby, this mature, respectful, understanding, compassionate person he seems to be now, is someone I really get on with. If I didn't, I wouldn't waste my time still talking to him. But there is still a part of me that wonders how much someone can truly change. I've been adamant in the belief that a leopard doesn't change its spots. In the past, I've made so many excuses for people's behaviours. So much so that I always end up being the one that gets hurt. That's why now, this whole thing with this new and improved Robby feels so difficult to wrap my head around. I don't hold resentment towards him for all the things that occurred in the past, but that still doesn't wipe away what had happened. Yet in that same breath, I need to work out if it is possible for someone to really change that much. I know for a fact that I've changed. I know my self-worth. I recognize the things I should have, things I deserve. How I should be treated. And if I don't get those things, then that person doesn't deserve a place in my life. So if it's possible for me to change this much, would the same apply to him?

Today has just been a nightmare of a day from the get-go. Zion and Kai were both in the foulest of moods this morning because their dad had promised to take them this weekend and listed the fun and exciting stuff that he apparently was going to be doing with them. Then last night, while I was cooking dinner, he called to cancel. When I pushed back on it, he just went on some self-pitying rant about how hard he has to work and how I shouldn't be trying to palm the kids off on him and use the excuse that they will miss out on his promise as the pretence. As always, the coward that he is, he didn't have the guts to tell them himself, so he left that task to me. I waited until we finished dinner to tell them. Zion stormed off into his room. I've seen how much he struggles to navigate the fragile and already dented relationship he has with his dad. Kai ended up having a complete meltdown. I think for him, the whole dynamic with his dad is such a difficult one for him to process. Both were miserable last night and it carried over this morning as I was trying to get them ready for school.

On top of that, I've had to get legal advice because I found one of my design templates on another website. I just hate that I'm going to have to deal with this, plus pay the legal fees, until we get it all sorted.

There is no better way of taking all that annoyance and frustration and letting it out at the gym.

By the time I finish my class, I'm absolutely dripping with sweat. It was probably also one of my best classes, as I just had so much fire within me. I was landing every shot, every kick. My reactions were fast and precise. I head over to the water fountain to refill my bottle and spot Robby talking to one of the other trainers. It's funny because before he left, I never used to see him at the gym. I didn't even know if he was sitting up in his office and I was attending class. But since he's been back, I've spotted him so many times. I've passed him in the corridors several times, he's been at the reception desk twice, and I could have sworn I spotted him looking in on the class once or twice.

Just as I'm closing the lid to my bottle, I feel someone approaching. Before I even look up, I already know that it's him.

"I was walking past the studio while your class was on and damn, you were on fire today," Robby says as I look up and see him rest his hands on his hips.

I huff a laugh. "Let's just say today has been one of those days. So the timing of the class was perfect."

I'm trying really hard not to look at his forearms. One thing that has always been a weakness of mine has been when a guy has prominent veins along his forearms. So the fact that Robby's are protruding, likely from him also having just worked out, is making it hard for me to concentrate right now.

"Hope it's nothing bad?" he asks.

"Huh?"

"I mean, I hope nothing bad has happened today which caused you to need to lose some steam?"

"I… it's just lots of shit going on at the moment."

"You wanna get a coffee or something to eat? We can chat about it. I'm happy to just listen if you need to vent."

I want to say yes, mainly because we have been civil and getting along fine, but where the boys are now going to be home this weekend, I don't have the time.

"I'd love to take you up on your offer, but the boys are now going to be home this weekend and with some of the shit that's happened, I'll feel bad if I get Amira to babysit."

I don't really want to get into the details here. Not because I'm ashamed, but there are several people around and I don't want to talk about my personal business at the gym. He must get a sense it's personal stuff, and I appreciate when he doesn't push the matter further.

"That's fine. Just know that you can always call or message me. Doesn't matter the time. I'll always answer."

Appreciation and warmth spread through me and again I just can't believe how much more caring this version of him is.

"Thank you. I think I will. And I'm sure we can work something out soon."

His whole face lights up at that and I can't help but feel a little giddy that even just a simple open-ended suggestion like that can get such a reaction from him. I won't lie. It feels pretty powerful and gives me the confidence and happiness boost I really need right now.

"I'll hold you to that."

Chapter 40

Robby

There haven't been many things that I've seen as missions in my life. To be honest, I spent way too many years just being unappreciative of so much, wasting time, energy, and so many opportunities.

It took me hitting rock bottom to really get a grip on my life. Allow all my wounds to open up and finally get the chance to heal. Letting go of all the anger, all the hurt and pain. Not just from feeling like my life was spiralling out of control, not just the agonising grief of losing Michael and Joseph and Mom, but also the fear and pain of feeling absolutely alone in this world. I'd never properly processed any of that.

I hate that through me not having allowed myself the time and space to work through losing them, not getting the help I clearly needed, not recognising that alcohol and I just don't mix well, I didn't see how harmful and damaging my actions were to Carina. I'd become so dependent on her, and that all somehow morphed into being so many things. She was the person who would always give me warmth, care, and compassion. I embraced the almost maternal concern she showed with how she always made sure I ate and helped me out with almost everything possible. She gave me sexual satisfaction whenever I wanted. Like she said in the letter, she gave me everything a partner would give. Yet I hadn't appreciated it. Didn't cherish every single thing she gave me, despite my not deserving it.

So that's why, when I fell apart and slowly put myself back together, I knew the things I needed to achieve. The important goals and accomplishments I want to achieve. The first is really doing everything I can to get the gym to its greatest potential. So it can go on and be the legacy my brothers deserve it to be. I also knew I needed to create something that was completely my own. From start to finish. My money, my ideas, my blood, sweat, and tears. That's what the restaurant will be. The ultimate mission I want even more now than I did before is to get Carina to fully and truly forgive me. I would love the chance to start again with her. Earning her trust, her respect, her care. I would give anything to feel her embrace, the soft touch of her lips against my skin. Have her eyes light up and be filled with happiness when she looks at me.

I won't allow myself to get carried away, simply because she's relaxed and has even bantered back with my flirting. I know I have a long way to go and can't just give her empty promises. I need to show consistent, reliable, and thorough actions that back up everything I say and feel. All the things I didn't do, how I neglected showing her how important she is to me. What an amazing woman she is. I know what I want, I just hope with enough time and showing her all the ways that I've matured, I'll be able to get a real chance with her again.

You didn't happen to make friends with a hit man while you were in Thailand, did you?

My eyes do a double take at the text from Carina and immediately call her.

"Hey." Her voice sounds resigned and a little fed up when I call her to find out what's bothering her too much.

"I'm gonna guess you were joking about a hit man, but something's clearly upset you. So what's happened?"

She lets out a deep sigh. "It's easier to say what hasn't happened."

"Remember what I said. You can always talk to me."

She pauses briefly, and I can hear a rustling in the background. "It just feels like at the moment things are coming at me from all directions. As soon as I put one fire out, another one starts somewhere else."

I wait a second in case she elaborates further, but when all I hear her deep breathing I get the sense she doesn't even know where to begin.

"Do you mean things with work and home?" I ask.

"Yeah. Last week I had to get legal help because a company has been using my content and is selling it as if it were their own. Today I heard from my lawyer, and she said they want me to prove that it is all my stuff. So I now have to put together a whole bunch of stuff, and even though I know I have the proof and those designs are mine, it's still annoying. I could just really do without that extra and unnecessary work. Plus, on top of that, I had a client this morning reaching out. I'd sent her the final mock up that I've been working on and now she wants to go with something completely different."

"Aww, man, that's annoying. Regarding the legal stuff, is it just documents that you need to gather?"

"Yeah, I need to print logs and metadata of when I was creating it. I know the software that I use has this function on it where it basically logs each step and basically transcribes it. So everything is date and time stamped. But it's still just a long and annoying thing I'm going to have to go through since I often jump between projects while working, so I'll need to really go through each and every detail, to make sure I can get all the correct things over to my lawyer."

"I never even would've thought that there would be things like this that you have to deal with. I get that it's annoying, but one good thing is that not only do you know that you're one hundred percent in the right and it's all your own work, but hopefully with that log thing you were saying is in that software will help you get that information easily and quickly."

"I know. I just hate that I have to do all these extra things, not only to prove that it is all my work but the fact that where they are a bigger company, I know this is just going to drag out longer than it needs to be."

I hate hearing how frustrated she sounds. Those assholes.

"And with that other client, do you know why they changed their mind?"

"No. Because I literally created exactly what she asked for. But I'm going to have to say that now that she wants to go with something completely different, we will need to add on an extra package since she'd agreed with me to make that design. So for her to do that, let me spend all those hours making it, then changing her mind after the fact, I've essentially wasted all that time for nothing."

"I wish there was something I could do. You want me to call her and tell her she's an idiot and should just be grateful that you even took her on?"

Her laugh is a little lighter now. "Thank you but no. I don't think that'll go down too well for me."

"The offer's there if you change your mind," I say reassuringly.

I'm glad I got even just a small laugh out of her.

"So, what's the other stuff that's bothering you?"

"Last week the boys' dad, Andrew, was meant to have them for the weekend, and unsurprisingly, he canceled. He called them a couple of days ago and made even more empty promises. I then gave him a follow up call, telling him he can't cancel this time because it's just not fair. He can't keep doing this to the kids. Which then led to a huge argument and I'm just so sick of it. I've always made sure not to let my anger out. Especially not letting the boys see just how difficult it is dealing with him. But sometimes I just wish I could tear that asshole apart."

I've never met that man, but from what she's told me, he sounds like not only an awful dad, but also just a terrible human. I grew up without my dad, and it took years for me to process just how much that fucked me up. But even now, looking back, knowing how much it affected me not having him around, I think it would have probably been worse if he'd been coming and going in and out of my life. So I can only imagine the type of damage it's doing to her sons. Hating that she has no way of letting her annoyance and stress out, an idea suddenly pops into my head.

"I'm sorry you have to deal with that. I don't need to

tell you the guy is a complete and utter tool. Like I've said before, let me know if there is anything I can do to help, but I understand that in this situation, it probably wouldn't help much if I intervened."

"Yeah, that'll probably just set him off more and make things worse," Carina says with a sad laugh.

"I do have an idea though. What are you doing on Wednesday?"

"Um… besides trying to get all this shit sorted, nothing. Why?"

"I know you said that you have no way of letting out your frustration, and I've got an idea. Why don't you come to the gym and do a sparring session with me?"

"Are you being serious? That's a crazy idea" Her tone rises and then she bursts out laughing.

"I'm being serious. I think it would be great."

"But I'd look like an idiot. You're a pro. You've been training and competing for years. It would be like an infant sparring with Goliath."

"Don't be silly. We wouldn't be putting on a fight. It would just be a sparring session. Not really any different from the ones you do in your classes. There won't be any specific or required combinations. I just think it'll be good for you to let some of that anger out in a safe way."

She's silent for several moments, and I don't think she's going to agree. I know for a fact it would be good for her. Too often she has to keep things inside. Protecting those around her, always at the cost to herself.

"Fine. I guess we can do that. I'm already warning you now that I'm probably going to embarrass myself, so at least you will have some amusement."

Chapter 41

Carina

I don't know why I feel nervous, but I do. Luckily, the parking lot is practically empty, so there's no one around to watch as I shake my head and fan my face to cool my warming cheeks down. It's not that I'm nervous to see Robby. No, not at all. We've spent enough time together and have eased into this newfound comfortability that I know it's not that. I think it's more the case that I don't want to make a fool of myself. This is his domain. He's the pro, the expert and I'm still just learning the ropes. If I was just having a one-to-one session with one of the usual teachers, I'd be fine. Wouldn't care. But I do feel like it's going to be an uneven keel between us. And that's what has me slightly doubting myself.

"Fuck it, just pull yourself together. It's only Robby," I mutter to myself before climbing out the car and walking towards the entrance.

Looking around, I'm a little perplexed because the place is completely dead. There's literally not a soul around.

"Hello?" I shout out, very confused.

What the hell is going on? I'm just about to pull my cell out of my bag and call him when I hear footsteps coming down the corridor. Turning, I see Robby approaching, wearing a white compression t-shirt and shorts. I have to make the conscious effort to not ogle his body.

"You came. I was worried you might change your mind and cancel."

"I… yeah. Um, why is it so quiet?" I ask, confused.

A smile spreads across his face and his eyes have this gleam within them I haven't seen so such a long time.

"I really wanted you to relax and not stress while we have our session. So I canceled all classes and closed the gym. We've got the place to ourselves until three."

Part of me feels massively relieved because I now know that should I end up embarrassing myself, at least there won't be anyone else around to witness it. But given the physical reaction I've just felt from having him approach me, as well as the fun little flirty messages we've started having, my pulse suddenly races at the thought of us being alone here, working out and getting into a sweaty mess.

"Oh, okay."

"If you don't want to or don't feel comfortable, we can just leave it. I'm sorry. I thought it would make you feel more comfortable. The last thing I wanted to do was make this awkward or anything."

The sudden panic and worry that mars his face is actually kinda cute. And instantly relaxes me.

"No, no, don't be silly. And you're right. I do feel more comfortable knowing that others won't witness my utter humiliation at training with you," I tease reassuringly.

His eyes once again light up and I'm glad that he not

only feels relaxed but also that he didn't take my initial reaction the wrong way.

"I've already told you, you're so much better than you give yourself credit for. So come on, let's get your hands wrapped and I'll even bet that you'll take me down at least twice."

We start the session with some stretches and a light warm up and several times I've caught him just as he has caught me checking him out. This just reminds me of those moments in high school when you first notice someone differently and then catch yourself noticing all those little things that you previously hadn't thought about. Once warmed up, we get into some basic foot-work, which I surprise myself with how comfortable I feel. It's weird though as this is the first time I'm seeing Robby in his element in the flesh. I've seen clips and videos of him training and a couple of his fights, but it's another thing when you see the drips of sweat rolling down his arms, or the way his nostrils flare when he breathes through a combo. The more I relax, the more I let go and put weight behind my movements.

"Alright, let's do jab, cross, and a roundhouse kick."

Stretching my neck from side to side, I shake my arms before starting the combination. We do a couple of rounds before he shouts out the next one.

"Now jab, cross, lead hook, cross."

My arms warming as my muscles burn.

"Double jab, cross to the body, right knee. Go. And I really want you to push that power through, ok?"

I nod as I pant, trying to catch my breath before resuming.

"Come on, Carina. I know you've got more power than that. Stop holding back."

He's right. I do feel like I'm holding back. But I just can't do it.

"Think. Think of every time you've been let down. Every time you've felt disappointed by someone. Imagine every connection is a way of stamping out that flame of frustration."

The more he talks, the more I feel myself letting go. I shout out every time I land a good connection. That only spurs him on further.

"Exactly. Just like that. Come on. Keep going. Don't get lost in your head. Just let it out."

And I do. I don't allow myself to fall back into the memories of the things that are bothering me. Instead, I just allow myself to feel. Using that anger, the rage and hurt and letting those feelings ignite me. I follow all the various combinations he shouts out. Grinding my teeth as I feel sweat dripping down my back. Every punch, every knee, every kick feels like it's closing something. Something deep inside me. It's as if my arms and legs can fight away the demons that are plaguing my mind. As thoughts of my ex-husband and the way he's just constantly letting down the boys, hurting them, disappointing them, sends me into a blinding rage. My arms and legs are on fire as I continue the combo without stopping. The only sound I can hear is the loud pounding of my heart. Tears roll down my cheeks and join the sweat that's dripping down my face as I fight through the struggle of helplessness I feel about not being able to change things for my boys.

I don't even realize Robby is talking to me until he

grabs my upper arms and tries to get me to focus on him. “Hey, hey, stop. Just breathe. Stop.”

The soothing sound of his voice finally breaks through the drumming in my ears. My tears continue to fall as I struggle to catch my breath. Robby drops the pads before taking my face in his hands, making me look him in the eyes.

“Carina. I’ve got you. You're fine. Just breathe. In through your nose, out through your mouth. Nice and deep. You're fine. Keep going. Just like that, focus on your breathing.”

His thumbs wipe away my tears before he pulls me into his chest. His arms stroke my back soothingly and I can feel his heart beating through his chest too, but it’s nowhere near as intense as mine. He continues saying soothing words and rubs his hands up and down my back as I finally feel myself calm down.

Once I finally feel like I’m able to breathe without hyperventilating, I let my arms and shoulders relax into his embrace. Each gentle stroke of his arms along my back soothing me back down to earth safely. Slowly, I lift my head and my eyes meet his. I’m sure mine look red and irritated, whereas his glow with a brightening tenderness, filled with so many unsaid words, and have me hypnotized.

“Carina I… I know I shouldn’t ask right now, but please can I kiss you?” he whispers, bringing his hand along my neck, stroking my chin.

Captivated by the raw intensity of this moment, words fail me, but I nod. Ever so slowly, Robby dips his head, first just brushing his lips against mine. It’s as if he’s using his lips to read my own. The way someone’s finger would glide across braille, his lips trailing a burning path along my own. Finally, he kisses me. Clasping the back of my head in place, he fuses his mouth to mine. He holds me so tightly, I don't know where he stops, and I begin. As his tongue explores and massages mine, I moan into his mouth. Every cell within me is lit with desire as he continues kissing me like his life depended on it. Frustration slowly builds as I struggle to get a grip on his body, my hands are still bound within the gloves. Like he can read my mind, without breaking the kiss he reaches down, pulls each glove off and starts unwinding my bound hands. Once they are finally free, I grip his compression top, wishing I could touch his bare skin. I let out a moan as he kisses his way down my neck, his thumbs brush across my nipples that have hardened under my sports bra. The slight stubble on his chin grazes against my oversensitive skin, adding another layer of friction. Guiding me backward, he continues to kiss along my chest, his tongue leaving a blazing trail in its wake.

Wrapping his arms around me, he holds me close as he gently dips me and lowers us down onto the mat. Resting his fists on either side of my head, he cages me in with his body. Sitting back on his knees, I watch as he pulls his compression top off, his chest rising rapidly as he looks down at me with such hunger, his eyes burning with desire. Hooking his fingertips into the band of my gym shorts, he looks at me first for approval and I nod, desperate to be free from the bindings of my clothes. Sliding my shorts and thong down my legs, he then throws them off, and they land beside us. His large hands grip my thighs, opening them wide.

"You have no idea how long I have been dreaming about this," he growls before sliding down.

The second I feel his tongue swipe against my swollen clit, I cry out. "Oh, fuck yes."

My eyes roll to the back of my head as he stiffens his tongue and works me into a moaning frenzy. His thick fingers join his mouth, and my walls clamp down on them as he pushes them deep inside. The pads of his finger brushing against the spongy ridge, making my legs shake.

"Oh… oh… yes… yes. Just like that. Oh, god yes… yes…" I pant.

Robby continues to devour me as if I were his last meal. The sounds of my moans, heavy breathing, and panting echo across the studio.

"More, please, I need more," I beg.

Reaching down, I pull at his arms, guiding him up. His mouth glistens with my juices, and I kiss him, tasting myself on his tongue and moaning into his mouth. His fingers find the zipper in the center of my sports bra, unzipping it before discarding it with the rest of my clothes. Slowly, he rains kisses along my shoulder, running his tongue along my overheated skin before gently blowing along the wet trail, making me shiver. Kissing his way down across the slopes of my breasts until latching his mouth onto my nipples. Licking, biting, and sucking on them as my hands brush down his arms, along his chest until finally I feel the bulge in his shorts.

Swimming in a sea of pleasure, I pour all the unspoken words I've yet to say into this kiss. My lips soften under the firmness of his as finally he matches my greed and takes possession of my mouth. As his mouth leaves mine, I am breathless, watching him shuffle his shorts and boxers down to his knees. My fingers trace along the swollen mushroom tip that's already leaking with pre-cum and memories flood me of the last time I had him; I forgot just how big he is. My pussy clenches as I know how delicious the feel of him stretching me will be.

"I'm clean. I've not been with anyone for a year," Robby says against my lips.

Thrills run through me not only because he hasn't been with anyone for a long time, but also that I get to feel him again skin on skin.

His chest rumbles with a growl as I wrap my hand around him and begin stroking him from root to tip.

"Fuck, Carina, I need you. I need you right now." The deep timbre of his voice only heightens my desire more.

His mouth finds mine again, and I can feel his want is just as great as my own as he kisses me, laying me back down onto my back.

Rubbing the crown against my clit, he teases me more, making my back arch against the mat. Finally, just when I think I can't take his teasing anymore, he lines himself up and slowly buries himself until our hips fuse together.

It takes me a moment to adjust to the stretching fullness of him. It's been so long since I've felt this full, this turned on, yet flashbacks flood me and it's like my body has muscle memory of him. Robby must feel the moment I relax as he slowly increases the pace of his thrusts. Reaching down, he pinches and rolls my nipples between his fingers before reaching under my thighs and resting them in the crook of his elbows, allowing him to drive deeper.

Every inch of my body feels alive as waves of pleasure continue to wash over me.

"You feel so good. I've missed this, miss you so much, Carina. I love the way you grip me tight every… single… time," he groans.

Leaning down, he bends me practically in half, the angle enables him to reach spots that have me screaming out at the top of my lungs. His rhythm and pace are relentless and my whole body tingles. Explosive euphoria erupts, and I cry out in ecstasy. My thighs tremble as I fall over into the abyss. Wave after wave of pleasure rushes through my veins as I ride out my orgasm. Kissing me and swallowing my moans, Robby keeps pumping in and out of me until I feel him swell, then comes deep inside me. His groans vibrate against his chest as my walls clamp down, milking every drop out of him.

We're both a mess of sweat and juices, and he slowly lowers my legs before covering my body with his own. Continuously kissing me, he rolls us to our sides and his fingers trace along my skin, which now shivers from over-stimulation.

It takes us both a few minutes to catch our breaths while my fingers trail along the intricate blues and greens of his large chest tattoo. Lifting my head, he looks deep into my eyes.

"Let's get you in the shower. I'm not finished with you yet."

Chapter 42

Robby

Every part of me feels like it's buzzing with the best high I've ever experienced. I take a towel that's on the ledge, wrapping it around her, and tuck one around my waist before threading my fingers between hers and leading her toward the ladies' locker room.

"Do you want it hot or just warm?" I ask, opening the shower cubicle door.

"Warm, please. My skin still feels too hot," she says with a grin.

I adjust the water to what I'm hoping to be the right temperature, and I think I've got it right based on the sound of her relaxed sigh as she steps underneath the cascading water.

Following her, I step beneath the spray and begin massaging her shoulders, arms, and back. Watching the contrast of my fair and pale skin against the rich, deep and dark hues of hers has been something that's always intrigued me. Not only that, but Carina is literally glowing. She's always been beautiful, but the effervescent way she has shone since I've returned hasn't gone unnoticed, which makes me feel that it was my fault, my presence that diminished her before. As my fingers glide over her lower back, I still can't wrap my head around the fact that she's here. With me. Naked in the shower after one of the hottest sexual encounters I've ever had with her.

I don't know if it's due to how desperately I have been wanting her, or that this was the first time she allowed herself to be completely bare to me. It was something that I'd never even noticed before. Never even thought of the fact that all the time we'd previously hooked up, she'd always still worn at least one item of clothing. I'd just always been so desperate to be inside her that it had never been something that bothered me. But I for sure noticed earlier, when she let me completely strip her down and not only be allowed to experience and enjoy her delicious body but also see it.

"Oh, I think I've got a knot there," she says, her shoulders tensing as I knead out the exact spot she's talking about.

"Mmmm, yeah, I can feel it."

I continue massaging my way down her body, focusing on her thighs and calves before turning her and gently leaning her against the wall. She lets out a gasp as her back touches the tiles. Getting down on my knees, I hook her leg over my shoulder and grip her hips firmly. Looking up at her as the water continues to pour down over us, her eyelids droop and she takes that delectable bottom lip between her teeth. Keeping my eyes focused on hers, I watch her eyes roll back as my tongue sweeps along her warm and wet core.

“Yes… oh, yes… Mmmm… that feels… so good.” She gasps as my tongue teases and relentlessly works her clit.

I love the way she reaches down and grabs a hold of my hair, keeping me firmly in place as I devour her. Despite my firm grip on her hips, they rock against my face as she chases her pleasure, only turning me on even more. My dick strains and bobs against my stomach and my balls feel heavy despite the fact that I got my release not that long ago, but this isn’t about me right now. I just want to give her pleasure. My eyes are glued to her as she lets go of my hair and teases her nipples. This has to be the sexiest thing I have ever witnessed in my life.

“Oh, Robby… oh, yes… yes… yes…” she moans.

Her thigh tightens around my head, and I know she’s close. Her cries as she finds her release echo around the shower cubicle. My mouth is filled with the taste of her essence and the water that still falling around us. I keep slowly drawing more and more moans from her before giving her a moment to catch her breath. I wait for her legs to stop shaking, before gently sliding her thigh off my shoulder and rising to my feet. Gripping her face between my hands, I fuse my mouth with hers. Kissing her, getting her to taste just how delicious she is. Trying to show her just how much I want her. How much I need her. This time it’s me who moans at just how much I love the feel of her on me, engulfing me, consuming me.

Taking a breath, I rest my forehead against hers, looking deep into her eyes. Hers are still slightly unfocused from her orgasm, but she must see something in mine as she suddenly reaches up and places her palm against my cheek.

“What’s wrong?” I can hear the concern in her voice.

Shaking my head, I run my hands against the back of her neck, threading my fingers in her wet hair.

"Nothing's wrong. I just… Carina… I-I just want you so much. I need you more than I need air."

Her eyes widen, then her brows crease. "I'm confused. You just had me."

"I know, but I don't just mean like that. I want more. I feel so torn as a part of me knows I don't deserve to even ask this of you, but I know I will forever regret it if I don't."

Her shoulders hunch up slightly and I'm sure she's probably confused with how unclear and inarticulate I'm being. Letting out a deep breath, I try to get control of the nerves that now flood through me.

"When I came back, there were several things I wanted to do. Wanted to achieve. Some of those I've already accomplished. Others, I'm working towards. But the one that has meant more than anything to me is you."

"What about me?"

Licking my lips, I tamp down the emotion I can feel is already building within. "My main, or I guess biggest hope from my return has been to get you to forgive me. Not just from me saying sorry though. I wanted to earn your forgiveness, earn your trust, and show you not only how sorry I am for all the things I took for granted before, but also proving that I have truly changed. I'm no longer the selfish and idiotic man I was back then."

She nods to my words and covers her hands over mine as I'm guessing she can feel my hands shake.

"Robby, I have forgiven you. I let go of the hurt and pain a long time ago. I've seen how much you've changed. The man standing before me now differs completely from that one from two years ago. And to be honest, I think you needed that time and opportunity to sit back to look and see what things you want and need in your life, really get a good plan and structure in place, and you've been implementing the changes that I honestly never would have pictured for you to alter."

"Thank you. Thank you for forgiving me. But that isn't the only thing. Carina, these past couple of months, yes I've been wanting to show you this new, improved, healthier both mentally and physically version of me but from the second I laid eyes on you in the parking lot, I knew I would do anything for you to give me another chance."

Her mouth opens in shock, her pupils widen as her eyes bounce between mine.

"I did everything wrong the last time. I approached the whole situation we were in wrongly. I didn't acknowledge my feelings for you and made nothing clear. But I will now, Carina. I would love to have a second chance with you. With us. But doing it properly. For us to have an actual relationship. To really try to give things a shot. I want to take you out on dates, I want to make you laugh, I want to make memories with you we will look back on and reminisce together. I want to earn you each and every single day. Give you whatever it is you need. If that's a safe place for you to be vulnerable, I will cherish that and enable you to let go and be there to hold you. Every day I will not just tell you but also show you what you mean to me. I want to be your friend, your lover, your partner. We can go at whatever pace you're comfortable with. We don't need to rush anything. But please, please give me—us—a proper chance?"

My heart is pounding so hard in my chest it feels like it's about to jump out. "I-I… I honestly never expected this," she stutters.

And I understand that, because I've never made it clear how much she means to me and that's just one of the many errors I've made in the years.

"Do you really mean it? Do you mean everything you said?" she asks.

For the first time, I see a slight hint of worry in her eyes, and I know that's only there because of how I treated her before. That worry, that doubt is all my doing and I hate myself so much right now that through my stupidness, I put that there.

"Yes. Every word. We can go at whatever pace you're comfortable with. If you tell me you want us to not sleep together for the next, I don't know, three or four months while I continue to show you how serious I am, then we do that. Yes, it'll be hard as I already want you all the time, but I need for you to know that it's not just sex. I want *everything* with you. I will gladly follow any rules or boundaries that you set to make yourself feel more comfortable. Whatever it is you need, I will give you."

Her chest rises and falls rapidly, and I would give anything to know what is going on in her head right now.

"I'm lost for words. I really am. Like I said, you have changed, but I have too. That's why I don't want to just give a quick answer right now. I need some time to think about it. I'm not saying no, that's not the case at all. But I do want to really think things through and make sure I'm making the right decision. Is that okay with you?"

My chest pangs slightly, but I fully understand where she's coming from.

"Yes, of course. You can take all the time you need."

And I mean that. Carina is absolutely one of a kind. I know for a fact that I will never meet anyone like her ever again. I don't want to just have some fleeting relationship with her. I want us to build a life together. So if that means she needs some time to think this through before she decides, then that's the best thing. Besides, like she said, she's not said no. And I hope that if it was something she really didn't want, then she'd have shut this all down already.

"Thank you," she says with a shy smile before pulling my face down to hers and kissing me.

Even this kiss already feels different. It's tender, caring, and full of hope.

Once we're all showered, I run and grab her bag so she can change and dash up to the office to put on one of my spare sets of gear I've always got here before walking her to the door and give her another kiss.

"Thank you. I don't know how long I need, but I promise I will think it through and let you know," she assures me.

It's been a week. Seven long days and Carina still hasn't decided yet. I'm not angry or annoyed and again I know it's completely down to her and I don't want her to rush anything. We've still been talking and messaging every day, which was something I wasn't sure she would do. There was a part of me that wondered if she'd need her space from me, while she made up her mind. But now every time my cell goes off with a message from her, I can't help the smile it brings to my face.

Trying to distract myself from the continuous thoughts of her, I focus back on all the emails I need to get through, not just for the gym but also for the restaurant.

I get about an hour's worth of work done before I'm interrupted by a knock on my office door.

"Come in," I shout.

Expecting to see Koa walking in, I'm pleasantly surprised when I look up and see it's Carina instead.

"Am I interrupting anything?" she asks.

"No, not at all. Is everything okay?" I ask, rising from my seat and walking over to the front of my desk.

"Yeah, everything's fine."

She closes her eyes, takes a deep breath, and then looks up at me.

"I said I needed some time because I really didn't want to jump or rush anything. Not only because in that moment you told me, I was still in a slight sex haze, but also because of everything that has happened before."

Leaning back on my desk, I brace my hands on either side of me as my pulse spikes.

"It took me a long time to let go of the past. Not just because it was difficult, but also because of how intertwined it was with other things I have gone through. I needed to see if I could separate the person you were then to the one that you are now, and I wasn't sure if I could. There was a part of me that was really worried that I'd fall back into my own habits and not stand my ground and all that. But in the last few days, I've realized I am strong. I know I won't put up with things I don't deserve."

My chest deflates as I get the feeling this is going to be her nice way of saying no.

"I also know that life is short. And there is just something about you. Something that I've always felt. If you were truthful and honest about everything you said, how you'd be happy for us to take things slowly, being completely open and honest, then yes. Yes, I want to give us another shot. A real one."

I'm truly stunned. Absolutely amazed, as I'd convinced myself she was going to say no.

"Are you being serious? You really mean that?" I ask, my heart in my mouth.

"Yes, Robby, I'm being serious," she says with the biggest, warmest smile spreading across her face.

I walk the two steps to her, wrap my arms around her, lifting her, I kiss her with everything I have. So grateful she's giving us a chance. Putting her down, I keep my arms around her and bend to rest my forehead against hers.

"Thank you. Thank you for giving us a chance. I promise I will make sure you don't regret it."

Chapter 43

Carina

It's funny because sometimes in life I feel you put things out into the universe, and whether or not you believe it, fate just manifests those things to you. Other times, you could just be keeping your head down, not wanting or needing anything in particular, and then bam, you're thrown the biggest curveball. One that you never could have expected, predicted, or even thought you wanted. And that's what my life has felt like the past six months since I told Robby yes to giving us a shot. Something I honestly never could have imagined happening.

I won't lie, in the first month or so I was convinced he was just going to go back into his old ways. Continuously believing that surely things couldn't end up being so different, so much better. But they have been. It's like he transported back in time and courted me at first, and then does everything he can to help, be there for me, care for me, and always lets me know how he feels.

It took us a while to work out our new dynamic, but we've really made it work. We have proper dates twice a week, and because of the kids, they vary and are often during the day. But usually once a week we've been able to do things like going out for dinner, bowling, comedy clubs; you name it, we've done it. My mom and Amira pretty much alternate watching the kids one evening a week and it's meant so much having them support me too.

I've still been consciously very protective of myself. It's not that I haven't enjoyed all our time together, but I guess there's just still such a big part of me that has a slight fear of getting hurt, so I've held myself back emotionally.

Which was really hard to do when he made a little picnic for us and was super cheesy doing a four-month anniversary lunch where we were just talking and enjoying each other and threw the bombshell when he told me he loves me. He didn't make any grand gesture, nor did he recite some sort of romantic poem or heartfelt plea. He just said it in the middle of the conversation. That he loves me and just wants me to know that. I honestly thought he was joking, but I could see from his expression he was being serious. I never responded. I couldn't. I didn't say it back. That's not because I don't care for him. It's not because I don't have strong feelings for him. I do. But I think I just keep holding that back because I know that the second I do, things for me will change forever.

Giving him my heart feels like the riskiest thing in the world and it scares me. So I've just stayed quiet. I do feel guilty about that, but like I said to him six months ago, I need to do things at my pace, at my time. And maybe one day I'll feel safe enough to say them back.

I give myself one last look over in the mirror. I'm wearing a fitted maxi dress that has a long slit along my thigh, allowing my tattoo to pop. Mom's sleeping at my house tonight to watch the boys because Robby is putting on a charity fight night at the gym. Despite this being the second charity event he's put on, it's the first one where I'll be attending with him.

"Alight, boys, behave yourselves for Nanny and if there's any problem, just call me," I say, walking to the sofa and giving them each a kiss on the head.

"Enjoy your night sweetheart," Mom says.

"But Mom, why can't I go? I train at the gym too," Zion complains.

Mom looks over at me with a grin.

"I know. How about we see if you can come to the next one?" I suggest.

"Okay, fine," he agrees, though he's not too happy missing tonight.

Giving Mom a wink before heading out to the car, I have to laugh at Zion's endless enthusiasm at wanting to integrate himself more and more at the gym. Training has really transformed his life. But it has been the one thing I have struggled with mine and Robby's relationship.

I've not told the kids yet that we are together. I guess I just want to wait until I know exactly what we are. I'd never want them to meet someone I wasn't sure was going to stay around. I would never do that to them. And because Zion trains at his gym, and I'm the one picking him up and dropping him off, it's been hard for us both to make sure we don't give each other lingering looks or are tempted to touch or kiss in front of the kids. We're fine doing that otherwise. I'm pretty sure everyone at the gym has known for some time now that we're a couple, but just not the kids yet. I asked Robby if it bothered him I haven't told them, but he said no. He understands that the boys are my priority and he's happy if he just falls behind. Again, it's just another demonstration of how much he has matured, and I know he's doing all of this just for me. To make me happy.

It's amazing what a few posters, a few rented tables and chairs, and a change to the lighting can do to transform a place. Don't get me wrong it's still clearly the gym, but it's got a slightly different air around the boxing ring. The place is already pretty busy and as I weave my way through the growing crowds, I wave and nod at people I recognize from class.

A tap on my shoulder startles me and as I turn, laughing at Koa's wide eyes at my reaction. "Sorry, didn't mean to make you jump," he says.

"Don't be silly, I was just in my own little world," I reply as my head cranes up to his huge six-foot-eight stature.

"I was just coming over to let you know Robby is sorting something out in the office, so if you want, you can head up there or you see that table over there? He's reserved that and the seats for a couple of people, obviously including you. I don't think he should be much longer, so it's up to you."

My eyes glance over at the table and already see a few guys sitting there. "Thank you."

He gives me a nod before disappearing into the crowd.

I only recognize two of the guys at the table as Robby's friends. I've been introduced to them and have chatted casually a couple of times, but I don't know the others. Not wanting to feel awkward, I make my way towards

Robby's office. I don't even get to the corridor by the locker rooms when I spot him coming out from behind the door.

His face lights up the second he sees me and makes quick strides over to me. "Hey, baby," he says, wrapping his arms around me and pulling me to his chest before taking my breath away with a kiss. "Have you been here long? Sorry, I should have messaged and said I was up there sorting some stuff out."

"No, I literally arrived a couple of minutes ago and Koa found me straight away and told me you were in the office," I reassure him.

I can't help but love the way he holds me. Since we've been together, he's never shied away from physical touch in public, whether they be innocent or when I know he's turned on. His large hands rest on the curve of my ass and my chin rests on his chest.

"You look beautiful, by the way."

I smile at his compliment. "Thank you. Do you still have more work to do, or are you able to join everyone and relax now?"

"Everything's pretty much all set. All the fighters except one are here and have probably already started warming up and getting ready with their trainers."

"Where's the one that's not here yet? Is everything okay?"

"I'm not sure. Koa said that he lives a little while away, so maybe he's just stuck in traffic or something. His trainer's here as he also trains one of the other guys that's fighting tonight, so I'm gonna find him in a little bit to see if he knows what's going on. Anyway, I'll deal with that in a bit. Let's enjoy ourselves for now."

Linking my hand with his, he gives me another kiss before we head back and join all the other attendees.

Koa comes over and whispers something in Robby's ear.

"Shit. Damn, that fucking sucks," Robby says under his breath.

I turn to gauge what's happened.

"No, we can't cancel that one. It's raised too much already."

I try to work out what they are talking about, but it's hard since I can only hear Robby's one-sided response to Koa.

"There's what, like, an hour till that one, right?" he says, looking and stretching his head before carrying on. "I'll do it. Yeah, there's enough time for me to."

Turning to me, he kisses the top of my hand before he faces the table. "Alright boys, I'm gonna have to leave you. Our main guy's car broke down and there's no way for him to get here in time. So I'm gonna take his place."

My mouth opens in surprise, and I get a small tingle of unease crawling up my back.

Robby's friends all cheer, obviously even more excited that they now get to watch their buddy fight tonight. I, however, don't feel the same type of excitement. Turning towards me, he squeezes my hand. "I'm sorry I won't be able to watch the others with you but I'm gonna have to warm up and get ready. Will you be alright here?"

I blink rapidly as I don't want him to think I'm annoyed that he's leaving me here, but I just don't know how I feel about watching him fight. Also not wanting him to suspect my worry, I plaster a mask over my face and give him a reassuring smile.

"Yeah, don't worry about me. I'm fine. You go and warm up. Focus on the fight."

Leaning forward, he pulls me in for a quick kiss before rising from his seat.

"Don't worry about Carina," William says across the table. "I'll make sure she's okay. Get your head in the game and show these boys how it's done."

He must have been both watching and listening to our interaction. The look he gives Robby, I can't quite decipher. Robby gives me a kiss on the head before heading off towards the locker room. I try to get myself to relax and join in the conversation with the others, but I can't shake this feeling in my gut that something bad is going to happen.

Just as the first fight is about to start, William takes the seat beside me. "There's nothing for you to worry about. Robby's gonna be fine," he says, leaning over so only I can hear him.

I look up at him in surprise. I thought I'd disguised the worry on my face. But from the way he lifts his brow at me, I'm guessing I didn't do as good of a job as I thought.

"Your whole-body language has changed since he told everyone he's fighting. Wasn't hard putting two and two together."

"Yeah, I guess it's just because I wasn't expecting it."

"I promise you he'll be fine. I've watched the guy he's up against before and he's nowhere in the same league. They might be the same height and weight, but Robby's got so much more experience."

I'm knocking back glasses of water like there's no tomorrow because my mouth just feels so damn dry. Just then, the announcer declares to the crowd that there has been a last-minute change because of the fighter pulling out.

"Taking his place, we have the man who has put this whole evening together, the owner of this very gym, he's undefeated with sixteen wins under his belt, the one, the only *Diamond Demon*," the announcer roars into the microphone.

The crowd erupts as Robby takes his place, bowing to each corner of the ring. Adrenaline pumps through me so intensely my fingers feel like they have pins and needles. Time feels like it's passing at a snails pace. I don't know what he did for his warm up, but his body looks pumped and ready. Sweat already pools along his hairline and the muscles along his chest and arms are clearly defined, even through the vibrant multicoloured print of the tattoos that cover them. His hands are bound and encased in his gloves, he swings his arms and stretches his neck from side to side. The air around us feels thick with excited anticipation. My stomach is in knots as I watch Robby bouncing on the balls of his feet. I smile when I notice the shorts he's wearing. They're the ones I'd gotten him two years ago for his birthday. That momentary sense of ease and happiness is extinguished the second I hear the bell ring, starting the fight.

My heart is in my mouth during the first round. All his friends sitting beside me roar him on with every punch, kick, and elbow he lands. The three minutes it takes for the first round feel so much longer. When the bell rings and he heads to his corner, I watch with anticipation as Koa wipes his head, giving him water and talks to him while Robby's nodding along as he gets his breath back.

As anxious as I feel watching him, I'm also fascinated. His entire demeanor, body language, the way he moves is just so different from anything I have seen before. He's absolutely in the zone. Focused solely on the fight. If I wasn't so worried, I'd be really turned on right now.

The smell of sweat and this indescribable fighting hunger fill my nose, almost making me feel lightheaded.

The bell rings for the second round and he dodges a kick but mistimes his step and catches the guy's left hook, which lands on the side of his face and knocks him down. Rising to my feet, my mouth drops open. Everything goes in slow motion. My ears ring with the loud beating of my heart. My fingers tremble as I lift them to my mouth whilst pure fear ricochets through me. He doesn't stay down for long, but in those moments that he was, I don't remember the last time I felt that scared. That's the moment that I realize just how much he means to me. How scared I was that he was hurt cemented my realization that despite how much I've tried to suppress it, I love him. There's a tug on my arm and it's William trying to get my attention.

"He's fine. He didn't get hit properly. He lost his footing. Was already on his way down from that, not the punch."

I can just about make out what he says over the loud noise around us.

Squeezing my hands together to stop them from shaking, my eyes zone in as Robby gains back momentum and lands a solid jab, cross, hook, and rear leg kick, ending it with an uppercut and knocking his opponent out. My chest hurts with how hard and fast my heart is beating.

The entire table gets to their feet as they cheer him on.

The ref ends the fight as Robby wins by knockout. He goes over and checks his opponent is okay and I can feel the relief of everyone when he nods, and his trainers help him back up to his feet. The entire gym erupts in a loud roar of cheers and celebration.

The next twenty minutes are a bit of a blur of everyone celebrating, Koa telling the crowd how much money was raised, and Robby reemerging, now wearing a clean pair of sweats and thanking everyone for coming and all their generous donations.

The first thing he does when he joins us is wrap me in his arms and kiss me until there are enough catcalls and whooping from his friends around us.

"You had her worried there for a second when you went down," William ribs.

Robby puts his arm around my shoulder, looking down at me sweetly.

"Were you worried, babe? You didn't need to be. I was fine. Felt more embarrassed than anything else that I hadn't planted my foot firmer."

"Yeah, I got worried there for a moment." I still feel a little overwhelmed by it all.

I stay close by his side for the rest of the night. Enjoying to just sit back and watch as he celebrates and relaxes with everyone around him.

Despite my protesting that he should take it easy and let me drive, he ends up driving us back to his place.

Once we get inside, Robby is pulling my dress over my head, leaving me in only my bra and panties, he begins kissing my shoulder as his hands wander and tease down my sides, along my hips, and around the lace edges of my underwear.

"Robby," I say, looking up at him.

"Yeah."

"When you went down, I was scared. I didn't think I would feel as worried as I did. And… well… it made me realize something."

"Oh, and what's that?"

"I love you. I know you said it to me a while ago, and I've not said it back. I guess I was just trying to protect myself. But there's no denying it. I'm in love with you."

I panic momentarily as he pauses, not responding, and I can feel tears prick the back of my eyes that maybe he doesn't feel the same anymore. Maybe it's too late. Fear wracks me that there's the chance he doesn't feel like that towards me anymore.

The biggest and most beautiful smile breaks out across his face and instantly relief washes over me.

"You have no idea how much that means to me. I love you so much."

Grabbing my face, he kisses me with such passion, such abandon. Both of us pouring the love we just spoke of into action.

Walking me backward until the backs of my calves hit his bed, he continues kissing me. My body tingles with both desire and endearment.

"I love you, Carina. And tonight, I'm going to show just how much."

Chapter 44

Carina

This is the first time since I've told Robby I love him that I'm taking Zion to his BJJ class, knowing that Robby will be around. I can't lie, there is a part of me that feels a little nervous, only because after I opened up and told him how I feel, it felt like the floodgates opened. Now that I've accepted it, all I want to do is bask in it. But I can't. Not here. Not right now. I still haven't told the kids yet and know, especially Zion, will have a strong reaction when I do. So I need to make sure it's done in a calm, safe environment, and not carelessly bumping into each other and giving it all away at the gym.

Robby isn't teaching the class, but I know that he's here in the building. Even if he hadn't commented on it earlier, I'd have known it in my gut. I can't explain it, but it's as if there's this hidden magnetic pull between us. Like I can sense his proximity.

Focusing back on Zion's class, I sit back and just enjoy being able to watch. It's actually been a really enjoyable and bonding thing for me and Zion since I've been coming to watch his classes. As he's gotten older, it's been harder and harder to not only find the time but also the common ground of something that brings us together.

All is going well when suddenly one kid in the class seems to have taken what the teacher said the wrong way. His reaction is extreme with the kid flying off the handle. Sean, their instructor, keeps his tone firm but not loud as he tries to defuse the situation. The boy is now just shouting at the other kid, trying to blame him for everything and I'm glad when I see Zion step back, making sure not to get involved.

I'm alert and watching but not getting involved. However, despite the teacher managing to get control of the situation and defusing it all, the parents of the two boys now have gotten into an argument. I don't know which belongs to which, but the tension they are now creating from their shouting has gotten all the parent's attention, with everyone watching.

I'm about to walk over to Zion when Robby comes over to the parents and begins talking to them. I can't hear what he says as there is still just the loud noise of the rest of the surrounding gym, but from watching his body language I can tell he's not impressed. He doesn't have his arms crossed and isn't talking animatedly. No, there isn't anything combative about him, he's just seems to take back control of the situation. He must sense my eyes on him as he moves off the mats and stands to the side as Sean talks. The class was already almost finished, but all of that turns into a blur as Robby and my eyes lock. Though no words exchanged, and no expressions are being made, there is still so much being said. I don't realize how connected, how engulfed I am in his eyes until Zion walks in front of me and starts talking.

"Well, that was an annoying way for our class to end," he mutters before taking a big sip from his water bottle.

Turning my focus on him, I hand him a towel to wipe the sweat off his face. "I know. It's silly. Do you know what even set it all off?" I ask.

"Not really, no. I think that Jamie kid thought he could do this move, but it wasn't in the combo we were practicing and could have been dangerous and argued that it was okay for him. Something like that, I think."

I nod. "Do you know that guy?" he asks, jutting his head to the side.

"What guy?"

"The tall one that came in and fixed everything? Is he like another teacher here or something?" he asks, and his eyes squint slightly as he looks around.

He focuses on Robby and the slight panic that had subsided earlier is now back.

"He's the owner. This is his gym," I answer.

Zion's head spins back to me, his eyes light up and the corner of his mouth lifts in a small smile.

"No way. That's the Diamond Demon?"

This time, it's my head that looks over in shock.

"How do you know that?" I ask.

"There are posters of him, or I guess his torso and tattoos are all over the place. The guy is cool. We've talked about him loads during class before. One guy told me he has loads of knockouts under his belt. Someone else said that they'd heard he's a former black special op now living here under a new identity as he was involved in some top-secret mission."

I can't help but burst out laughing at that, which has everyone looking over at me, including Robby. Zion's eyes widen in embarrassment.

"I'm sorry, but that's ridiculous. Who on earth told you that?" I ask, still laughing.

"I can't remember. But someone else said apparently every tattoo he has is about a fight he's won."

Looking over, my eyes scan Robby's arms and I have to suppress the shiver when I think about how up close and personal I have gotten with all his tattoos.

"I don't think that's true either."

"Still, the guy is cool. We've all heard of him, and someone showed us some of his fights, but we've never seen him before. Have you met him before like when you do your classes and stuff?"

I struggle to keep my face neutral. Although I don't want to lie to my son, this really isn't the time or the place to tell him about us.

"Yeah, I know him."

He takes another swig from his bottle, and I follow his line of sight and see that he's watching Robby now talking to the instructor.

"Can I meet him? You know him so it wouldn't be some weird and random thing, plus it would be really cool if I could meet him properly."

At that same moment, Robby looks over at us. I can feel from Zion's energy he is both desperate and determined to meet him. Completely oblivious as to who this is. Unaware of the significance. I know that if I try to brush it off and make a big deal about not introducing him to this so-called legend he and the other kids believe him to be, Zion will not only find that weird but is likely to be more suspicious.

Taking a few deep breaths, I look over again at Robby, who is still talking to Sean.

"Okay, fine. But we will not interrupt him while he's talking."

I pack up my bag, now finding it a little amusing the way Zion is eagerly waiting for a window for us to walk over. He doesn't have to wait too long when Sean goes to talk to some other parents and Robby then turns and scans around before his eyes land on me.

"Come on, Mom, he's free now," Zion says, before already beginning to stroll in his direction.

My heart beats faster, and even from this distance, I can see the confusion on Robby's face.

Gathering up our things, I walk with Zion towards him. Now it's his turn to have just the slightest look of surprise in his eyes. Again, I don't think anyone else would even notice it, but I do. Zion's steps slow, and I can feel the sudden shyness that he used to have when he was little start to show. That spurs me into action. Pushing my shoulders back, I take the last few steps until we both stand before him.

Chapter 45

Robby

"Hiya, so this is my son, Zion. Zion, this is Robby the owner. Robby, apparently you have a bit of a reputation amongst the younger gym goers, and Zion was keen to meet you," Carina says. My eyes blink rapidly as I feel both confused by her statement and also nervous about meeting her son.

"Oh, well, I hope it's not bad things. It's nice to meet you, Zion." I reach out my hand and I appreciate when he returns a firm handshake.

"Yeah it's all good stuff." His voice is deeper than I'd imagined, and he's only a couple of inches shorter than me, with the two of us dwarfing his mother.

"So is it only BJJ you're interested in, or do you think you'd ever be interested in trying some others too?" I ask.

"Well… I love BJJ, but I've been watching loads of videos on MMA and that just looks insane," he says animatedly.

"Zion, no. You're not doing that." The sternness in

Carina's voice makes me think the two might have had a similar conversation before.

"I have a question. Is it only in like boxing and Muay Thai and MMA that you get like a nickname? 'Cause your's is really cool, and it would be so sick if one day I could get one too," Zion asks.

I have to bite my lip as I think about how to answer that. "You see, when I was younger I had a nickname that started when I was in high school that then carried on into my fighting competitions."

"Really? What was it?" he asks curiously.

"The Emerald Giant. Well, my buddies would sometimes call me The Shamrock Giant."

"Why? Are you Irish or something?"

"No, no, it's just green has always been my favorite color, and I used to always wear green shirts, like every day and I was always the tallest amongst my friends. So half of them would call me some variation of green, the others 'giant' and one day my best friend was ribbing me and shouted out emerald giant and it stuck. Everyone else called me that too."

"So what made you change from that one, then? As that's pretty cool, too."

Glancing over at Carina, she quickly looks down at her shoes, but before she does, I see a big smile on her face.

"I… uh… well, I changed it only a couple of years ago. Someone really important to me actually came up with it. It also kinda started out as a joke, but eventually, it became the most important name I've ever been given because it changed my life. See, I even got the original design tattooed here," I say before lifting my shirt and showing the highlighted diamond and horns that sit on my ribs by my heart.

Zion stares at it, then tilts his head slightly, glancing up for the briefest of seconds at his mom before looking at it again and nodding at me.

"That's pretty cool. It's good that you've got special people in your life that give you cool names."

I don't know why, but I almost get the feeling his words mean something else. As he straightens back up, his eyes have a different look to them. Instead of just looking at me like he was before, it's as if he's trying to look deep inside. It isn't menacing or even negative, but there's something. I can't quite put my finger on it. Looking over at Carina, I check to see if she's noticed it, but she's sorting out his gym bag, and I don't think she's picked up on anything.

Walking them to the vending machine, I get him a drink and a protein bar, which he eats in two bites. We talk for a few more minutes before I make my excuses that I need to head up to the office. I can feel myself struggling not to reach out and touch her while she's so close. Zion gives me another handshake as they leave. This time it's even firmer than before. Carina gives me a nod and a smile before they make their way out to the parking lot.

I'm not in my office for long when my phone goes off with a message.

> Thank you for how you dealt with that little interaction. He was desperate to meet the notorious legend that apparently you are. Plus, it was funny watching him trying to act cool and mature. Oh and no, don't get any ideas about trying to suggest that he take up MMA. There is no way my blood pressure could handle watching my son step into the octagon. I'll call you later. Love you x

Leaning back in my chair, I rest my feet on my desk as I type my reply.

> Was a pleasure. He's a very polite young man, and I already knew it before, but just seeing you interact together only confirmed what a great mom you are. Alright, I won't suggest any MMA, but how about we arrange another 1-2-1 session for just the two of us on the mats? Call me whenever you're able to. And if that just so happens to be a video call while you're in the bath, I'll be more than happy with that. Love you xx

Chapter 46

Carina

One thing I've always been adamant about is the happier a mom or dad is, just within themselves, the better and easier it is to be a good parent. Children really absorb and bounce off your energy. The more I smile and relax, it's so clear to see that they do too. It took me a really long time to understand and cement the notion that I don't need to chase the approval or love or attention of a man to feel happy. That I need to feel and believe within myself. But having someone to love and care for you is just an added bonus.

That's how I feel right now. My career is only going from strength to strength, I have more time that I get to enjoy with my kids, I've got a good and solid network of people around me, and to top it off, I have a partner who loves me and shows me just how much at every opportunity he can. The next goal is working out how I can merge my worlds together.

Although I'd given him my spare keys, he still rings the

doorbell instead of using it. Rising from my chair with a smile, I answer the door.

"You know you could just use the key?" I chuckle as he kisses me and walks in.

"I know, but I still just don't feel right using it. I don't want to use it and then shout out, 'Babe I'm here,' or something even more graphic, while you're in the middle of a meeting," he jokes back.

"It would be possible for you to just come in without shouting anything," I tease.

I follow him into the kitchen as he unloads the bags of food he's brought.

"Mmmm, that smells delicious. What did you get?"

"Well, I know you're bummed that you can't come tonight, so I thought even though you're going to miss out this evening, I could at least bring what you'd have likely eaten now to make up for it."

I hug him and kiss his chest in appreciation. The chef who's going to be running Robby's restaurant is having his last night in his food truck before closing. He's doing a little street party with him, serving his specialties one last time and having a few drinks and all that. Robby invited me, but tonight is Zion's parent-teacher conference, so I won't be able to go. But the fact that Robby grabbed lunch from there makes both my tummy rumble and my heart swell.

"That was delicious. I can't wait to try every single thing he puts onto the menu for you," I say, leaning back on the couch as Robby pulls my feet up, resting them on his legs before he starts slowly massaging the soles.

I moan in pleasure as he kneads and rolls.

"I just hope you won't be moaning like that while you eat his food there," he jokes still focusing on the TV.

Satiated from the food and the soothing feel of him rubbing my feet, my whole body feels weightless as I melt further into the couch and can feel my eyelids growing heavier by the second as I struggle to keep them open.

The next thing I know, I can feel my shoulders gently being shaken as my eyes slowly open.

"Hey, baby, I would have let you sleep longer, but I wasn't sure if there was anything you needed to do or sort before you do the school pick up," Robby says softly.

Pushing myself up, I knock down the throw blanket I hadn't realized been on me.

"Sorry. I didn't mean to fall asleep," I say, still slightly groggy.

"Don't apologize. You never nap, so I knew you must be tired."

As I finally get my bearings, I notice Robby must have taken his sweatshirt off as he's now only in his t-shirt.

"How long was I asleep for?"

"Only about an hour. I cleared away the stuff from lunch and the washing machine finished as I did the washing up. I checked the stuff inside and moved them over to the dryer and put the load you had in the basket in front of the machine in for a cycle."

Appreciation and gratitude warm me at his thoughtfulness.

"Aw, thank you. That's so sweet."

"I've told you before. I enjoy looking after you. It's not often I get the opportunity to since you're usually ten steps ahead and sorting everything out yourself. So any chance

I get, I'll take," he answers lovingly as he strokes my thigh.

Casting the blanket onto the floor beside me, I push up onto my knees before straddling him, running my fingers through his thick jet-black hair.

"I'm a very lucky woman," I say, peppering kisses along his jaw and the corners of his mouth.

"Mmmm, I think I'm a lucky man," he replies, pulling my hips close as he grabs my ass.

My lips brush against his, the tip of my tongue tracing along his lips with a featherlight touch. Wrapping his arms around me, he pulls me closer, and I can feel him harden as I grind myself down on his lap. Kissing him, we both moan as I continue rolling my hips, getting the perfect friction as my core rubs against his throbbing length.

Instantly, the tension and passion between us ignites like an inferno. Hands, mouth, teeth, lips in a seismic rush.

"God, your body is the most delicious thing in this world. The mold was broken with you," he says between kisses.

Pulling my tank top up over my head, he stands with the unexpected strength of being able to lift me before laying me back down on the couch and peeling my leggings and panties off in one swoop.

"If I could, I'd spend hours every single day worshipping every single inch of your body."

"You've already spent many hours studying my body," I say breathlessly, captivated by the intense and sexy way he's looking down at me.

"Baby, even if I had you for every minute of every hour of the day it still wouldn't be enough. Now, why don't you be my good girl and just lay back and let me get my fill of you before it's time to leave?"

Just as I'm about to give a cheeky retort, I can feel his wet, hot tongue licking its way across my entrance, making me moan out loud. Working me up in a quick frenzy with his talented tongue, his fingers join as they tease and massage me from within, making my back arch and my thighs shake. The way he knows and understands my body is a wonder, playing it like a skilled musician who's been doing it for years. It takes him only moments before he has me climbing and I feel like I'm going to explode. The sounds of my ecstatic moans echo across the room as my eyes squeeze shut and I see multicoloured spots dancing as I erupt with my orgasm. My skin feels hot to the touch and sweat beads on my chest. In the daze of my release, I feel him move himself back onto the couch and the next thing I know he's pulling me onto his lap and sheaths himself in one swift thrust.

"Oh fuck. You're gripping me so tight," he says through clenched teeth.

Pulling me in for a bruising kiss, I can taste myself on his tongue while I rock, grinding myself on his thick length. Wrapping his arms around so he has a tight locked grip, he fucks me from below hard and fast. Each and every thrust hitting just that right spot and I have to bite down on his shoulder, which only seems to spur him on further. The grip he has on me is bruising, and I love it. Knowing that in the days to come, I will feel that reminder of this moment. I can feel the vibration of his growling moans through his chest. The veins along his neck bulge as he fucks me at this unrelenting pace.

"Fuck… so good… fuck, yes," he cries as he finds his release.

He continues rocking into me as we both try to catch our breath again.

"I love you so much," he says softly, just above a whisper before kissing me.

The tenderness of his declaration is such a juxtaposition from the intense way he just fucked me. But it only goes to show the intense and un-limiting love we have for one another. One doesn't diminish the other, it only heightens the all-encompassing affection we share.

"I love you too. More than I ever knew I could."

Chapter 47

Carina

"Zion, do you wanna grab the popcorn? I've got the chocolates and sweets ready," I shout out as I load the bowls on the coffee table to move the throw blankets off the couch and onto the pouffe that Kai is resting his feet on.

"Did you also get my Twizzlers and lollipops?" Kai asks, making himself comfortable beside me.

"Yes, I did. See, they're here," I reply.

"So which movie are we going to watch?" Zion asks as he walks in holding the bowl of popcorn and his can of pop.

"I told you, if the two of you can agree on one then we can watch that and play UNO after, but if you can't decide on one, then you get to pick one each and we watch both but you each have to watch both of them. So the choice is yours."

I head back to the kitchen to grab my glass of water, hearing the two of them bickering. My phone pings with a message so I quickly grab it out of my pocket, checking it before I go back.

> Just remember, if you don't feel comfortable or ready yet, I fully understand. You don't need to tell them yet. Just do what feels right. Love you babe and call me if you can later xx

I breathe out a deep breath. Besides having a nice movie night in with the boys, I finally want to tell them about mine and Robby's relationship. Making my way back to the living room, I'm pleasantly surprised to see that the boys seem to have agreed on a movie.

"Well, I guess we'll be watching this then playing UNO," I say with a smile and make myself comfortable between my two no longer little babies.

I had to refill our snacks after the movie and the three of us have been in hysterics playing UNO. Honestly, tonight has been one of the most fun nights we've had in such a long time. There's a part of me that's apprehensive about potentially spoiling the evening by telling them, but I know it's the right thing to do.

"So, before we start another round, I wanted to tell you both something."

Kai takes another bite out of his Twizzlers and Zion, refilling his glass with pop, looks up with concern etched across his face.

"Mom, what's wrong? Is it something bad?" His voice hitches and I feel bad that his natural reaction is to think that the news I have to share is going to be bad.

"No, honey. It's not bad," I reassure him.

Looking both of them in the eye, I smile and reach out my hands.

"As you know, since your father's and my relationship ended, I haven't had a partner or boyfriend or anything like that."

"Yeah, because you've got us, Mom," Kai declares with a nod.

My heart warms at his sweet answer.

"That's not what Mom means, silly," Zion retorts at his brother.

Looking at my eldest, I try to gauge if there is any underlying tension or annoyance to his tone, but nothing on his face gives that away.

"I know, I am very lucky that I've got two of the most amazing boys that fill up my heart and make me the happiest mom in the world."

I have to bite my lip and suppress a laugh at the way Kai is nodding and smiling, along with every word I say.

"Now, as much as I know how lucky and grateful I am that I have the two of you, I've also had the chance to meet someone who also means a great deal to me. I want you both to know this isn't some sort of fast and silly thing that I've jumped into. I spent a long time really thinking about what is best for me and us as a family."

Zion has this smirk on his face and for the life of me, I can't work out what it means.

"I understand that this will probably take some time to get used to, and I never want either of you to feel or worry that simply because I now have another person I care deeply about, that it in any way takes away from how much I love you."

"What's his name?" Kai asks, slightly bored and not very interested.

"His name is Robby."

"I knew it," Zion barks with a laugh, making my head snap over at him at the same time Kai replies, "Who's Robby?"

"I… um… you know where Zion does his BJJ?"

"Yeah."

"The man that owns that gym. That's Robby."

"Ok cool," Kai answers, taking another bite from his Twizzlers.

"How did you know?" I ask Zion.

Leaning back in his seat, he rests his hand on the back of his head, suddenly looking much older and more mature than his sixteen-year-old self.

"Well, I suspected you were seeing someone for a while. In the last couple of months, you've had Amira babysit Kai more often in the evenings than you had before. Then that time when you were watching my class, and that argument broke out and he came to fix the situation and you introduced me to him, that's when I worked out it was him."

"How did you work that out?" I ask, genuinely curious.

Relaxing back, he has this air of satisfaction about him. "Do you remember when he was telling me about his tattoo and that initial design he on his ribs?"

"Yeah, what about it?"

"He said something about how the person who designed it was really important to him and changed his life or something along those lines. It obviously looks slightly different to the one that's all over the gym and the merch. And it took me a second to realize I recognized that one but couldn't work out from where. Then it hit me. What, like two and half years ago I remember passing your laptop and it was open on some software thing, and I saw that logo. I thought it was cool and just something you were working on for your job. Then when I saw it again, and he explained what it means to him, I put all the pieces together."

My mouth drops open in shock. I can't believe he worked that out. Not only that, but I can't believe he hasn't said anything since.

"Why didn't you mention anything at the time?"

Tilting his head, he studies me for a moment. Suddenly I feel like I'm the child and he's the parent.

"Well… I was kinda confused at first. One, it was weird to think that you might be in a relationship with someone." He shudders slightly before continuing. "You've never been in one, so that was something new that I needed to wrap my head around. Then I started thinking back and vaguely remember there was a time when you were really upset, and I'd thought maybe you were dating someone and it didn't work out. I wondered if it was maybe him. So then I was confused, and I didn't want to ask you. But I guess none of that matters now."

Surprise engulfs me. Not only from just how perceptive he has been, but just the extent of his awareness. I'd been so convinced that I'd hidden just how much I was struggling back then. But I guess I hadn't done as good of a job as I thought.

"Are you annoyed? How do you feel about it?" I ask nervously.

"I think he's cool. Obviously, I don't really know him beyond the stuff from the gym, but that's all pretty sick stuff. Plus, now I'll have more of a chance at getting into

MMA, as I'll have him back me," he says as his eyes light up with amusement.

"I don't think so, Mr.," I retort.

"I know, I'm joking. But still. Once the initial weirdness of the fact that you're in a relationship wears off, it will be kinda cool. As long as he makes you happy, then that's all that matters. And if he doesn't, I don't care that he's a former fighter, I'll still take him on," he says, puffing out his chest.

"Thank you. That means the absolute world to me." I stretch out my arm and give his hand a squeeze.

"Yeah, Mom, as long he doesn't take away my iPad and games then it's okay," Kai adds.

"Thank you. And I promise he won't be taking any games or anything away from you."

"So, when will we meet? Like I know I've met him and seen him now several times at the gym. But when will we properly meet him as your boyfriend?" Zion asks.

"Well, that is completely up to you. There is absolutely no rush. You both are in control, and it'll only happen when the two of you are ready and comfortable."

"Considering Dad has already canceled again for next Friday, could we maybe go out for ice cream and pancakes or something after school instead and he join us?"

I'm surprised by Zion's request. I don't know why, but I thought he'd want to take longer to get used to the idea. "Kai, how do you feel about that?" I ask, worried talking about his dad cancelling on them again will trigger him.

"Yeah. I love ice cream and pancakes. Will I get a double scoop with sauce and sprinkles?" he asks.

"If that's what you want. But are you sure you'd be okay with meeting Robby?"

"Yeah. I don't mind."

"Please, Mom. At least that'll be something fun for us to do, instead of sitting at home thinking about the fact that Dad can't be bothered to drive up to see us."

Although he's trying to come across as nonchalant, I can see the pain in his eyes. I hate how much this affects them. Hate the fact that Andrew neither cares nor sees just how painful and damaging it is when he continuously lets them down. Never having to bear witness to the suffering he is causing.

"Okay. As long as you're both comfortable, then yeah, we can do that."

Chapter 48

Carina

It's crazy to reflect on how, only three months ago, Zion and Kai officially met Robby—a moment that unfolded with surprising ease and warmth. The colorful fidget spinner Robby brought Kai immediately charmed him, its constant whir a quiet distraction amid the buzz of introductions. Meanwhile, Zion unsurprisingly assumed the role of steadfast protector, a role so genuine and heartfelt it softened every corner of the encounter. Robby quickly picked up on this dynamic and, with a relaxed smile, allowed Zion his moment to shine. It wasn't long before Robby's initial nervous energy melted away; soon he and Zion were engrossed in animated conversation, with Zion enthusiastically scrolling through his phone to show off montages of past fights, rattling off statistics on his favorite fighters, and immersing himself in each shared detail. As the evening gradually shifted and the restaurant filled with the hum of excited chatter, I felt like the reluctant bad guy when it came time to leave—Kai was visibly overwhelmed by the escalating noise and crowd, yet Zion still clung to the night, keen for it to stretch on a little longer.

True to his word, Robby has since become a regular addition to our outings. He's been with us on trips, shared in our dinners and movie nights, and even stepped in to help when Kai was bedridden with a tummy bug. On one particularly challenging day when I couldn't take Zion to school or his regular classes, it was Robby who volunteered his help—a gesture that, after a quick chat to ensure Zion was comfortable, filled my heart with so much love.

I'm still awestruck at how seamlessly everything has melded together—particularly given that the whole arrangement was brand new for the kids and for me. Venturing into this uncharted territory of blending families and relationships, I found myself without a handbook to guide me on how the boys might respond to having a significant other in their lives. For someone who had long believed that love would eternally elude me, I now pinch my arm in wonder at the sheer luck that has brought this new, joyful chapter into existence. I honestly couldn't ask for a better life, and tonight is exceptionally significant as we celebrate the grand opening of the new restaurant.

In the moments leading up to the opening, I've been taken aback by how composed Robby has remained—even as the day built to a crescendo of emotions. I watch him while he drives us all there; his calm exterior gave way to tiny, nervous taps on the steering wheel that betrayed his inner jitters. I reach over and stroke his arm reassuringly. "It's going to be great. Don't worry," I murmur, confident in his abilities.

He responds with a modest smile, "I know. I did it the right way. I knew I couldn't do it alone, and the team has been amazing, tackling every issue and hurdle that came our way."

Meanwhile, Zion and Kai sat animatedly in the back, their faces lit with anticipation for the evening ahead. My heart swelled when, while I was getting ready, Robby carefully packed a little bag for Kai filled with his essential comforts—his iPad, headphones, fidget spinners, pens, a notepad, and even his beloved stuffed toy. It was a small act of thoughtfulness that spoke volumes about how deeply he's embraced Kai's needs. Witnessing such a remarkable transformation in Kai—who typically shuns change—was nothing short of heartwarming; he has bonded with Robby almost effortlessly, like a duck taking naturally to water. I deeply appreciate the way Robby has forged genuine, individualised connections with each of the boys, never overstepping into parenthood or forced camaraderie, but simply adapting his natural self to nurture the evolving dynamics between us all.

After parking the car, we make our way inside, and I can't help but admire yet another considerate gesture from Robby. He has already rummaged through Kai's backpack to take out his headphones in anticipation of the lively, chatter-filled atmosphere that awaited us. Our waitress then guides us to a cozy booth tucked away in a quiet corner. In that moment, as I turn to plant a quick kiss on Robby's cheek, I notice how thoughtfully he has arranged the lighting—just enough to dim the harsh overhead lamps and ease the noise, creating a peaceful little haven for Kai. William and Koa are already here, waiting with warm smiles; Amira wraps Robby in a congratulatory hug before squeezing me and high-fiving both boys with infectious excitement.

"Congratulations. The place looks amazing," Amira exclaims, eyes sparkling with delight as she declares, "And I've been eavesdropping—people are absolutely blown away by it." Kai, with his uncharacteristic eagerness, quickly joins her in the booth, settling comfortably beside her.

"Dude, you've done incredibly well," Koa chuckles, patting Robby's back enthusiastically before pecking me on the cheek.

"Honestly, I'm so glad you all arrived—the food smells divine, and I'm starving to try it all."

Across from us, a cluster of Robby's friends and some of their partners have gathered, while at the nearby table, one of Robby's aunts sits with her husband alongside a couple who, if I recall correctly, are Robby's godparents.

Every detail, from the artwork, the staff's uniform, the décor, and menu to the thoughtful way Robby has allowed everyone who's worked on this project to not only shine but also be celebrated tonight has made it one I won't forget for many years to come.

Amira takes a picture of me, the kids, and Robby and as I look down on it I don't think my heart has ever felt so full.

I think Zion might have a bit of a crush on one of the waitresses because he hasn't stopped looking at her since she began serving us our food. Plus, I think he was a little jealous when she made a bit of a fuss of Kai as the chef, bless him, made him his own little plate of the limiting foods he eats. When I saw what was on his plate I instantly looked over at Robby who was already looking at me with a soft smile on his face. How did I ever get so lucky to be with someone that not only is there for me, loving me and supporting me, but also for my kids? Words fail me to describe just how blessed I feel.

As the evening wraps up and both Robby and I notice Kai struggling with all the people around, he rises from his chair and, using his knife, taps his glass to get everyone's attention.

"I just wanted to take this quick opportunity to thank everyone for coming and I am so proud of the hard work every single person has put in to get ***Naiads*** up and open. I'm going to keep this quick and PG," he says, his voice carrying across the restaurant as everyone around us chuckles.

"We've had our fair share of things going wrong, but never once did anyone drop the ball and that was simply proof of just how good this entire team is. Like I promised I'm making this quick, so if everyone could raise their glass. Here is to every single person who has worked their asses off, thank you. Lee, you and your team, I honestly couldn't have done this without you. To my friends who supported me, even those who initially laughed when I told you about this idea. And yes, you know who I'm talking about." Several raised chuckles come off the table with all his friends.

"To my family, those that are here and those that are gone. I love you all. And lastly and most importantly to Carina. If it wasn't for you, I would've never had the confidence or drive to put my dream into reality. You lit that match within me and that small fire has morphed into this blazing sun that we all get to bask in. I love you, baby. Thank you. Cheers, everyone."

Chapter 49

Robby

"Anyone want any more?" Carina asks as she rises from the table and refills the jug of water.

Kai shakes his head as he finishes his fries and nuggets. Zion however snaps his head up and nods enthusiastically.

"Yes, please, Mom."

She looks over at me with a smile.

"You know I'll never say no to more," I confess, also handing her my plate, she grabs both our plates and gives us each another helping of brown stew chicken and rice.

Since I moved in about eight months ago, Carina and I came to a deal. We will always alternate who cooks. I remember when I first suggested it to her. Her eyes widened, and I think there was a part of her that didn't believe me. But I meant what I'd said when she first asked if I'd like to move in. We are a partnership. That goes with everything: cooking, cleaning, housework, plus helping with the boys.

In my head, I hadn't pictured us moving in together for

some time. Not because I didn't want to, but because I didn't want the boys to think I was overstepping. So I was so surprised and honoured when I'd told her I was going to renew my lease for another year, and she mentioned that she, Zion, and Kai had chatted and the boys were the ones that suggested I move in. Especially as I was over at the house every day as it was.

The first couple of weeks were a bit of an adjustment. I'd tried to take note and remember every routine and timetable and felt bad when I'd gotten it wrong. But being the amazing woman that she is, Carina reassured me it wasn't a problem, and we just worked through it.

"Tomorrow, Robby is going to take you to your class, Zion, since I've got a meeting at Kai's school. So I thought we could just grab some takeout. Then on Friday, I know you've got Henry coming over. And you and Kai are off to your dad's on Saturday."

I hate that the second there is a mention of the boy's dad, the whole atmosphere changes. As much as I'm excited to have a nice and relaxing weekend with Carina all to myself, I don't like that the boys aren't looking forward to seeing their dad. One time when I'd picked Zion up from school, he'd actually confided in me and said that the only reason he still agrees to see his dad is because he wants to be there for Kai. He said his dad doesn't pay attention to Kai or accommodate his special needs and Zion said if he didn't go with him, then Kai would be left alone, and god knows what would happen. He made me promise not to tell Carina, and I felt bad, but said I would only stay quiet on one condition. If ever he feels uncomfortable or anything happens, then Zion is to call me instantly, day or night and I will pick them up straight away.

These boys are such good kids. I don't know what's wrong with that asshole. He should be begging to see them more often. Be dying to spend more time with them. But he's too stuck up, too selfish to put them before himself.

"How about tomorrow after Zion's class we'll grab some food on our way back then after we eat we'll have a games night? Then on Friday when Henry comes over, you guys can game upstairs and chill. And Kai, how about we do a Super Mario go-cart competition?"

That instantly gets his attention. "Yeah. I wanna do that. Can we set up a leaderboard? And Mom, will you join in too?" he asks, his eyes open wide.

"Of course. I won't be any good, but yeah I'll join in."

"Yay," he cheers.

"Don't worry, Mom, if you're really bad, Henry and I can join, and we can do teams," Zion adds.

I think I did the trick with my suggestions since both boys are much more animated, and everyone's mood is massively lifted as we get through the rest of dinner and desserts.

"Thank you for that at dinner," Carina says, taking a seat beside me on the couch once the kids are in bed.

Wrapping my arm around her shoulder, I pull her close. "It was nothing." Kissing her temple, I run my hand along her arms, relaxing back into the couch.

"It wasn't nothing. You noticed how they both went quiet the second I brought up their dad. And you didn't hesitate at coming up with something that not only were things you knew they'd enjoy but also that would cheer them up in the moment and keep their minds preoccupied and not dwell on them not wanting to see him."

She turns in my arms, leaning down on me and I'm trying to stay focused but it's difficult as she got changed when she was upstairs and she's no longer wearing a bra and all I can think of is how I can feel her nipples as they rub against my chest.

"You're getting that look in your eyes," she retorts with a smile as she raises her brow.

"No. Yes. I mean, of course I was going to cheer them up. It's not as if I suggested anything overly exciting or extravagant. I am trying to be good right now but you're making it very hard to have a serious conversation, baby. The feel of you on me is eliciting very inappropriate thoughts right now."

"Oh, is it?" she asks with a purr, knowing full well what she's doing.

My mouth is dry as she reaches her hand down and strokes me through my sweatpants. I'm already semi hard and it only takes a few seconds before I'm throbbing in her hand.

"You, Carina… are insatiable."

I pepper kisses along her jaw before pulling her in for a bruising kiss. My fingers imbedding in her coily hair that I love so much.

"How about we go upstairs, and you show me just how insatiable you think I am?" she says against my lips.

"Mmmm, you don't have to tell me twice. But we need to be quiet. So why don't you get the shower on in the ensuite and get undressed and I'll join you there after I've closed everything off down here?"

"Sounds good to me. And who knows, I might even

match your generous mood. We haven't used the plug to warm me up for a while" Her eyes sparkle at her suggestion before she gets up to head upstairs.

I grab her ass as she stands, not wanting to waste a second, especially with that teasing little add-on she left me with. Damn, that woman could ask me to crawl over broken glass, and I'd do it if it would make her happy.

Chapter 50

Carina

I tried calling, but there was no answer. The boys are running about thirty minutes late as there was a long queue at the barbers. Hopefully, they'll be back soon.

I send the message to my ex-husband and continue with the housework I'm wanting to get done. To my surprise, they are staying with their dad this weekend, and he hasn't canceled, so where Robby and I will have the place to ourselves, the last thing I want to do is waste any of the time doing housework. The plan is to stop at ***Naiads*** for either dinner tonight or lunch tomorrow and the rest of the time I'm hoping we stay either in bed or on the couch, preferably wearing as little clothing as possible.

Loading up the dishwasher, I wipe down the kitchen counters when the doorbell rings. Checking my phone, I see that Andrew still hasn't opened or responded to my message, so I'm guessing it's him.

I don't even make it two steps before the doorbell rings twice again in quick succession.

"Jeez, I'm coming," I shout.

As I open the door, my grumpy and miserable ex-husband greets me with a scowl. His face is tense, and his brows are furrowed, acting as if it's the worst day instead of the excitement he should have about spending the weekend with his children.

"How long does it take you to open the damn door?" he mutters in annoyance.

"I literally just heard the bell ring like three seconds ago," I reply, trying to keep my voice calm despite his attitude.

He rolls his eyes and lets out an exasperated huff as he leans against the doorframe.

"Are they ready? I want to get going. Today has already been a shit show and I'm not in the mood to be stuck in traffic," he complains impatiently.

"No, they're not. I tried calling you and sent you a message. They're running late because they're at the barbershop. But they should be here soon."

"For fuck's sake. You always do this. I bet you planned for them to be late so you can play the martyr and be the good guy," he accuses, his agitation growing.

I let out an exasperated sigh and shake my head in disbelief.

"That's utter bullshit. It's not my fault or theirs that there was a long queue. Why would I intentionally tell you the wrong time? It makes no sense," I argue back, feeling frustrated by his constant accusations.

"You always mess up my plans. You do it on purpose just so you can seem like the victim," he continues to rant, ignoring my logic.

Frustrated beyond belief, I finally snap back at him.

"This is ridiculous. I will not stand here and argue with you. You have two options—you can sit on the couch and wait for them to arrive or go wait in your car. The choice is yours, but I will not waste my time listening to your nonsense," I say, trying to keep my voice calm and controlled.

He stomps his way into the house and slams the door shut behind him. Not wanting to deal with his moody behavior, I retreat upstairs to grab the boys' rucksacks that I had already packed earlier. Bringing them downstairs, I leave them by the door and take a deep breath, trying to calm my frayed nerves before facing my ex-husband again.

Just as I walk back towards the kitchen, I spot Andrew looking at the pictures on the mantel. Something within me feels possessive and irritated when he picks up the picture of Robby's opening. It's my favorite and Zion was the one that secretly got it printed and bought a frame for it with his pocket money. So seeing Andrew's grubby paws on it sets my teeth on edge.

"Can I help you?" I ask, not even trying to disguise my annoyance.

"Has your little boyfriend experienced the real you yet? Or is he still just getting the fake, phoney version?"

My nostrils flair as anger bubbles beneath my skin. "Firstly, there is nothing little about him." I say, glancing first at his groin area. "Secondly, my relationship has nothing to do with you. You have had a slew of women you've been with over the years. Not once have I cared or even asked about them."

"What the fuck is that supposed to mean?" he barks.

"You know exactly what I'm talking about. Robby is a better man than you will ever be. Not only does he treat me with love and care, but he already cares so much about Zion and Kai. He's there for them. Supports them. Helps them. And that's a hell of a lot more than you do. So don't you dare try to say anything about him. You should be lucky and grateful that there is someone in *their* life who is around to show them how a man should behave. Now I'm not going to have you be in my house and say this fucking bullshit. So you can wait for the boys in your fucking car."

I walk towards the hall, ready to hold the door open for that asshole to leave, but I only make it a few steps when he shouts. "Don't you fucking walk away from me, you stuck-up bitch." His hand clamps down on my upper arm.

"Get the fuck off me," I shriek, pulling away.

I go to turn and block him, but I turn too slowly, still in shock that he's put his hands on me again after all these years, when he grips my ponytail and uses it to bend my head and slap me across the face.

The sharp, burning sting of his palm against my cheek brings tears to my eyes. I desperately try to free my hair from his iron grip, but his fingers only tighten around the strands. In a last-ditch effort, I deliver a swift kick to his shin, causing him to momentarily loosen his hold. Seizing the opportunity, I land a hook and an uppercut on his jaw; something I've never had the courage to do before. Surprise flickers in his eyes, but it quickly turns into rage. Instead of backing down, he charges at me with wild abandon and tackles me to the ground.

I continue to fight back, adrenaline coursing through my body as I land blow after blow. This is the first time I have ever defended myself against him; usually I would just curl up into a ball and endure the pain. But not today. As we roll and struggle on the ground, I can feel bruises forming under his knees, digging into my thighs. The sounds of our grunts and shouts echo through the room as we engage in this vicious battle for power.

"Aahh, get the fuck off me," I scream.

My arms flail as I scream from the pain of his knee digging into my quads. Burning, searing pain explodes across my face as he punches my cheek, making my teeth rattle. My eyes struggle to focus. The metallic tang of blood drips into my mouth. My ears ring. The world spins as my vision blurs, a nauseating dizziness overtaking me as warm blood trickles down my temple. Through the haze, I hear his ragged breathing, see his silhouette looming over me. Panic surges through my veins, giving me a burst of desperate energy and I begin kicking out wildly. My foot connects with something solid—his chest, maybe—and there is a satisfying grunt of pain. But he's on me again in an instant, his weight crushing the air from my lungs as he straddles me.

"You stupid fucking bitch," he snarls, his face contorted with rage. "You think you can fight me?"

His hands wrap around my throat, squeezing. I claw at his arms, gasping for air, black spots dancing at the edges of my vision. My lungs burn. My arms and legs feel like lead. Digging my nails into the back of his hands, I think I pierce the skin as he screams out and pulls them from my throat. Coughing and struggling to catch my breath, my throat feels like it's on fire, but somehow I drag myself up and try to scramble away from him. I don't make it far when he wraps his arms around the backs of my legs and as he pulls me down, my head hitting the side of the coffee table.

My vision swims in and out of focus, a disorienting haze that refuses to clear. I open my mouth to scream, but an oppressive silence swallows my voice, leaving me mute and panicked. A relentless ringing fills my ears that feels like it's drowning out all other sounds. Blood trickles into my eyes, the warm, coppery liquid stinging and further distorting my sight. My limbs feel like they belong to someone else, heavy and unresponsive, as I struggle to regain any control over my body.

"You fucking bitch. Who do you think you are? Look what you made me do. This is your fucking fault," I hear him shouting in the distance, in a muffled tone. It feels like I'm under water.

My head throbs as I struggle to stay conscious. I try to move my arms and legs, but my eyelids just keep closing. Every inch of my body aches and hurts. I'm losing my fight to stay awake and fight but can only think I hope he doesn't kill me. It can't end like this. This can't be happening. I can't leave my boys like this.

Then I succumb to the darkness.

Chapter 51

Robby

"At least it was worth the wait," I say, quickly glancing in the rearview mirror at Kai, then over at Zion in the passenger seat, looking at their fresh trims.

"Yeah, and that playlist they had on was sick," Zion says, looking up from his phone before pulling the visor down and checking himself out in the mirror.

"Now, I know we won't be able to eat, but why don't we quickly stop and grab some snacks that you two can have in the car with your dad?" I ask them both.

I see Kai nodding in the mirror, and Zion agrees as he opens his window.

As we stop at the store, I let the boys pick out whatever they want and pull my cell out of my pocket to message my girl.

> We're just grabbing some supplies for them on the road. We should be back in 5. Love you x

I still have no response from her by the time I pull out of the parking lot and drive the final stretch to the house. She's probably in the shower or something. I can't wait for us to have some quality time together. Plus, I've planned a couple of fun surprises for her I really hope she loves.

As I pull up to the house, I recognize their dad's car already parked there. Shit. I can't see him sitting in it, so I'm guessing he's inside. "Do either of you need to use the bathroom? Your dad's already here"

"Nope," Kai says from the back, still glued to his device.

"Nah, I'm good," Zion says as he unbuckles his seatbelt.

"Why don't I quickly grab your bags and I'm sure your mom will wanna come out and say goodbye."

They both nod and I make my way to the front door. As I open it, the weirdest feeling washes over me. The coldest shiver runs down my spine and I shake myself at the unexpectedness of it.

"Carina?" I shout, but all I hear is a faint grunting noise.

As I stride toward the front room, my eyes catch sight of jagged shards from a broken vase scattered across the floor. Rounding the corner, I see him crouched on the ground. But what arrests me mid-step is the haunting, motionless form of Carina lying amidst a pool of blood, her face surrounded by an ominous crimson halo. A blinding, searing rage ignites within me, burning hotter than a forge.

"You fucking piece of shit!" I scream, charging at him with a fury that propels my fist straight into his jaw.

My arms are alive with a fiery intensity as my fists collide with his ribs, each punch delivering a satisfying thud against his bones. He collapses to the floor, and only then do I realize the primal roar echoing in my ears is pouring from my throat. He attempts to shove the coffee table toward me, but it barely registers; I simply kick it aside, my focus unbroken. To my surprise, he staggers back onto his feet, but I quickly land a solid cross on his biceps and follow it with a swift jab to his cheek.

"Fuck you, you fucking asshole," he shrieks, blood spewing from his mouth as he flails in futile attempts to strike back.

I deliver a powerful kick to his stomach, sending him sprawling back onto the couch. Just as I'm about to finish him, a soft groan from the floor captures my attention. Peering down, I see Carina's head twitch slightly. My entire being shifts focus to her. Rushing over, I crouch beside her, frantically checking for a pulse. It's strong, but her eyes remain closed, blood oozing from a gash on her head.

"Baby, baby, I'm here. I've got you. I'm here," I murmur, my voice a soothing balm amidst the chaos.

Stripping off my shirt, I press it against the wound, desperate to stop the bleeding. My fingers grow slick with blood as I gently wipe it from her face.

"You're gonna be fine. You're gonna be fine. I promise. I've got you. Baby, I've got you," I whisper repeatedly, unsure if the words are for her sake or mine. I don't even know if she can hear me.

A piercing, guttural scream reverberates through the room, cutting through the tension like a knife.

"Stop!" Zion's shout breaks the moment, and I glance up to see his dad brandishing a jagged piece of wood, likely from the broken chair, poised to strike me. But Andrew hesitates, his eyes flicking to his son, whose face is flushed with emotion, tears streaming down his cheeks.

Time seems to freeze, the world suspended in a tense

stillness. Zion's chest heaves with laboured breaths as he struggles to find words.

"How? How... could you... do this?" he stammers, voice choked with disbelief and pain.

"I... Son, I..." Andrew falters, unable to finish as Carina groans again in my arms, her eyes fluttering open. I continue to gently clear the blood from her face, my heart pounding with a mix of relief and urgency.

"Get out. I never want you near her again," Zion commands, his voice resonating with an unfamiliar strength that echoes through the room. His presence is formidable as he steps forward, positioning himself like an unyielding shield between his mother and Andrew.

"I said get out!" he shouts, the words crackling with intensity.

Andrew, resembling a shamed, pathetic rat, scurries away without even a last glance backward, his departure as silent as it is swift.

"Is she okay?" Zion asks, his voice quivering as he drops to his knees. His hands tremble as they gently brush his mother's arms, searching for reassurance amid the chaos.

"I'm not sure. I think so. She's got a cut to her head. I don't know where else she might be hurt. I need you to call an ambulance. And tell them we also need the police. Can you do that for me?" I request, striving to project a calm façade that belies the turmoil within.

"Yeah. I... yeah," he whispers, his voice barely more than a breath.

I am struck by the strength and maturity he displays as he speaks calmly to the operator, detailing the incident with clarity. His hands are still shaking when he finishes the call.

"Buddy, you did a great job. I'm really proud of you.

I'm going to keep hold of her, keep her as still as possible until they get here. I need you to do one more thing for me."

He nods, his eyes wide with the shock of seeing his mother in such a state.

"Can you go to the car, get your brother, and bring him in, but go through the back door? Take him upstairs to either your room or his. I don't want him to see this. And if you can just stay in there until the ambulance arrives that would be best for Kai. Once they're here, I'll come get you and let you know what they say. Can you do that?"

I watch as his Adam's apple dips with a swallow, and determination washes over his features.

"Yeah. I can do that."

Tears prick my eyes as he leans over, tenderly kissing the small patch of her face untouched by blood.

"I love you, Mom," he whispers before making his way outside, a young boy shouldering the weight of courage.

Chapter 52

Carina

My head is pounding so intensely it feels like a stampede of elephants is trampling over me. I can't tell if I'm caught in some twisted dream or harsh reality. A dense fog clouds my mind, making every thought a struggle. My arms and legs are as heavy as lead, and every attempt to move them sends searing pain shooting through my body. The surrounding noises are distorted and strange, like I'm submerged underwater, unable to make anything out clearly. At one point, I think I hear shouting, a distant echo that seems familiar. Though the voices are muffled, something deep inside tells me it might be Robby. I try to open my eyes, but even they feel impossibly heavy, as if weighed down by invisible chains. "I've got you. I'm here," Robby says, his voice cutting through the haze.

I attempt to open my eyes again but instinctively shut them tight as something drips into them.

"Aahh," I cry out in discomfort.

Time becomes irrelevant as seconds stretch into minutes; I can't be certain of which. Gradually, I feel myself becoming more aware. Pain ricochets through me, yet the moment Zion's voice reaches my ears, something within me stirs. Battling through the oppressive fog, I summon every ounce of strength to concentrate. Someone is gently patting my face with a damp cloth, and finally, I manage to open my eyes. To my right, I see Zion kneeling beside me, tears streaming down his cheeks like tiny rivers. Ignoring the pain, I try to lift my arm to touch his face, but they remain stubbornly heavy. On my other side, Robby cradles me in his lap, his expression a storm of mixed emotions. My eyelids grow too heavy to keep open, but the next time I raise them, I notice his hands are stained with blood. A question forms in my mind, but my throat constricts as memories of Andrew and our fight come rushing back.

"Shh, shh, it's okay. I've got you. You're safe. We're here. An ambulance is on its way," Robby reassures me softly.

"I… where's Zion? Where's Kai?" I croak, finally finding my voice.

"They are fine. Zion's taken Kai upstairs. The ambulance shouldn't be too much longer now, baby. Can you tell me where it hurts?" Robby asks tenderly, his voice a soothing balm amidst the chaos.

I attempt to catalog every painful area, but the task feels overwhelming, like trying to count stars in a stormy sky. Sensing my struggle, he leans down and kisses my forehead, his lips warm and reassuring against my clammy skin.

"Don't worry, it's fine. Just stay as still as possible. I don't want to risk any further damage. I think the bleeding from the cut on your head seems to have slowed down, which is good. The rest we'll just wait and see. I've got you. I love you so much. So, so much, Carina."

Tears glisten as they slowly trail down his cheeks, and only then do I notice the depth of his despair etched into his features, like a shadow that refuses to leave.

Zion rushes over, his footsteps a soft patter on the floor, and kneels beside me, taking my hand in his, his grip both gentle and firm as if to anchor us both in this turbulent sea.

"Mom. I'm so sorry," he chokes out between sobs, his voice a fragile whisper.

"Shhh. Don't, this isn't your fault. Don't say sorry. I'm sorry you had to see this."

Never have I seen such raw pain, such profound sorrow on my sweet little boy's face, and it tears me apart inside that he's now witnessed the monster Andrew is. No child should ever see their parent in such a state. I don't even realize I'm crying until I feel two hands gently brushing away my fallen tears.

"I let Kai play that F1 game he's always bugging me to let him play in my room. I've told him he needs to wear the headphones and listen to the instructions. He's so excited, I don't think he's going to move a muscle," Zion says, his voice still tinged with brokenness.

"That was a great idea, buddy," Robby tells him, a proud note threading through his words.

"I also called Amira and told her what happened. She said she's on her way since I know we wouldn't all be able to come in the ambulance."

Fresh tears trickle down my cheeks as my heart swells

with pride for my son. I wish he never had to be in a situation like this, but I can't deny how amazed I am by his quick thinking.

"I'm so proud of you," I say, finally able to reach up and stroke his cheek, feeling the warmth of his skin beneath my fingertips.

Chapter 53

Robby

The hours have blurred, and I've never in my life felt as helpless as I do right now. Just sitting here, waiting and watching as the doctors and nurses clean her up, run various tests on her, and the only thing I can do is hold her hand. I feel like a volcano, ready and waiting to erupt with emotion. The adrenalin that had been keeping my veins buzzing earlier has now worn off. Pain and anger pummel me as they talk through each and every injury she has sustained.

My heart sinks when I think of what further damage could have happened if she'd been left there on the floor any longer. Every time the nurse looks over at me she gives me this look, like she can see that I'm really struggling to hold it all together. Which I am. That's why I'm hardly speaking. I'm too scared. I need to be strong for her. Be her pillar of strength when all I want to do is explode. I wish I'd have beaten him until his bones turned to mush. Never in my life have I hated someone as much as I hate him. What he has done to Carina is fucking sick. Doing that to the mother of his children, the woman who put up with his bullshit for years, who's raising the boys a million times better than he ever could. To do that in her home, knowing the boys were on their way back, that they would witness it. The fact that Zion actually witnessed the horrific sight has me boiling even hotter. If I ever see that pathetic piece of shit again, I'm going to kill him.

My knee bounces as I try to channel my frustration.

"Hey, I can feel your anger all the way from here," Carina croaks. Making me stop bouncing instantly.

"I'm sorry," I say, lifting her hand and kissing the back of it.

"Don't apologize. None of this is your fault."

I just can't agree with that. If I'd have simply left with the boys instead of us waiting for the barbers, I'd have been there and nothing would have happened. If I hadn't have stopped at the shop, maybe I'd have been able to stop it. I'm meant to be there for her. Protecting her. Supporting her. And I wasn't.

Needing to snap out of this selfish mindset, I focus my attention back on her and gently sit beside her on the hospital bed.

My eyes prick with tears. "I love you so much. I'm so sorry that you went through this." Despite trying to keep my voice in check, the first tears fall down my cheeks.

"Babe, don't be sad. It's over now. I know I probably look like shit, but it's over."

I hate that she's the one to be reassuring me. When I should be doing that for her.

"You don't look like shit. You always have and always will be the most beautiful woman."

She goes to laugh but winces in pain. Just then, two

police officers knock on the door and enter to take her statement.

"You've been through a lot. And although some things you have told us, we won't be able to prosecute him on, there are several that we can. And will. Along with this, we are charging him with felony assault. That, along with his previous criminal record, he will be going down for a very long time," the officer explains.

Carina burst into tears, and I lean over, holding her as close as I can, trying not to hurt her. It takes her several minutes to calm herself down. The officers leave their details and let us know they will be in touch soon.

When they leave, I help her dress and almost choke on overwhelming emotion as I map her injuries.

"Carina, I love you with all of my heart. I know I've fucked up so bad in the past, but I promise I will never let you down ever again. I want to wake with you in my arms and fall asleep kissing you every night for the rest of our lives."

"I love you too. It's all finally done now. He's gone. Will be out of our lives forever. I just want to go home. I want to hug my boys. I want you by my side. I just want us to live our lives filled with love and each other."

Her eyes fill with tears, and I can only imagine the magnitude of emotions she must be feeling.

"Then that's what we're going to do. Let's go home, baby."

Epilogue

15 years later

Robby rises from his seat, glass in hand, and gazes out at the table full of loved ones. My parents sit to one side, smiling warmly at me and my husband. Across from them are Zion, Kai, their partners, and our two closest friends, all chatting and laughing over glasses of wine.

I am struck by how much time has passed since our wedding day. Fifteen years ago, we stood here with our loved ones around us, promising forever to each other.

"I know it's not just me," Robby says, gesturing towards me with a loving smile, "but also my beautiful wife Carina. We are so grateful that you have all joined us to celebrate our anniversary."

I look up at my husband with adoration, marvelling at how quickly time has flown by. It feels like just yesterday we were falling in love. But now, as I gaze around the table at our family and friends gathered together, I am filled with a deep sense of gratitude for the life we have built together.

"There was a time many years ago when I never could

have imagined or dreamed of having the life I have now," Robby continues. "I am so blessed to have found my soul mate—the woman who changed my life from the moment she entered it." His words bring tears to my eyes as I reach for his hand and give it a gentle squeeze.

In this moment, surrounded by love and togetherness, I couldn't imagine my life without him by my side. And as we raise our glasses in celebration, I am reminded once again of just how lucky I am to have found my true partner in life.

Reaching down, he takes my hand and kisses it.

"My love, we have been through so much together. Overcome hurdles that most could never imagine. On our wedding day, I promised to always show and tell you just how deeply and fiercely I love you, and to express my gratitude for your love and support. In my darkest moments, you have been my guiding light. I am grateful for every moment spent by your side, and I cannot wait to celebrate many more decades of loving you."

His voice cracks slightly at the end, and I squeeze his hand tighter. He has always been an emotional diamond demon, easily moved by moments like this.

"To Carina," he begins, raising his glass in a toast. "The most beautiful woman, the love of my life, the best mother, and my best friend. Happy anniversary, baby."

"Happy anniversary!" everyone echoes as we clink our glasses.

Leaning down, he presses his lips tenderly against mine. Even after all these years, I still get butterflies every time he kisses me.

"Happy anniversary," I whisper back, gazing into his cerulean blue eyes.

Taking his seat beside me, we dig into the delicious spread of food before us. We are on the terrace of our dream home nestled in the hills of Ko Samui; a place we fell in love with during our honeymoon. It was my fourth time visiting this paradise, and with each trip, I understood more and more why Robby was captivated by its beauty. We stumbled upon this piece of land while hiking during our honeymoon and purchased it. After several years of planning and getting permits, we built our dream home here. It took three years to complete, but managed to visit at least twice a year for family vacations. After Kai went off to college, we moved here permanently. It was an adjustment at first, being so far away from my family, but we make it a point to visit them in the US and take family trips in Europe as well.

"Thank you for organising this surprise anniversary celebration. I can't believe no one let it slip," I say, brushing my lips against Robby's ear. He places his hand on my thigh, causing a tingle of excitement to shoot through me.

"We knew you would figure it out, which is why everyone took an oath to keep it a secret," he replies with a grin.

I give him a playful kiss on the cheek and my eyes trace over the large tattoo on his forearm. It depicts a mermaid who looks uncannily like me, floating gracefully in the water with curly hair that matches mine perfectly. He surprised me with it while I was recovering from injuries, and it brought tears to my eyes.

"You all did an amazing job. I couldn't be happier. Thank you," I say sincerely.

"I will always do everything in my power to make you

smile and bring joy to your life. You deserve the world, my Carbonados Mermaid," he says lovingly.

"And I love you, my Diamond Demon," I reply with a smile, feeling grateful for every moment spent with my loving husband by my side.

The End

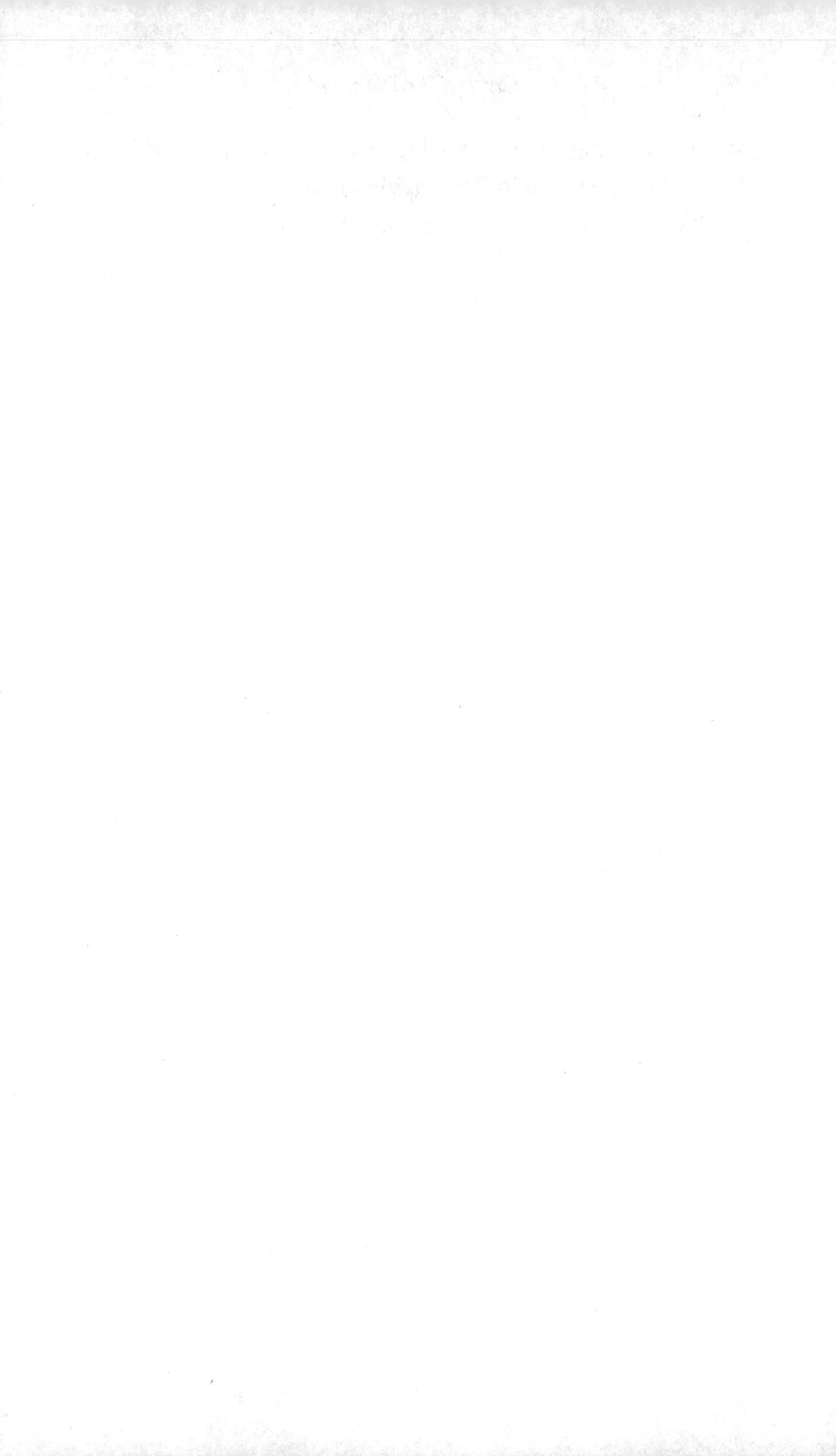

Acknowledgments

I have to start with Mr O, you know who you are. Obviously I wouldn't have been able to write this story if it wasn't for you. Now there's a part of me that's convinced you'll never read it, but then the other part has pictured you flicking through the pages, wearing your elephant trousers, eating Key Lime Pie and using your massage gun as an array of emotions (probably several negative ones) flit through you as you read the words which mean so much yet only shows a fraction of all that transpired. Now you can add muse to your Diamond Demon title. Time will tell if you ended up reading it.

As always, I would never be able to get any of my books published if it wasn't for the little village of amazing women I have that support me through all of this.

My unbelievably talented graphic designer, Samantha @smashdesigns, where do I even begin? I know this one was probably a pain, especially considering my naïve and slightly skewed thought of what would work for this story. But in all seriousness I had such a specific image for this cover, and I know it would have been easy for you to just put that together, but it just wouldn't have worked. I never in a million years could have hoped, guessed or come up with the absolutely breathtaking idea for this cover the way you did. You managed to dig deep into the story and create something so beautiful and captivating, you really made this the perfect window into this emotional love story. One thing I've realized is your art, your creativity honestly gives me the drive to write. Just so I can get another absolutely stunning cover from you. My problem is I just need to get faster at it hahahah. Thank you. You know what this book, what this story means to me and honestly once again you have done such an amazing job!!

My editor Sarah @wordemporium, I know you were hesitant with how this story would not only go but also how the readers would take it. You understood the weight of the words in this book and helped cut it down but also find the gem inside. Thank you for your patience, for your understanding and for not screaming at me for all those long drafts and 10minute long voice notes.

Kerri, Kerri, Kerri. You are more than just a proofreader. You're a magician, a therapist, a negotiator and a detective all rolled into one. The way in which you are able to find the smallest of things, those little snippets or cracks that completely go over my head, yet you shine a light on them and helped me wrangle it into something that works for both the readers and stays true to the heart of this story.

To my PA Natasha JPA, I'd said from the beginning that this one was going to be the hardest one so far. Not just for me to write, but also in how we work out how to shine a light on a story that isn't all rainbows and joy. Thank you for being there, for supporting me, for picking me up when I was drowning in self-doubt.

To Rowena, I know your opinions on Robby Black. We have had so many conversations about who, what and how this character should be portrayed. Hopefully you approve this version. But thank you as always for being there and supporting me no matter what. Even on the numerous occasions I was a fool and didn't listen to your advice.

I want to say another huge thank you to Hollie from Pages Of A Bookish Girl. Wow, I honestly don't have the words to say how much I appreciate your care and support. You know how much this story means to me and I am so glad this has brought us together. You really are an angel. Thank you for being you, for listening and for seeing the real heart of this story.

Just as ever I wouldn't be able to do any of this without the unwavering support of my parents, and my children. I know I was on a rollercoaster whilst writing this one and I am so grateful to the support and always reminding me why it's worth being true to myself and the stories I write.

Most notably, I need to thank my readers. Those of you who have continuously supported me, the ones who took a risk on this little unknown author, I thank you. The book world is filled with so many amazing stories and I will forever be grateful that you've allowed me and my words to be a part of reading experience.

This book will forever hold a huge part of my heart and life in both the best and worst of ways. Thank you for being a part of this wild journey and I cannot wait to share more of the crazy and wild stories I'm planning on releasing.

Also by Natasha Allen

Decisions and Destiny Series

Beyond Expectations

Entangled Paths

Book 3 - Coming Soon

The Pursuit of Pleasure Series

The Perfect Stranger

Enticing Choices

Heady Desires

Searing Need

Lasting Impression

The Pursuit of Pleasure

About the Author

Natasha Allen is a contemporary romance author born and raised in London, now based in East Sussex.

Inspired by the works of Sylvia Day and Kennedy Ryan, she loves to write about diverse and interracial relationships.

When she's not crafting steamy love stories, Natasha can be found lost in a good book.

With a focus on diversity, Natasha strives to create inclusive and relatable love stories that reflect the world around us.

Keep an eye out for her upcoming releases, as she continues to enchant readers with her heartfelt tales of love and desire.

instagram.com/natashaallenauthor

amazon.com/author/UK

www.ingramcontent.com/pod-product-compliance
Lightning Source LLC
Chambersburg PA
CBHW050607170726
48283CB00001B/139